Luck Is Just the

Beginning

Celeste León

FLORICANTO PRESS

Berkeley Press is an imprint of Inter-American Development, Inc.

FLORICANTO^{TM} PRESS

7177 Walnut Canyon Rd.

Moorpark, California 93021

(415) 793-2662

www. FLORICANTOPRESS. com

ISBN-13: 978-1517716578

"Por nuestra cultura hablarán nuestros libros. Our books shall speak for our culture."
Roberto Cabello-Argandoña and
Leyla Namazie, Editors

Cover design by Carol Purroy, Gay Jardine, and Elena Friedman. Cover photo and author photo by Pete Rezac, Photographer. Photos in frame on cover: *Doña* Chepa, circa 1950, Ramón and Lila, circa 1928.

Ramón León Carrasquillo tending the store.

For Elena

Inspired by a true story

"If one is lucky, a solitary fantasy can totally transform one million realities."

--Maya Angelou, *Poems*

CHAPTER 1

Maunabo, Puerto Rico

November 17, 1944

Ramón León Carrasquillo had a powerful premonition. Something extraordinary was about to happen.

Just that morning, he shot an unprecedented seven free throws in a row. He watched the seventh ball soar into the air and sail through the tattered net when numbers appeared, high in the sky above the palm tree that held the faded backboard nailed to its mighty trunk. A fourteen, trailed by three zeros pulsed red above the clouds, so vibrant that Ramón believed God Himself must have painted it.

His heart fluttered in his chest like a moth caught in an oil lamp. He could scarcely breathe before the vision faded away in the breeze. A trail of gooseflesh swept up his arms until his mother's voice broke his trance, calling him to work at her *tienda de ropa*. Ramón tucked his basketball under his arm and hurried across the plaza, the only paved area in his village.

He passed the whitewashed colonial Catholic church and the enormous ceiba trees shading park benches. This morning, Ramón was the only person in the plaza, but the benches would soon be occupied by young boys who polished shoes for a penny and old men too frail to work in the sugar cane fields.

Ramón stepped into the store, legs trembling—had he imagined that vision in the sky? Would everything suddenly look different? No, the shelves were lined with the same bolts and rolls of cotton, broadcloth and muslin from which his mother fashioned shirts, pants or skirts that villagers ordered when they could afford it. He placed the basketball under the counter where he tallied purchases, and washed his hands in the old ceramic basin. He began to press and straighten the rolls of fabric tight against one another when the tarnished brass doorbell jingled to announce his first customer, an elderly *jíbara* from the *barrio*.

Ramón nodded to acknowledge her. He wondered: what did it mean, the number above the clouds? What other extraordinary things might happen today? When the peasant woman laid seven brown buttons on the worn counter and counted fourteen pennies, a revelation struck him like a fist: fourteen cents, seven buttons, and seven free throws. He was the seventh child to survive after his beloved mother lost her first eight babies, the lucky one, born in a caul on the seventh day of the seventh month.

"I hope Caimito comes today. It's lottery ticket day, and my husband's been saving two dimes to play," the woman declared.

There was no reason the lottery vendor wouldn't roll into Maunabo in his battered old truck. Hurricane season had passed, the roads were clear and the sky electric blue. The tropical breeze carried the scent of the sea.

At that moment, Ramón felt the gooseflesh again. Now he knew what those numbers meant. He must play that number in the lottery.

§§§

Honk, honk, honk! Caimito blared the horn of his rusty Ford truck. After years of monthly trips to Maunabo from San Juan, the horn sounded like the braying of an old donkey. Ramón heard the squeals of the children who chased the jalopy and the engine's coughs as it rattled to a stop in the plaza.

Several minutes later, Caimito lumbered up to the counter with a painful shuffle, courtesy of a bullet to the left foot from a spurned lover.

"Ay Ramón, I've been coming here for how many years, more than ten? Probably since you were no taller than my knee, helping your mamá. Are you finally going to buy a ticket today? Surely you can spare twenty cents for a portion. Everyone does once in a while. So . . . how many will it be?"

Ramón thought about that morning, the number he had seen: 14,000.

It was worth the risk.

"I'll buy a *complete* ticket," Ramón blurted, his stomach full of caught butterflies. "I want 14,000, and even better if there's a seven."

"No kidding—you're going to loosen your purse strings?"

"Yes," Ramón said, trying his best to sound resolute. "And I want the whole sheet."

"This is a day in history. Buying your *first* ticket, and the whole sheet at that, six dollars for all thirty portions! I've never sold one of those to anyone but a rich man. And guess what? It's your lucky day. I just happen to have one, number 14,217. Señor Trujillo from Yabucoa has been playing this number for *years*. He *was* my best customer, but he didn't play today. If you want it, it's yours, but I do have other customers to see . . ."

Caimito shrugged, removed a crisp white handkerchief from his pocket, and dabbed at the sweat on his forehead and fleshy, full-jawed face.

A complete ticket. 14,217. That's it. That number's meant for me!

Electricity spread down Ramón's arms all the way to the tip

of his fingers, and for the briefest of moments, he felt a glimmer of heat.

"I'll take it," Ramón demanded.

Ramón pulled his tin box out from under the counter, his hand trembling as he counted six dollars: three single bills and the remainder in coins, mainly nickels and pennies. The money piled up on the center of the counter, faded from dark brown to the color of nutmeg from decades of coins passing there.

"Hey, why's your hand shaking so hard?" Caimito asked.

"So what if it's shaking. Don't mention it again unless you want me to change my mind," Ramón retorted with a strength in his voice that surprised him.

Ramón thought of the dozen years it took him to save this money, of the trips to the sugar cane fields he started when he was seven. He could still feel the basket of pastries he carried on his head to sell to the cane workers for a penny a piece, the tang of salt as sweat trickled down his forehead to his top lip. The *macheteros* wielded their razor-sharp machetes as they worked the cane, their muscles rippling as they sang *plenas* passed down from their *jíbaro* grandfathers.

Ramón admired those men, but he wanted more.

"*No problema,*" Caimito replied as the money disappeared into his leather pouch quicker than a lizard's tongue catching a fly. "Good luck, Ramón. You never know, aye?"

The ticket seller embraced Ramón and clapped his back before he handed over the sheet of tickets. He tipped his straw hat and hobbled out the door as fast as his lame leg could carry him.

It was done.

Ramón bounded into the back room of the store, where Doña Chepa made alterations on her Singer sewing machine, her fingers dancing as rough bolts of cloth grew collars, cuffs, hems and ruffles.

"Mamá, I just bought a *complete ticket* from Caimito. I had a vision of a number that must have come from God. Caimito had a number *so close* I bought it—I think I'm going to win the jackpot!"

Ramón let his racing heart slow as hope flooded his heart.

Doña Chepa's foot stilled on the treadle. She looked up, her eyes wide as she declared, "*¡Dios mío!* A complete ticket? You spent *everything?*"

"Well . . . yes, but what if I inherited your gift, your visions? The number was so bright it was like the fireworks Papá talked about on that day in San Juan—the day we became citizens. I bet that number's been waiting for me for years, probably since I was born!"

Ramón saw the concern in his mother's expression and added, "Mamá, you told me I was born on the seventh day of the seventh month, that seven was my number. And the number I bought, it's a multiple of seven. I had to buy it."

"Ay, that took some courage. You know what I've always said about you: 'That boy was born in a caul. He'll be lucky all his life.'"

She made the sign of the cross and a secret smile played across her face.

"If God wills it, you will win. May He bless you."

§§§

Ramón sat in the kitchen that evening with his sister, Lila, for a dinner of fried plantains, rice and roasted chicken—a former pet named Chi Chi. Lila had married her *novio,* Jorge, a year before, and now lived eight houses and three hundred paces away. Yet that night she ran to her childhood home for the evening meal to hear Ramón's news.

Hours earlier, their mother prepared the meal in her usual fashion. She held the bird upside down by its feet and thanked it with soothing authority for the privilege of eating it. Then she spun it in wide circles to disorient it before a merciful slaughter. Now Doña Chepa bustled about, ensuring her children's plates were full before she sat to join them.

The three sat with heads bowed and hands folded in front of them as Chepa prayed: "Merciful God, watch over my beloved, brave sons, Isidro and Rafael. Return Your devoted children safely home from war."

After each made the sign of the cross, Ramón announced his news. "Lila," he said quickly, "I bought *a complete ticket* from Caimito. I think I'm going to hit the jackpot!"

Lila stopped her fork midway to her mouth as she cried, "A complete ticket? *¡Dios mío!* What did you do, rob a bank? No one's ever won with a full sheet before. And you—the first man in the family to finish high school. I thought you were smarter. You're *loco*, Ramón."

She shook her head, clucked her tongue, a gesture learned from Chepa.

"Well . . ." Ramón sat up straighter and defended, "A number flashed across the sky, and Caimito just happened to have a number so close to the one I saw, I had to buy it. It was meant for me."

"I can't believe it. All that money gone in a second," Lila scoffed. "Why didn't you only buy a couple portions? The money could be used for fixing the roof of the latrine, or—" her voice fell to a whisper, "a new pair of shoes for Mamá."

"Ay, let him be. The deed is done," Chepa interjected with a

12

wave of her hand. She stood and retrieved the pot of rice from the *fogón* to spoon another serving on all their plates.

Ramón swallowed hard. He pushed his food around on the plate.

"The message in the sky *must* have come from God," he insisted. "If I'd only bought a portion, it would be like I didn't trust Him."

§§§

Ramón rose with the sun on Wednesday, November 22, the day the winning lottery number would be posted in San Juan. A Puerto Rican parakeet squawked—a good omen, as the exotic birds were seen only in the deepest interior of the rainforests. He threw back the mosquito net, and then pulled on one of his two pairs of trousers and the white, short-sleeve shirt his mother had washed in the river, pressed and hung on the back of his door the night before.

Ramón entered the kitchen and kissed Doña Chepa on the cheek.

"Good morning, Mamá. Don't we need merchandise, so I can go to San Juan today? You'll be okay without me?"

He couldn't wait to check the number, had thought of little else.

"Go ahead. Your brother can help me at the store. We need a dozen dress shirts and fabric. Get five yards of blue and white cotton and a dozen brown buttons."

The entire time she talked, Chepa never stopped moving. Two guava pastries and two mugs of steaming *café con leche* materialized on the table.

"Whatever happens, remember, it's God's will," she reminded Ramón.

§§§

The mud-encrusted bus to Yabucoa pulled up in a sputter of smoke. Ramón's friend, Herman Steidel, hung his head and arms out of the window, swinging his hands like a monkey.

"¡*Oyé*, Ramón!" he shouted.

"¡*Oyé*, Herman," Ramón yelled back as he climbed aboard. "I'm on my way to San Juan, and I'm going to win the lottery!"

In a rare show of confidence, he held up his complete ticket, waving it proudly.

"You bought a full sheet!" Herman bent over, clutching his midsection and snickering like a hyena. "What a waste—you're a fool!"

All the kids joined Herman in ribald laughter, and even the few adults looked at the floor and covered their mouths to stifle chuckles. Heat flooded Ramón's face as he took a seat near the back.

He spent the remainder of his morning traveling the fifty miles to San Juan. After the school bus, he transferred to three different dilapidated *públicos*, where he squeezed between passengers carrying parcels and pigs or chickens meant for their dinners. The rickety bus bounced side to side and up and down on the dirt roads filled with potholes the size of stray dogs. A chicken clutched by Ramón's seatmate squawked and flapped its wings, striking Ramón in the face. A mother with dusty clothes cradled a crying infant to her breast as her two other children leaned against her.

Ramón could barely think over the noise and heat. He moved closer to the broken window to allow the salt air to dissipate the

14

musky scent of sweat from a trio of *macheteros,* one who sat with his eyes closed, cradling his hand wrapped in a bloody bandage and moaning quietly.

Looking out the window at the endless blue sea, Ramón's heart sank as he worried Herman and the others were right. He had squandered all his savings, what took twelve years, over half of his life, to earn. Dread filled him with the thought: *was this all his life might be?*

The air began to smell like rain as dark clouds slid in and turned the sea an oily gray. It would be one of the last rains before the dry season. Ramón gazed at the clouds and thought of the picture of New York City he had seen in the newspaper, the place where the skyscrapers kissed the clouds and men strolled down the streets with fine silk suits and top hats. Those who'd visited there spoke of the city with reverence. If this vision amounted to anything, perhaps he would get to see it for himself.

The *público* driver honked the horn and shouted at a farmer herding a dozen goats and sheep across the road. Ramón tuned everything out, the jingling of bells, the mewling of the flock, and remembered the man who changed his life.

CHAPTER 2

Ramón's mind went back in time to the day, at age eight, when he went to see the dentist from America for a terrible infection. The pain in his tooth became so intense that Ramón could hardly eat, so Chepa ordered his brother, Rafael, to take him to the other end of the village to the man everyone called "*humanitario*."

Ramón and his brother trudged for an hour in silence. With each step, Ramón's jaw throbbed. He kept his head down, trailing Rafael's sandals as they kicked up plumes of dust that filled his nostrils. The boys saw a man astride a donkey approaching them from the opposite direction, a *jíbaro* who gave them directions. Rafael led Ramón down a well-trodden path with weeds on either side that brushed his small shoulders. It ended at a tumbledown cottage in a clearing surrounded by jungle pungent with guavas.

The boys knocked on the door, and an old gentleman answered. Ramón had never seen someone so ancient, so bent over that Ramón could have touched the top of his head without reaching up. The man used an ebony cane with a tarnished silver head. His hair was the color of whitecaps on a stormy day, his face so deeply lined it reminded Ramón of his papá's old work boots.

The dentist held his hand to Ramón's cheek. He nodded and uttered, "*inflamado*" but his eyes smiled and Ramón forgot his fear. He followed the stranger to a table covered with gleaming instruments. Even the strange implements failed to alarm Ramón when the dentist patted his shoulder, motioning for him to sit.

The old man spoke in halting Spanish, with a heavy American accent, telling Ramón he had an infected molar. Before he prepared a syringe of Novocain, the dentist washed his fine-boned hands at a porcelain sink stained with rust. With a calm and determined countenance, he injected the drug. When the dentist's hand brushed Ramón's cheek, he detected a faint medicinal smell. The man's hand was wrinkled, with thick blue veins twisting across the back, but unlike Ramón's *abuelo*, the dentist's palm was clean and soft, whereas Ramón's grandfather's palm was thick with calluses and dirt caked under his fingernails from working the fields.

The dentist gave the tooth a few gentle tugs, pried it loose and placed the decayed thing on a piece of gauze for the boys to see. He then put a clean piece of gauze over the hole in Ramón's mouth and gave him a vial of hydrogen peroxide to rinse with. Ramón had felt the sting of the needle, the pull of tissue on his gums, but in moments, blessed relief for the first time in days! He leapt up and hugged the dentist; his body was as frail as a tree branch, but he had performed magic. Ramón felt a sudden release of all the tension from his small body. He longed to cry out to God, *I want to be able to do that!*

He ran ahead of Rafael back down the path, feeling so light he believed he could fly. The flowers lining the path were as if God had become giddy with His paintbrush: magenta Hibiscus, golden and tangerine Bird-of-Paradise, blood red flamboyan. Why hadn't he noticed such huge splotches of color before?

Every Saturday after that, Ramón went to Doctor Robert's cottage on the way home from the sugar cane plantation. He watched the dentist work, mesmerized by the dexterity of his hands as he treated patients. The man had a gift, like the artists who created the paintings in his neighbor Don Cadiz's magnificent art book that Ramón loved to study, and Ramón wanted that gift.

By Ramón's third visit, Doctor Roberts asked him to be his

assistant: "Hand me the dental mirror, thank you." Minutes later, the dentist handed back the mirror. "Now the extractor, then the scaler, please."

Ramón memorized the names of the instruments and within several weeks, in a shift that was nearly imperceptible, anticipated his mentor's needs with merely a glance or a single word.

Ramón became accustomed to the man's rudimentary Spanish and interpreted for patients. The two became a good team. Other than the occasional gifts of coconuts, grapefruits, or a chicken, Doctor Roberts accepted no payment. When they had no patients, Ramón taught Doctor Roberts how to play dominos and helped him improve his Spanish to near fluency as they sat for hours at a small table under the shade of a mango tree.

On a day four years into Ramón's apprenticeship, when the old dentist's steps became halting and he needed assistance getting up from his rickety chair, Ramón, then twelve, arrived at his cottage to find his mentor confined in bed.

Doctor Roberts patted the side of the mattress for Ramón to sit next to him, cleared his throat and said in a strained voice, "You're like a son to me, and I've never seen someone learn so fast. Remember Señor Sarabia? When we taught him to clean his teeth, it helped his heart disease. The paleness of his skin improved so much that he got a job. It changed his life, improved his health. There are so many more like him to help."

Doctor Roberts stopped talking to cough into his handkerchief. It alarmed Ramón to see the white cloth covered in spots of blood when Doctor Roberts pulled it from his mouth, but the old man's voice gained strength.

"You have a way with people. Never forget that! I dreamed of opening a large clinic here but I'm running out of time. You must take the torch and grant an old man his last wish. When you grow up, you can help your village and become a healer. *You* can make the world a better place."

Tears blurred Ramón's vision. He rubbed his wrist across his eyes, praying and hoping that when he opened them, everything would be fine. Doctor Roberts would be okay, old but spry enough to take his daily stroll down to the road and back.

"You can't leave me," Ramón croaked, his voice a hoarse whisper.

"I see you accomplishing great things," Doctor Roberts affirmed.

Ramón's ears rang and his heart raced at his mentor's words. Warmth radiated through his body as he remembered all that he had learned.

"I will!" Ramón exclaimed. "Everything you've taught me, I'll never forget. I'll set up a clinic one day that will make you proud. I'll teach people how to take care of themselves—I promise!"

After Ramón helped Doctor Roberts out of bed and they treated a few patients, he rushed home, as if sprouting wings, to tell Doña Chepa of the promise he made.

§§§

The *público* lurched to the side as the driver swerved to avoid a large washout from the last hurricane, pitching Ramón into the window to disrupt his treasured memory. Then he remembered how Doctor Roberts had taught him the way to visualize.

"Ramón, close your eyes. Imagine taking over my work, *our* work. Imagine it, and it will come true," Doctor Roberts told him years before.

At night, when the rest of the family was asleep and the only sounds were the chirps of the *coquí* frogs outside his bedroom window and the creaks of the house settling, Ramón fantasized that he was a dentist as skilled as his mentor, with a waiting room full of patients who smiled to show off their perfect white teeth, wearing fine clothing they could afford since they had obtained good jobs after coming under his care and improving their health and looks.

Ramón reached into his pocket to feel his ticket. It *had* to be the winning number, to grant him the money to make his promise to his old friend come true.

Ramón would arrive in San Juan in two hours, when the bells of *Nuestra Señora de Lourdes Chapel* tolled for the noon prayer. The words, *make the world a better place,* rang in his head. He wondered: would the bells toll for him, too?

CHAPTER 3

In Santurce, San Juan's business district, Ramón dashed down a narrow street teeming with traffic, pedestrians, and stray dogs. He hurried past the small dry-goods store with rice and beans filled in wooden barrels on the sidewalk and a bar with an open doorway, its jukebox blaring a song about lost love and liquor. He arrived at the shirt wholesaler, a single-level cement building, and ran inside.

The owner, Señor Mendoza, stood behind his workbench, and greeted Ramón with a smile.

"Ah, good day, Ramón. Always a pleasure. What will it be today?"

Ramón removed his cap and nodded.

"A dozen men's shirts, single pocket, short sleeves, and oh—" he rushed on, "I need six blue, six white, please."

Señor Mendoza reached under his metal work counter and began to retrieve shirts one by one and place them in a pile, smoothing and pressing the front of each in turn.

Ramón wanted to take over, to somehow make the man's hands move faster. "Do you know the winning lottery number?" he blurted.

"It's posted by now, the cigar store, three blocks west. All I know is, it's not my number."

Señor Mendoza shook his head and sighed as he grabbed a ball of rawhide string and began to tie the shirts together in a neat pile.

Ramón gasped. He felt his face flush. Beads of sweat popped

out on his forehead. He wanted to grab the string and tie the shirts himself.

"Isn't this what you wanted?" The merchant secured the knot on top. "You look like you may faint."

"Yes—thank you!" Ramón urged.

His hand shook as he felt in his pocket to make sure his ticket was still there, something he'd already done hundreds of times. He threw two dollars on the counter, thrust his cap back on his head, grabbed the shirts and sped out of the store.

Ramón's pulse raced as he sprinted three blocks to the cigar store.

He stood at the rear of the crowd. Taped to the glass window, a piece of brown wrapping paper fluttered in the breeze. Hoping it would be a day of good fortune, dozens of people had gathered to read the five-digit number scrawled there minutes earlier by the store owner. Ramón craned his neck to see over the crowd. The printing was too difficult to make out.

People in front walked away, tossing their tickets to the ground like confetti and muttering in disgust. A small commotion erupted as some tried to push their way in front of others. Unable to wait any longer, Ramón squeezed himself between a man with a straw sombrero and an old woman. The shade cast by the man's hat blackened the paper, making it still unable to decipher. Ramón nudged the man and the woman aside, with a breathless, "¡*Perdóneme* (Excuse me)!"

The man flashed an annoyed look. Ramón took one, two, three steps. His heart pounded so hard he imagined everyone around him could hear it.

Everything led to this moment.

Ramón stood for a moment with his eyes closed, saying a

quick prayer, until a man shoved him aside.

"Move out of the way, you've had your turn. Let the rest of us see," the man snarled.

Ramón opened his eyes, his entire body trembling with anticipation. There it was: 14,217. He blinked twice and looked again to make sure his eyes weren't playing tricks. He checked his ticket again.

I won. A miracle.

His whole body tingled as if shot with electricity. He felt as if his feet were not touching the ground, yet if he didn't move as fast as humanly possible, his knees would buckle beneath him. He sprinted across a wide bustling avenue. Cars honked their horns. Ramón ran for two blocks as if he were floating through someone else's life before he stopped, laughed, pulled his cap off and tossed it in the air.

He felt heart-throbbingly alive. Wait until Caimito heard, surely his ticket sales would increase tenfold—a day of prosperity for them both!

A distinguished elderly couple walked by, arm in arm. Ramón had to tell someone his news.

"Señor, look, I have the winning ticket!" Still breathless, he waved the ticket in the man's face and sputtered, "I've just seen my number, 14,217!"

Ramón's joy was so profound his entire body shook.

The gentleman leaned in close to Ramón and grasped his hand, pulling it down to conceal the ticket, then whispered, "Bravo, young man, but be careful. Don't shout the news. Someone may knock you over to steal your ticket. Find someone you trust, quickly now."

"Splendid idea. *¡Gracias!*" Ramón blurted.

He shoved his ticket back into his pocket, looking around to make sure no one was watching.

Ramón bolted down the street, faster than he had run in his life as he imagined all of San Juan chasing him to steal his prize. He ran into a store that sold fabric and sewing notions where the proprietor, Alberto Gómez, knew the Leóns well.

Ramón waited seconds before his breathing slowed.

"Señor Gómez look, the winning ticket—I won the jackpot!"

No other customers were shopping. Ramón felt safe waving his ticket and shouting his news.

Alberto's eyes opened as wide as silver dollars. "Are you sure?"

Ramón danced a jig and embraced the older man.

"Yes, I've seen it, with my own two eyes as sure as the sun comes up every day!" Ramón shouted.

Alberto held Ramón at arms' length and smiled.

"I believe you. What a day!" Alberto kissed both of Ramón's cheeks and let out a joyous wallop. "Let's call the lottery office. I've never known a winner before, but they'll tell us what to do."

Good old Alberto. When he smiled, his eyes smiled too, crinkling at the corners all the way to the touch of gray at his temples.

Ramón paced the aisles filled with bolts of fabric, spools of thread and rows of buttons. The array of colors of merchandise in blue, black, brown, red, and white made him feel dizzy and light-headed. He barely heard Alberto relay the information that *he*, Señor Alberto Gómez, had the winner in *his* store, Gómez and Sons, Incorporated. Alberto hung up, giddy, to announce: "We must go to the office to confirm the ticket and collect your prize. Hurry!"

The merchant locked the door and flipped the CLOSED sign over before he and Ramón ran to his car.

§§§

Ramón stood in the lottery office, feeling the check in his hand: $18,000. The jackpot. He wondered if he'd blink and rouse from a beautiful dream. But it was real. In his head, he tried to do a quick calculation of how many years he would have to work to make such an exorbitant amount, but after figuring at least decades, he gave up.

The paper was light in his hand, yet felt heavy with the promise of a future that before now, he could only imagine.

He turned to Señor Gómez. "It's all happening so fast! I need to do something with this check, go to a bank, but I've never been to one before," Ramón exclaimed. His words had trouble keeping pace with his reeling mind, and he found it nearly impossible to stand in one place.

"Of course—I know just the place!" Señor Gomez announced.

Ramón heard his friend making his second phone call for the day, this time to *Banco Público*. Alberto hung up. "The bank is about to close, but when I told the manager who was coming in, he agreed to stay open. Let's go!"

§§§

Señor Gómez ushered Ramón through the large glass and metal doors of *Banco Público* where a tall man in a gray double-breasted suit was waiting.

The small rectangular name tag pinned beneath his lapel read: Señor López, Manager. "Congratulations, young man," he said, and beamed as he shook Ramón's hand. "We are so pleased to have you as a customer, and let me assure you, *Banco Público* can meet all of your financial needs."

As in the lottery office, employees came over to shake his hand and congratulate him.

"And now, my senior teller will open an account for you. Right this way, please," Señor López indicated with a slight bow of his head and turn of his hand.

The group of employees parted to allow Ramón to make his way forward. Sensing all eyes following him, Ramón stared straight ahead as he approached the mahogany counter. The teller, a man who looked as important as Señor López, stood waiting. Ramón handed his check over and after several minutes of pressing numbers into an adding machine, the teller issued Ramón a blue pass book. On the first crisp page, was typed his name: Ramón León Carrasquillo, with the numbers $18,000 in the upper right hand corner and the date: November 22, 1944.

It was the day before Thanksgiving, and Ramón couldn't believe all he had to be thankful for.

The passbook was the same size and color as Don Pablo's passport. Ramón never owned one but he remembered the places Don Pablo talked about visiting: New York, Chicago, Paris, and Madrid. Now, Ramón may have the opportunity to go to those cities. When he signed his name on the designated line, the employees clapped, smiles all around.

Ramón withdrew seventy dollars in cash. He stared at the seven ten-dollar bills in amazement before folding them and placing them in his pocket. It had taken years to save a mere six dollars, and within seconds, he had over ten times that amount, what a cane worker in the fields would take months to earn.

Alberto and Ramón danced down the sidewalk, their smiles

as wide as alligators', tipping their caps to everyone. Many turned to watch as they passed, shaking their heads in bewilderment or amusement.

Ramón stopped and turned to his friend.

"*Dios,* I missed the last *público* to Maunabo. My mamá will be sick with worry. I need to get word to her but there are only two phones in Maunabo, and I don't know their numbers."

"You *must* send Doña Chepa this news. Come—to the telegraph office!"

"Mamá never gets telegrams, and she doesn't read well. What if she thinks that one of my brothers was killed in the war?" Ramón said, his thoughts racing.

"Someone can read it for her. Let's go!"

"But telegrams are expensive," Ramón insisted.

"That won't be a problem for you anymore!" Alberto threw his head back and laughed.

Ramón's hand trembled as he wrote this message in view of the astounded telegram operator:

WON JACKPOT Stop HOTEL TONIGHT Stop HOME TOMORROW Stop GOD BLESS Stop RAMÓN.

§§§

That evening, Señor Gómez and Ramón enjoyed a sumptuous meal at *La Mallorquina*, the finest and oldest restaurant in San Juan. A tuxedo clad waiter escorted them to a table covered by a starched white cloth laden with white dishes rimmed in gold—actual gold on plates that people used for dinner. A candle flickered in the center of the table, its light reflected in the floor to ceiling baroque mirrors.

Ramón had never imagined such opulence. Compliments of the Puerto Rican lottery, they dined on exquisite foods he had never even dreamed of: asparagus laced with melted butter and steak imported from New York. Ramón's taste buds danced on his tongue when he bit into the watercress salad drizzled with blue cheese dressing, the combination crisper and creamier than anything he had ever tasted.

Waiters with perfect posture and spotless white napkins folded over their forearms hovered, using phrases such as, "At your service" and "It is my pleasure to serve you, señor." These men made water glasses fill, hot foods materialize or a clean linen napkin appear at the table like magic. Ramón had never been treated with such respect by men older than he, men polished and efficient at their jobs. The other patrons in the restaurant joined Ramón and Alberto in a toast to Ramón's new fortune. The rum slipped down Ramón's throat like silk.

After buying a round of drinks for everyone in the restaurant, and the telegram, Ramón paid three dollars for a hotel room. It was the first night he had ever spent away from home.

Ramón lay down on the firm bed and clasped his hands behind his head on the pillow. At home, it often took an hour or two to fall asleep from the heat. Now he felt the caress of air on his body from the swirling ceiling fan, his thoughts keeping him awake.

He remembered how his father, Juan Bautista, would puff out his chest and brag that he was named in honor of the first name given to Puerto Rico, San Juan Bautista, by Queen Isabel of Spain in Christopher Columbus's time. Juan Bautista always claimed that he was a direct descendent of Spain's royal family.

Ramón felt a smile spread across his face when he remembered how Juan Bautista tried to discipline him as a boy, swinging at his bottom with a stick carved from their mango tree. His father would always miss—Ramón now knew it was on purpose—and stroll away, his laughter rich and rolling. Villagers claimed Juan's tenor voice was the glory of the church's choir. People even claimed the dogs and *burros* stopped to listen.

Ramón felt an unnamable tenderness toward his father and his mentor, Doctor Roberts, both gone many years. He would give anything to bring them back, to embrace them, to celebrate with them.

It took a long time for Ramón to fall asleep that night. He stared at the ceiling fan and marveled at this turn in his life. *Thank you, God, for this miracle. I will make my family proud. Now I have this wealth, and the means to fulfill my promise. Yet . . . will I be up to the task?*

CHAPTER 4

Sometime in the gray period between dark and dawn, Ramón drifted off to sleep. He woke to the cacophony in the street, honking horns and sputtering engines, so different from the sounds of laughing gulls and tiny *coquís* to which he was accustomed. The smell was different, too. Diesel fumes seeped through the open window, rather than the sweetness of the grapefruit and mango trees outside his home.

Light filtered into the room, but not the way it usually did, bright and clear from his bedroom window. It was more subdued as it peeked between wooden blinds. He rolled over in bed to notice a lamp on the nightstand. He clicked the switch on and off three times. Electricity—amazing—so much brighter than his oil lamp at home!

Ramón's brain registered the information in seconds: *I'm in a hotel in San Juan.* A memory of the day before flooded over him. For the second time, he thought it all a dream. He heard the shouts of vendors delivering their wares in the business district outside the hotel. He sat up quickly and trembled. *No, it's real, it's real! I've won! Thank you, God!* Ramón wanted to shout his news to the world.

It was Thursday, November 23, 1944. Thanksgiving Day, "*El día de Acción de Gracias,*" a day to give thanks and praise for all that's good with the world. Ramón wished he could fly home to embrace his mother, instead of taking four old *públicos*. Then he remembered the yards of fabric and buttons he was supposed to buy. In all the excitement, he'd forgotten to buy them from Señor Gómez. Since it was Thanksgiving Day and Puerto Rico had begun to follow mainland customs, the store would be closed. Considering his reason, Chepa would forgive Ramón for returning home with only the bundle of men's shirts. With it, he had a bank account holding almost $18,000.

In the bathroom, Ramón twisted the hot and cold faucets and watched the water gush into the porcelain sink. Giddy, he cupped a handful and splashed water on his face, hot running water, unlike the lukewarm rainwater from the metal drums on the roof at home. He pulled on his shirt from the night before, the cotton rough against his skin. Now he could afford to buy the types of shirts he sold to his customers! He grabbed his checkbook from beneath the mattress, where—heeding the warning of the old man on the street— he'd stashed it before going to bed. He checked out of the hotel and sprinted to the bus stop in Santurce, grateful that the buses ran on the holiday. Ramón boarded the *público* and sat down to catch his breath.

The man sitting across from him smirked. "Hey, are you the one I saw running away from the cigar store yesterday faster than a jackal? I heard somebody won with a full sheet, and for the first time in years! It was you, wasn't it? I saw that look on your face!"

The man was missing his two front teeth. His remaining teeth were rotten, making his smile look like a dark hole in the yellow moonlight.

Ramón remembered the old man's warning and merely shook his head.

The man smirked again and said, "Are you sure? You look familiar, *compadre*. You know, I got no job. How about a loan, so I can fix my car and travel in style, rather than in this old rundown bucket of bolts? I'll be your driver, and I got a sister, she's sooo beautiful, how about you meet her?"

Ramón thought of the lizards that his cousin, Albertito, used to dangle live off his earlobes. "No, that wasn't me," he said, keeping his voice low.

Ramón turned away and moved closer to the window, yet not so far as to allow space for the man to sit next to him. If the *jíbaro* had dental care, would he be in such a predicament? This man was the type of man he could help, yet not with money, rather with improving his health and his looks. Ramón glanced back at the fellow to see his lecherous grin. Was it his imagination, or had the man moved closer?

The *jíbaro* got up to exit in Caguas, but before he stepped down off the bus, he turned to hiss, "Watch your back, *compadre*."

§§§

The *público* let off its remaining passengers and began to ascend *La Pica*, the treacherous nine-mile dirt road named for the great mountain towering over Maunabo. The road had long been the only way into the village and was so narrow and full of switchbacks that the driver kissed his Saint Christopher medal before tackling it. He honked the horn around each hairpin turn to warn unseen vehicles coming from the opposite direction, though it was hardly necessary as there were only three dilapidated trucks in all of Maunabo.

As the *público* rolled into the plaza, Ramón spotted dozens of people. Typically, the plaza's occupants were stray dogs sleeping in the sun, pigeons pecking the ground for seeds, a few old men napping or playing dominos in the shade of the African palms, or boys playing basketball after a day in the cane fields. Ramón heard laughter and conversations, and for a moment he thought everyone must be celebrating Saint's Week. Yet that was impossible, for the annual celebration was held in June.

As the bus sputtered to a stop, shouts drifted through the open window.

"Here he comes—he's here!"

Is this possible? Could everyone be here for me? Of course, it was the telegram—the delivery man had broadcast the news, which must have exploded through the village faster than one could say "Boriken," the aboriginal name of Puerto Rico.

The entire village cheered and clapped. Even the *público* driver thrust his head out his window and hooted along with the crowd. Only Ramón's brothers, Isidro and Raphael, still at war, were missing.

In the front of the crowd stood his mother, Doña Chepa, who placed her hands on either side of her face and began to weep.

When Ramón saw the relief and joy wash over his mother's face, something inside him welled up. He felt as if the rays of the sun of the most brilliant of days would burst out of the tips of all his fingers and toes. Doña Chepa, who had suffered more heartache than most could imagine, who had buried so many of her babies after they died of malaria or dysentery and not only survived but learned the healing arts to become the finest *curandera* in the region, certainly deserved to share in this moment with him. As soon as Ramón stepped off the bus, his friends and family rushed forward. Young boys gazed at him, eyes wide with admiration and envy. Girls threw flower petals in the air.

For that moment, Ramón believed the applause could carry him as high as the clouds. His heart danced a pirouette in his chest as the sky filled with a kaleidoscope of color.

CHAPTER 5

Ramón ran into the arms of his mother. "Mamá, I did it, I won!"

"I knew this would happen," she whispered. The two stayed locked in a tight embrace as villagers clapped and cheered.

"Maunabo's son is home. *¡Gracias a Dios!*" everyone shouted.

"Ramón, Ramón!" they chanted.

Meat smoked and sizzled on the spit of a grill. The delectable aroma of pork, garlic and onion wafted through the air. As soon as Ramón let go of Chepa, Señor Uribe, el *carnicero,* grabbed him to pull him into the crowd and shouted, "God bless Doña Chepa, who killed her Christmas pig just for this occasion!"

Every New Year's Day, Chepa chose a piglet, which she fattened up all year for their Christmas dinner. Yet for this day, the butcher had prepared it for a feast. Ramón thought of what he had done the night before: spent nearly seventy *pesos* on a lavish dinner while his mother had killed the two-hundred pound sacrificial pig that could have fed his entire family, brothers, wives, and neighbors for a week. He experienced a moment's pang of guilt, when, before he knew what was happening, he was lifted by the arms of the strongest villagers and carried through the crowd. When he was back on the ground, everyone lined up to embrace him.

Herman Steidel slapped Ramón on the back and handed him a full glass of rum. "You did it, Ramón, you won, you lucky bastard!"

Ramón threw his head back and gulped the amber liquid. It tasted finer than the rum in *La Mallorquina.*

For the first time in his life, Ramón felt like a king.

His brothers and dozens of townspeople embraced him and kissed each cheek, and then a woman walked toward him through the crowd. Elsie Miraflores.

Ramón was thirteen when the new police chief moved to the village with his wife and eleven-year-old daughter, Elsie.

"That girl's already a beauty! She's one to watch," villagers had declared.

Ramón would never forget the first day he saw her. Working in the store one afternoon, he decided to take a break. He was leaning against the door jamb when he watched a woman and the most exquisite girl he had ever seen cross the plaza. He blinked as the sun glinted off her copper curls, like a new, shiny penny, so unlike the hair of the girls from the *barrios*, as dark as roasted coffee beans. She wore sandals with red flowers on the ankle straps. Their tapping created a delightful rhythm on the pavement. She was clearly from a noble San Juan family; the local peasants wore crude *chancletas* or no shoes at all.

Ramón's heart raced when he realized she was about to walk into the store. He prayed her mother would make several purchases so he could impress her and her daughter with his quick calculations.

"Ca-can I help you find anything?" he stuttered.

Elsie's mother politely declined, telling him she had heard of Doña Chepa's skill as a dressmaker and had come to inquire if she would fashion dresses for the upcoming wedding of her sister.

Ramón had never seen his mother work so hard to produce frocks of the finest ivory silk. How he wished he could have danced with Elsie at that wedding!

Now, Elsie walked toward him. He tried not to stare but that was as futile as trying to stay dry in a monsoon. His heart drummed in his chest as he held back a gasp, for now, at seventeen, she was a sight: the effect of her white ankle-length summer dress against her honey-colored skin and slim hips was stunning. Pure sunlight was woven into the locks of her hair.

"Ramón, congratulations! Everyone's been talking about you since Doña Chepa got your telegram," Elsie marveled.

Elsie smiled, excitement brightening her emerald eyes. If she had noticed his staring, she was kind enough to ignore it.

Ramón felt beads of sweat pop out on his brow and felt like that tongue-tied thirteen-year-old. "Ah . . . it's great, isn't it?" he said.

"Yes!" Elsie nodded.

She bit her lower lip and tucked a copper curl behind her ear. Ramón watched a blush bloom across her cheeks. Was it possible? Could *he* actually be making *her* nervous?

"Well, now what do you think you're going to do—" she began to ask.

It was either the glass of rum he'd gulped, the maracas someone started to play, or the fact that he had a bank note for nearly $18,000 in his pocket, but leaving all traces of that shy thirteen-year-old boy behind forever, Ramón held his shoulders back and boasted, "I'm going to college—to be a dentist."

"Oh—I bet you'll be a great dentist!"

Ramón couldn't believe his ears. Such a compliment from the woman whose beauty could stop a herd of wild horses in their tracks, and the smile that accompanied it!

"Thanks, you look great tonight," was all he could manage.

Incredibly, Ramón heard himself say, "Elsie, would you like to go to the town hall dance with me sometime?"

"Oh," she murmured again, her cheeks a deeper scarlet, "I'd like that."

As they spoke, Ramón felt the collective glances of the partygoers. Those gathered grew hushed, and Ramón felt sure they listened in on his conversation with Elsie. Here he was, talking to the most sought-after girl in the village and not even in the presence of her parents. He needed to be more careful. Gossip blew through town faster than the winds of a hurricane.

Ramón was about to say more when, as if summoned, Elsie's father, Capitán Miraflores, appeared at his side.

"This is a lucky day for you and your family. Congratulations." The police chief offered his hand.

It was the longest sentence the most uncompromising man in the village had ever uttered to Ramón, who held his shoulders back as he returned the man's firm handshake.

"Thank you, Capitán Miraflores, for celebrating with me. Please, enjoy some rum and pork, compliments of my mother and *el carnicero!*"

The sun dropped behind *La Pica,* and the celebration became more heated. Someone set up poles with blazing torches around the edges of the plaza. A never-ending number of well-wishers, many of them strangers, filtered in and out of the party, waiting their turn to congratulate Ramón. The León brothers brought out their instruments: Juan, the eldest, with his trumpet, Francisco, with his maracas, José Luis with his prized *barril de bomba* and little Juanito, Ramón's ten-year-old nephew, with his *güiro.*

People danced as couples and in groups to the rhythm of *son* and mambo: girls with their grandfathers, parents with their children, women with women, and boyfriends with girlfriends. The women lifted their ruffled skirts and swished them to the beat, daring to show bare ankles and knees as they twirled around the plaza.

Ramón might have dared ask Elsie to dance, but his guests scarcely left him alone, and he had downed a few more tumblers of rum. The ground began to sway slowly under his feet, and he wanted their first dance to be special, not drunken. He had already committed a blunder when he asked her to the town hall dance, without requesting her father's permission first. And the way he offered food and drink to the police chief; he had never acted so brazen.

Yet no one could prohibit him from *looking* at Elsie. Ramón glanced across the plaza to see her talking with his sister, Lila, and hoped the two would become friends. Then a sobering thought followed: had Elsie only approached him because of his good fortune?

No, it was a party. Everyone was joyous and laughing, and he had to admit, the way Elsie looked at him made his heart soar. She laughed again, and it sounded like church bells, spilling over him like a waterfall.

§§§

That night Ramón kissed hundreds of cheeks, embraced total strangers. He had another tumbler of rum to feel light again. Then he noticed a man at the edge of the plaza in a wide-brimmed linen hat. In the flickering torchlight, his face remained shadowed, and Ramón sensed something almost sinister emanating from the man's eyes. It made his heart pound, but not in a pleasant way like when he watched Elsie. Was it the same man from the *público*, come back to make good on his threat? No, this man looked far more portly, and wore a fine hat few could afford.

Ramón was about to approach the fellow when someone

clasped his shoulder from behind. He turned to find Antonio Díaz. With his jet black hair and a highly polished shine in his city shoes, Antonio was Maunabo's Casanova.

"Ramón León, did you make a deal with the devil to win that prize?"

"Nah, an angel. Now I can go to college in the states, like you. Tell me, what's it like?"

Antonio smiled, and Ramón couldn't help envy the man's perfect, dazzling teeth.

"Michigan State is full of pretty girls, with no eagle-eyed fathers watching over them." Antonio cocked his head toward Elsie and raised one eyebrow. "But who's not to love right now?"

A lot, thought Ramón. *Lots of pretty girls who speak only English and hard college classes in English.* Ramón thought of the book he picked up in the hotel lobby the night before, *The Little Prince.* A family of tourists had probably left it behind. All that time studying English in high school, and he couldn't even read a damn kid's book—but he'd never admit that to Antonio.

Instead, he said, "Leave it to you to notice the women. I'll go there, too!"

"You're in luck again, *amigo*, because I know a lovely lady who works in a very important office. I'll give her a call and have her send you an application. And I'll give you my old dictionary."

"Wow—thanks!"

"That's what friends are for." Antonio flashed his award winning grin again. "But the school is tough, and there's the matter of the essay . . ."

"Essay?" Ramón swallowed hard, the tempting co-eds forgotten.

"You didn't know about the essay, *amigo*?"

At that moment, in spite of the merriment surrounding him, Ramón wished he were invisible.

"You know," Antonio suggested, "I can write it for you. I've done it before. But all this work . . . calling my lady friend, working on the essay, I'm afraid my time isn't free. I'll do it for twenty *pesos*."

Antonio grinned wider. "You can afford it."

Twenty pesos—an exorbitant amount! Ramón was about to say "no thanks," but thought of *The Little Prince* and the fact that Antonio had just graduated from that college in faraway Michigan and knew a lot more English than he did.

"But I only have five *pesos* on me, left over from dinner," Ramón blurted.

"That's a start. Consider it a deposit," Antonio jested before he put his arm around Ramón and slapped him on the back.

A Chinese firecracker exploded above the palm trees into a sizzling bouquet of yellow, red and blue. Ramón felt an adrenaline rush. Surely, such a display meant something. After all, Antonio was a man who could get things done, a man who always had a beautiful woman on his arm and wore fine suits.

Before Ramón could change his mind, he reached into his pocket and thrust the bills into Antonio's hand.

"Don't worry about anything, *amigo*—here's to your future!" Antonio shouted above the boom of the firecrackers.

Ramón lifted his glass in return. "To the future!"

He then looked to the edge of the crowd, to search for the man in the wide-brimmed hat. For a moment, Ramón experienced the same sensation he had in the store right before he bought his ticket, the electric hum that spread across his shoulders. Yet this time, it was foreboding, as if something dark loomed.

The man seemingly had evaporated, nowhere to be seen.

CHAPTER 6

The following morning, a crowd stood outside the store, waiting for it to open. Ramón had never seen anything like it. He made his way to the entrance through a sea of applauding customers, many he didn't recognize. No sooner had he pulled up the louvered doors and windows when people began to push inside.

El carnicero shoved aside a short man in a tan suit, growling, "I was here first."

If he didn't create order, Ramón feared a fight might break out.

"All right everyone," he called out. "What's going on here? Calm down. Form a line. There's no need to push!"

Ramón stepped behind the familiar worn counter. A dozen men and women queued up. The line stretched outside the door.

El carnicero knelt and removed his straw cap.

"Don Carrasquillo, thank you for blessing me with your presence on this fine morning, in this fine establishment. As you know, I have an old truck. It can barely crawl up *La Pica*. Please be so kind as to loan me a few doll—"

The baker stepped in front of the butcher to declare, "My *panadería*, Don Carrasquillo, my good man, is in need a new roof. If you could find it in your heart to pay for it, I would rename it in your honor!"

The butcher stood and pushed the baker aside.

"Give him a chance to answer me first," the butcher snarled.

For a moment, Ramón had the absurd notion the two men would fight over who could kiss his hand first. And calling him Don

41

Carrasquillo? Ridiculous. That was a term of honor and respect, one that had to be earned.

Señora Sarabia, a stoop-shouldered, old woman, pushed between the men. Ramón recognized her pale yellow dress as one of Chepa's creations, now faded from being washed in the river and dried in the sun over the years.

"My husband, he needs an operation. He's got a bad stomach. A few extra dollars to see the doctor would help an old *amigo*."

Ramón was amazed at the woman's gumption to position herself between the two men and said, "Señora Sarabia, my mother will take care of your husband, like she always does. You know he gets a stomachache when you use too much *adobo* in your chicken. Does he really need an operation?"

"But the doctor—" she pleaded.

"You heard him," shouted the baker. "Your husband is fine. You don't need his help—I do!"

After a minute, a slight man approached Ramón, the man the butcher had shoved aside when they all came rushing through the door. His dark mustache twisted into small curlicues at each end and his tan suit was worn thin from too many pressings. He smelled of cheap cologne.

"Don Carrasquillo, I'm Señor Peña, originally from Cuba. Today I came all the way from Ponce. If you make a contribution for my daughter's *Quinceañera*, she'll make you a wonderful wife. She may need someone to fix her teeth a bit, but after, she'll really be a beauty! She's a good girl." His grin pushed at the tips of his mustache.

"I'm sure she is, señor," Ramón replied. "But if she's only fifteen, make sure she finishes school before she becomes a wife."

"Free—everything should be free today—I need a new shirt!"

42

called out the hunchback who cleaned the church.

Everyone called him *Trepado* because his left leg lurched to the side at an awkward angle when he walked, giving him the appearance of climbing over an imaginary boulder.

A lady with black hair down to her waist agreed. "Yes, he's right. I haven't had a new pair of shoes in years. You can spare the money—you're rich!"

Ramón glanced down at her feet. Her *chancletas* were tied with rawhide string around her arches and toes. Her tattered brown shirt hung loosely off her bony shoulders.

Everyone squawked at once like a flock of seagulls, their chatter ricocheting off the walls of the store: "Yes—yes—that's right!"

Ramón couldn't think. His head began to throb. For merely a second, he looked down and closed his eyes, rubbing his temples in circles, wishing he hadn't drunk so much rum the night before.

He opened his eyes as a young mother stepped up to the counter. A little girl with matted dull brown hair held the woman's hand. Her legs were so skinny Ramón was surprised they could hold her up. The mother supported a baby boy with a runny nose and wet diaper on her hip.

"My babies are hungry, and they need more clothes."

The woman looked to be sixteen or seventeen. She stared at Ramón in a way that made him feel dizzy, overwhelmed. What could he say to this young mother—give her money and not the others, the villagers who had known his family since before he was born?

A memory flashed in Ramón's head: at age three, lying on his cot at night, hearing the sighs of his five brothers sleeping next to him and seeing the stars through the webbing of his mosquito net after *Huracán San Felipe* ripped off the roof. His father had worked side-by-side with the baker and the butcher to rebuild their roofs and walls before he repaired his own. Ramón would never forget how Papá carried him and Lila through gale force winds to the neighbor's house to squirrel them away in the dirt-packed crawl space while the hurricane destroyed the village. His father was a hero that day.

Ramón cringed over what he was about to do.

"I'm sorry." He swallowed hard, his throat dry. He cleared it before he continued. "I . . . I don't know what to say. I can't give you money. I need it for college, to become a dentist. Don't you all remember *el humanitario*, the dentist? He helped many of you. I can go study and come back to pick up where—"

"College!" a man near the door interrupted. "But isn't there enough for us?"

"Yes, what about us?" someone else shouted, throwing up his hands.

Murmurs and nods of agreement followed. The baby began to whimper in his young mother's arms.

Chepa hurried into the store after finishing her morning chores: scrubbing the laundry against the metal ripples of the washboard before hanging it in the sun, and picking herbs from her garden, *culantro* for indigestion and arrowroot for spider bites. "Ay, what's all the trouble?" she exclaimed.

The butcher and the baker resumed their bickering, like the back and forth dance of a matador and a bull. Both men pressed his needs upon her over who would be heeded.

"Stop," Chepa demanded. "Both of you."

"Yes," Ramón agreed. "You two have been friends for years. I've seen you helping each other's businesses." He made direct eye contact with each man. "Do you want to ruin all that? Apologize to one another. Right now."

El carnicero looked down and held his hat in front of his

stomach, like a boy in trouble at the principal's office.

The baker took his handkerchief from his pocket and wiped the sweat off his brow. He shrugged his shoulders and put his hand back in his pocket.

"Ah, sorry," he mumbled.

The butcher held back. He glanced at Ramón and then at Chepa, who gave him a look, narrowing her eyes slightly.

"Me too," he murmured.

"Everyone, please listen," Chepa announced. "If you're here for alterations or would like to order something, we can help you. You've always been happy with my work, and Ramón's work, and that won't change. But if you're here for money, my son needs time to adjust to everything that's happened. So you can go, please."

It was as if the air were sucked out of the room. No one spoke. Chepa's word was absolute.

People began shuffling out until only Ramón and Chepa remained.

"Come, sit with me for a moment, in the back. We're closed for the rest of the day," Chepa sighed.

"But we never close early," Ramón said.

"Today, I'm making an exception. Let them all come back tomorrow, or not." Chepa gave a dismissive wave of her hand. "I helped the midwife with a breech birth last night until early this morning. *Gracias a Dios* the mother and baby survived. That's what's really important."

She and Ramón took seats in the back room.

"*Dios*, Mamá, those people were acting crazy, but still, I could have helped them and that woman with the babies . . ." Ramón leaned forward and buried his face in his hands.

"You can't stop bad things from happening to people by

45

handing them money. We don't live in that kind of world. What you *can* do is go on being a noble man; one who can go to college like you've always dreamed and come back and help everyone, not just a few who will likely squander their money. That's not selfish."

"It's practically all I've thought about for the past two days. I can still hardly believe it, but I'm worried. I wish Doctor Roberts was here. I wish Papá was here."

Chepa placed her palm on Ramón's chest and said, "Your papá will always be with you. Part of him is in you."

Ramón sighed, remembering his father, his bravery. What would Juan Bautista do if he were in Ramón's shoes?

"And *el humanitario*? I'll thank that man all of my days for what he did for you." Chepa made the sign of the cross.

Ramón remembered those last days with his mentor. "I made a promise to him a long time ago. What have I done to keep it? Nothing. But now that I have this money, I don't know if I can do it. I feel . . ." Ramón dropped his chin to his chest.

"Ashamed?" Chepa whispered. "Afraid?"

"How did you know?"

"I know."

She could read him like no one else. "I have something for you. From your father."

Chepa reached into the pocket of her simple brown dress and pulled out two small squares of brown cloth attached by a string. His father's Lady of Mount Carmel Scapular. She pressed it in Ramón's hand and closed his fingers around it.

"It will protect you. Things won't be easy from now on. Many will be unhappy with your fortune." Chepa's brow wrinkled on her wizened but lovely face. "Don't allow this money to change you. Remain a good man, not perfect, but noble."

Ramón felt her hand around his. Her bones were as fragile as those of a bird, the skin like parchment paper. When had his mother become so frail?

"But what will you use, Mamá?" he asked breathlessly.

"Ay, don't you worry about me. I know I'll be safe." She smiled her wise, contented smile and gave Ramón's cheek a gentle pat. "Doctor Roberts could have chosen some other boy, but *he chose you*. He knew it was your destiny to carry on what he started. You cannot deny that a divine force was guiding you to buy that complete ticket. Have you ever had a vision of yourself working in my store for the rest of your life, or your brothers' stores, or starting one of your own?"

"No." Ramón sat up ramrod straight, and felt his pulse quicken as he remembered his vision. "I've seen myself in a dental clinic, *my clinic*."

"Yes," Chepa affirmed. "I had a vision of *you* healing people, a picture of what was to come. Belief and faith are very powerful. Never forget that."

Powerful. Power. Ramón heard the words. Now that he had it, fear crept in his heart that he'd disappoint people. They had all shouted at the party that he was Maunabo's son. What if he failed?

Chepa squeezed his hand. Ramón was amazed at her strength. Although fragile at age sixty-six, she still had the force of a lioness. She embodied their name, León. Maybe he would, too.

"There's a reason God kisses some people and not others." Chepa let go of Ramón's hand. "It would be a sin to deny His gift."

CHAPTER 7

Antonio Díaz lived on the *Calle de Los Blancos*, the mile-long road that ran through the center of Maunabo. The Leóns lived at one end of the street and Antonio and Elsie's families at the other with a scattering of homes in between. The remaining families lived in the *barrio* in clapboard shacks with dirt floors and hammocks.

Ramón hadn't been to the Díaz's house since he was a child of seven, when he delivered the pennies owed to Señor Díaz from selling pastries to the *macheteros* at the sugar cane plantation. Antonio's father, who owned the plantation, would ruffle his hair, and say things like, "Ay, such an earnest boy!"

And he often gave Ramón a nickel or a whole dime for a tip. Sometimes Antonio would be there. He was five years older than Ramón and Ramón always looked up to the older boy. After Ramón started working in the store when he turned ten, he and Antonio hardly saw one another. Until now.

When Ramón was a boy, he thought Antonio's two-story stucco hacienda with red-tile roof was a mansion. It didn't loom so large now but Ramón couldn't help but compare it to his own house, barely large enough to hold a kitchen with dining area, a trio of small bedrooms, and a back porch with a sink and mirror. A dozen window panes were cracked and random tiles of the zinc roofs on the house and the latrine had blown away in hurricanes; his family always spent money on keeping the store running before they spent it on home repair. Ramón made a mental note. The next shopping trip to San Juan, he'd buy new tiles.

Antonio yanked open the large oak door as if he'd been waiting.

"Perfect timing, Ramón. I was just about to go out, to call on a charming young lady as a matter of fact. How's the luckiest man in Maunabo, besides me, of course?"

"Great, Antonio, just great. I came by to remind you to call the college. How long will it take for the application to get here? Is there just one essay or two?"

"I'll call first thing Monday morning, because we made a deal, right?"

"Yeah, I paid for the phone call, but I don't know about paying for the essay. . ." Ramón shook his head.

"Do you really think your English is good enough?" Antonio probed. "You don't want to ruin your chances, do you? I've done it before for other guys, just last semester for a guy in Yabucoa, and it worked great. Trust me, it'll pay off. And I trust you so much, I'll even start writing it. You can pay me the rest of my fee when I'm done. In the end, it'll hardly cost you anything."

Ramón reasoned: he bought his ticket from Caimito in a heartbeat, didn't that pay off? Maybe this would too. Should he let Antonio help him? Still, it didn't seem right.

Antonio must have sensed his reservation.

"Don't let it ruffle your feathers, *amigo*. You look so worried, your hair's gonna' fall out! Put your energy into chasing that skirt, the policeman's daughter! I saw you two at your party. It looked like things could get real cozy, right?"

Antonio cast a lascivious grin.

"Yeah, sure," Ramón muttered.

Ramón thought of Elsie. Was it fair to start something if he'd be off to the U.S. in a few months? Then he remembered how Elsie looked in that dress at his party, the way her eyes met his, the hint of teasing in her smile when she agreed to go to the town hall dance, the way *he* made *her* blush. Surely there was no harm in getting to know her better. That's how he could spend his time, not writing English essays.

"Yeah, just like I thought. You've been hit hard, *amigo*, hit by the thunderbolt of love." Antonio chuckled.

It was uncanny how he could read Ramón's mind.

"Okay, Antonio, we got a deal. But how about that dictionary you said you'd give me?"

"You're some guy, Ramón, to think of a dictionary over a girl. Don't worry," Antonio repeated. "I'll get it right now. Hey, you're so studious, you'll go straight to Michigan and do just great!"

§§§

That afternoon at the store, Ramón dealt with the lingering crowds. Chepa's word had spread, for rather than ask for money, they came to shake Ramón's hand, everyone except an American who strolled in. The man wore pressed gray suit pants, his white dress shirt stuck to the sweat on his back. He tried to sell them a phone, but Chepa waved him away.

"Ay, I'll never learn to use one of those things," she declared. "And who would I call when the only man with a phone is Don Pablo? Why call him when I can walk next door?"

For a moment, Ramón was frustrated. After Chepa sent the salesman running off, Ramón considered chasing after him to buy that phone. Then he remembered the girl from the day before, the one he denied help to, barely a woman but already with two babies.

And to think, he lamented he couldn't have a phone when the young woman barely had enough to eat. Was the money changing him already?

Ramón told Chepa he had to leave for an hour and dashed to visit Señora Lepe, the postmistress who ran the makeshift post office out of her run-down adobe house near the plaza. The woman made it her business to know everyone else's. As Ramón expected, she knew the young woman; her name was Esperanza.

Ramón went to her tin-roofed shack in the *barrio* after he purchased a sack full of items he'd hoped she'd like: a loaf of sweet fresh bread, white cheese wrapped in wax paper, roasted garbanzo beans and papaya candy suckers for the little girl. Ramón knocked at the flimsy wood door. It opened a crack. His heart beat faster. He had agonized over what to say to her. *Sorry, I hope this helps* didn't seem enough. Esperanza opened the door wider and stepped outside.

"Ahh, here's something for you." Ramón thrust the package at her.

She took the bag. "Thank you."

Something flashed in her eyes. Before, they had seemed vacant, sad. Now they had depth, a glimmer of hope.

Ramón shifted his weight from one foot to the other, wondering what else to say before an idea struck him and he asked, "Would you like a job?"

Her eyes opened wider, more alert, and expectant.

"What kind of job?" she asked with a trace of suspicion.

"An apprentice to my mother. She's been teaching sewing to young ladies for years, but she doesn't have any students now and my sister, Lila, just took a job at the new public health clinic in Yabucoa and will probably have her own family soon. My mother needs someone new to train. Mamá's been sewing so long that she's getting arthritis in her hands. You'd be helping her and me, too. We can't pay much, it will depend on how many orders we get, but I'd feel a lot better knowing someone is picking up some of my mother's work."

"But what about my babies?"

"You can take them to the store with you. Mamá loves having babies around. And once you get more skilled, I can bring some of the work to you here."

"Oh, I'd love the chance to work with Doña Chepa," she said, her voice lighter. "Everyone talks about how good she is, with her sewing, and her herbs. My baby boy has colic."

"She can help you with that, too," Ramón assured. It felt right to help her.

The daughter peered out at him from behind her mother's skirt and said in a tentative voice, "Mamá says Papá is with the angels. Are you an angel he sent to help us?"

The little girl's chocolate brown eyes grew bigger.

Esperanza stroked the top of her daughter's head and whispered, "He is, *m'ija*." She locked eyes with Ramón, took his hand and kissed the back of it. "God bless you, *Patrón*."

Heat flooded Ramón's ears and face.

"My pleasure. I'll talk to my mother and set everything up." Ramón tipped his cap before he left.

He had not only helped her with a few groceries, but with something much more; she'd learn a skill that would allow her to support herself and her family. Esperanza was a year or two younger than he. Her life was hard beyond measure, yet she was still capable of tremendous gratitude. Before he went back to work, he stopped at the bakery and the butcher's to arrange for a weekly delivery for Esperanza with her donor to remain anonymous. She was the kind of person he needed to help.

§§§

The rest of the day passed with little fanfare. Perhaps the news of Ramón's winning had begun to settle. After Chepa sold two yards of muslin to another well-wisher, the store emptied of customers.

"It's quiet again, and my back is aching with all this business. I'm going home for a rest," she said.

Happy to be alone, Ramón picked up the dictionary. There was no better time than the present to start studying. He flipped it open a few pages into the "A" words, memorizing them as he tried say each word out loud, his tongue twisting over the strange combination of a, c, and h: ache, achieve, achievement.

Not even sure if he was pronouncing the words correctly, he absently turned a few pages. His eyes focused on the word *alluring* with its Spanish translation: *seductivo, encantador*. He daydreamed of Elsie standing next to him at the party, her shapely thigh, the honey skin above the delicate hollows of her collar bones.

Tomorrow, Ramón decided, he would visit the Miraflores home and request permission to take Elsie to the town hall dance on the following Saturday. Asking a week in advance was respectable, so how could the police chief refuse? His stomach fluttered at the thought of being with her.

When the doorbell jingled, Ramón's fantasy of kissing her lips and the soft skin on her neck and shoulders was interrupted. A man strode into the store. He wore a white linen suit and matching fedora, unusual for a villager. Another customer or well-wisher, perhaps.

Annoyed at the intrusion, Ramón said, "Señor, I'll be closing in a few—"

The man rushed forward and smacked his hand on the

counter. The dictionary jumped. The water glass that Ramón had sipped from minutes earlier rolled off and shattered.

"Why you?" growled the man. "I bought that ticket for *years*, and the *one day* I didn't . . . I had to see you, to prove you exist, because this is all so unbelievable!"

He was the man from the party, the lurking figure at the edge of the plaza. Ramón remembered the feeling of the man's eyes boring into him from under the brim of his hat.

Ramón felt the color drain from his face. An eerie prickling spread its fingers across the back of his neck and shoulders. If this man could make the dictionary jump like a cockroach, what else was he capable of?

"Tell me!" the man shouted. "Why you, and not me? How did you do it? What sort of trickery did you use?"

"I had a vision of a number and Caimito had it. It was no trickery!"

The man moved closer. Ramón felt his glare like the heat of the blistering tropical sun. The man's breath smelled of stale rum.

Ramón squared his shoulders.

"Señor, look around." He made a sweep with his arm. "This store is all my family has. My mother puts everything into it. She lets our customers buy things on credit and pay us back when they can. My family has gone without to keep this place running. We've sacrificed. I've sacrificed. Maybe that's why I won."

"It was *my* number. How did you know it? Did you perform some type of math magic? Did you bribe the lottery officials? As God is my witness, I want what's mine!"

"No, it's mine," Ramón said, his voice steely. "Caimito went to a lot people that day before he came to me. You could have bought the ticket, but didn't."

Francisco materialized. Ramón's heart had been pounding so hard he hadn't heard his brother enter.

"Señor, we're closing. *Please leave now.*" Francisco, twenty pounds heavier and a decade younger than the intruder, puffed out his chest and glared.

Ramón stood next to his brother and held his chin higher. "Yes, leave now," he stressed.

"This doesn't end today. I'll ruin you and your family. I will run this store out of business!" the man threatened and glared before he retreated a step.

Ramón watched him walk out of the store and turn the corner. He was surprised at how hard his hands trembled as he kneeled to pick up the broken glass. Francisco grabbed a rag from under the counter and knelt to soak up the water.

They both stood. Ramón tossed the broken glass in the small trash container where it shattered into more pieces, making him jump.

"Damn, that was Trujillo," Francisco told him. "Everyone's talking about how mad he is that he bought that number forever, and that *you're* the one who won with it. He's the biggest merchant in Yabucoa, but I heard he's been spending his profits on more than lottery tickets, on the ponies, and cockfighting and liquor."

"*Dios Mío*—that was Trujillo? He looks so different that I didn't recognize him. He used to be respectable."

Ramón remembered the first time he had seen Trujillo, when Ramón was twelve and Chepa took him on a trip to Yabucoa. The merchant had paraded through the streets, and everywhere people tipped their hats; some kissed his hand. The butcher ran out of his shop to gift el señor his best cut of meat, the fruit vendor with his best mango. Señor Trujillo's mere presence demanded respect.

"People say his best friend is Bacardi Superior." Francisco shook his head, clucked his tongue, the habit he inherited from Chepa. "If I was in his shoes, losing like that, I'd go crazy, too. I guess there's a wolf in all of us, waiting to get out."

Together, Ramón and his brother closed the louvered door and windows to secure the store. Francisco took the key from Ramón, whose hand was shaking so hard he could barely maneuver it in the key hole. He couldn't stop seeing the look in Señor Trujillo's eyes, feral, like the rabid dog that attacked Ramón when he was five, just enough past crazy to tear him in two.

"He threatened me, our family. Should I go to the police?" Ramón said, his throat so tight he could barely speak.

"He hasn't done anything, so the police will only laugh at you. Plus, a man like Trujillo probably has one or two *policías* in his pocket. Juan can keep his eyes open when he's working at the court, since it's only a block from Trujillo's store. The guy's just blowing smoke. It'll pass."

Francisco patted Ramón's shoulder.

They had shut the store, but Ramón could not shut down his dread that Señor Trujillo would be back. He reached up and pressed the scapular to his chest. It had protected him in the encounter just now, but what about next time?

CHAPTER 8

"Cultivo una rosa blanca
En julio como en enero,
Para el amigo sincero
Que me da su mano franca."

I cultivate a white rose
In July as in January
For the sincere friend
Who gives me his hand frankly.

It was their custom. Every evening after dinner, Chepa asked Ramón to read to her as they sipped peppermint tea. She insisted both the words and the herb helped their digestion and improved sleep. When they started the custom years before and Lila still lived at home, she and Ramón would take turns reading, but the task more often fell to Ramón. The words flowed out him like the trickle of a gentle river, as if he were born to recite. He often read from a school book or the newspaper. Tonight Ramón selected poetry from a volume loaned by Don Pablo.

"You're the smartest person in the neighborhood, and all this reading will continue to improve your mind for when you go off to school. Ay, you have so many chances I never had. I'm so happy for you," Chepa extolled.

Ramón warmed to her words, needed the calming effect of their time together, with the fresh memory of Trujillo's threat. Yet he wouldn't share the incident with Chepa. She had looked so frail a few days earlier, after villagers showed up at the store and a fight nearly broke out over Ramón's money; he didn't want to burden her with bad news.

The poem he recited was by José Martí, a Cuban national hero, a poet, philosopher, essayist and journalist. Martí fought for liberty and Cuba's independence from Spain. Chepa told Ramón how she admired the man and would never tire of hearing his poems.

Their pet cat, Gigi, rubbed against Chepa's leg, her loud purr mixing with Ramón's soft voice. Stray cats savvy enough to escape the village cur dogs wandered in and out of the yard, and most Chepa shooed away. But this lucky cat had snuck into their house weeks before. The bones of her spine poked through her matted fur, but she never stopped purring. Chepa fed her once and now she trotted into their kitchen every night at dinner. Her bony frame filled out and her soft gray fur shone.

Darkness descended into the room, and Chepa lit a candle that cast a shadow of the book across the kitchen table as Ramón continued to read:

> "Y para el cruel que me arranca
> El corazón con que vivo,
> Cardo ni ortiga cultivo,
> Cultivo una rosa blanca."

And for the cruel person who tears
Out the heart with which I live,
I cultivate neither nettles nor thorns:
I cultivate a white rose.

"Such beautiful words," Chepa began. "I know you'll be studying science in school, but you should take a class in reading and writing. What do they call it?"

"Literature," Ramón said.

"Yes, of course, it helps balance the mind. Tell me, *m'ijo,* what do you think the poem means?"

Ramón paused before answering. "Maybe he should have used a poisonous flower, rather than a white rose. But maybe not. I think Martí is saying to repay evil with good."

He thought again of Trujillo—how much evil was he capable of? Then Ramón pushed it into the back of his mind, not wanting to poison the moment.

"I think you're right. You see, all that reading you did in school, getting there so early every morning, it was worth it," Chepa pointed out.

"Yeah, once I got used to getting up at four every morning, I never regretted it."

Ramón recalled his final two years of high school. He had transferred from his crumbling school in Yabucoa to a new high school in Guayama, one that had fresh paint, new textbooks, and teachers recruited from San Juan or even the U.S. mainland to provide a better education. But it was a longer trip on a rutted road, and cost ten cents fare for a *público* that was often late or didn't show. So Ramón found a solution: he woke at 4 A.M. to catch a ride with the newspaper delivery man, who was thankful that Ramón kept him awake with their chatter as they watched the sun rise over the palm trees. Ramón would arrive at school two hours early to study. He could even fit some studying in on the *público* ride home (the evening service was more regular). He was always tired, but it was a well-deserved fatigue, because he fell in bed every night satisfied with the fullness of his days.

"Think, months from now, you'll be studying books and

poems, science, medicine," Chepa remarked, her voice joyful.

It sounded exciting, but overwhelming, too.

"But I'll miss this time we have together," Ramón admitted.

"Ay, you'll be too busy learning new things."

Yet knowing there may not be anyone to read to her in the evenings filled Ramón with melancholy.

"No, Mamá. That will never happen. Of course I'll miss you."

She nodded. A comfortable moment of silence followed. By the wistful look on her face, Ramón knew Chepa was thinking of the future alone, too.

Before Ramón could start another poem, Francisco burst through the door. His face ruddy from rum, he spoke in the lofty voice he used when he had been drinking.

"Well, isn't this cozy? The favorite son, with his fancy book."

The cat darted out of the room.

"*Sinvergüenza* (without shame), don't talk such nonsense," Chepa chastised as she stood.

Ramón stood next to her. "Brother, unless you're here for a good reason, you need to go home and have some coffee."

"Actually, I am," Francisco sneered. "Trujillo's making good on his threat. On my way back from Yabucoa, I heard he was promising free food and gifts for anyone who shops at his store, and stays away from *our* stores—mine and Mamá's"

Francisco wagged his finger at Ramón to say, "Little *brother*, you won all that money, and you'll take it and go to your fancy college, but what about the rest of us?"

What Francisco said was rawly honest. A sense of doom began to mushroom deep in Ramón's stomach. How could something nearly miraculous have come to this?

"I can't believe Trujillo would do this!" Ramón felt the anger in his voice.

"What are you talking about, Francisco? What threat?" Chepa implored, her eyes darting from one son to the other.

"Oh," Francisco scoffed. "The prodigal son didn't tell you what happened?"

"Mamá, I didn't want to worry you," Ramón defended. "Trujillo showed up at the store a few days ago. He was furious I won and he didn't."

"Yeah," Francisco interjected, "and he threatened to ruin our family and now it looks like he may just do it."

"Let it go," Chepa insisted. "We'll survive. People won't listen forever. This is big news for now, until something else happens, good or bad. Sadly, they'll move on to the next piece of gossip, and eventually, you'll be forgotten," she finished as she nodded at Ramón.

"As for you," Chepa turned her attention to Francisco. "I repeat, let it go. Take yourself home, throw some cold water on your face, and go to bed. No more talk of this."

Francisco's jaw tensed.

"Fine, but Trujillo's threat better not turn into something more," he grumbled before he turned and left, his feet not quite steady beneath him.

"Mamá, I didn't mean for any of this to happen." Ramón shook his head, the pit in his stomach growing larger. "Maybe I should pay the man, give him some money to make this go away."

"No amount of money will help him. His heart is poisoned with envy. Stay away from him."

"But I should go see him, reason with him!"

"Don't. He won't listen to you. Promise me you'll stay away

from him. If you don't, things will get bad. I have a feeling about this, a bad one."

"But the store—" Ramón tried to say.

"Things will be fine in the store. Plus, we sold more than usual with all those people coming to see you. And people will always need my herbs, my cures. Sadly, they still get sick and will call for me. I need to hear your promise."

Ramón nodded and swallowed hard.

"Fine!" he vowed, a fierceness in his voice that surprised him.

Then, regretting using such a tone with his mother, he continued in a softer voice, "Mamá I don't feel like reading any more tonight. Is that okay?"

Chepa embraced Ramón and gave his back a gentle pat before letting go.

"This shall pass. You need to get some rest, too. Go on to bed. Sleep well, *m'ijo*."

Yet Ramón didn't sleep well. The news from Francisco wasn't good. Not at all. What if Trujillo made good on his threat? He was after not only after Ramón, but his family. And what of Chepa's warning to stay away from the man?

And the way Francisco was drunk tonight? It was painful to see him change, like a split personality. Ramón would have to formulate a plan to keep them all afloat. The plan would have to include Francisco, who stayed sober when he had something more pressing to do. Ramón had seen it, the time when his brother didn't touch a drop of alcohol when his five-year-old daughter had awful bronchitis, when Chepa and Francisco together kept it from turning into pneumonia with her herbal teas of pleurisy root and echinacea.

It was a lot to take in. Then Ramón thought of Elsie. After winning the lottery, seeing her again was one of the best things that had happened in the past few days. He wanted them to be together, he wanted her to be the rose among all the thorns that were piercing his heart.

CHAPTER 9

The next evening, Ramón stood in front of the oval mirror nailed above the sink on the back porch. He combed a dab of pomade into his freshly washed hair. When he told Chepa he was going to ask Capitán Miraflores if he could escort Elsie to the town hall dance, she clucked her tongue and shook her head. Yet she produced Juan Bautista's finest black tie, which she had kept all this time.

"*Cuidado, m'ijo* (Be careful, my son). Don't get hurt. That family and ours are not the same. Think twice before things get too serious," Chepa said, knotting the tie for him before she left to prepare dinner.

Ramón heard her warning, but didn't want to listen. He needed Elsie. He thought of Trujillo's visit and his threat. Elsie could be antidote to his fear, to all the worries that kept him up at night as he contemplated the future.

Ramón looked at his reflection in the old mirror with a crack across the top. The face that looked back at him had chiseled features, smooth olive skin, and dark hair clipped short. For the first time, he considered himself handsome. He and Elsie would make a fine pair at the dance. Ramón looked down and straightened his father's tie, admiring how it contrasted against his pressed white dress shirt.

Before walking the mile to the other end of *La Calle de Los Blancos*, Ramón picked a bouquet of rose colored hibiscus from Chepa's prized tree.

§§§

The Miraflores home, Spanish Colonial and two stories high with a portico graced by spiral columns, was even finer than the Díaz's. Ramón walked up the four front steps, exhaled deeply, knocked on the massive arched front door and waited.

Señora Miraflores, a plump woman barely higher than Ramón's shoulder, answered. "Oh, Ramón, what can I do for you?"

"For Elsie and ahh . . . you, Señora."

Ramón thrust out the bouquet. *Why didn't I think of picking two?*

"Oh, beautiful!" she bubbled.

Her mouth formed a perfect O, and her double chin wiggled like coconut flan.

"What's the occasion?" she asked.

Suddenly, Ramón's mouth felt as dry as the scales on a lizard's back.

"Could I have something cold to drink?"

"¡*Sí, sí*!" she exclaimed.

Ramón followed her through the reception room. They walked across a polished floor covered in black and white checkerboard tiles and entered the kitchen. Señora Miraflores retrieved a glass bottle from the small electric refrigerator. The Miraflores were the first family in Maunabo to get one. Ramón tried to pronounce the label in his head—*Free-gi-daire.*

Beads of sweat popped out on his forehead. The woman busied herself with taking a vase out of the cabinet and placing it with the flowers on the center of the table, which was huge and made of dark wood polished to a high shine. Ramón leaned over to actually peer at his reflection. La señora then retrieved a drinking glass and filled it with ice and juice—ice not chipped from large chunks like they had in the ice box at home but from their fancy refrigerator and shaped into perfect little cubes!

Señora Miraflores handed Ramón the glass of mango juice and napkin. He dabbed his forehead and placed the napkin on the table. He took a sip of juice, held the glass and swallowed hard.

"Is Elsie home?" he mumbled.

"I'll get her."

She left the room. Ramón heard whispers behind the closed door. He wiped off more beads of sweat with the napkin before Elsie and her parents entered the room. The police chief nodded a hello but stood silent and imposing. He seemed like Goliath to Ramón's David.

Ramón's heart did a cartwheel. Elsie wore the same white dress as the day of his party.

"Hi, Ramón."

"Hi," he managed to say.

Ramón placed his glass on the table. "That juice was delicious!" he said in an attempt to make the moment less awkward.

Ramón looked down. The bottom of the glass was sweating almost as much as he was. La señora gave him an exasperated look. She stepped forward and placed the napkin under the glass.

Ramón groaned inwardly. What if the glass left a mark on that fancy table? At his house, they didn't have to worry about such things.

Ramón steeled himself and then faced the chief.

"I came by to ask if I could take Elsie to the town hall dance next Saturday."

Not sure what to do with his hands, Ramón thrust them in his pants pockets.

Elsie's father stood like a statue. The large black hands of the wall clock ticked mercilessly.

"¿Papá?" Elsie turned to her father expectantly. "I'd really like to go."

Ramón saw the look in the police chief's eyes, a softening almost undetectable, as he turned to Elsie. He prayed the man would concede.

In the awkward moment of silence before the police chief had the chance to reply, Ramón pulled his left hand out of his pocket and knocked over the glass. It crashed to the floor and shattered, spilling a rivulet of orange fluid.

"*Dios*, sorry!" he stammered.

He grabbed the napkin and crouched to clean the mess.

"Oh, let me get it," Elsie said breathlessly.

Elsie retrieved a dish cloth and knelt beside him. She placed her hand on his arm to stop him, almost a caress. Ramón felt heat, electricity. He didn't want her to stop.

They stood. Elsie held the towel with the pieces of glass within its folds, her face flushed. Against her caramel complexion, Ramón believed the color was more stunning than anything that existed in nature, even more beautiful than the flowers. As if reading his mind, she smiled a hint of her teasing grin again, and said, "Thanks for the flowers."

"Yes, you may escort my daughter to the dance," the police chief said, finally giving the faintest smile, his eyes crinkling at the corners.

Ramón had the absurd notion to dance a few steps right there in their kitchen. Instead, he stood straighter.

"Thank you, Capitán. I have only honorable intentions. I'll be back at seven on Saturday."

The man's smile faded as he demanded, "Have Elsie home before eleven."

Even so, Ramón could hardly believe it. He bid them good bye and bounded down the front steps. Just as he landed at the bottom, he saw a shadow looming over the sidewalk. Ramón turned, to see el Capitán hovering tall at the top step.

"I'll be watching you," the police chief warned. "It's my precious daughter you'll be taking out."

For a moment, Ramón felt as small as an ant, about to be squashed under el capitán's shiny black boot, but no, he had come here with honor.

"As I said, Capitán, I have only the best intentions." Ramón removed his cap and nodded. "Thank you again."

He thrust his cap back on his head. As he walked away, he sensed Elsie's father's gaze on his back and straightened his spine. The policeman's statement made him think of Antonio's words: "*to chase that skirt*." Ramón would never think of Elsie that way.

He also thought of the way the glass broke, the second one in two days! And Trujillo's threat, and the police chief's warning. Bad luck comes in threes. He continued on, trying to ignore the trembling of his hands as he shoved them in his pockets. That was the superstition of peasants, and he would soon be studying to be a man of science.

Yet part of him dreaded, what would come next?

CHAPTER 10

Toot toot toot. The driver honked the horn to greet another bus coming from the opposite direction and pulled aside. The two *públicos* slowed down so much, that, as was the custom, the passengers stood and shook one another's hands through the open windows. Today, when the two villagers from the opposing *público* shook hands with Ramón, they shouted congratulations.

"Ah, so you're the fellow I heard about who won with a complete ticket—the dentist," Roberto, the driver, called out.

Ramón laughed and told him, "I'm not a dentist yet, señor. It'll take years of study first. I'm going to Michigan."

"My cousin's cousin is in the states, too, in New York! You should look him up."

"I've had so many people tell me to see so many other people, if I visit them all, I'd never get to class," Ramón quipped.

He laughed again, enjoying the feeling of doing so. He had been worried about Trujillo and about Francisco, so when Chepa asked him to go to San Juan to purchase chiffon and linen, he'd leapt at the opportunity. A group of three women who had come from Patillas to congratulate Ramón ordered dresses for a wedding, and Chepa had no fabric as fine as chiffon. Such an order was one of the benefits of all the extra foot traffic.

The driver laughed along with him when suddenly, the bus hit a gigantic hole in the middle of the road that any fool could see. The *público* lurched to a stop.

"Ay, another flat," the driver declared and stepped out.

Ramón and the only other passenger, his old friend, Herman Steidel, followed.

The three stood at the front of the bus. The rusted rim was already embedded in the dirt, with a tire as flat as a tortilla. The driver removed his straw hat and scratched his head.

"I used my spare last month. We'll have to wait for the other *público* to come back this way and help us."

"How long will that take?" Ramón asked.

The driver shrugged. "He's making a run to Patillas and back, two, maybe three hours."

"Three hours!" Ramón gasped. "I need to get back. My mother's got a big order of dresses to fill!"

"Why are you on this old carcass of a bus anyway? You could buy your own car, my bus, or hell . . . every bus on the island!"

Before Ramón could answer, Herman scoffed, "He's saving his money for school, to be a dentist, remember?"

The driver nodded and removed three small cigars out of his front shirt pocket.

"Well, I don't know about you boys, but I'm gonna' have one of these and take a *siesta*. That looks like a good spot," he said and pointed to a grassy area in the shade of a ceiba tree.

"Come on, Ramón," Herman suggested. "Let's have a smoke. You better get used to them—you can afford them now! I don't want to go to school today anyway."

"No thanks. Those things are bad for you."

Ramón wished he had Antonio's dictionary so he could at least use the *two*, or even, *three* hours to study.

He decided to walk until another bus came along and told the others.

"Suit yourself," the driver and Herman chimed in unison.

70

They settled under the ceiba tree. Ramón started walking and turned around once to see the two men in the supine position, tendrils of smoke lazily drifting above them.

§§§

The first half hour of the walk was pleasant enough, with only the sounds of a few laughing gulls and crickets to accompany him. Then Ramón began to feel a slow trickle of perspiration from his underarms. Rolling up the sleeves of his dress shirt, he wished he had worn a short sleeved one. Over the next hour, he passed three rusted cars, whose only occupants were lizards darting in and out of their broken windows. He remembered what the driver said: *Why are you on this old carcass of a bus anyway?*

Ramón rationalized, *don't I need a car? Maybe that's why the público broke down. It must be a sign.*

There were only three cars in all of Maunabo, owned by Capitán Miraflores, Don Pablo and *el carnicero,* although the butcher's old jalopy of a truck hardly counted. Plus, if he had a car as fine as Capitán Miraflores, wouldn't that elevate him in the police chief's eyes? And how could he take Elsie out on a date *on foot?* Ramón imagined the two of them driving off in some fine car into the sunset, maybe an Oldsmobile like her father's.

Having a car made perfect sense for his trips to and from San Juan. And when he left, he could give it to José Luis or Francisco to continue buying trips, or even sell it and get back his money, and then use the money to improve the store. A car would be an investment, wouldn't it?

§§§

Ramón arrived in San Juan three hours later than expected, hot and frustrated. The other *público* had eventually rolled along and picked him up. The new driver chuckled as he told Ramón he woke Roberto and Herman up from their naps before he gave them a spare tire and left them there, swearing and huffing to fix the flat in the blazing heat.

Heck, Ramón reasoned, if those two were still there when he made his return trip in his new car, he'd even offer them a ride.

He hurried through his shopping, buying two bolts each of chiffon and linen. His arms ached from carrying a heavier load than normal. A car would solve that problem, too.

Ramón headed down a street clogged with pedestrians, bicyclists, and a man leading a donkey with a bushel of hay on its back. The shouts of vendors rang in his ears, men selling *bacalaitos fritos,* fried plantains and beer. At the end of the street was a car lot.

A black Buick sat at the end of a line of a dozen cars. The sun glinted off the sleek hood, where the polished V-shaped ornament perched on the front like a bird of prey. The Buick emblem was fixed to the grill. Ramón walked over and stared.

An American man dressed in a gray pinstripe suit materialized next to him and pumped his hand up and down.

"Young man, you have excellent taste. You've chosen the finest vehicle on my lot." The salesman waved his large hand in admiration. "A 1942 Buick Super, nearly new, barely used—you'll love it! Care for a test drive?"

Ramón hesitated, tapping his left foot on the pavement. A test drive meant this man would discover he didn't *really* know how to drive. Ramón silenced his foot to hide his nervousness. After all, he had watched the drivers of the *públicos* for all these years, and *el carnicero* had let Ramón practice driving once on his old truck. "It already has lots of dents," the butcher had claimed and shrugged. "What's a few more?"

"Well . . ." Ramón straightened his spine. "It's a beauty. How much?"

"I suppose I can let her go for $1,900. After all, I have to pay a steep import tax—it nearly kills me. But once you get behind the wheel, you'll see. It's a fair price." The man nodded, grinning like a court jester.

"I don't need to. I'll take it," Ramón blurted before he lost his nerve.

Ramón ran to *Banco Público* to draw money out of his account. Of course it should be saved for college, but this represented only a little over ten percent of what he won. He could afford it, couldn't he? And there was the practical matter of owning a car.

The teller looked bored when Ramón stepped up to counter. "Next, please," he said in a flat voice and stifled a yawn.

The man's eyes were bloodshot, and Ramón guessed he had been out late the night before, probably at a fancy night club. Other than his coming home party, Ramón hadn't had a night out since he won. Didn't he deserve some fun, and a car, too?

"I need nineteen-hundred dollars in cash," Ramón announced, handing the teller his bank book. When he had opened the account weeks earlier, the bank manager explained he'd earn interest, so he reasoned he'd even have a little more money by now. He could buy himself something.

The teller's eyes flew open wide as he uttered, "Yes, señor. I'll need to see some identification. Your license please."

The man was a few years older than Ramón, yet he treated him with respect.

"I don't have a license. That's all I have." Ramón pointed to the bank book.

"Oh, I'll have to get the manager then. Excuse me, señor."

The bank teller rushed off.

An image flashed in Ramón' mind, their family store empty of customers if Trujillo's threat came true. Should he dare buy a car? Then he thought of Elsie—the car could be for them. *He . . . they deserved it. They would go in style to the town hall dance.* And he hoped it would be the first of many dates.

Señor López, the same manager who welcomed Ramón the day he won, hurried to the counter.

"I'm sorry for the inconvenience, Señor Carrasquillo. Will that be check or cash?"

"Cash," Ramón insisted.

He couldn't believe how easy it was. After he took the wad of money, he shoved it in his pocket and ran back to the lot.

§§§

When the salesman turned over the keys to Ramón, their metallic jingle sounded magnificent. *Dios, being a rich man is amazing—he sold me the car and I don't even have a license, and that treatment at the bank, too!*

The salesman stood six inches over him, but on that day, Ramón felt like a giant.

When Ramón stepped into the car, the smell of the upholstery filled his nostrils. The chocolate brown leather seats felt cool under his legs. He turned the key in the ignition, and the engine roared to life.

After releasing the clutch, Ramón shifted into first too quickly. Embarrassed, he glanced in the rearview mirror to see the salesman laughing as the Buick bucked and lurched out of the lot. By something short of a miracle, he shifted into second gear, then finally, third. The eight cylinders purred.

Despite his earlier display of bravado, Ramón's heart pounded. He slowed his breathing and repeated the mantra: "*Clutch, shift, gas, clutch, shift, gas . . .*" as he drove through the towns of Caguas, Humacao and Yabucoa. Caguas was one of the largest towns outside of San Juan where cars filled the road, but as Ramón drove farther, traffic thinned. The two lane road became single and dirt packed. The foliage became so thick that he drove under a canopy of leaves where it almost seemed like nighttime.

The hoots and cries of a parakeet replaced the tooting of horns. Chickens squawked and flapped their wings as they scrambled out of the way of the Buick. In Yabucoa, swayback donkeys outnumbered the cars. The villagers astride them turned their heads and pointed when Ramón drove by. He guessed most had never seen such a vehicle.

When Ramón reached *La Pica*, his heart pounded harder. He uttered a prayer for every switchback he came to, and on his eighth one, he rounded the tight curve and nearly collided with a wild horse grazing by the side of the road.

Ramón slammed on the brakes. The car began to skid. In that split second, Ramón imagined hitting the horse, killing it, or even himself. *My God, it can't end this way, it's too soon!*

In an instant, the horse's brown head shot up before it snorted and galloped into the forest. The car landed in a rut, the engine dead, the front fender two feet from the trunk of an enormous mango tree.

Ramón's heart stopped hammering. He turned the key in the ignition and pressed his foot on the gas. The wheels spun in the dirt. *Slower . . . maybe if I press it slower, I'll get out of this.*

He tried once. Twice. Three times. Nothing. He stepped out and stared at the car, as if that would get it to move. Sensing someone behind him, he turned. An old peasant approached with a basket of mangos and papayas on his head.

"Need a little help, son?"

Ramón felt the heat creep up his face and pleaded, "Yes, if you don't mind."

"I used to work for a man who owned a car. I know what to do, but surely a man with a car as fine as this can spare something for an old beggar like me."

The man slipped the basket off his head and smirked to reveal four missing teeth.

Ramón reached into his wallet. He had two dollars, what this man would earn in a week delivering fruit.

"This is all I have. You're welcome to it." Ramón handed the bills over. They vanished into the peasant's pocket as fast as a cockroach in a beam of light.

"My bones ache all over. You're a young fellow. Move in front. I'll start the car. You push when I holler so I can back it out," the man explained.

Ramón stepped in front and put his hands on the hood as he braced one foot against the trunk of the mango tree. The old man hopped into the front seat as quickly as the bills disappeared. He turned on the ignition and shouted, "Now!"

Head down, Ramón grunted and pushed, then pushed again.

The car backed out of the rut. He looked up the see the peasant snicker. *Dios, he's going to steal my car!*

The car moved another three, four feet. Ramón sprinted to the driver's side door, grasping the handle with the same strength he had used to push his car.

"Got it!" he gasped.

The peasant smirked again as he got out of the car.

"Take a driving lesson, son." He laughed and retrieved his basket before lumbering down the road.

Ramón felt the sweat trickle down his cheeks the entire way home. By the time he rolled into Maunabo, his shirt was even more soaked to his back than from his walk. Realizing he'd hardly been breathing, he exhaled.

He made it.

When he pulled up in front of his house, he shifted into first gear too quickly. The car jerked to a stop. He bounded up the two front steps and ran into the kitchen. The door banged behind him.

"Mamá, I'm home! Come quickly—wait 'till you see what I bought!"

Silence greeted him. Since he had driven home, even with the *público's* delay, he arrived earlier than usual. Chepa was at the store.

Voices filtered in from the street. Someone must have spread the news already.

In his bedroom, he pulled off his shirt and grabbed a new one. He ran to the sink on the porch, threw cold water on his face and underarms, dried himself, and quickly donned the new short-sleeved shirt. When he jumped down the front steps, he almost collided with Guillermo, his best friend since childhood. Diego was there, too. Adrenaline flooded Ramón's chest when he saw who accompanied them. Elsie.

His friends circled his car, admiring his purchase.

Guillermo whistled. "What a beauty!"

He opened the passenger side door and reached in to stroke the rich leather.

"You actually did it. *El carnicero* said he saw you rolling into town, but I didn't believe it until I saw it with my own eyes. Let's go for a ride," Diego called out.

"It's beautiful." Elsie ran her fingertips along the hood. "My father's Oldsmobile's not even as nice as this."

"Thanks," Ramón stammered, glad he had changed his shirt.

"Let's stop standing around and see how this baby handles," Guillermo said.

"Yes, to the light house!" Diego suggested. He punched Ramón's shoulder. "You're a good driver, aren't you, Ramón?"

"Yeah—sure I am." Ramón felt his ears burning.

"Let's go." Elsie's face flushed, excitement filled her voice.

The four friends hopped into the car, Ramón and Elsie in the front seat, Guillermo and Diego in the back. Elsie stroked the leather under her legs. Ramón could tell she was impressed. Surely, he was justified in buying the car.

Still, he secretly begged God to let him start the car smoothly this time. Ramón eased into first, thanking his hands for their steady obedience, and the group started their journey to the Maunabo Lighthouse at *Punta Tuna*, a bluff several hundred feet above the ocean. His heart raced as he kept his eyes on the road and off the curve of Elsie's thigh under her full-length ruffled skirt. He gripped the steering wheel like a vise, occasionally letting go to wipe the sweat from his hands onto his pants.

"Quick, Ramón, pull over. The sun is about to set." Guillermo pointed to a grassy down slope leading to a cliff in front of the lighthouse. It was one of the finest views of the Caribbean Sea as the last rays of the sun caressed the horizon, pink and blue serpentines streaking the sky. It was also one of the steepest drops on the island. Ramón slowly pulled off the dirt road, stopped the car, and turned off the ignition.

Everyone got out except him. For a moment, he drank it all in: Elsie, showing up to see him again, the smile she flashed when she said, "let's go," the never ending rose colored sky above the sea.

Then he stepped out of the car after his friends. He'd walked about ten paces when Diego screamed, "Look—the car!"

Ramón turned and realized—with horror—that he forgot to set the hand brake. He watched as the finest thing he owned rolled forward, about to catapult over the cliff. And it wasn't even the old peasant that would steal his car. He'd manage to lose it all by himself.

He bolted forward, leapt in the front seat and slammed on the brake. The tires spit chunks of gravel as the Buick skidded to a stop, the front grill two feet from the abyss.

Ramón let out his breath as his body stopped shaking. His friends started clapping. Ramón heard a voice. At first, he thought it was Guillermo or Diego, but then realized it was the voice of his own conscience: *Mamá said not to let this money change me. And I went out and got this fancy car. My God, what have I done?*

"¡Hey, *pendejo*!" Diego shouted. "That car cost a fortune—you could have bought a house with the money you spent!"

Ramón leaned back in his seat. All that money spent, which should be saved for college, or for the store if sales plummeted. And he almost lost his life, too. It should have been the second luckiest day of his life, saving the damn car, but he felt his cheeks burn.

Ramón swallowed hard, and tasted shame.

CHAPTER 11

The tale of Ramón's Buick spread almost as fast as the news of his fortune. Ramón's brothers had come to Chepa's house to ogle his Buick the night he returned from *Punta Tuna*, teasing him about his poor driving skills. But after too many tumblers of rum, Francisco turned nasty.

"Showing off, little brother? And what if people listen to Trujillo and stop coming to us? What then?" he said, his mouth grimacing as if there were a bad taste in it, his face reddened.

Chepa silenced Francisco with a look, as always, and sent him home to his wife, Isabel, to sober up.

Chepa's reaction to his purchase wasn't what Ramón expected either. She didn't agree it was a good idea, but shook her head and clucked her tongue, her trademark gesture that meant he should have known better.

The next day in the store, people teased him, calling him "slippery fingers." But with many it was worse. The butcher, stinking of fat and blood, came in with a scowl and mentioned again that his truck needed fixing, an essential thing, not a luxury. He said villagers were talking: if Ramón was going to spend money like water, would he have enough for that fancy college?

Ramón felt so guilty that he drove to San Juan to try and sell the car back, even though he didn't have a license yet. The salesman laughed.

"No one wants to buy a car during wartime," he claimed, "And with the way gas is rationed, I don't need another car on the lot. Thanks, but no thanks."

Instead of people raving over his car like Ramón fantasized, they were raving that he had spent money on a Buick that he almost drove off a cliff.

From all the talk, Ramón's nerves were on edge. Trujillo's threat and the incident between them kept coming back to haunt Ramón as if the man were still in the room. When an unfamiliar customer had pulled a quarter out of his back pocket, Ramón saw a hint of silver and gasped, thinking it was a henchman sent by Señor Trujillo wielding a knife. When the man left, sales dwindled to nothing.

How different it was all turning out than he expected.

At least he had his date with Elsie to look forward to. She didn't tease when she saw the car. She loved it, and he wanted her to love him in it.

§§§

The following morning, Ramón drove to Yabucoa and passed his driver's license test. Amazing how a couple dollar bills and a freshly slaughtered chicken for the examiner's dinner made the man forget to ask how Ramón got to the test in the first place.

Then something happened. Customers stopped coming into the store. After all that activity, the rest of the morning dragged like a dog with three legs.

Trujillo's threats were coming true. It had taken several days, but villagers were listening. The merchant must be promising a lot, for Ramón knew people were catching rides or taking the *públicos* to Yabucoa to shop at Trujillo's store.

Ramón flipped the CLOSED sign and ran across the square to Francisco's store. His brother had a small hardware store whereas

Chepa's store sold clothing, shoes and fabric used for alterations. Offering different merchandise seemed to work well, until now.

Ramón stepped inside to find Francisco sitting at his front counter, the same type of stained wood counter in Chepa's store, with his accounts book flipped open in front of him. It was not quite noon, and Francisco had a cup in front of him. He reached for it and Ramón noticed his scar, a thick, pink line starting in the center of his palm and ending in his forearm in the shape of a star. It was the remnant from the injury when at age fifteen, Francisco stopped that rabid dog from attacking Ramón when he was five. The incident with Trujillo wasn't the first where Francisco saved him.

Francisco sipped from his cup and placed it back down with a plunk. Thank *Dios* it contained only black coffee.

"Anything been going on here today?" Ramón asked. "No one's been in since I opened this morning."

"I've only sold an oil lamp. And the past couple days haven't been a lot better. If it keeps up, I don't know what I'm going to do."

Francisco's eyes looked puffy from sleeplessness, with deep lines at the corners that shouldn't be there for a man of almost thirty.

"I know what we're going to do," Ramón affirmed. "Close shop. We're going to San Juan, to buy more merchandise. If we pick up more inventory, it will be cheaper, and we can pass the savings on to our customers. We'll beat Trujillo at his own game."

"But that costs money." Francisco stood and turned his hands upward in a frustrating gesture. "I can't do that right now."

"I'll cover it."

"But what about saving all that money for college? Mamá will never agree," Francisco said.

He looked so different when he hadn't been drinking, contrite even, paternal. At that moment, it dawned on Ramón how much Francisco's eyes resembled their father's. Ramón truly loved his brother when he was sober. He had to find a way to help him stay that way.

"Let's just say I'm sure I'll get it back when our sales increase," Ramón assured. "I trust you, Francisco. Pay me back when you can. I got the damn car, I might as well use it. Let's drive to San Juan." Ramón paused. "Hey, you know I regret buying the Buick, don't you? I tried to sell it back, but I'm stuck with it. You can't imagine how sorry I am."

"Yeah, I know," Francisco said in a gentler tone. "And you know what Mamá would say? The deed is done." He laid his hand on Ramón's shoulder. "You know what? In your shoes, I would have done the same thing."

§§§

They spent the afternoon in San Juan, running between four different warehouses and buying a half-dozen men's shirts and trousers, a half-dozen women's blouses, gingham beach dresses, skirts with trouser pleats, scarves for women to tie in their hair for parties and lace *mantillas* for them to wear in their hair for Saint's week. They placed an order from a thrilled Alberto Gómez for five dresses of the newest trend with wide belts that cinched the waist and shorter, daring hemlines that fell to the knee. After Alberto told them they'd have had to wait several weeks for the dresses, Ramón and Francisco purchased a few gold and silver belts for their customers to practice with.

"Ay, it's so good doing business with my favorite customer," Alberto exclaimed. "People have been coming in to see the store where the jackpot winner came to that day. Even in these times, my sales have never been better!"

Ramón and Francisco also ordered five men's suits. Ramón knew families saved money for years for their sons to purchase a single suit when they turned eighteen. The same suit could be worn for weddings, funerals, or the town hall dances, and now his families would be able to buy one for a few *pesos* less.

They bought bolts of rayon, a new fabric for Chepa to work with. For Francisco's store, they bought paraffin, oil lamps, mosquito nets, nails, lumber, hoes, shovels and zinc tiles, and a few extra tiles for Chepa's roof.

Ramón hadn't seen Francisco so animated in weeks as he joked with each merchant, claiming, "My little brother hit the jackpot, and now I have too!" Francisco acted drunk with excitement.

The brothers drove home with the trunk full of merchandise and two brooms and planks of lumber the size of small trees sticking out the back seat window.

"You know what?" Francisco said as he propped his arm on the passenger side window. "It feels good to be working like that again, to have my head clear. Thanks."

"It was good for me, too."

Ramón felt a relief of the tension he had been holding in his shoulders. A memory bubbled to the surface, from years before when Francisco took him to the old theater in Maunabo and splurged an extra two cents for seats in the front with a better view of the screen. They saw *Tarzan the Ape Man* over six installments. Ramón loved the experience and knew his big brother did, too.

For the first time in weeks, Ramón saw Francisco smile. He prayed to see that look again and again, happy and unbroken.

CHAPTER 12

Ramón began the drive to his former high school in Guayama. The Christmas holiday and the school's two-week break were fast approaching and he needed a copy of his grades to send to Michigan with the application. Antonio had actually kept his promise and called the college. The application would arrive after the first of the year, and was due in February for the fall semester of August, 1945. It seemed an interminable time to wait, but Ramón found some comfort in the fact he continued to study the dictionary as far as the "Bs".

He replayed in his mind the words he tried to pronounce a few hours before: *betray, betrayer, betrothal,* how ironic those words were listed one under the other. He thought with a growing sense of unease of Trujillo, then with a far more welcoming thought of Elsie.

The Buick bumped along on the rutted roads, while cur dogs chased the tires, barking at the dust the wheels kicked up. Ramón thought of his family's livelihood, the money spent on the extra merchandise to keep them going. He would have to spread the word, maybe through Señora Lepe the postmistress?

In Patillas, he rolled down the window and propped his elbow on the window sill. He listened to the sound of a waterfall that tumbled down to the sea from the cliff nestled into the mountain and breathed in the heady scent of papaya and mango.

Ramón passed a dilapidated *bohio* and broke hard as a naked, brown-skinned boy ran to the edge of the dirt road to chase a mangy chicken. As Ramón drove away, the boy watched with eyes wide open and waved. Ramón smiled and waved back, remembering that as a boy, he would have been just as amazed to see a Buick.

He continued on past the clapboard shack of a former customer, remembering the woman who invited him and Francisco in every Saturday for coffee and pastry; how happy she was when she had two dollars to purchase a blouse or skirt fashioned by Chepa, even though it was only two times a year.

Ramón pulled the Buick over. He heard the cries of a mockingbird, the pinging of the car as it cooled.

Ramón thought of that morning in the store and how slow it had been. Only one woman came in. Like most customers, she strolled in to gossip about friends and enemies. Yet she didn't buy anything, despite the extra merchandise, despite Christmas being so near.

Chepa must have noticed the despondency on Ramón's face.

"Things will pick up," she insisted. "We'll manage. Go to your school like you planned. I can use the time to teach Esperanza. So go."

It had been the best moment in Ramón's day; to listen to Chepa in the back room as she taught Esperanza to sew an apron, how to cut the correct shape of fabric and then gather it to make the waistline. He loved hearing Chepa and her young charge gloat over how well Esperanza's infant son was doing as he cooed from inside the straw basket Chepa gave the young mother. Chepa prepared *culantro* tea and showed Esperanza how to spoon a teaspoon on the baby's lips or rub it on his gums. The treatment worked.

"He's so much happier!" Esperanza had told Ramón. "Thank you again, for everything," she exclaimed before Ramón left for his trip. At least he did something right, inviting Esperanza into their lives.

He allowed his eyes to rest on the panorama and took it all

in: sugar cane fields spread like a sliver shimmering carpet in every direction and towering African palms dancing in the wind. His land, his home. The same, yet utterly changed. The scene was one he would never tire of, but his life would undoubtedly take a new turn. He would leave this place he loved, the only home he had ever known.

And he had to assure everyone's well-being before doing so.

§§§

In the school's office, a middle-aged secretary sat behind her small desk. A ceiling fan whirred overhead but did little to dissipate the heat as she alternately swatted at a fly and fanned at her neck and face with a folded newspaper.

"Can I help you?" She chomped on her gum.

Ramón remembered her from his school days; she wore her black curls piled high atop her head and always chewed gum. He wondered if he should tell her it might cause cavities.

"Yes, thank you. I'll need a copy of my grades. I'm applying to Michigan State College."

"Michigan? Well, aren't you something!"

She stood and walked to her rusty file cabinet. The door screeched as she opened it. "What's your name, kid?" she asked.

"Ramón León Carrasquillo."

"Ohhh . . . You're the one who won the lottery. It's big news around here. People are saying you're going to be a great doctor, or something. Good luck with that," she harrumphed, bent over the cabinet and fingered through files.

The principal stepped into the office.

"Well, look who's here! I thought I heard a familiar voice. It's wonderful to see our graduates, especially one who's so famous—a future dentist! Do you have a minute to come into my office?"

Ramón answered, "yes" before the principal turned his attention to his secretary. "Anacleta, can you bring us two glasses of *guarapo* juice please?"

She rolled her eyes and tromped out of the room.

Ramón followed the principal across the hallway into his office and took a seat across from him.

"It's nice to be back," Ramón began, "but I don't think your secretary was happy to see me."

"I'm sorry, but Anacleta's still angry, going through a difficult time. Didn't you hear?" He paused. "Her nephew was murdered."

"Murdered?" Ramón swallowed hard.

"*Sí*, a terrible tragedy. Jesús was our last student who went to the states, to New York. He was a smart boy who, sadly, got involved in gangs and drugs. Then, miraculously, he fought his way out. He started taking college classes. But one day, he was walking down the street and was shot. In cold blood. We think it was a case of mistaken identity. The police have done nothing to solve his murder. They probably think 'one less spic to worry about.'"

"¡*Dios Mío!*" Ramón gasped, sinking back into his chair. *That poor kid, that poor woman, no wonder she acted the way she did.*

"It's a hard life for us in the states, Ramón. You'll face prejudice. Even though you have money, it's going to be difficult, in so many ways. Please, make the right choices. Study hard and don't get involved with the wrong crowd."

They stopped talking as Anacleta came into the office and placed two glasses of sugar cane juice wordlessly on the desk along with a carbon copy of Ramón's grades. She looked at Ramón and her face softened. She let out a small sigh before she left.

"I promise," Ramón uttered to the principal. "I won't let that happen."

On his way out, Ramón stopped at Anacleta's desk.

"I'm sorry about your nephew, señora," he said.

"Well, good luck, you're going to need it." The tone of her voice changed from sarcasm to sincerity. "My family was thrilled to have one of us start a new life, but it only brought us heartache. I'll pray for you, kid. Don't let the same thing happen to you."

§§§

Before driving home, Ramón strolled into a roadside *cantina.* He had skipped lunch and was famished. He ordered his favorite meal from his school days, a *bocadillo,* the scent of the Mortadella wedged between two slices of fresh bread so pungent his mouth watered.

Someone had left a dog-eared copy of *El Mundo* on the wooden, peeling table. The newspaper was from the day before, December 18, 1944. Ramón read as he ate. The headlines weren't good. He said a silent prayer for Glen Miller, whose plane was missing over the English Channel, and for Rafael and Isidro, and the soldiers in Belgium, where the Germans had launched a major offensive.

He'd realized how much he'd miss his times in the plaza, reciting the newspaper to the many villagers who couldn't read. Ramón was the most requested reader in the village.

He finished lunch and stepped outside. By then, school was letting out and he watched students exiting the building. A couple came down the front steps holding hands. The young man wore a shirt faded from too many washings, probably worn by a few older brothers. The boy certainly wasn't a lottery winner, but

Ramón couldn't help but envy the way the girl looked at him, with unconditional adoration.

It made him think of Elsie again. Hadn't she had looked at him at his party and at her house with a hint of the same? Or was it his imagination? What were the words that made him think of her? Alluring: *seductivo, encantador*.

It was a lot to take in: Jesús's murder, wartime casualties, Francisco's drunkenness, and Trujillo's threat to his family's business. He didn't know what the man was capable of. And he'd made yet another promise, this time to the principal, on the heels of his promise to Chepa to stay away from Trujillo.

This should have been the happiest time of his life, but Ramón's emotions were in tumult. He remembered his mother's words, *there's a reason God kisses some and not others*. He fingered the cloth square of the scapular below his collar bone. He wanted solace and he knew the one person in whose arms he could find it. In four nights, with Elsie, at the town hall dance. He could hardly wait.

CHAPTER 13

Ramón closed his dictionary and placed it under the counter when the doorbell jingled and someone came into the store. He'd been studying for an hour, free from interruption. When he looked at the extra merchandise on the shelves, the scarves in brilliant patterns of red and black flowers, orange and cobalt blue swirls, they seemed to mock him. He decided he'd go to the post office later and put up a sign telling customers of the new items they were offering.

He had to admit he was happy to see his sister-in-law, Isabel León, walk into the store and not Trujillo. Ramón breathed easier.

Isabel wore a knee-length scarlet dress that revealed a body full of curves, cinched with one of the gold lamé belts he and Francisco had brought back from San Juan. Ramón had insisted Francisco give one to her. "She can advertise for us," Ramón had claimed. But the dress; Ramón had never seen her wear such a creation before.

She approached him and Ramón smelled a whisper of rose. He had never seen her hair or skin gleam so. It made him nervous, wondering if she went to such lengths for him. His breath caught in his throat.

"I heard you went back to your old high school, that you're going to leave for college," she said. Her voice rose an octave. Ramón suspected she might be as nervous as he.

"Ummm, well, after I get the application and send it."

"It's so brave of you to go off to school, but I wanted to warn you, Francisco is upset you're leaving. When he drinks, he says things, like it's your fault things are slower at the store, that you should stay and help Chepa."

"But he seemed so much better that day we were in San Juan," Ramón said, then rushed on, "He hasn't hurt you or the kids, has he?"

"I'm not surprised you'd worry about me."

She reached up and placed her hand on top of Ramón's, shocking him. "I wish Francisco could be more like you."

He wanted her to take her hand away, yet was amazed at its softness.

"You look beautiful," he blurted, surprising himself.

Heat flooded his face, and the other end of his torso. He was ashamed. For them both.

"Thanks." Her voice sounded different, breathless. She squeezed his hand with a firmness that surprised Ramón.

"What are you doing?" He yanked his hand away.

Her eyes fell. Her face flushed. "It's just that everyone was talking about how you're going to the same school as Antonio Díaz, to become a dentist." She rambled on, "But I'm afraid for you. I've heard of people having a terrible time trying to make it in the states. Maybe you should think of staying home. I'm sure Chepa would be happier."

For the briefest of seconds, he wondered if she were right.

No.

Ramón steeled his shoulders back.

"Isabel, go back to your husband. What you're doing, coming to me like this; it's not right. Francisco needs you. I know it's tough in the states. Believe me. I've heard. But I need to go and make something of myself, to keep the promise I made to come back and help people."

"I should have known. You would keep a promise above all else." Isabel looked down at the floor.

"I'm sorry, but, umm, before you came in, I was studying my English dictionary. I'd like to get back to it. Please . . . go check on Francisco."

"Of course," she whispered before she left.

It was distressing how people changed around money, and worse so when it was someone from his own family.

Within a few minutes, Señora Lepe walked through the door.

"I was just about to come see you," Ramón commented. "To post a sign telling customers about the extra merchandise we brought in."

"You got another letter today."

She clutched a single white business sized envelope.

"Ah, come to grumble some more? At least it's only one today," Ramón teased, enjoying the lighter moment.

Maunabo's postmistress, accustomed to only a handful of letters a month, had complained about the piles of letters Ramón received, people from as far as Caguas asking for money, yet Ramón knew she was thrilled with the importance it afforded her. Even these had started to dwindle, though.

Señora Lepe shook her head. The look on her face told Ramón the news wasn't good.

"What is it?" Ramón asked quickly.

"I'm sorry," she whispered. "I'm just surprised it took them this long."

She handed him the envelope. The words "United States Draft Board" were emblazoned on the upper left corner.

Ramón opened it. The notice was in English, but he knew what it contained. Rafael and Isidro had received them. The paper felt thick in his hand. Across the top was the emblem of an eagle holding an olive branch in one talon, and arrows in the other. He read the words he feared most:

> ORDER TO REPORT FOR INDUCTION
> *The president of the United States is summoning Ramón León Carrasquillo for service in the Army, to report to Fort Buchanan at 9:00 A.M. on the 8th day of January, 1945.*

There was more small print, something about transportation and an examination.

Señora Lepe squeezed Ramón's hand briefly before she left.

How could this be happening, and at this time in his life? Ramón felt disembodied. He felt his dream slipping away, no, being snatched. He remembered how Chepa had cried, wailed even, when first Isidro and then Rafael had sailed away to war.

He also remembered an episode with Doctor Roberts. After the dentist had completed filling a young man's tooth, his eyes misted with tears. "That boy reminded me of my son," the old dentist said, his voice hoarse. "I lost him years ago in the war. You know something?" he confided, "In every language, there are words for widows and words for orphans. But there are no words for a parent who has lost a child. It never gets easier. I pray that you never have to go to war."

Ramón was dumbfounded. Only ten, he had never seen his mentor so emotional. Shortly after that day, Doctor Robert's health started to decline.

Both his mentor and his mother were fiercely against war. And after he saw its effect on Doctor Roberts, although just a boy, Ramón was, too. He could never imagine killing. And know he would be faced with it, right at time he should be preparing to leave for Michigan to change his future, to become a healer.

Yet, Ramón knew men and boys who were happy to go fight for the allies. Was it his turn to fight alongside them, his own brothers even?

He felt a tingle spread through him, but unlike the uplifting warmth when he saw his number, and bought the ticket, this was a sinister tingle, icy fingers crawling up his back. He shivered.

He had a premonition. He was in the Catholic church. A funeral. A plain wood casket covered with plumeria and flamboyan was displayed in front of the altar. Chepa and Elsie, ashen-faced, held each other, sobbing. The casket was closed. Ramón dared not allow his mind to open it. He knew who was inside.

If he went to war, it would be him.

At that moment, his stomach lurched. How could he fulfill his promise, come back and help people if he lay dead in a casket?

Ramón rubbed his eyelids to sooth a looming headache. He thought of Señor Trujillo's threat, the store, his brother, and his brother's wife ready to betray her husband. He hoped things couldn't get worse. But this was worse.

Much worse.

CHAPTER 14

December 23, 1944 was the last Saturday before Christmas, the night Ramón was anticipating when he'd escort Elsie to the town hall dance. He would not jeopardize it and pushed the arrival of draft notice to the back of his mind. He had made a promise of sorts to her, too. He suspected she was looking forward to it as much as he.

With its impressive façade of a mahogany arched door, large glass-paned windows fronted with balconies and a massive two stories high, *Casa Alcaldía* was the finest building in Maunabo and home to the monthly dance, the most popular event in the village.

Ramón had only been inside a few times. As a boy, he believed it was a castle built for a king. That evening, when he entered the front door framed with columns and a Romanesque arch, he had the enchanting Elsie Miraflores on his arm. Even the songs of the *coquís* sounded sweeter.

Partygoers made their way to the large room on the second floor, moved tables and chairs aside and scattered Ivory laundry flakes over the floor to smooth it for dancing. Guillermo brought his record albums. Before playing one on the phonograph, he cleaned it with a chamois, the way a man caresses a fine car. A dozen couples whirled across the scuffed old planks to the tunes of "In the Mood," "Moonlight Serenade," and "Chattanooga Choo Choo" by Glenn Miller.

As the third song ended, Guillermo shouted, "Hey, everyone, my brother bought some punch, and spiked it with rum!"

Good old Guillermo, he had tried to put up a tough front, but on that night all his selected songs were in honor of his favorite composer who died when his aircraft disappeared over the English Channel. Ramón could have sworn he witnessed Guillermo wipe a tear when he bent over to clean his treasured Glenn Miller record.

Elsie interlaced her fingers in Ramón's as dancers headed to the punch table. He felt a warm tingle spread all the way up from his fingertips, from the way her hand felt nestled in his.

She wore a sleeveless knee-length dress the color of jade, elegant for a girl from Maunabo. The scoop neckline complemented her delicate collar bones. The dress revealed tiny freckles dusting her upper arms that matched the spray of freckles on her nose. He imagined kissing them. He and Chepa heard rumors that she'd gone to the finest dressmaker in San Juan to have a dress fashioned for the New Year's Eve party she would attend in the capital with her parents, yet she chose to wear it first that night. For him.

"I've never had rum before, just don't tell my father," she said, flashing that smile again, playful dimples on full display.

Just as Ramón and Elsie arrived at the table to wait their turn in line for a glass of rum punch, Antonio strode over. The crowd parted.

"How's the richest man in Maunabo, besides me?" Antonio chuckled and put his arm around Ramón. "Can I borrow him for a minute?" he asked Elsie.

Ramón squeezed Elsie's hand and said, "You'll be okay?"

"Sure." She nodded.

Elsie's hand floated to her face to tuck a loose strand of hair behind her ear. Her bracelets jingled and slipped down her slender forearm to her wrist, like golden honey. At that moment, with the way she beamed at him, Ramón knew: she *wanted* him to like her. He could fall in love with this enchanting girl. Completely. Maybe he already had.

Antonio pulled Ramón away from the group.

"I told you things would get cozy between you two. She's a beauty all right, but imagine being on a campus with hundreds like her!" Leering, Antonio added, "You're lucky, Ramón, I bet you'll find a college gal to keep you warm at night, and no strict fathers to worry about."

For a moment, Ramón wanted to defend Elsie, to tell Antonio how he felt about her. Instead, he replied, "Leave it to you, to notice the women."

Despite Antonio's experience in another world, Ramón guessed he had never been in love, and felt sorry for him, for his cavalier life.

"Everything's still in place for our deal on the essay, right? It will be quite a year, won't it?" Antonio said, as he raised an eyebrow, flashed a grin.

Dios. Next year. Ramón would be at his army physical a week after the first of the year. He had more pressing problems than an essay.

"Yeah, sure," he retorted dismissively.

He wanted to go back to Elsie.

She patted the seat next to her when Ramón approached the round table where three other couples sat drinking punch and nibbling on guava jelly with *queso blanco*.

"So, everyone says you two are the golden couple," Armando Lepe, the son of the postmistress declared. "Any New Year's resolutions? Everyone knows about you going off to school, Ramón, but how about you, Elsie?"

All conversation ceased and the collective eyes of the table turned toward Elsie. Her cheeks colored. Ramón wished there was something he could do to pull her away, to save her. It felt good, imagining he could be her savior.

"Well . . . I think I want to be a school teacher," Elsie said tentatively.

Ramón saw a few eyebrows rise around the table, and heard Armando's girlfriend, Sophia, humph and inquire, "Oh, so you're going to school, too?"

"Well, eventually, I suppose so . . . yeah." Elsie bit her lower lip.

Ramón knew how nervous she was. It was quite a declaration for a girl from Maunabo, probably one whose parents were grooming to marry well, not to have a career.

"Imagine, the two of you, going off to college. You really are the golden couple," Armando repeated that phrase, *golden couple*.

Guillermo, God bless him, must have noticed Elsie's nervousness too and shouted, "Hey, quit chattering like a bunch of myna birds. Let's dance!"

Ramón laced his fingers in Elsie's and led her back to the dance floor. She walked with a quality of movement so different from anyone, lithe, graceful, no wasted steps. The final song of the evening, fittingly, was "At Last." Ramón held Elsie close and felt the rhythm of her heart through the silk of her dress, perhaps in a promise of love, at last. He knew where he had to be on January 8, and dreaded the evening to end.

§§§

After the customary good-byes, Ramón and Elsie left holding hands. A shiny black De Soto idled on the street alongside the building. How strange, there were only four cars in Maunabo and no De Sotos. Something must have made Elsie turn as well.

"Who's that?" she asked with a twinge of suspicion.

Ramón saw the outline of a hat, dimly lit by the moon, but he knew in the light of day, that it was white, the same hat worn by Trujillo. Ramón's heart accelerated. He squeezed Elsie's hand.

"I don't know," he lied. "Let's go."

They almost stepped into a carpet of broken glass on the side of the road. A smashed rum bottle. Ramón could still make out the label, Bacardi Superior. Only the finest, it was Trujillo's. Had the merchant meant for them to walk over it, to hurt themselves? Or worse, had he meant to throw it at them?

And the third broken glass, a bad omen. First at the store, then at Elsie's house, and now. An icy shiver ran up and down Ramón's spine.

"Look at that," Elsie said as she held Ramón's elbow to stop him. "Someone made a mess, we should clean it up."

"No, leave it," Ramón insisted.

The De Soto continued to idle. Ramón heard the engine begin to rev, only slightly.

"But someone could get hurt, all the girls are wearing sandals. I'll get a broom, be right back," Elsie said before she ran back into the building.

The car moved forward. Ramón stayed rooted to his spot. His hands opened and closed, then balled into fists.

As the car rolled by slowly, Ramón felt the merchant's sharp gaze upon him, feeling like prey cornered by a predator. Trujillo's eyes bore into Ramón, his lips and teeth curled into a snarl. Ramón watched the red taillights slowly grow smaller as the car rolled away.

Elsie came out with a broom and dustpan. "I'll get this real quick."

"No, let me," Ramón said, happy for the diversion. He took

100

the broom from her, knelt and swept up the glass fragments. "Done. I'll bring these back in."

Right before he left Elsie's side to return the broom and dustpan, Ramón glanced up and down the street. Nothing, no De Soto. He felt safe leaving Elsie alone for a moment, relieved she hadn't recognized the merchant.

Ramón came back outside and he and Elsie continued on holding hands. Ramón focused on listening to the chorus of cicadas, and no vehicle idling up next to them.

"That was strange, that car," Elsie commented.

"It's nothing. Don't worry about it."

Ramón stopped and turned to Elsie. He faced her as they stood under a coconut tree, in a shadow cast by the light of the full moon. He needed to focus on something other than the hate on Trujillo's face.

"You look beautiful, Elsie. Thanks for being with me tonight. I had a great time."

"Me too," she whispered.

"I'm sorry Sophia made you uncomfortable, questioning you like that."

"I've never told anyone that I want to be a teacher," Elsie admitted. "The idea came to me when I was thirteen. My mother would be furious for telling you this, but that's when I taught her how to read. And you know what? I was *good* at it. Madre was embarrassed that she didn't know how to. When I used to bring something home from school for her to look at, she'd say, 'Oh, you read it to me, honey.' She never spent much time in school, her parents only wanted her to find the right husband."

"You'd be a great teacher," Ramón interjected. "You never knew this, but a few years ago, when I picked my nephew up from

101

school one day, I got there early. I watched you read to him and the other kids. You were so good with them, they loved you. You had just moved here, and I had never seen anyone like you. Neither had those kids."

"Really? Thanks." Her face flushed in excitement.

Ramón took a deep breath and exhaled.

"I haven't told anyone either, but I got my draft notice. My physical is in a couple weeks."

"¡*Dios mío, no*! Can't you get out of it, tell them you're going to college?" she pleaded.

Ramón shook his head. "No, I don't even have the application yet. Elsie, I despise this war, the violence, the casualties, but, *Dios*, I have to go . . . I saw something."

Ramón remembered how she looked in his vision, grief-stricken. He remembered the closed pine box.

"What did you see?"

Ramón heard the fear in her voice. He couldn't tell her of his premonition. He didn't dare say it out loud, for his own fear there was an inkling of truth.

"*Dios,*" she repeated. "I can't believe it. Come see me afterward, no matter what time. My bedroom is on the second floor around the back of the house. It's the window nearest the big mango tree, the one with the nest of *reinitas* who sing to me every night. You can get a pebble from the rock garden under the tree. Just throw it at my window, and I'll come." She paused. Her eyes misted over. "I hate the idea of you being drafted. I'm scared for you. I don't want you to go . . ."

For the briefest of seconds, Ramón allowed his thoughts to bombard his brain: the draft, leaving the island, Trujillo's threats, the merchant's jealous obsession.

Then he looked into the eyes of the beautiful woman with him *now*, caring about him, the most sought after girl in the village. He reached up to wipe a single tear from her cheek.

Summoning the courage, he asked, "I've been waiting all night to ask. Can I kiss you?"

"Yes," she said, almost pleading.

Ramón pulled her close. When he held the back of her head and leaned in to kiss her, the pins fell out of her bun, and her hair spilled over his hand. He breathed in the scent of her shampoo and perfume, as sweet as orange blossoms.

She trembled as she returned his kiss, her lips softer than a butterfly's wings.

CHAPTER 15

January 6, *El Día de los Reyes Magos* was the evening when Ramón's brothers, wives and their children came for the celebration of lighting candles and singing carols dedicated to the kings. That would be the time to make the announcement of his draft notice. Ramón knew how devastated Chepa would be, but hoped that having all those she loved around her would act as a buffer.

Chepa insisted that no matter the age, as long as her children lived in her home, they continue to observe the tradition followed by all Puerto Rican families since long before her time. So, on the evening of January 5ᵗʰ, Ramón placed hay under his bed to feed the camels of the three Magi, and the following morning, Chepa replaced the hay with a piece of homemade papaya candy wrapped in a silk square, fabric she set aside each year for her children, and now her grandchildren in their homes.

After dinner the family gathered outside, the adults holding lit candles on tin plates. White light from the crescent moon spilled into the courtyard. The children sat on the grass and quieted, as even they were satiated from Chepa's *paella*. It was the one time of the year she purchased costly saffron for the plentiful dish. Juan began to strum a carol on his guitar and the voices of the family soon added to his melodious one:

> *Los tres Santos Reyes, los tres y los tres,*
> *los tres Santos Reyes, los tres y los tres,*
> *Los saludaremos con divina fe,*

los saludaremos con divina fe.

Los tres santos Reyes, yo los sé contar,

Los tres santos Reyes, yo los sé contar,

Gaspar y Melchor y el Rey Baltazar

Gaspar y Melchor y el Rey Baltazar.

The three holy kings, the three holy kings

We greet them with faith, we greet them with faith

The three holy kings, I know there are three

Gaspar, Melchior and King Balthazar

Ramón was too distraught to join them. He cringed when he imagined how they would be all be here again the next year, following this revered custom, and he wouldn't be, most likely hiding or waiting in a ditch somewhere for the onslaught of the enemy, or worse: in the simple pine box he saw.

After the final stanza, he blurted, "I got drafted, for the army. I have to go to a physical."

Chepa's face fell. Her knees wobbled and she nearly fell.

Ramón ran to her side to support her arm, to keep her upright.

"When . . ." Chepa managed to say.

"In two days, I have to go to Fort Buchanan. They're sending a bus."

"But you have to tell them about college," Isabel insisted, "that you're going to Michigan. That must count for something!"

Francisco turned to his wife and said, "You think you know how the army works?"

"Easy, *hermano*, she's only trying to help," Ramón defended.

"When I'm gone, you'll need to help Mamá more. I'll be counting on you, okay?"

"Yeah, okay, sorry. The important thing is, what are we going to do about it?"

Thank *Dios* Francisco listened this time. When his eyes flashed an apology, again Ramón was reminded of their father. If only Juan Bautista could be there now.

Everyone spoke at once. Chepa cried that the war was taking another one of her sons.

"Don't cry, Mamá, it will be all right!" Ramón exclaimed, trying to reassure her, but he didn't believe his own words. Surely it would not be all right. His mother looked so distraught, that it reminded Ramón of how sick Doctor Roberts was that day years ago, the day he extracted the promise from Ramón to carry on their work. *Dios*, how could he keep it now? Ramón felt sick.

His family surrounded him, tried to offer words of comfort. Esperanza was considered family, and she was there, too.

"Oh, Ramón, after everything you and Chepa have done for me, I wish there was something I could do!" Esperanza cried.

Juan took his turn speaking: "Things are turning for the allies and surely this war is gonna' end soon. So Ramón will probably never see a battlefield and Rafie and Isidro will come home soon. And Ramón can talk to his C.O. or someone in charge about all that time he worked with Doctor Roberts. I bet they could use him as a medic."

Ramón knew they were only trying to help, yet he remembered the pine box. There he stood, encircled by his family who loved him, yet Ramón had never felt so alone in his entire life.

§§§

At 6 A.M. on January 8th, Ramón kissed Chepa goodbye. She was unable to speak as she cried and clung to him. Reluctantly, Ramón let go and trudged to the plaza. He would have preferred to drive, but the draft notice, translated by Don Pablo, had instructed: "This local board will furnish transportation to the induction station." Ramón didn't argue. He had more pressing things on his mind, like trying to get out of this, like staying alive.

In the plaza, two other young men waited. Neither had attended school with him but Ramón recognized them from the few times they had been to the store and knew they lived in the *barrios*. He nodded hello to each and took a seat on one of the park benches. No one spoke as they waited, each lost in his private thoughts and fears.

The olive drab bus rolled up, and they boarded. There were a dozen other young men from the neighboring villages, Patillas and Arroyo, maybe as far as Ponce. With only sporadic conversations among the riders, it was quiet. Ramón stared out the window with a heavy heart as the bus rolled along on the dirt road to its destination. Stray dogs ran alongside, kicking up dust and barking in the wind. Ramón breathed in the smell of the salt air, as heavy as perfume. The sun made its slow ascent over the sea and stained the sky cobalt blue, as brilliant as an oil painting. He would miss these smells and sights. He shuddered, wondering what death smelled and looked like.

After three hours, they arrived. With head down and hands in his pockets, Ramón shuffled into the barracks at Fort Buchanan. He felt a load on his shoulders, as if he had been one of the pallbearers of

107

his father's coffin years before. A few dozen young men filed into the building. They all gathered in a barren room to sit on metal folding chairs beside long tables to take a written exam. It was in English so Ramón barely understood some of the questions. *If I flunk, maybe they won't want me.*

Then it was on to the physical exam. A male nurse pointed to the bathrooms and ordered Ramón to urinate into a plastic container. Afterward, the nurse led Ramón into a small examination room where he was instructed to strip down to his underwear. Nearly naked, Ramón sat on the hard exam table. The fan on the ceiling chattered above him. With each revolution, it seemed to warn "you're doomed, doomed, doomed . . ."

Ramón shivered, exposed, naked, and very much alone.

The doctor entered the room. The man looked like he hadn't slept in days. He barely looked all 150 pounds of Ramón over and brusquely gave orders to bend over, squat down, and raise his arms. Although Ramón was thin, his legs and arms were strong from playing basketball.

The doctor nodded, declaring, "You're fit." He left the room as quickly as he came in. Ramón dressed slowly.

Another nurse extracted a sample of his blood. For two hours, Ramón paced and looked out the small, grimy windows. The hallway held the scent of mildew and sweat, probably from the men, like he, who had waited for test results that could decide their futures. Ramón thought about what he would do in combat. What if he, God forbid, had to kill someone? And what of Elsie? Would she wait for him? And what was he to do about Trujillo? And what about the store? And Francisco, who was sober a couple nights before, but how long would it last? Ramón had seen his bother relapse before.

The same doctor strode down the hall toward Ramón,

interrupting his misgivings. He directed Ramón back into the exam room and gestured for him to sit on the hard exam table. The doctor remained standing, a stern, tired look on his face and told Ramón, "Your samples show schistosomiasis, snail fever. You must have been swimming in contaminated rivers. The worms from their eggs settle in the bowel, bladder or blood. Have you had any blood in your stools or urine?"

"No, doctor, but I've had more stomachaches lately. They always get better with my mother's *culantro*," Ramón explained.

"Sometimes it takes months to show symptoms. But it's serious. The longer you have it, the more it spreads. This parasite can lodge in your lungs and liver and cause permanent damage. If it gets in your brain or spinal cord, it can lead to seizures, paralysis, in the worst cases, death. You need to see your personal doctor, or go to the Tropical Institute . . . " He rambled on and declared, "***You are not fit to serve . . . We're declaring you 4F . . . ***"

The words rang in Ramón's head so loudly that he could barely hear the doctor's instructions: "Young man, did you hear what I said? You need to get this treated."

The doctor thrust a piece of paper in Ramón's hand, not unlike the draft notice Ramón received in the mail. It was in English. Ramón shook his head and tried to focus. He saw black letters stamped across the paper: **4-F.**

"Get the medicine, Faudin, as fast as you can," the doctor finished.

On the walk out of the building, it was as if Ramón were hovering outside his body. He sat immobilized on the trip home, the same *públicos* he took before he bought the Buick. He could hardly believe what had just occurred. He had come so close to serving, to fighting. He believed it was wrong, but he would have done what was required, as other men before him. But now, he was unfit to serve. Saved by a parasite. He swam in the Maunabo river only weeks before; that must be where he contracted it. He didn't feel sick, not physically, but he had a serious condition.

Was it God's hand that did this?

And what about Juanito? Didn't his nephew swim in the river sometimes? Could the boy be infected, too? Ramón would have to make sure Juanito was okay.

Thoughts bombarded Ramón's head at rapid fire, of everything that had happened to him. First, his vision, then his winning ticket, and being with Elsie, who was so concerned about him, who insisted he come tell her the outcome of his physical. He heard the doctor's words again, *not fit to serve*. Ramón mused over what Chepa had said: was there a divine force guiding him to his destiny, to the promise he had made long ago?

CHAPTER 16

Elsie's room was the farthest to the right of three arched windows, set back above the red-tiled verandah surrounding the Miraflores home. Ramón supposed the expansive porch was built to take in the grand sweep of lush valley surrounding *La Pica*. He experienced a sweet vision of him and Elsie in the future, sitting on that same porch surrounded by their children, a girl, and two boys, the girl with the same copper curls as her mother.

He arched a pebble from Señora Miraflores' manicured rock garden. It landed with a ping, bounced off the side of Elsie's window and rolled back down to the garden. He tossed another. She appeared, opened the window and leaned out. Her hair spilled across the front of her shoulders. When she saw Ramón, she waved, the joy evident in her face. A tingle spread through Ramón's entire body. He wanted to see that look again and again.

Ramón motioned for her to come down. She nodded.

She ran into the garden, and they embraced. Ramón breathed in the scent of jasmine and rose, from la señora's flowers and Elsie's perfume.

Glancing back to the house, Elsie took Ramón's hand and pulled him into the shade of the mango tree.

"What happened? I've been thinking about you constantly," she said, breathless.

"I'm unfit to serve, Elsie. They rejected me. The doctor at my physical said, umm . . ." He hesitated, wanting to spare her the details.

"*¡Gracias a Dios!* How?"

"I have schisto . . . something."

"What's that?"

"It's snail fever. I guess I got it from swimming in a river with, umm . . . bad snails."

Rather than being repulsed, Elsie hugged him again. Ramón loved her all the more for it.

"I'm so happy!" she cried.

"I've been thinking about you, too, ever since the dance, about how you want to be teacher. Let's make a promise to each other."

Ramón took her face in his hands. Her skin was as smooth as the finest silk his mother used decades ago for those fancy wedding dresses. He couldn't imagine anything in nature felt more exquisite.

"I'll get the medicine, get well, and we'll both go to college. We can both follow our dreams!" Ramón exclaimed. He never wanted to let go.

"And I want you to know, you're booked every month for the town hall dance, and I want to take you dancing to *Parque Florida*, Friday night, to hear my brothers' band. I want the whole world to know about us. I want you there by my side," he affirmed.

"I want that, too, but . . ."

Elsie stepped back and looked down, scuffed the toe of her sandal in the dirt and bit her lower lip. "I'm not sure how my father will feel about me going to college, but maybe Madre will be on my side." She looked up, frowning. "I'd love to go dancing with you, but I've been worried about you for something else, too."

"What now?"

"Señor Trujillo came to see my father," she told him, then pressed on, "He wanted Papá to arrest you for cheating in the lottery. He's not making any sense. And he's been telling people to stop shopping at your mother's store. It was him outside the dance the other night, wasn't it?"

Ramón's chest tightened. He stood silent a moment, not wanting to admit he lied to Elsie that night. Finally, he confessed: "Yeah, that was him."

"He looks terrible. It's hard to believe—Madre and I used to shop at his store, and he always acted so refined."

"Why won't he just leave me and my family alone?!"

"My father told him he wouldn't do it, that he knew you as an honest young man, that the idea of cheating was absurd. Then my father told him to let you go about your business in peace."

"I'm grateful for that. But, Elsie, I have to go see that man, I have to clear my name."

Ramón remembered the promise to his mother to stay away from Trujillo, then pushed the thought aside.

"But my father did that for you!" Elsie insisted.

"¡**No!**" Ramón shook his head. "I'm thrilled that your father thinks well of me, but I can't let him fight my battles. I'm tired of Trujillo accusing me." Ramón hesitated, then said, "But enough of that, because you know what? I love the way you worry about me. Let's seal our promise to each other."

They pressed together again and kissed deeply. Her lips were so inviting, full, yet soft, and he wanted more. Before his hands dared to roam, right there in her mother's garden, Ramón pulled away. He looked into Elsie's eyes but he saw something in them akin to fear. He took both her hands in his.

She held his hands tighter.

"Be careful, Ramón. I . . . I think I'm falling for you, and something tells me Trujillo's going crazy."

CHAPTER 17

Ramón and Elsie planned a night of celebration, for Ramón's avoiding the war, and for their budding love. Ramón had obtained the medicine, Faudin, from the pharmacist who worked with Chepa. Señor García handed Ramón the amber bottle of tablets with one condition: Ramón promise to be retested for the parasite after taking the two-week supply. The kind pharmacist also warned Ramón of the side effects of jaundice and nausea, which may become quite severe, but thank God, Ramón didn't have them, at least not yet.

Ramón put these troubling thoughts aside, for when his brothers, Juan and José Luis, played with the Caribbean Kids at *El Parque Florida* in Patillas, it promised to be a sell-out.

The dance floor, measuring forty by forty feet, took up most of the venue and was already filled with couples when Ramón and Elsie arrived. A small crowd was ordering drinks at the metal-topped bar. One couple sat so close with their hands and arms entwined and eyes locked that it looked like they were glued together on the same chrome stool, as if no one would ever break them apart.

Typically, someone would have put a nickel in the *vellonera* to play a bebop tune by Coleman Hawkins, but this night, the band was already on the stage, in full swing. Ramón and Elsie made their way through the throngs to the center of the dance floor. Couples moved and gyrated to the throbbing beat of *Guaracha*. Music reverberated off the walls.

Ramón admired The Caribbean Kids. They were quite a force

on the stage, dressed in their blinding white trousers and shirts, the only hints of color the black bands on their fedoras and their black belts. Juan blared his trumpet. José Luis played his *pandereta* and his prized *barril de bomba,* the drum he crafted from a large rum storage barrel with a goat skin stretched across the mouth. Ramón's brothers were accompanied by three more members of the band playing maracas, *güiro* and Spanish guitar.

Ramón's steps became effortless. He and Elsie had never danced so well, their hips and shoulders moving like a mirror image. Ramón noticed many of the other dancers watching them, the most admired couple on the dance floor. He had never felt so alive with a lightness radiating from his toes all the way to his fingers. He wanted to cry out, that for now at least, he was safe, he would not be shipping off to war. He and Elsie were so in sync that surely they were meant to stay together forever. Why would God make them fit so perfectly, only to break them apart?

After two more numbers, the band took a break. Elsie and Ramón made their way to a quiet area outside, picking a small table tucked under an African Palm. The stars looked like a million tiny holes punched in the vast night sky. The moon lit up the sea. For a moment, the only sounds were Ramón and Elsie's breaths as they recovered from dancing and the lapping of waves on the shore below them. They were the only ones in the courtyard, not that either would have noticed.

They sipped piña coladas, and Elsie told him of the movie her aunt had seen in San Juan, the film version of *For Whom the Bell Tolls.* She was waiting for a Spanish translation of the book. After all, it was written by Hemingway in Cuba, why was it published only in English? She would love to read it in her native tongue and share it with her students, someday, if she ever became the teacher she dreamed she would be. She admitted she envied her aunt's cosmopolitan life in the capital.

Ramón talked about his days with Doctor Roberts, how the dentist had such wonderful and skilled hands, and did amazing things like hypnosis and acupuncture. He shared his dreams, too. He wanted to be as revolutionary as his mentor.

Before they knew it, they were dancing again. The final song of the evening was a romantic Bolero, a slow dance that for many couples was a prelude to a night of passion.

Ramón held Elsie close. Her perfumed hair fell softly to her shoulders, framing her face. Her hips and chest pressed against his, separated only by the thinness of her white summer dress. He had seen her wear it before, but tonight, it was even more enticing. He breathed in the intoxicating scent of her, the light sheen of her perspiration mingled with her rose perfume. He ran his hands up and down her back, drinking in the feel of her body with the fit of his.

"You're the most beautiful woman here," he whispered as he nuzzled her ear. "People can barely take their eyes off you."

Ramón hoped he had said the right thing. He had never been so bold with his hands and words. When he looked into Elsie's eyes, they shone. He *had* said the right thing.

"It's you they're looking at, too. I've never seen you look so handsome," she whispered back, her voice soft, intimate.

As soon as the song ended, he took her hand and led her out of the club. He remembered what she said several nights before, "I think I'm falling for you," and felt the thrill, the near dizziness when someone first speaks those words. Would they seal their love tonight?

As soon as they walked out the front door, Ramón spotted a man across the parking lot. Trujillo. Standing. Watching. Stalking.

Ramón thought he'd felt an odd presence when he and Elsie were enjoying their drinks earlier under the palm tree but the moment was so delicious, he pushed the thought out of his head. Had Trujillo been hiding, spying on them as they shared their wishes and desires?

Ramón felt Elsie tense. She saw him too. Ramón couldn't lie this time.

He was about to stride forward to confront the man when Trujillo hurled an empty rum bottle. Ramón and Elsie ducked. With shocking force, the bottle smashed against the cement wall of the building and shattered. Ramón threw his arms over Elsie to shield her from flying glass.

They stood and he quickly checked her. "*Dios*, are you okay?"

She was uncut but shaking. Ramón held her as a blinding rage washed over him. He was desperate to go after the man, but Elsie clung to him with a ferocity that shocked him. He had a vision of hunting down the man but wouldn't dare leave her side.

Seconds later, Ramón's brothers ran outside with a group of patrons and the bartender. They must have heard the explosion of the bottle. The De Soto's engine roared as Trujillo peeled out of the parking lot and sped down the street.

"What happened?" shouted Juan.

"It was Trujillo. He threw the bottle at us and took off, the coward!" Ramón yelled, with a fury he never had before. He shook with rage.

"So it's true, the guy's going crazy and has it out for you. What are we going to do?" José Luis asked. "Should we go after him?"

"Yes!" Ramón shouted.

"Yeah, the bastard. Let's go. Get the car, Ramón," Juan demanded.

"No, please—Ramón, can you just take me home?" Elsie's

voice was small, tremulous.

Trujillo will have to wait, Ramón thought.

"Calm down, everyone," growled the bartender. "He's gone. I don't want any trouble tonight."

§§§

Ramón was a ball of pent-up energy, fueled by anger, as they drove home.

"The coward," he repeated as he pounded the top of the steering wheel with his fist. He would have called him a bastard too but kept that to himself, out of respect for Elsie. "It's bad enough that he rants on about me, threatens me, but tonight, if he'd have hurt you, I swear . . . "

"Maybe I should talk to my father. That man is capable of real violence," she said and shook her head, bit her lower lip. "I better not, though. My father's not too happy about us. We were having such fun tonight that I didn't want to tell you, but I heard my parent's talking the other night in the kitchen. I missed most of it, but Papá was saying he wanted me to meet a man in San Juan, a son of his *associate*. It made me so sick that I gasped and they heard me behind the door. I told them I didn't want to meet that man, to leave us alone."

"Then don't talk to him, don't give him any more ideas about pulling us apart. I could go to the police in Yabucoa or . . . I don't know what I'm going to do, but I swear, I gotta' go see the guy and put a stop to this!"

"I heard he has men working for him, bad men. He may have the police in Yabucoa on his payroll, too. Trujillo is powerful. Be careful, Ramón," Elsie pleaded.

118

Ramón thought about the bottle ricocheting off the wall, shattering, more broken glass. Bad things come in threes, but in fours, did it become something even worse?

CHAPTER 18

Ramón woke with a start. Sunlight beamed into his room in a golden circle that pooled on the floor. Already late morning. He pulled the mosquito net back and jumped out of bed, chastising himself for oversleeping. The night before, when he dropped Elsie off, she begged him to wait until things cooled off; he tossed in bed, his mind churning over how to handle Trujillo, and what to do about the awful conversation that Elsie overheard between her parents. When he reasoned an answer may come to him in the light of day, when his mind was fresh, he finally fell asleep past dawn.

The house seemed too quiet. Ramón was filled with an eerie sensation that he should have told Chepa what happened, warn her of some impending doom, but she had been asleep when he arrived home.

He dressed quickly and dashed to the store. When he stepped inside, he saw something that made the blood pound in his temples. Chepa stood in front of the counter, facing Trujillo. Ramón had a sudden vision of a lion tearing apart another lion who threatened his family, how it would feel to rip flesh.

He saw Chepa's hand moving in a balletic motion, her head nodding, like she would do when she was explaining a treatment or counseling a patient. But Trujillo was no patient.

"Leave my mother alone." Ramón's voice sounded like bones snapping.

Trujillo turned toward him. He wore the same white linen suit as the day weeks earlier when he barged into the store, but now it looked like he had slept in it. There was a quarter-sized brown stain on the lapel, coffee or adobo sauce. Red spider-like vessels twisted like a road map on his bulbous nose.

Ramón moved closer, fists clenched. Chepa shot a look toward him that said, *calm down, let me handle this.*

The sour stench of Trujillo's sweat assailed Ramón's nostrils, the odor of stale rum seeping out of the merchant's pores.

"How dare you come here! Leave my mother alone," Ramón repeated.

Chepa spoke first. "I'm trying to reason with Señor Trujillo. I told him about you using the money for college, that he must not let this obsession with you ruin his heart, his constitution."

"You think this is easy?" the merchant hissed, his jugular veins popping out as thick as tree twigs. "Do you know what it feels like to be *so close* to something, then have it stolen away? I played that number *for years*! There were times when I was so close to winning, a number off . . . and then *you* came along! How did you defeat me? How did you do it?"

"Like I told you before, you could have bought the ticket that day. Caimito came to you first. I saw a number, and because I had a hunch, I played it. No cheating or trickery. Go to San Juan, to Alberto Gómez's store. Go to the lottery office. They'll tell you I didn't cheat. It's not my fault you sent Caimito on his way that day." Ramón heard the venom surfacing on his tongue. "Stay away from my family."

"I can't. I need to recoup the money I lost. I'm running you and your family out of business. I'm offering free merchandise, free food—I've told people about you, how you're blowing through your money on frivolities for this family, on cars—"

"Señor, please, there is enough business for all of us," Chepa begged. She leaned forward to place her hand on the merchant's shoulder, to reason with him.

Trujillo snatched Chepa's hand away as if it burned. "NO!" he bellowed. In one motion, he grabbed the front of her shoulder, flung her down and ran.

Ramón felt a blinding anger course through him. He sprinted forward to charge the man.

"¡¡Ayyy!!" Chepa cried out like a bird in pain.

The plaintive sound pierced Ramón's heart. For a millisecond, he was paralyzed with indecision. Go after the man or help his mother?

"¡Mamá!" he shouted, and turned and ran back to her.

Doña Chepa grimaced in agony on the floor. She lay frozen for long seconds.

"I'm fine, just bruised," she insisted. She turned to her side and winced when she tried to push herself up.

Ramón reached under her shoulders to help her. They felt smaller and lighter than he remembered. When had his mother become old? She had always been the strong one.

On this day, of all days, why couldn't Francisco or José Luis have been there to help Chepa so Ramón could go after Trujillo? This time, he wanted the merchant to feel like prey, but for now, he couldn't leave Chepa.

He rushed to retrieve the chair from her sewing room.

"Mamá, I'm so sorry. It's me he hates, why did he have to push you?"

Chepa squeezed Ramón's arm as he lowered her into the chair.

"I'll be fine. I just happened to be the one in his way. Let him go."

As if reading his mind, she made a dismissive wave with her hand. Then she closed her eyes, as if to will away the pain.

"Last night he showed up at the club to spy on me and Elsie.

He threw an empty rum bottle at us, now he comes after you. He's taking business away, what you've worked your whole life to build. Enough is enough. I have to do something!"

"I'll talk to Capitán Miraflores," Chepa declared. "This is a police matter. Don't tell your brothers what happened. I don't want things to get out of hand. Let the police chief handle it."

Ramón wanted to get his brothers to hunt down Trujillo. But this was *his* problem. If things did get out of hand, why involve them? No, this was something he needed to do on his own.

"*Fine.*" Ramón heard the sharpness edging his voice, much more than he intended. Once again, he was amazed how easily the lie came.

CHAPTER 19

Chepa was bedridden for two days. An angry black and purple bruise spread across her back. Ramón applied the same remedy she had used on her patients: a tincture of arnica, aloe vera and chamomile. He massaged the injured area as gently as possible, as he had observed her do. Everyone claimed his mother's fingers were magic, but now, no one could perform the same wonders on the magician.

Ramón brought chamomile tea to her bedside table after one of his treatments and begged her to take back the scapular.

She insisted he keep it, murmuring, "Leave me now, *m'ijo*, rest is what I need."

Ramón tossed that night in bed and went to her room to change her mind. She slept so soundly he didn't dare wake her. In the morning, he tried again only to stop outside her door and listen to her humming her morning prayers. When he peeked inside to plead with her to take his father's scapular, she waved him away.

When he wasn't taking care of Chepa, Ramón worked in the store, although he needn't have bothered, for no one came. At least Francisco's store had a few customers. It appeared as if Chepa and Ramón were Trujillo's main targets.

Ramón waited until the next morning, the third morning after the assault, when Chepa was able to get out of bed and move about comfortably. He started the trip to Yabucoa, alone. He couldn't risk exposing anyone else to danger. It would be difficult, but maybe he and Trujillo could settle things civilly.

On *La Pica*, he drove past two boys using long sticks to prod oxen that pulled a cart filled with plantains, pumpkins and sweet potatoes. The boys were laughing, carefree, in no rush. Part of Ramón wished he could go with them, rather than to where he was going, but he continued. His anger fueled him.

He arrived in Yabucoa and parked outside the wide *Plaza de Recreo*. The tires of the Buick crunched over the gravel surrounding the paved plaza. He cut the engine, which pinged as it cooled. The bells in the high church steeple rang, signaling the noon hour. They were much bigger and so much louder than the bells of the church in Maunabo that it made Ramón jump in his seat.

He sat in his car and watched, from across the plaza, the front entrance of *Ana's*, the store Trujillo named in honor of his wife. The store was fronted by a large wooden porch. Weeds sprouted from the cracks of the floor planks, and the poinsettia hedge was wildly overgrown. Ramón recalled how well tended and clean it used to look. He watched customers stroll in and out, mainly women and girls, gossiping or giggling. They all came out carrying stringed bags of merchandise. So it must be true, more people were shopping there.

Suddenly a large cloud passed over the sun and the sky darkened. When no one entered or exited for five minutes, Ramón made his move.

He entered the store. Trujillo stood behind the counter with its shiny steel cash register. The merchant had looked so large in Ramón's seven-year-old eyes. Now he appeared smaller, disheveled.

"You!" he hissed. "You've got some nerve showing up here, unless it's to give me back my money!"

Ramón's face burned. He took a deep breath and squared his shoulders. All his muscles quivered.

"Don't you look at me like I'm a leper—I've done nothing wrong to you. The way you shoved my mother, the way you threw a

125

bottle at me and my *novia* was despicable," Ramón fumed in a deep voice, "This has to stop!"

An animalistic growl escaped the merchant's throat: "Never! Your mother deserved it, because she bore YOU! You've ruined me. I despise you!" Trujillo glared at Ramón with neck corded and teeth bared.

Anger more pure and heated than anything he had ever felt burst in his Ramón's brain. Vengeance thickened the air.

The merchant came out from behind the counter, pointing his finger like a judge pronouncing the death sentence and bellowing, "If you don't have my money, get the hell out of here!"

Ramón looked into the face of a lunatic. The merchant's eyes were rimmed in red, the pupils dilated black. Trujillo charged him, his hands reaching for Ramón's neck.

They tumbled to the floor.

With a sudden burst of strength, Ramón pushed up from the ground and pinned Trujillo underneath him. Rage bubbled like hot lava. He wanted to hurt the man more than he had hurt Chepa. Make him pay, make him feel infinite pain. He grabbed Trujillo's throat. His forearms shook as he squeezed the man's neck and the cords of his windpipe.

Time seemed to slow down, as if Ramón were standing outside his body to watch someone else strangling the man with the strength and rage of a lion.

It was the bluish cast of Trujillo's lips, the gurgling sound that brought Ramón to his senses, the wheezing, agonized gasps. The man's final breaths.

What am I doing? The words rushed into Ramón's head. *I'm killing him.* He envisioned his father's face on his deathbed, mirroring Trujillo's now. Then, Elsie's face, Chepa's face. What would they say if he actually did it . . . committed murder?

Ramón released his grip and fell back. Trujillo continued to cough and sputter, his jacket stained dark with dirt from the floor.

Ramón's legs trembled as he pushed himself up to stand. He heard the tatter of his own breath. Señor Trujillo tried to stand before his legs buckled and he fell to his knees. Weariness seemed to pour into the merchant's body. He broke out in another spasm of coughs, spewing saliva and sputum on the floor, trembling like a mouse in a cat's claws.

Ramón felt sick. *"¡DIOS!"* he shouted.

He stumbled out of the store and down the steps. With the adrenaline still coursing through him, Ramón had to move. So he ran. He ran faster than he had when he won the lottery. He ran until his chest felt like it would explode.

He stopped and coughed, his lungs protesting from the strain. Was violence the answer? He had sunk as low as the merchant. He limped back toward his car. The outside of his right ankle throbbed. He must have twisted it when he catapulted down the steps.

Ramón found himself in front of the Catholic church. If Chepa were here, she would tell him to pray for guidance. He proceeded up the stone steps. The old wooden door groaned when he entered, the interior dimly lit. Near the altar, a nun was changing flowers at the feet of the Virgin Mary. Ramón heard her scissors clicking as she cut the stems on a bouquet of plumeria. She looked up when she heard him enter. She wore a black habit which encased her body to make her look tiny as a girl, but her face and eyes were lined with wrinkles and emitted kindness, even wisdom.

"I need to see the priest," Ramón sputtered and coughed, his throat and tongue parched.

The sister looked aghast at his ashen face and dirty, sweat-stained shirt, then nodded quickly and hurried out the back.

Ramón made the sign of the cross and genuflected at a pew. The heady scent of incense, sweet yet suffocating, permeated the walls and stone floor. He leaned forward and cradled his face in his hands, praying for forgiveness. After minutes, he looked up. From above the altar, a wooden Christ on a cross looked down on Ramón with an agony Ramón understood. At the right side of the church, candles illuminated a statue of Madonna with child. The Virgin Mary stared at him vacantly. Ramón felt as cold as the stone from which she was carved.

He reached up to place his hand over his father's scapular below his collarbone but now, he felt undeserving of it.

Ramón thought of Doctor Roberts, his gentle, kind mentor, who'd be appalled at his behavior. He remembered the day the package came from Doctor Robert's son, five years earlier. In it was a letter, translated by Don Pablo, telling Ramón the dentist had died peacefully in his sleep. The package also contained Doctor Robert's framed diploma. On his deathbed, the old man asked his son to send it to Ramón.

He also remembered what Chepa said to him that day: "It's hard when you lose someone you love, but you still carry them with you, in your memories, in the choices you make in life. *El humanitario* understood that. After all those years you spent together, I see you carrying on his work."

Today, Ramón had fallen far below his mentor's expectations. And Chepa, he had promised her he'd stay away from Trujillo, and then almost killed him. When he felt Trujillo's life almost slip away, for the merest fraction of a second, it felt good, which filled Ramón with shame.

He heard footsteps and looked up.

Ramón saw a figure looming above him, in a black cloak, and like with the nun, focused on the priest's face. He knew the priest's eyes had witnessed a lifetime of events, his ears had heard a lifetime of stories.

"My son, what is it that troubles you so? Are you ready to talk of it?" the priest asked.

"I . . . I attacked Señor Trujillo. If I didn't stop, I may have killed him. He hurt my mother badly, tried to hurt my *novia*. He wants to ruin my family. I lost my head."

The priest was silent a moment before he took a deep breath and dropped down on the pew next to Ramón.

"My son, this is not good. Yet in moments of great passion, sometimes a man lashes out in ways he cannot understand."

"I've never done anything like that, I want to help people, heal them, not . . ." Ramón's voice cracked, "hurt them. And I made a promise to a great man a long time ago to become a healer, and the promise to my mamá, that I would stay away from him, Trujillo, I broke it, and . . ."

Ramón was unable to continue for the raw feeling in the back of his throat, one of grief, shame.

The priest nodded in understanding and put a gentle hand on Ramón's shoulder.

"I see your remorse. This experience, assaulting another man in a moment of weakness and anger; it's possible to lose control. Acknowledging these feelings may make you a better man. Señor Trujillo is suffering. Pray for him, for his family.

"There may be a way to turn this around. His youngest son is so vulnerable and seems to be suffering. Perhaps you could help the boy in some way. People think it's hard to do the right thing. But

129

that's not the problem. It's knowing what the right thing is. Pray the answer comes to you."

The priest grew silent for a moment to let Ramón reflect.

"Are you ready to make your confession?" the priest asked.

The priest's tone had been so reassuring, his eyes so soulful, that Ramón trusted him.

"Yes."

They entered the confession booth. Ramón could no longer see the priest, but imagined that same look on his face, one of compassion and love.

"Forgive me, Father, for I have sinned. My fury was so great that I wanted a man dead. I almost killed him . . . *Mi Dios*, what does that make me?"

Fingers of shame and fear clawed at Ramón's heart when he uttered these words.

"Through the power invested in me, in the name of the father, the son, and the Holy Ghost, I absolve you from your sins. Most importantly, you must forgive yourself, for God has forgiven you. For penance, say the sorrowful rosary and ten our fathers."

"Thank you, Padre," Ramón whispered.

Ramón left the church with an inkling of peace, a balm applied on his mental wound, yet at the same time, he sensed that his life was divided into two halves—before that day in the plaza when he had his vision and after. So much had changed. He had the money and the means to fulfill his promise. He had fallen in love with Elsie and she with him. Yet a madman had entered his life, his family's lives. Some of that madness touched Ramón. The words echoed again in his head and his heart, those spoken by his mother: *There's a reason God kisses some and not others.*

And the words from his mentor: *Make this world a better*

place because of the work you do, make your life count.

He must do what he promised.

After he descended *La Pica*, Ramón pulled over the Buick over and leapt out to vomit. He retched at the side of the road until there was nothing left but the taste of bile and with it, shame.

By the time he arrived home, Ramón shook with chills and nausea. He parked and looked across the plaza at the Catholic church. The two small bells in the steeple that he had known since childhood morphed into four. *Dios mío, what's happening to me? I'm hallucinating.*

His father's scapular began to burn above his chest. Ramón pulled down his shirt collar to check to see if his skin was really on fire and looked in the rearview mirror. A face stared back at him, yellow, sickly. Señor García warned him of it, jaundice, a side effect of the Fuadin. Ramón had been on the medicine for five days. How ironic that the side effects surfaced now. It must be a penance for everything, his agreeing to pay Antonio to write the essay for him and nearly killing a man.

Ramón hardly recognized himself.

CHAPTER 20

Days passed in a haze of nausea, vomiting and hallucinations. A burning swept up and down Ramón's legs and arms and the back of his neck to his scalp. It was as if the parasites were crawling out of his pores. He scratched his forearms so hard that when he pulled his hand away, he saw blood, inhaling the scent of a rusty penny.

Chepa employed all her knowledge and skill: *culantro*, coriander and ginger tea for nausea, and poultices of mashed arrowroot and aloe for the severe rash on his forearms, covered with a dressing to keep Ramón from scratching.

Every time he tried to stand, Ramón felt so dizzy and weak that his legs nearly collapsed and he was confined to bed. Esperanza came by to sit with him.

"Don't you have your children to take care of?" Ramón asked as he turned his head from the pillow toward her. It was a strain just to get the words out, robbing him of what little energy he had.

"I want to be here. I begged your mamá to let me sit with you while she watches them. Little Alfredo is taking a nap for a couple hours. I love working for you and Chepa; she's taught me so much. This is the least I could do. Rest now, okay?"

Esperanza wiped the sweat off his forehead with a cool cloth before he drifted off to sleep.

Ramón drifted in and out of consciousness, exhaustion settling over him like a lead blanket.

Sometime later he woke to someone touching his arm. When he opened his eyes, a figure came slowly into focus. Ramón expected to see Chepa, Esperanza, or Lila. Instead, it was Isabel. A rectangle of sun filtered through the open window, highlighting the flecks of gold in her brunette hair. By the way the light came in, Ramón guessed it was morning.

"Oh," she said, startled. "I hope I didn't wake you. Chepa showed me how to change the dressing. The rash is a lot better than last night. And your eyes don't look so yellow."

She fixed a new dressing in place with a gentle touch, discarding the soiled one in the trash basin.

Ramón had no memory of it. "You were here last night?" he asked.

"Actually, it's been a few nights that you've been out."

"A few?" Ramón croaked, pain needling his throat.

"Yes, you've been in and out, mainly out. I took over for your mother so she could go into the store. It's been slow, so she closed it for a few days, but she's there now," Isabel explained as she grabbed a glass off the night stand and held it to his lips. "Take a few sips before you try to talk."

Ramón swallowed a few mouthfuls, relieved he could hold the water down. "Why are you being so nice to me, after I sent you away?" he managed to say.

"Because you have what people want, dignity. You're using your money to better yourself, to come back and help us with a clinic. It's noble. And since the children are in school every day now, why wouldn't I help? I need something to do."

"Francisco can't be too happy about this, you being here."

"No." She shook her head. "But when I told him your mother needed me, he didn't argue."

"Did you say my mother closed the store?"

It took the news some time to register. Ramón felt frustrated by the fogginess in his brain.

Isabel nodded, furrowing her brow. "Not too many people are coming in these days. Francisco offered to take over, but Doña Chepa said she didn't need him. It's been the only good thing of Trujillo telling people to stop shopping; she's hardly left your side."

"No, this won't do. I should go help her!"

Ramón tried to get out of bed. He tottered, his vision blurry. He shook with a new wave of nausea.

Isabel jumped up and helped him to sit back down. "Careful," she cautioned. "Chepa says you need to eat and drink before you try to get up, strict orders. She wouldn't be happy if we didn't follow them. You had us all scared. You were *really* sick."

Ramón exhaled. "Wow, I didn't expect that. I almost passed out." He trembled and put his hand up to his forehead, which felt clammy and cold.

"I'll get you some tea and broth," Isabel said. "That's all your stomach can handle. I'll go tell Chepa you're awake. Don't try to get up before she comes back, okay?"

Too tired to respond, Ramón simply nodded.

§§§

"*¡Jesús, María, Y José!* You're better. Eat—you had nothing for days, *m'ijo!*"

Chepa fluttered around Ramón's bed like a dove attending to her chick. Ramón had a fleeting memory of her concerned face hovering over him. He liked this version of her better, joyous, and playful. She propped him up in bed with pillows and placed a warm roll and a fresh cup of chamomile tea on the bed table, both issuing ribbons of steam.

Ramón bit into the bread. Saliva filled his mouth, the taste buds dancing on his tongue. He didn't know how long it had been since he'd eaten solid food, but after three bites, his stomach revolted.

"Mamá, how long have I been in and out like this?"

"Four days. Your eyes were as yellow as a sunflower, now I see they're nearly back to normal, like the bright eyes I named you for. That means your liver is recovering from the Fuadin. *¡Jesús, María, Y José!*" she repeated.

"*Four days?*" Ramón exclaimed. Isabel had made light of how long it had been.

"Yes, and Elsie visited every day. She made *polvo de amor*. I see the way you look when you talk about her, and I saw how worried she was about you. I never thought things would get this far. And I wonder, as hard as it may be, if you should say a kind good-bye. Remember what I said, our families are different."

Yet things had already gotten far.

"I want to see her again . . . I *need* to see her again. Mamá, please, I know what I'm doing!"

The effort of sitting up, talking and even eating had taken its toll and Ramón had to lie back down.

Chepa's face softened and she reassured, "All right, but tread carefully, *m'ijo*. Antonio came by, too. He's got your application. He mentioned he did something else for you."

"Oh, I'm sure it's nothing much," Ramón said, managing to keep his voice light.

Of course. The essay. Ramón was feeling better, but his stomach seized up again with the lie. Yet he knew he had to act quickly.

"Mamá, tell them to come back. I need to see them—I need to get that application done!"

§§§

Somehow, Ramón got up the strength to walk to the kitchen table to receive Elsie. She threw her arms around him. His legs wobbled before he had to sit down.

"Oh sorry, I've been so worried. I'm so glad you're up and around," she exclaimed as she sat next to him.

"Me too, but I can't believe how weak I feel."

"Your strength will come back. I brought you this. It's one of my favorites, because the first poem made me think of you."

She handed him a book, *Versos Sencillos*, by José Martí.

The book's spine felt right in Ramón's hand, a perfect fit. He opened it and flipped through the first few pages, which were worn smooth. Elsie had obviously loved the book and the fact that she had entrusted it to him made his heart accelerate.

"José Martí. He's my mother's favorite, too!" Ramón said.

"You want me to read it to you?" Elsie asked.

Ramón nodded and slid the book on the table back toward her.

She cleared her throat and recited:

> *"Yo soy un hombre sincero*
> *De donde crece la palma,*
> *Y antes de morirme quiero*
> *Echar mis versos del alma.*
>
> *Yo vengo de todos partes,*
> *Y hacia todas partes voy*
> *Arte soy entre las artes,*
> *En los montes, monte soy."*

A sincere man am I
From the land where palm trees grow,
And I want before I die
My soul's verses to bestow.

I'm a traveler to all parts,
And a newcomer to none
I am art among the arts,
With the mountains I am one.

Ramón closed his eyes. Elsie's voice was soothing, lilting. What he said before on that night of the dance was true. He'd never met anyone like her. He opened his eyes and said, "Thank you, Elsie, that was beautiful."

Before Elsie could respond, Antonio sauntered into the kitchen and exclaimed, "I heard you were bad off, but you look worse than I thought—like hell!"

"Your timing isn't the best," Ramón sighed. He was trying to be funny, but he was so tired.

Antonio pulled up a chair next to Ramón and said, "Sorry, *amigo*. I have your application. It's due in a few weeks. You know how long letters take to the mainland. We need to send it out— *today*."

"It's okay, this is more important right now," Elsie said and squeezed Ramón's hand. He felt a warm tingle. "But you look so tired, don't overdo it."

She stood and pushed her chair in.

"Come back soon. Your man needs you," Antonio said and

raised his eyebrows.

Elsie kept her eyes focused on Ramón. "I'll be back tomorrow."

"Thanks, I can't wait," Ramón answered.

After Elsie kissed the top of his head and left, Ramón asked Antonio, "You got it, the essay?"

"You bet. You still need to fill in a few things."

Antonio pushed the application toward Ramón, indicating where to fill in his name and address. Ramón's hand shook when he started to write, making the first letter nearly illegible.

"Let me do it," Antonio ordered. "They won't be able to read it. After all I've done, let's not screw it up."

Ramón recited his biographical information while Antonio filled in the blanks: name, address, high school, intended course of study. Ramón shuffled back to his room to retrieve the copy of his grades. He got out of breath just bending over to search in the drawer of his bed table, where he also had a ten and a five dollar bill tucked, the rest of the money for Antonio. The fact that he had allowed Antonio to write the essay for him made him feel even sicker, if that were possible. All those hours spent studying in high school mocked him. Before now, Ramón would never have paid anyone to do something for him, and especially something of this magnitude.

By the time he got back to the kitchen, a headache surged at the base of his skull. He massaged the back of his neck.

Antonio turned to the last page of the application.

"Here's the essay, as promised." He slid the paper in front of Ramón but kept his hand on it. "And the rest of my fee, *amigo*?"

Ramón's hand shook as he handed over the money. He tried to focus. The words blurred, even harder to read in English. "I can't concentrate," he admitted.

Antonio thrust the money in his pocket and commented, "You

look worse than when I got here."

"You wrote I was third in my class, right?" The headache wrapped around into Ramón's temples. He closed his eyes and rubbed them.

"Yeah, and I told them it was your lifelong dream to be a dentist, that you were willing to work hard, blah blah. Don't worry, your grades are better than mine were. They admit lots of international students—you'll get in."

"If you say so . . ." Ramón said as the blood pounded in his head. He hoped he didn't lose the three bites of bread he had consumed. "I need to lie down. I can't do this right now. Just send it. God forbid if I miss the deadline."

CHAPTER 21

After two more days, Ramón was able to hold down a bland meal of white rice and unseasoned beans and felt well enough to walk across the plaza to the store. It felt like ages since he'd been there. He glanced at the sign above the door, *Rafita*, slightly askew and faded. He took some comfort in the fact that it still hung there. Chepa was in the back working on a garment in a shade of sky blue cotton. She lifted her foot off the treadle and looked up when Ramón entered.

"Mamá, what's this I heard about you closing the store?" he asked.

She clucked her tongue, and waved his words away with a flip of her hand and assured, "It's been slow here and a little slow in Francisco's store too, but I was able to close for a few days and take care of you. It will pick up again."

"We can't survive without customers. And it's affecting Francisco, too."

Ramón had to sit down from the effort of talking and walking.

"I talked to Capitán Miraflores," Chepa began. "He said he'd talk some sense into the man. Despite what he's done, I hope the police chief lets Trujillo keep his pride. The man's health is failing." She paused and made a sign of the cross. "This will be a dress for Señora Sarabia. She came to the house when you were sick and brought chicken soup, and she gave me an order, paid in advance.

"Esperanza started the job since my hands felt a little worse the past few days. That girl is learning fast. She thanks me every day, and tells everyone what you did for her. People say her work is good. So, see? We still have a few orders, we'll manage. Plus, people will stop listening to Trujillo. Jealousy and bitterness are ruining him. I heard he yelled at his son at his baseball game and dragged him off the field."

Chepa shook her head and said, "That boy was his father's pride and joy."

Trujillo's young son, the priest had mentioned him. Ramón remembered the merchant's venomous face as he lunged across the counter. Did he let loose the same anger on his own son? Ramón also remembered how it felt to choke the man, and could no longer contain the story of his attack on Trujillo. The events of that day spilled out.

"Mamá, the priest was right. He said that when people are overcome by anger, or passion, they often lash out. It's tragic that Trujillo hurt you and his own son, but I did something horrible, too." Ramón exhaled all the air in his chest, and covered his mouth to keep from a sob from escaping. "I want to be a good man."

"You are, *m'ijo*," Chepa said as her face softened. "There may be a way to make things right. For if you give love, you will receive it."

§§§

That evening, an urgent rapping at the front door interrupted dinner. Lila had come over for dinner and she, Ramón and Chepa stopped eating *asopao* and glanced uneasily at one another.

"Mamá, stay put, and you too, Lila," Ramón ordered. "I'll get it. If someone wanted to hurt me, he wouldn't knock, but still . . ."

Feeling stronger than he had in days, Ramón got up to answer the door.

It was Capitán Miraflores.

"I need to talk to you, Ramón."

Ramón felt a thudding in his chest. Visits from the police chief were rare, unless it meant trouble. "Come in, please," he said.

Capitán Miraflores followed Ramón into the kitchen. He removed his cap, placed it on the table, and nodded to acknowledge the women.

Chepa stood. Ramón saw her try to hide a grimace. Although she was faring better, he knew moving too quickly still pained her.

"Can I get you something, tea, something stronger?" Chepa asked the police chief.

"No. But perhaps I should speak to Ramón alone."

"Anything you say to me, my mother and sister can hear, too," Ramón affirmed.

"After Doña Chepa came to see me to tell me what Trujillo had done to her, I paid him a visit. Imagine my surprise when I saw the welts around his neck."

Ramón felt the red flush of shame spread across his face.

"I caused those bruises. I went to see him, to reason with him. Things got out of hand. I'll regret what I did for the rest of my life," Ramón admitted.

Ramón heard a gasp from Lila. This was the first she'd heard of it. He said a silent prayer of thanks that he had already told Chepa what he did.

Again, as if reading his mind, Chepa interjected, "My son told me everything. He went to see Padre Pérez in Yabucoa, he went to confession, said the sorrowful rosary."

"Considering what the man did to you, Doña Chepa, I'll forget I saw those welts if Ramón gives me his word that he'll stay away from him. Let's just say he won't be coming to Maunabo anytime soon."

"I'll stay away from him, if he stays away from me," Ramón said gravely.

"Good," the police chief uttered and grabbed his hat. He locked eyes with Ramón, knitted his brows together as if to put weight to his words: "I gave you permission to court my daughter. I'm wondering if I did the right thing, but she speaks very highly of you. She begged me to let her keep seeing you and I agreed, for the time being. Don't make me regret it."

Ramón swallowed the knot in his throat and said, "You won't."

A heavy silence followed for a few seconds.

"Well, I'll let you get back to your meal," Capitán Miraflores declared.

"Ramón, please show Capitán to the door," Chepa requested.

The men left the room. Before he headed down the front steps, the police chief said something that chilled the blood in Ramón's veins.

"Trujillo has a lot of people in his pockets, and he's not taking any of this well. He'll stay away for now, but he's ordered the Yabucoa police to come after you, to arrest you. He may just pull it off, and of course, he'll omit the fact he attacked you first. Watch your back."

The knot in Ramón's throat got even bigger. "I will," he pledged.

CHAPTER 22

"Mamá, I'd like to go to San Juan today. I need to get tested again for snail fever, to make sure the medicine worked. Juanito needs to get tested, too. And I have those ads I cut out from the newspaper, with pictures like some of Francisco's and our new merchandise. I'll hang them at Señora Lepe's and at the post offices in Yabucoa and Caguas, too. We need to advertise, try to get things going."

Ramón wished he could claim that he needed to shop for the store, but with no customers and the extra merchandise purchased, the shelves were full already.

Chepa agreed. "Some signs will help. My back's aching but I'll go into the store today. A boy brought in a pair of pants for me to hem for his little brother. Esperanza insisted on doing the job; she's getting better every day. Don't worry, things will pick up."

Of course, she could read his mind.

He wanted to tell Chepa of the warning from Capitán, but he knew she was still in pain, and he wanted time to figure things out. Should he go to the Yabucoa police, tell his side of the story?

And what of the snail fever? Ramón had promised Señor García that he would be tested and suspected the test would be negative, but it provided little solace. There was so much at stake right now: dwindling business and the future of the store, his relationship with Elsie that their families didn't approve of, and most paramount, the threat the Yabucoa police were after him. If they showed up and arrested him, what of the promise to Doctor Roberts from so long ago and Chepa's assurance that he would fulfill it?

144

The problems were spreading as fast as fire in a field of dry grass.

For a moment, Ramón wished he could go to San Juan alone, to blend in with the crowds and wait a few days for things to blow over, to avoid the police, and then come home. But he remembered the warning from the army doctor how serious snail fever was; he had to get Juanito tested.

§§§

The lab was located in a drab gray building on a side street in the capital. A small sign on the door read: "*Laboratorio Clínico*".

A nurse dressed completely in white, with a skirt, long-sleeved blouse and starched hat that looked like it was about to salute them ushered Ramón and Juanito into an exam room. After she took Ramón's blood, she turned to Juanito with a large syringe in her hand.

Juanito put up a brave front despite the way he glanced at Ramón, wide-eyed.

"It will be okay," Ramón assured when he saw the pained look on his nephew's face. Ramón thought the boy may cry, but only heard a sharp intake of air as the nurse injected the needle and drew Juanito's blood.

It took only twenty minutes for Ramón and Juanito to receive the results to the blood samples: Negative.

One less thing to worry about.

§§§

They spent the afternoon walking and eating *frijoles negros*

145

and beef *empanadillas* at a cantina. Juanito jabbered about his first visit to the capital, about the stores and bars with open doors and blaring jukeboxes, and the streets clogged with cars and vendors selling fruits and vegetables that in Maunabo they could pick off the trees.

On the way home, they stopped at the post offices in Caguas and Yabucoa, and then at Señora Lepe's makeshift post office at her adobe home. Ramón tacked up another ad he had clipped from *El Mundo:* it depicted four young smiling women strolling down a New York City sidewalk wearing fitted knee-length dresses in pink, light green and navy cinched with belts with gold buckles. Under it he wrote: *Come to Rafita. See our new fashions and low prices. Saving is easier than ever. Only $1.99!*

An ad for Francisco's store pictured new oil and paraffin lamps and the price of new zinc tiles: *a package to cover your entire roof, starting as low as $5.99!*

The entire time in the car, Juanito continued on about how well the people dressed, in suits and shoes—made of leather, no sandals or barefoot *jíbaros!* The chatter distracted Ramón, but when they drove over *La Pica*, he constantly looked in the rearview mirror and held his breath around every turn, wondering if he would see a police car. When he dropped off Juanito at home and gave him a hearty hug, Ramón wished he could keep driving off into the horizon, far away.

But he went home. When he stepped into the kitchen, Chepa lit a briquette on the *fogón* to heat a pot of tea and remarked, "So you're both fine. I knew you would be."

"Yeah, but how did you know?"

"I knew."

Ramón sat at the table to ask, "How was the store?" He

146

disguised the anxiety in his voice. If the Yabucoa police came by, she would have mentioned it immediately.

"Esperanza finished the pants and we started Señora Sarabia's dress. Like I said, the work did me good."

The teapot blew steam. Chepa filled his mug and said, "The important thing is, you and Juanito are healthy." She handed him his mug and joined him at the table. "Why don't you look happy, what's wrong?"

"Nothing. Juanito and I walked so much, he tired me out. He hardly stopped talking the whole time."

Ramón hid his face behind the tea mug and sipped.

He thought of telling her about the police, but remembered how frail she felt when he lifted her off the floor after Trujillo knocked her down. And by the way she moved in the kitchen, a few paces slower than normal, Ramón knew she was in pain. No, he wouldn't say anything. Not yet.

"Are you sure you're okay, Mamá? Can I get something for your back, some of your wintergreen gel? I can make some ginger tea," he suggested.

Chepa shook her head. "I'm feeling better every day. But there's something you're not telling me," she added.

"A big part of me is relieved that I'm cured, especially that Juanito's okay. But, part of me thinks I should join the army, report that I'm okay," Ramón said, then thought of the coffin, his vision.

Chepa reached over and patted his hand. "*No,*" she told Ramón. "But I'm not surprised you'd think that. Do you know how good you are? God made you noble and good. All that work you did with *el humanitario*, you have abilities that others don't. You're meant for something else, not war."

"I'm not out there like my brothers . . . I feel like I'm cheating them," Ramón admitted.

"What about your life is the truth?"

"That I made a promise, to Doctor Roberts and to you, that I'm prepared to do whatever I can to keep it."

"We'll pray for peace," Chepa assured. "People are saying the end of the war may be coming soon. What have I told you before?"

There were so many tidbits of wisdom Chepa shared with him, with everyone. Ramón remembered one of the most powerful.

"You told me there's a reason God kisses some and not others."

§§§

Ramón had to tell Elsie he was cured. She always made him feel better by her mere presence. He ran to the Miraflores home and banged the large iron knocker on the front door. He had a fleeting image of Elsie's father arresting him, but that was absurd. El Capitán had tried to warn him.

Señora Miraflores opened the door. "Oh, Ramón. Is there . . . umm . . . anything I can do for you?" she asked.

Nothing, there's nothing you can do, just give me your daughter.

Ramón removed his cap to say, "I was wondering if Elsie would like to go for a walk."

She hesitated. "I'll ask."

She closed the door. Odd, she didn't invite him in.

Minutes passed. Ramón wrung his cap like a wet rag. Elsie opened the door and stepped out to greet him. She had her hair pulled back in a ponytail. Her face was luminescent; her caramel-colored skin glowed against her white short-sleeved blouse with scoop neckline. Ramón inhaled her rose perfume.

His heart fluttered.

They strolled down *La Calle de Los Blancos*. The gravel on the roadside crunched under their feet.

Ramón talked first. "I came by to tell you, I'm cured, no more snail fever, and Juanito's okay, too."

"Oh, that's good."

She sounded relieved, but he expected more. He wanted her to embrace him, as she had done when he told her he actually had the disease.

They continued on for a few minutes. The only sounds were *coquís* and cicadas, no police car coming up behind them. Ramón relaxed slightly, grateful for the calming effect Elsie always had on him.

"There's something else on my mind. I did something I'm not proud of," he admitted.

"My father told me you hurt Trujillo, and Trujillo's been telling everyone. There were welts around his neck." Elsie sounded brusque.

Ramón felt like a donkey had kicked him in the chest. He had wanted to explain everything, how Trujillo hurt Chepa, but he was so flabbergasted by the tone in her voice, he felt at a loss for words.

A silence fell between them.

Elsie stopped. Ironically, they stood together under the same coconut tree where they shared their first kiss. She touched Ramón's elbow, turned him toward her.

"I was shocked. My father didn't want me to continue seeing you, especially when I told him about that night Trujillo threw the bottle at us. I don't know what to think. I feel terrible about everything, and I need some time to think."

"But he tried to hurt my mother, and he tried to hurt you when he hurled that bottle. I had to do something, and I lost my head, it was awful . . ."

"I know you want to defend your family," she interrupted, "but part of me doesn't want to get in the middle of this. It may get dangerous. My parents are upset, and I need some time to adjust to this, please, can we just go?"

Ramón heard the pleading in her voice. He was glad for the shadows from the coconut tree that hid their faces.

"I'll walk you home." The inside of his mouth had turned to cotton, and he couldn't say any more.

CHAPTER 23

Ramón trudged along in the waning light, feeling empty and hollow with the sting of Elsie's rejection.

When he arrived home, some instinct made him slow before he opened the front door. Who was there waiting to receive him, the police?

When he stepped into the kitchen, it was Francisco sitting at the table. Ramón was in no mood to talk to anyone, but shouldn't he tell Francisco about the threat of the police?

"Francisco, there's something I need to—" he began.

Francisco stood and turned. A half-empty bottle of rum sat on the table in front of him. His eyes were bloodshot. It looked like he had slept in his clothes. He walked toward Ramón drawing his lips back in a snarl.

"*You*, with your fancy car, your talk of going to some college, you think you're better than the rest of us. I saw the way my wife looked at you, practically crying that you shouldn't be drafted, running over to take care of you when you were sick. For all I know, you're sleeping with her!"

Dumbstruck, Ramón defended, "You're insane, I would never!"

So quickly that Ramón never saw it coming, Francisco punched him across his mouth. A tremendous blow, it sent Ramón reeling. Somehow, he stayed upright. He tasted blood.

Francisco looked down at bloody gashes on his knuckles. He shook his hand, hollering, "*Pendejo,* you cut me!"

Ramón felt like a matador facing a raging bull. With strength he didn't know he could possess, he planted his feet and struck his brother back, squarely across the mouth. *Dios*, he couldn't imagine how this was happening, after what he did for his brother, their day in San Juan. He thought they were getting along, and with the sting of Elsie's words so fresh, he exploded.

Francisco's head snapped back just as Ramón flew at him. The two fell to the floor, kicking and punching each other's ribs, shoulders, and chests. Ramón landed more punches than his brother; Francisco's movements and aim were slowed by alcohol. Their tussle lasted only seconds before Francisco stood and shuddered. He began to retch and ran outside to vomit. Ramón followed his brother, who looked up at Ramón with sweat pouring off his brow and shame that fell across him like a heavy cloak, his mouth a bloody mess with traces of vomit.

Ramón felt rage, but pity, too, when he saw his brother's suffering.

"Go home, Francisco, and sober up. How dare you think I'd sleep with your wife!"

Francisco wiped his mouth with the back of his forearm and stumbled off. Ramón watched his brother's retreating back and shouted, "You don't even know what I'm going through! And all I've done to help you!"

Francisco didn't answer, as if there was no fight left in him. Ramón traipsed back to the kitchen and dropped into a chair. An intense sadness filled him, squeezing out all other sensation in his body. He grabbed the empty glass and held the cool surface to the gash on the side of his face. His brother had helped him that day in the store when Trujillo charged in, now he attacked him. His girlfriend was ashamed of him and he was terrified the police from Yabucoa would show up next. In the quiet of the room, Ramón understood that an uneventful day was a gift. He poured three fingers of rum into the glass and finished it in one gulp. It tasted so different than he remembered at his celebratory party—bitter instead of sweet.

CHAPTER 24

Ramón snapped awake, despite having hardly slept. The events of the previous night crashed in on him, and he groaned. Chepa had come home from a villager's house after tending to the colic of his youngest son and was shocked when she saw the gash on Ramón's left cheek. He told his mother of the fight and despite trying to hold them back, tears welled in her eyes. After putting a salve on Ramón's wound, she went to Francisco's house to berate him, throw out all his bottles of rum, and ultimately forgive him. She had returned home exhausted, well after midnight.

So this is how people disappoint one another, Ramón thought as he sipped *café con leche*. Ramón thought again of his and Francisco's treasured time together at the old theater, watching *Tarzan the Ape Man*. How he'd like to escape to the movies now, yet the rain from tropical storms had leaked through the roof and caused enough damage to the old screen that the owners could not afford to replace it. Like many other things in the village, it sat silent and vacant. Before, he'd had a fantasy that when he came home a dentist and opened a fine clinic that Maunabo would become more of a destination, and that he might even help reopen the old theater. Now he was filled with dread that it would never come to pass.

The house was quiet. Thankfully, Chepa still slept after her long night. Ramón made a decision. He would go to work in the store and when Chepa got up and came in, he'd tell her the police may show up. Together, they may come up with a solution. They could talk to Juan, and with his position as a clerk at the district court in Yabucoa, could he in turn talk to someone?

In the back room, Ramón laid out fabric on their wide table to finish the laborious task of tucking and stitching the pleats of Señora Sarabia's dress that Chepa and Esperanza had started. As Chepa claimed, Esperanza was learning fast. At least things with their new young apprentice were going well. Ramón fondly recalled how nice it was to go to her *bohío* in the *barrio* on several occasions, to drop by with some work. She didn't have much but she'd always offer him something like fresh squeezed guava juice, and Ramón always brought papaya candy for her little girl. They enjoyed each other's company, discussing simple things like sewing and the weather.

He heard the doorbell jingle, interrupting his work. Could it be Chepa, or better yet, a customer? He put his work aside and hurried out to the front.

Two men stood, arms crossed. Ramón took in their blue police uniforms, their ramrod straight backs. So this was it. Somehow he believed he'd have more time before they came for him. The room seemed too small for the three of them. He wished he was in the movies and could escape out the back door, but there was no back door and this was his life, not the movies. Ramón's gut twisted into a knot. It took all his strength to keep his knees from giving way.

Each man had a holster on his waist with .38s. One was a hulking light- skinned man whose eyes sunk into his fleshy face like a weasel and bored into Ramón. The other was darker, lean and hawk-nosed, with a deep scar that pulled his face into a frown. They weren't customers.

"Ramón León Carrasquillo, come with us. NOW," the large one ordered.

"Where?" Ramón fought to keep the terror out of his voice.

"You attacked Señor Alvaro Trujillo." His voice cut like steel.

155

"Did you think you'd get away with it? We're taking you to the jail in Yabucoa."

Ramón had never heard anyone use Trujillo's first name before. It alarmed him that these men knew the merchant on that level, had probably done his dirty deeds in the past.

The bigger man strode toward Ramón as he reached back and took handcuffs from his belt.

"Is that really necessary? I did what I did because Trujillo attacked me first. He knocked my mother down, threw a glass bottle at my *novia*," Ramón said. He heard the urgency in his voice, yet prayed the men didn't notice his knees shaking.

The large policeman yanked Ramón's arms back so violently he thought they'd pull out of the sockets. The brute snapped the cuffs on tightly. Ice-cold, they sliced into Ramón's flesh. The policeman laid his hand on his revolver and snickered, "You try anything, I'll blow your head off. Just give me any excuse."

Ramón thought he might vomit.

They dragged him outside, toward their idling vehicle.

Ramón glanced across the plaza, secretly thanking God Chepa wasn't there to witness the scene. He had been so close to telling his mother. This was not the way he wanted her to find out. The only person present was an old *jíbaro* sitting on a bench smoking a cigarette. The man ogled, mouth agape as the larger policeman thrust Ramón into the back seat. Even the peasant's mangy dog stopped scratching his pitiful ribs to watch.

§§§

"Golden boy, with all your gold and money, you don't look so golden now," the larger policeman said, cackling like a hyena. He poked Ramón with his baton to force him to the back of the police station in Yabucoa. He opened a rusty steel door to expose a filthy room. Light flooded the windowless cell as a rat scurried across the floor and into a crack in the wall.

"There's a roommate for you," the big policeman scoffed. In the car ride over, Ramón had heard the smaller one call the larger one Boudreau. It must be his surname, probably American or European; there was a guttural sound to his Spanish, as if it came from deep in his throat.

The ten-by-ten enclosure contained a cot with a grimy blanket, a small sink coated black with mold, and a hole in the floor with a dark stain encircling it. The air smelled foul, sweat combined with stale urine and fear. Ramón shuddered as Boudreau tore off the handcuffs and kicked him into the cell with his heavy boot. Ramón felt a searing pain and heard a rib crack on his left side, maybe two. A cockroach scurried into the same hole as the rat.

Boudreau smiled malevolently as he said, "You're going to be here until it's decided what to do with you. Have fun."

Ramón grabbed his ribs, wondering if they were broken as he tried to breathe.

"I'm starving. This dirty business made me hungry. I'm going for dinner. As for you, you get nothing," Boudreau hissed as he spat at Ramón and left.

The smaller one named Marco remained seated on a bench outside the cell. "Well, well," he scoffed. "I heard you're the guy who won the lottery. You don't look so rich now. Trujillo says you cheated, that you're wasting your money at *Las Monjas*, that you tried to kill him."

"I lost my temper but Trujillo's losing his mind, and I didn't cheat. How could I have? And I never spent a penny at the race track—never been there in my life and my money's in a bank. All I want is to go to college and to come back here to help people."

The effort of talking made Ramón breathless. He felt a cough coming on and dreaded it, bracing for the feeling of a sword between his ribs, adding to the pain from Francisco's blows.

Marco chewed on tobacco, looking as if he were pondering Ramón's version of events. He spat tobacco onto the floor, then said, "Well, an order's an order."

"I'm thirsty. Can I have some water?" Ramón whispered. His lips had gone dry. He licked them. His tongue was dry, too.

Marco shrugged. "There's a sink. You got hands."

Ramón couldn't imagine drinking water from that sink, not after his bout with snail fever, not unless it was a matter of life and death. The sweat from his fear soaked through his shirt and chilled him.

Marco got up and left, slamming the door behind him and plunging Ramón into blackness. Only a sliver of light came through the crack in the wall. He couldn't imagine being in a worse situation. Two months before, the day he won the lottery, Ramón had prayed he wouldn't wake from a dream. Now sitting in this cell, he prayed he would.

Who would have thought he would pay such a price for a moment's loss of self-control? Despite the stifling air in the room, he shivered. Would his dream end here in this cell, or worse—a prison in San Juan?

Dios, what if the college found out about this? Surely not, the application must be there by now, sitting on someone's desk. And what of his reputation? What would people think of him? His ribs and cheekbone throbbed, but bruises and broken ribs healed. Reputations did not.

The crushing weight of loneliness bore down upon him.

Ramón let out a sob, hitching gusts of air. The knife in his ribs plunged deeper. From the street outside, he heard the honk of a car, the shrill blast of a policeman's whistle. He concentrated on the sounds, to allow them to drown out his sobs.

Ramón thought of Doctor Roberts, his mother, his promise to them both. He tried to hear his father's voice soothing him when he fell off his bike as a little boy, and had a long ugly gash on his elbow, yet the memory of his father's voice had faded over the years.

He thought of Trujillo and understood the agony the man was going through. The rich merchant had bought the same numbered ticket for years, had come *so close* to winning, and that one day, through his own actions, decided not buy it. Similarly, Ramón was so much closer to achieving his dream yet through his own actions, had landed himself here.

Like Trujillo, would he lose it all?

Moments passed, then an hour.

He couldn't let things end this way. What would Chepa do? Or his father and Doctor Roberts? He waited for an answer. Of course, visualization, his old friend.

Despite the dark, Ramón closed his eyes and focused on his ribs. He imagined a white, shining ball of light moving into them, healing the cracks in the bones. He concentrated on slowing his pulse and breathing evenly. He tuned out the sounds of another creature scurrying across the floor.

His thirst grew, and a headache began to pulse at the base of his skull. A pain shot through his cheek and he realized he had been clenching his jaw. He visualized the ball of light going into his throat, head and face, too, softening the tense muscles.

He pictured Elsie's face, the way her luminous eyes looked

when they were on the dance floor at *El Parque Florida*. He had to get out of this situation, to win her back. He wanted to find comfort in her arms, feel the softness of her skin as she pressed against him, soak in the mesmerizing essence of her. Even her breath carried the scent of flowers.

A scene popped into his head, one from two years earlier. A woman had come to their home for Chepa's help after she had lost her fourth baby in a rush of scarlet tissue, crying there were no more babies in her future. His mother cleaned her with the utmost tenderness, and made tea with *culantro* and ginger for cramps, and led the woman to her bedroom. The two sat at the edge of Chepa's bed, where Chepa held her patient, rocking her until she quieted.

Ramón stood unseen at the edge of the bedroom door. He couldn't look away; the transformation in the young woman was complete, her whole body and face relaxed, melting into Chepa's arms.

Chepa held the tea to the woman's lips. "I want you to do something," his mother advised. "I've seen you look at young mothers and their children with envy. Change that. Look at them with love, with happiness. Imagine yourself with a baby, how sweet she'll smell after a bath, the feel of your breasts giving milk, the softness of her skin against yours. Can you feel it?"

The woman nodded.

"Don't believe in only the things you can see," Chepa continued, "For believing in the unseen is a blessing. Imagine how your baby will feel in your arms, as you rock her to sleep. Focus on these thoughts before you and your husband lie down together."

Embarrassed at witnessing such a private moment, Ramón crept away.

160

Months later, the woman had visited again, visibly pregnant and glowing, deeming it a miracle. In another three months, Chepa was summoned to deliver the baby, a healthy girl.

What would his mother advise now? To replace his feelings of despair, hate and fear with hope and love.

"It's not what happens to you, but how you react that counts. Let go of anger, like a hot coal, it burns you," she would tell him.

He thought of Francisco, the two of them loving one another again as brothers, their businesses thriving.

He thought of war, and he visualized peace. Rather than becoming a soldier, Ramón visualized himself a healer, like he used to do.

He thought of Marco's comment about spending his money at the race track. On this, the worst night of his life, Ramón felt divided like two horses going down different tracks: he could sink into despair and try to get revenge or he could pick himself up, become stronger from this experience.

He knew somehow, these thoughts would allow him to survive the black night, and he made another promise. He prayed to God, that if he got out of this dire situation, he would do the right thing, as the priest told him. Trujillo had done something nearly unforgiveable, but the man was losing his mind, and Ramón would help him and his family, and he would fix things in the store. He reached for his father's scapular, where strangely, the area was unbruised. His father's talisman, two pieces of brown cloth, had done its job.

§§§

Sometime in the night, sleep overcame Ramón. The door creaked open in the morning, nearly blinding him as sunlight spilled into blackness. He blinked multiple times. He was still thirsty, but his headache was gone, the pain in his ribs less.

As his vision cleared, Ramón saw something: the corner of a black cassock as a man swept into the room, the priest from Yabucoa. Chepa was behind him. Padre Pérez tenderly helped Ramón to his feet and led him from the cell. His mother folded Ramón in her arms, crying quietly and thanking the priest for his help. Ramón's mind felt as blurry as his vision; he heard snippets of Chepa thanking God that the old *jíbaro* from the plaza had told her what happened.

Slowly, the smaller policeman, Marco, came into focus.

"You're a lucky bast . . . oh, *perdóneme,* Padre," Marco muttered, and then lowered his voice so only Ramón heard. "Padre Pérez asked me to get you out of here. He talked to Trujillo too, and I bet the old *diablo* wouldn't have listened to anyone else."

It took a minute for Ramón to register what Marco said, as if his words were traveling underwater, and then it dawned on him— he was getting out! He thanked God for sending Padre Pérez. He also thanked God the priest had sought out Marco, who showed a mere hint of decency, rather than the more vengeful Boudreau.

As they proceeded out of the police station, Ramón felt so drained, he began to stumble. Padre Pérez reached over and supported his elbow to help Ramón to Don Pablo's Oldsmobile. The don sat in the front, smoking a cigar. His brow knitted in concern for a moment, followed by the flash of an enormous smile, one of both joy and relief.

In spite of the stiffness in his back and legs, the ache in his beaten body, Ramón felt lifted by love when he saw the emotions play across the don's face. So Chepa had gone to their neighbor for help. Despite what Ramón had endured, God put another friend, another savoir, in his path.

Now it was Ramón's turn to fulfill the promises he had made.

CHAPTER 25

It took half a week for Ramón's pain to subside and for the purple shades to fade to yellow. He was amazed his ribs were bruised and not broken.

One morning, Francisco shuffled into the kitchen, hands stuffed into pockets, chin dipped to his chest. Ramón saw him searching for the right words.

"I heard what happened, that bastard, Trujillo, sending those guys after you and what they did to you. I'm sorry."

Francisco looked up and it was if Ramón were looking in the mirror. His brother's face showed the same bruises, the same sickly shade of yellow dispersed with broken blood vessels. Surprised that he had inflicted so much damage, Ramón wondered which one of them looked worse.

Francisco took his hands out of his pockets and held them up, almost in a pleading motion and explained, "I was jealous. All of a sudden, you had everything. Everyone looks up to you, even my wife. I couldn't stand it. You'll start a new life, and I'll still be here, in my store, doing the same thing, day after day. So I started drinking more, thinking I would forget. The day I attacked you, the kids had been real noisy, and God forbid, I almost hit one of them. And then I took it out on you. It took me getting to the bottom to realize something. When the booze wears off, nothing changes."

Ramón looked at his brother's face and understood the depths of his sorrow. "Francisco, you made some mistakes, and now you want to make good. I'm proud of you for that. I'm *so sorry* for what

164

happened between us. And you know what?"

Ramón put his hand on his brother's shoulder as he continued: "Your work is important. You've run your store with the honor that Mamá taught us. You helped grow your business, and Mamá's too. You know I'd never do anything with Isabel. And right now, I need your support. I've been through hell and back, and the thought of my family is what got me through the night in jail. I need your help, Francisco. I'm going to do something big, and I need you there."

"I'll be there, for whatever you need. Because after I came after you like I did, something in me snapped. And made me stop drinking."

"You don't look a whole lot better than me right now, big brother, but there's something in your eyes that I've always noticed, ever since I was a kid. You're honest, *hermano*, and you've always told like it is. There's a lot of good in you, more than in most people. You're going to get through this with me, and you're going to be okay."

The two brothers embraced.

Ramón then told a plan to Francisco, which he had formulated during that long night in jail. He would hold a meeting to appeal to their customers and the villagers of Maunabo and Yabucoa to clear his name, help restore the family livelihood. Francisco wholeheartedly agreed.

Ramón also knew the fastest way to spread news was through the postmistress, Señora Lepe. When someone told her a rumor or received noteworthy mail, the news traveled faster than the swiftest horse at the *Las Monjas Hippodrome*.

165

§§§

Later that day, Ramón stepped into the postmistress's "office" in her small adobe house.

"Any letters today, Señora Lepe? How about something from the college?"

"Aye, it's only been a few weeks, give them time, Ramón, quit moping around with your comb down like a rooster!"

"You're right, señora. But you know how important a letter from the college is for me. By the way, you haven't you come to my mother's store in the past couple weeks. We'll have those new dresses soon," Ramón said, pointing at the ad that was still placed on the wall. "You need to come see them, try one on."

Her face flushed. She looked down and commented, "Well . . . Trujillo may have offered me a stuffed goose if I shopped there. How could I turn him down? I've never had a goose in my life! And I only bought a pair of socks."

"Señor Trujillo and I have had problems, and I need to tell *my* side of the story. I figured this Sunday would be a good time, a day of rest from work. What do *you* think? Do you think people would come if I held a town meeting in the plaza?"

Her face brightened. "Oh, I don't see why not!"

Ramón strode away. The first part of his plan had worked. The excited look on Señora Lepe's face assured him the word would get out. After he accomplished his first task, he decided he would contact Trujillo's son. Ramón had been ordered to stay away from the merchant, but he could try and help the son. Ramón remembered Chepa's story of how Trujillo had humiliated his son and dragged

166

him off the baseball field, how Padre Pérez talked of the son that day in the church. Ramón had an uncanny feeling that the boy, a couple years younger than Juanito, would need him, that they would somehow matter in each other's lives.

§§§

After both Chepa and Francisco had agreed with his plan, Ramón decided to tell Elsie, too. He went to the same spot he had been at weeks earlier and tossed a pebble at her window. Like before, she came down to the garden and asked quickly, "You look terrible! What happened?"

It was no wonder. Ramón hadn't slept well in days. The last time he looked in the mirror, he was shocked at the pale color of his skin, the gauntness that hadn't been there before along with the healing bruises.

Now Ramón could tell her everything, including how Trujillo came to the store and pushed Chepa, the fight afterward, and how he spent only the second night in his life away from home, this time in a jail cell.

"It was the most miserable night in my life," he told her quickly, "And I don't know if I would have made it without the thought of you, Elsie. Don't you know how I feel about you? You're the most important person in my life right now. I don't know what I'd do if I couldn't be with you anymore."

The anguish on his face must have registered along with his words.

"*Dios*, that's terrible!" Elsie cried as she leaned forward and hugged him. "I'm so sorry for what I said before. I didn't hear the whole story. Do you forgive me?"

167

When Ramón saw the features soften on her face, he felt all the tension leave his body.

"I couldn't imagine not forgiving you. Elsie, I'm through with violence. I want to solve this fight the right way. I want people to hear my story, not Trujillo's. I'm going to tell everyone this Sunday. Can you be there with me?"

"Of course. I wouldn't miss it."

Elsie beamed, and it filled Ramón with the warmth of the sun after a hurricane.

§§§

Señora Lepe performed her due diligence by spreading word of Ramón's meeting at the plaza. His family and confidants accompanied him: Chepa, Juan, Tía Amanda, José Luis, Tía Marina, Francisco and Isabel, Lila and Jorge, Elsie, Esperanza, and Don Pablo and his wife, Rosario.

When the group arrived at the plaza, a crowd of about fifty villagers, about half from Maunabo, and half from Yabucoa, had already gathered in the center. A few stray dogs ran about and both humans and mongrels made room as Ramón proceeded to the front. His heart raced, drumming in his chest.

"I see the word got spread to come here today, and I'd like thank you all for being here," Ramón announced, nodding at Señora Lepe before he continued.

"As you know, I won the lottery. I've never gambled in my life, but something incredible happened that made me buy my first ticket ever, the whole sheet. I saw a number in the sky, I played it, and the amazing thing is, I won. You've heard I spent the money on gifts for my family and the horse races, but that's the farthest thing from the truth. You see, I won for a reason. Years ago, I spent four years learning from a man who inspired me like no other, *el humanitario*. His sense of duty and joy were one and the same. Doctor Roberts and I, we took care of some of you. I made a promise to him and my mother, Doña Chepa, that I would carry on that work."

Ramón looked out into the group and saw a few heads nod in agreement.

"That's what the money's for," he explained. "It's sitting in a bank. I'll use it to pay for college, to become a dentist and come back and build a clinic."

He stopped for a brief second. The next part wouldn't be easy.

"I did something I'm not proud of . . . I attacked Señor Trujillo when he came at me. He was full of rage, but I was still wrong. I hope he can forgive me, for I have forgiven him for telling lies about me, for hurting my mother, and for trying to hurt my *novia*. He's suffering, and I pray his suffering ends soon."

Ramón glanced at Elsie, who beamed at him. His heart pounded.

"He says that you spent your money on a car, that you tried to kill him!" a man in the front declared.

"I'll regret that for as long as I live. As for the car, I regret that, too. I tried to sell it back and the salesman refused. My brothers have agreed to use it when I leave to study and they'll add whatever they can to my college fund. I figure it will take eight or nine years, and that's far from free."

Ramón heard a few gasps in the crowd.

"Many of you used to come to my mother's store, and I'm shocked that you'd listen to Trujillo, and stop coming to her," he continued.

"He gave me a free blouse—I needed that. I don't have extra

money," a woman who stood a few rows back announced.

"I know times are hard, but my family has always done business with our hearts, not our pocketbooks." Ramón paused as he made eye contact with every face in the crowd. "We've always treated you with integrity. We put a lot of care into our alterations, and they're always on time. Our prices are fair—my mother lets many of you take clothing on credit, to pay back when you can! And she's taken care of nearly all of you when you're sick."

A few people shifted on their feet. More began to look at one another and nod.

Ramón directed his gaze at a *público* driver near the front and said, "Señor Martínez, you told me once that my mother cured your papá from a terrible bowel affliction, and gave him a poultice for a gash in the leg from working the cane. You told me that he worked himself to death with lung disease, and my mother helped him die with dignity, right?"

"Yes." Señor Martínez's eyes fell.

Ramón turned to another man. "And didn't my mother save you from a scorpion bite, Señor Herrera? Did she even charge you for the treatment?"

"Yes, I mean, no, she didn't charge me," the man answered, crossing his arms in front of his chest.

A pregnant lady stepped forward holding a toddler on her hip. Ramón could hardly believe it. It was the same woman he remembered that night he spent in jail.

"Doña Chepa's a saint," she shouted and turned so those in the back could hear. "She helped me have a baby, and look—there's another one on the way, thanks to her!"

The woman rubbed her protruding belly with her free hand, adding, "I don't have a lot of money, but I'm going to have

Doña Chepa deliver this baby and make the christening dress. I couldn't imagine going to anyone else."

Ramón's heart soared with pride when he saw the determination and love on the woman's face. That's why her image came to him that night, a premonition that she would speak out on behalf of his family. It took a moment for him to control the emotion in his voice, to keep it loud and steady. "I'm sure many of you can tell stories like la señora, so let me ask you, why turn your back on me and my family?"

Then Esperanza took Chepa's hand and stepped forward.

"What Ramón says is true." Esperanza's voice rose. "He was my savior. He took me in, offered me a job. I'll never forget what he did for me; I just wish I could repay it. My life is so much better since he and Doña Chepa taught me a skill I'll use the rest of my life. I don't know what I'd do without them."

Esperanza was so overcome with emotion she took a moment to continue. "They're my new family."

Ramón was dumbfounded by the unabashed warmth, love even, on her face. And she looked better, too. She stood taller. She wore one of the new skirts he brought back from San Juan, a camel color than complimented the sky blue blouse she sewed with Chepa's help. They fit perfectly on her new, filled-out frame. The word was going around the village; people had witnessed the change in her.

"And speaking of family," Ramón said, "I want my brother, Francisco, to join me now. We have new and better merchandise in our stores and we've lowered our prices, for you. And Francisco was a big part of it."

Francisco stepped forward and stood ramrod straight with Ramón.

"We improved our inventory and you won't find better places

to shop. We want you all back," Francisco called to the crowd.

"If you can be happy through the good fortunes of your friends, and not listen to quarrels; if you allow love and selflessness to blossom in your heart, your every burden will seem lighter and your joy will spread. Love thy neighbor as you love yourself, and extend to each person all the kindness, understanding and forgiveness that you can muster. That's what my mother taught me. That's what my brother taught me," Ramón proclaimed.

The crowd went completely quiet, like the expectant moment between thunder and lightning.

Francisco began to clap. After three claps, every person present joined him. The air filled with a rhythmic outburst of support. Francisco and Ramón embraced in a wordless embrace, Francisco's ultimate apology.

Elsie ran forward and grabbed Ramón's hand. He held her in his arms.

The applause grew louder.

His family came up and joined Ramón first, and then the rest of the crowd surrounded them. They clapped Ramón on the back and embraced him, some with tears in their eyes.

Antonio threw his arm around Ramón's shoulder and exclaimed, "Bravo—people are talking about Trujillo, someone said he may be going a little crazy! Don't you see, Ramón—you've won!"

Hadn't Chepa said when you give love and encouragement to others, it will come back to you multiplied? Here he was, surrounded by love. Ramón was filled with an enormous sense of peace, and despite everything that had occurred, with a wave of sadness for the merchant and his family—he knew they didn't have such an outpouring of support. He remembered what the priest said that day in the church; the man's family was suffering. There was one person

Ramón knew he must go see.

CHAPTER 26

The next afternoon, Ramón drove to Yabucoa to see Trujillo's son, knowing they were destined to meet for a reason. He asked a *jíbaro* sweeping the steps outside the church where he could find Leonardo.

"There's the boy. It's bad business, what's going on with that family."

The man shook his head and pointed to Señor Trujillo's youngest son sitting on a bench in the shade across the plaza. "Bad business," he muttered again when Ramón turned and headed toward Leonardo. The boy sat with slumped shoulders, absently throwing chunks of torn bread to a flock of pigeons.

"Leonardo?"

The boy looked up. "Yeah?"

"I'm Ramón León Carrasquillo."

"Oh, you're the one everyone's talking about, who made that big speech. Did you come here to give me a speech, too?"

"Nope," Ramón answered and sat on the bench next to the boy. "I did something I'm not proud of, and I . . ." Ramón paused. "I spent the night in jail. I paid for what I did, and now I'm here to see if there's anything I could do to help you or your family."

"Get me a new father."

"You don't mean that," Ramón said and grabbed a pile of stale bread pieces to toss at the pigeons, too.

"Do you know what he did to me?" Leo asked, his voice with a hint of a crack.

"I heard some things, but you can tell me, if it helps."

"He yelled at me, in front of everyone when I struck out at

174

my last game. I don't know what happened. I can't remember the last time I did that, especially when that street dog kid, Ernesto Montaña, is pitching. He's a third grader, two years younger than me!"

Leonardo shook his head.

"My father screamed 'What are you doing? You're useless!' He named me Leonardo, after Leonardo Da Vinci. He used to say I was destined for greatness, like some big artist. He pulled me off the field in front of everyone. I don't even know him anymore."

"He's going through a bad time," Ramón explained. "Be patient with him."

They finished feeding the pigeons.

"Leo," Ramón began, "I'd like to be your friend. I think I could be a good friend to you. Would that be all right?"

The boy flinched when Ramón touched him gingerly on the shoulder, then nodded.

"I'm not a baseball player, but I'm decent at basketball, and I brought a ball. You want to play one-on-one?" Ramón asked.

Leo nodded again, and stood. Ramón joined him and they made their way to the basketball hoop. Ramón moved slowly at first due to the pain in his ribs, but the heat and the exercise loosened him. He and Leonardo sweat hard and removed their shirts in the blazing sun. It warmed the boy's disposition as it did his body; when he won the fourth game with twenty-one points, he yelped in delight.

"Hey, you're pretty good. You should join the basketball team, too," Ramón yelped back. He wiped his forehead with his handkerchief and put his shirt back on. "You wore me out. How about I buy us a couple Cokes?"

"Why not? You can afford it!"

Leonardo punched Ramón's arm affectionately.

They walked across the plaza toward the cantina. Ramón said, "After, I'll show you how to catch lizards. You know when my cousin, Albertito, was your age, he used to catch them and hang them, dangling, from his earlobes—live!"

"No kidding? You guys from Maunabo are *locos*!"

Ramón chuckled. "You've never caught lizards before? You got a lot to learn, kid."

They spent the rest of the afternoon together until the sun dropped into the sea, far off in the horizon. Ramón couldn't believe how quickly the day passed, and he could tell Leo thought the same.

Ramón embraced Leonardo good-bye. "Let's do this again next week, on Sunday. If you need to talk, call Don Pablo in Maunabo. He'll come get me." Ramón tore a small piece of newspaper that had been left behind on the table, wrote the number down and handed it to Leo.

"You mean there's no phone at your house?" Leonardo asked, incredulous. "You didn't buy one with all your money?"

"No, I tried to buy one for my mother, but she just laughed, saying she had no one to call. The only family who owns a phone is Don Pablo's, and why would she call them when she can walk next door?"

"Well." Leonardo shrugged. "I guess that makes sense."

Leo's eyes had seemed empty, saddened before. Now there was brightness, a glimmer of hope.

"You know, I thought you'd be different, but you don't act like a rich guy. You're all right," Leo assured.

"I'll use that money for college, and I'll be back to help people when I'm a dentist. So I guess you could say I am rich, because I'm going to live my life for others, and that makes life worthwhile."

"Wow, a dentist. That sounds kind of cool, but hard. I guess I should say good luck."

Ramón wrapped his arm around the boy's shoulder.

"Thanks, Leo. I should hear from the school soon. I'm excited, but it means I gotta' leave my family, my *novia*. And then taking all those courses in English, something tells me I'm going to need a lot more than luck."

CHAPTER 27

Life resumed its routine as February slid into March. The tension with Trujillo seemed to ease. Ramón worked in the store. Business resumed at a brisker pace than ever before since his declaration at the square. The dresses arrived from New York, and Elsie and Señora Lepe bought one to be the "village models."

Villagers spread the news: "Ramón Carrasquillo is a noble man, a man you can trust like a brother," and "Ramón spent the night in jail, and came out a different man."

A rich owner of a coffee plantation from Patillas heard about Francisco, the other Carrasquillo brother, the one who stood next to Ramón, and came to Francisco's store to put in order for enough lumber, wheelbarrows and sacks of cement to build a new storeroom for his supplies.

Profits increased more than ever in both stores.

After waking every morning in a panic that he'd get another draft card, Ramón decided to change his inner thoughts. He visualized peace and the end to the war. Like Doctor Roberts had taught him, he visualized himself in his own clinic. When his feet first hit the floor near his bed, he said, "Thank you *Dios*. Thank you for sparing me thus far, and for sparing my brothers. And thank you to Doctor Roberts for teaching me such valuable skills." He even acknowledged that his night in jail had strengthened him.

Ramón continued his studies, reading all the way to *kindred spirits* in his English-Spanish dictionary: *espíritus afines*. He had coffee with Francisco every night after work and played basketball weekly with Leo. Every Sunday at 4 P.M., Leo would sit and wait for

178

him at the same bench where they had first met. The boy was never late, always with his basketball tucked under his right arm, always with a smile.

Ramón witnessed a transformation in Leo from the sulking boy he first met in the plaza. Now he bubbled with never-ending chatter about school, friends, and his beautiful pinto pony. Only once did Leo mention his father, when he told Ramón that Trujillo came home from the racetrack "stinking like rum." When Leo got to the point in the story where his mother screamed at his father he was wasting all their money and his father threw a glass at her, he started to cry.

Ramón folded Leo in his arms until his tears dried.

That same day, when they ate at the cantina they patronized every week, Leo had merely picked at his chicken *empanada*.

"Aren't you hungry, Leo? Usually I can barely tell what's on your plate before it disappears!"

"I'm not hungry today, Tío Ramón."

For the first time, Leo called him "Tío," the word meaning "uncle," used to show endearment and respect from one male to another. The tender familiarity touched Ramón.

After dinner, they left and saw a man across the street. They had seen him before, but today, the *jíbaro* looked thinner, his filthy clothes hanging off his frame like a scarecrow that had long stopped fooling the crows. He was probably a cane worker that had grown too frail to work the fields, and like so many other men in his predicament, would spend the end of his days in squalor. It reminded Ramón how important his mission was; these were the people he was meant to help.

Leo approached the man with his leftover empanada wrapped in butcher paper. "Señor, I have something for you. It's really good."

The man grinned to reveal he had no upper teeth.

When Leo handed him the food, he reached over and patted the man's shoulder. It was such a tender move that it left Ramón breathless: the boy showed unabashed affection for the old beggar.

Ramón felt grateful that their time together made the boy happy, but he never expected the reward he got: if he ever had a son, he wanted his boy to be as compassionate as Leo.

§§§

As Ramón's feelings deepened for Leo, they did even more so for Elsie. They had become a well-known twosome, dancing in Patillas or at the Maunabo town hall nearly every weekend. When she wasn't with him, Ramón felt incomplete. When he helped a customer in the store, he wanted it to be Elsie; when he studied his English-Spanish dictionary, his thoughts drifted to her, the way she bit her lower lip when deep in thought, the spray of freckles across her nose that no one else had, the curve of her breast under the white ankle-length summer dress.

At night before he drifted off to sleep, the memory of the softness and rose scent of her skin filled his mind, how her body felt pressed against his. Their embraces and kisses had become more heated. He wanted to make passionate love to her, imagining the way she would cry out in pleasure, how the skin between her breasts would taste, and how they would lie together afterwards, limbs intertwined, satiated, blissfully tired. But would he dare experience the pleasure, knowing it would dishonor her?

Spending time with Elsie filled Ramón up and broke his heart all at once, for at times, he found himself in a near panic, fearing what life in the states would be like without her.

§§§

For weeks, Ramón had been anticipating two things. The first was his letter of acceptance from Michigan State College. Don Pablo had called the college; Ramón trusted his friend's English far more than his own, and stood by as the don generously made the call. The admissions office acknowledged the application was under review and a letter would be sent within weeks. Ramón begged the postmistress to bring him it to him as soon as it arrived. Naturally, she was happy to oblige.

The second anticipated event was Elsie's eighteenth birthday: April 12, 1945. Ramón fretted over her gift. On a trip to San Juan, he went to the best jewelry store recommended by Alberto Gómez and purchased a string of pearls with a luster so fine they seemed to glow from within. It was an extravagant purchase yet the look on her face as she opened the black velvet box would be worth it.

On the evening of her birthday, Ramón donned the same suit and tie he had worn when he had asked permission to court her. This time, he picked *two* bouquets of plumeria for Elsie and her mother before driving to the stately Spanish colonial home on the other end of *La Calle de Los Blancos*.

Ramón walked up the front steps feeling equal parts nervousness and excitement on the first time he was invited to the Miraflores home for a social occasion. The family had canceled the large birthday party they had planned in deference to Elsie's uncle who had been wounded in the Battle of Luzon. After stepping on a land mine, he'd return home a decorated soldier, minus his right lower leg.

As Ramón pounded the large iron knocker, a conversation

played in his head from years earlier. Before his confirmation in front of a crowd of thirty in the Maunabo Catholic church, Padre Basilio had asked him, "Are you nervous, my son?"

When Ramón nodded, the priest answered, "Good, because that means you care." Ramón felt that very same way now.

A maid in a crisp black uniform and starched white apron answered the door.

"Vivi, I can't believe it's you! What are you doing here?" Ramón exclaimed.

For a millisecond, Ramón expected Lila to appear behind Vivian, her best friend. As girls, they were inseparable and even up until the day Lila moved out, the two women sat for hours at the kitchen table sipping tea or mango juice, the room buzzing with laughter.

"Ay, they hired me just for the night, for this dinner. I can't believe you're here!" Vivi said, then glanced back furtively before she lowered her voice. "I heard the parents talking earlier in the kitchen. Señora showed me how to set the table and it took me so long that they probably thought I wasn't listening. I don't think they know we know each other, because they talked about *you*. They said they're only letting Elsie see you because of that fancy college you applied to. You better hope you get in!"

So that's it. That's why I'm here. And I thought it was because I was honorable. A bead of sweat broke out on his upper lip. Ramón reached into his back pocket for a handkerchief to wipe it off.

"Well, you're coming in, aren't you? They'll start wondering what we're doing out here." Vivian lowered her voice again, motioning with her hand for Ramón to hurry and enter the foyer.

Ramón steeled himself to step inside. *It's Elsie I'm here for. She doesn't think that way.*

He followed Vivian into the dining room, an entire room in which to eat other than the kitchen. A long table was set for eight with starched table cloth, crystal glasses, and ivory china dishes etched with blue and pink flowers. Ramón panicked. At each place setting, there were more forks, spoons, and knives than he'd ever seen, each one with a fancy curlicue on the end. And two more spoons above the plate. However would he choose the right one?

He did a quick calculation, why eight settings? Of course, Elsie's Tía Sylvia from San Juan would be present with her two children. He silently chastised himself for not picking three bouquets—would he ever get it right?

Capitán Miraflores entered first to shake Ramón's hand, followed by Elsie. She had told him she and her mother had shopped for a dress for her birthday, but how she looked in the creation, a soft blush *peau-de-soie* with scalloped hem and neckline, nearly stole his breath. Neither he nor Chepa had ever used such fine silk in the store. The pearls would be perfect. At least he had done something right.

They took their seats, Capitán Miraflores at the head, Señora Miraflores to his left, Tía Sylvia to his right, Ramón next to Tía and Elsie across from him. Seven-year-old Esteban and six-year-old Marta sat at the ends. The other head was unoccupied but with a place set in honor for Victor.

The evening started with the discussion of the inevitable end of the war due to the Allied army's advancement into Germany and the Soviet's control of Poland. Ramón noticed how Sylvia glanced at her husband's empty place setting and turned to her. "I'm sorry about your husband. If I can help in any way, I'd be happy to, or have Victor come see my mamá for anything. She's a wonderful *curandera*."

When she thanked Ramón with startling blue eyes that seemed ready to smile, he saw a younger version of Chepa, and he warmed to her, someone in the family on his side.

Vivian entered and served a salad laced with asparagus sprinkled with buttered bread crumbs. No rice and beans—no salted codfish!

Ramón's mind flashed back to a day in grammar school, the day a lady visited, an *Americana* wearing a stiff white cap and nurse's uniform. She brought strange looking foods: asparagus, carrots, broccoli, pears and apples. A student asked, "Where are the mangos and the rice and beans?" All the kids giggled, and someone threw a spitball and a carrot. When she requested in a funny Spanish accent that they take some food home to their parents, no one took anything, and she never came back.

Vivi placed his salad plate down and looked directly at Ramón with a slight roll of her eyes. *I bet she remembers that day, too. She was there!* That was the last time Ramón had seen food like this, except for that night at *La Mallorquina*. He also remembered it was one of the last times Chepa had spanked him after he came home from school that day to tell her about the "silly *gringa* food." She berated that he should never belittle the kindness of others.

Ramón watched Elsie use the fork on the far left and did the same.

Vivi brought the second course with even a more daring eye roll. Ramón was relieved the conversation turned to the emigration of islanders to the mainland U. S. looking for better jobs and opportunities, for it gave him the opportunity to try and figure out what the devil it was that Vivi plunked before him. He knew it was a slab of meat; he'd had New York Steak at *La Mallorquina*, but this steak was sitting on some red, congealed fluid.

Just as the thought that he may be consuming something lying in its own blood made his stomach turn, Elsie exclaimed, "Oh Madre, filet mignon with red wine sauce. What a treat, however did you manage it?!"

Red wine sauce, *Gracias a Dios*. He never imagined this was how he would taste wine for the first time, but it made Elsie happy and the white potatoes that accompanied it looked as fluffy as clouds. The steak was so tender he could almost cut it with his fancy fork alone. When he watched Elsie slice small pieces, savoring each morsel after she moved her fork from left hand to right, it was like a well-rehearsed dance, and Ramón had a moment's thought that she might be a great dental assistant.

Just when Ramón was savoring how the round green vegetables the size of mini lizard eggs melted in his mouth, Capitán Miraflores leaned back in his chair and asked, "So, Ramón, what news do *you* have of your travels to the states? I expect you'll be leaving us soon?"

Ramón thought he might choke. He squirmed in his seat and felt the heat creeping up his neck.

"I sent my college application a few months ago—they tell me I'll hear any day now."

He ran his index finger along the inside of his starched white collar. In truth, he hadn't stopped thinking about it. When would he hear?

He had started a daily ritual: despite what he asked Señora Lepe, he trekked across the plaza to the post office to see if his acceptance letter had arrived, yet every day, he came home empty-handed, his gait a little slower. He thought by the time he received something, he might leave a permanent path on the only paved area in town.

For a moment, the only sounds were the tinkling of forks and spoons against china. Ramón wished Elsie's family was more like his, who squawked all at once like Puerto Rican parakeets.

"Ramón graduated from high school in third place, and he'll be going to Michigan State College to study dentistry. He'll be a wonderful dentist," Elsie informed the table proudly as she sat up straighter, mainly directing the information to her aunt.

Ramón panicked again. *Does Elsie think about me like that, too? Is that the only reason why she's with me—because I'm applying to college?*

When the toe of Elsie's pink sandal brushed his ankle under the table, and she flashed him a secret smile, daring and almost seductive, an electric jolt filled his body. *No, that's not the reason she's with me.* He could hardly wait until they left for their own private celebration, a night of dancing at *Parque Florida.*

They finally got to the last course, dark chocolate pudding molded into stars, and a sweet, pink ice cream (thus the reason for two spoons above the plate, two desserts!).

Ramón was thrilled when dinner was over. As he thanked Elsie's parents profusely for inviting him to their home, a thought nagged at him: Elsie's and his family were so different. He fantasized a future with her, but would he ever be comfortable in her world?

CHAPTER 28

By the time Ramón and Elsie arrived at *El Parque Florida*, Ramón felt the tension from the evening begin to lift. When it was just the two of them, he didn't have to worry about what fancy fork or knife with curlicue to use.

Sitting across from one another in the Buick, Elsie opened her gift. Ramón had waited to present it to her when they were alone. Her mouth formed a perfect *"O"* and she gushed, "Oh, they're the most gorgeous pearls I've ever seen!"

She kissed him tenderly, and it was just as if this was always as it should be. Just the two of them.

Elsie reached behind her head to twirl her hair into a coil for Ramón to clasp the pearls in place. Her skin was warm to the touch, smooth and unblemished. The necklace fell perfectly into place against the delicate curve of her collarbone, her honey skin.

She intertwined her forearm in Ramón's as they entered the dance club, crowded for a weeknight. They danced to two numbers of *Guaracha* before the club owner ran out into the middle of the room waving his hands like a sheep herder chasing away a heard of wild dogs.

"Stop the music, stop the music," he shouted.

"Here, listen!" He ran over to the side of the stage and turned on the battery operated radio the club used for background music when the bands took breaks. He turned up the volume for a bulletin from an announcer in San Juan: "*It is with great sadness that I bring you this news that has traveled all the way from Washington D.C. At 3:35 p.m. today, at The Little White House at Warm*

187

Springs, Georgia, Franklin Delano Roosevelt, the 32nd president of the United States, slumped over in his chair, was carried to his bed, and declared dead from a massive stroke. The entire country will mourn the death of our beloved leader and the founder of the New Deal Coalition, who led the Allied army against Germany and Japan. It is the end of an era. Decades from now, men will thank God that Franklin D. Roosevelt was in the White House. As our esteemed president said in his final speech: 'Let us move forward with strong and active faith.'"

The club owner switched off the radio and walked away in a daze, head down. A ponderous silence fell. People glanced at one another, connected in grief, searching for solace. Ramón took Elsie in his arms as her eyes misted. Other couples did the same. The band began to pack up their instruments, the happy mood squashed.

Ramón and Elsie filed out of the building with the other patrons. Ramón kept his arm around her until he helped her into the car. They sat in the Buick in silence before Elsie spoke. "I can't believe it. I'll never forget this birthday."

"Me neither, but I'm glad we're together."

Ramón watched Elsie absently finger her pearls. They glowed against her skin. Thoughts filtered into his mind: the duality of life—how his good fortune was accompanied by Trujillo's decline. He imagined how families in America were taking the news of the president's death. On the continent, they had known for hours, had probably been grieving while he and Elsie's family were feasting. He thought about grief, about Victor coming home forever damaged. About how so many families, fathers, mothers and wives had suffered the dismemberment and deaths of their loved ones. About loss.

In a brief moment of clarity, he knew: he didn't want to lose Elsie. He wanted, no, *needed*, her to come with him.

He took her hand. "Elsie, I've never met any woman like you. I'm in love with you," he said and released her hand, stroked her cheek. "When I touch your skin, my whole body ignites."

"I love you, too." Her voice trembled. "I love the way you respect me, how you encourage me to follow my dreams. I see the way men look at me, and it makes my skin crawl. I cringe inside when I imagine what they're thinking. You've never done that."

They kissed. A deep, complex kiss, one in which Ramón wanted to be lost. His heart raced, missing beats.

Ramón pulled away, his lips still warm from hers, to proclaim, "I want to spend the rest of my life with you. Marry me. Come to Michigan with me. You can go to college, too—we'll go together!" The words came out quickly, and it felt so good, so right.

"But I'm scared," Elsie admitted. "How can I go with you? Your English is better than mine."

"No, it's not. I'm scared too. When I listen to an English program on the radio, it sounds like gibberish, like they're choking on chicken bones. I still have a lot to learn—we'll learn together!"

Ramón knew, in Michigan, it would be just the two of them. They'd struggle together, as equals, and he wouldn't have to worry about fancy china and silverware.

"But, for me to leave . . ." Elsie wondered out loud as she bit her lower lip and looked down, shaking her head. Before she turned away to look out the window, Ramón saw her lips press together. He waited one, two seconds. Would she deny him?

She turned back with her face flushed, joyful and cried, "Yes, I'll marry you! I'll go away with you!"

"You make me the happiest man on earth!"

Ramón put his hand behind her head and kissed her again, slowly at first, then eagerly as if satisfying a hunger. Ramón felt her heart pound through the silk of her dress. She moaned. His hand caressed her breast. He wanted more. It was dizzying, yet at the same time, forbidden. Ramón forced himself to stop.

"I . . . I need to take you home. I want our first time to be special, not here. Please, don't tell your father I asked you to marry me. Let me ask his permission first, okay?"

"Yes," she repeated, this time, breathless.

§§§

The house was dark by the time Ramón arrived home. He thought of waking Chepa to share all the startling news of the evening but decided against it. She needed her rest, and tomorrow was only hours away.

He envisioned Elsie's and his life together, their wedding day, bounding down the aisle as the golden couple, heading to their future. He could feel the smile on his face, and couldn't stop it, didn't want to. He wanted to dream of her.

Instead, he dreamt of his teeth falling out. First they crumbled, then turned to dust. He woke in a sweat. It filled him with foreboding.

He stumbled out onto the back porch to look into the mirror over the sink, expecting to see lips curling over toothless gums. Of course, his teeth were intact. It was just a dream. A nightmare. Many would say it was a bad omen, a sign of impending doom. But those were the foolish superstitions of peasants. He soon would be a man of science.

He tried to convince himself it meant nothing.

CHAPTER 29

"Ahh, it looks like you had a good time last night!" Chepa declared when Ramón practically bounced into the back room of the store. She looked up from sewing a blanket stitched button hole on a blouse the color of saffron.

"Mamá, I have wonderful news and very sad news, too."

"Ay, I already heard about President Roosevelt. Such a great man, such a great loss."

Chepa closed her eyes and made a sign of the cross. "I've already been to mass this morning to say a rosary. There was barely a seat left. It won't be so crowded now. Why don't you go, too?"

"Yes, of course." Ramón bowed his head and waited a respectful second before blurting, "I asked Elsie to marry me last night, and she accepted!"

Chepa's face collapsed.

"What's wrong?" Ramón asked quickly. "It's all I can think about—I can't imagine my life without her, and she wants to come with me to Michigan, to study to be a teacher. I thought you'd be happy for us."

"*Lo siento, m'ijo* (I'm sorry, my son)," Chepa said softly. "I'd hoped things would never get this far. Elsie is a beautiful girl, but Capitán Miraflores will never consent. I'm surprised he let your relationship go as far as it did, most likely due to a father's indulgence of his only daughter. He'll never let her leave with you and go off so faraway to school. In their world, marriage and family are all a girl like Elsie can envision for a future. And how do you think that family can dine on fancy food and afford a maid, on the money el capitán makes from his job alone? He does favors for some men, looks the other way, and is rewarded in ways I or you can't imagine. Do you want to be part of that life?"

Ramón felt dizzy. He reached for the table to steady himself then crumpled into the chair. He shook his head and made a fist so tight that his fingernails bit into his palm, turning it white.

"There has to be a way to change his mind. Elsie said yes!"

"*Lo siento*," Chepa whispered, "I don't think so."

"But Mamá, I told her I loved her. That's the first time I've said that to any woman. She makes me want to be a better man!"

"*Dios*, how the world has changed, even from when I was young and married your father. I loved him, God rest his soul. We married when I was fifteen; he was eighteen. I'd never been with any other man, and never will be. I had no other choices, nor did he. *But you do.* I am so happy you've been able to love Elsie, and when I saw how you lit up when you talked about her, it broke my heart." She placed her hand over his heart. "These are the lessons we learn in life. You can't let anything, or anyone, stand in the way of your dream, your destiny, and I don't think Elsie will be a part of it."

Chepa's words were like a lead weight had dropped on Ramón's heart. His mother had more wisdom than anyone he knew, the reason why so many people came to her with their problems.

He prayed and hoped this time, she was wrong.

§§§

Ramón shuffled into the church, more humble than the one in Yabucoa, yet more welcoming. There was a single alcove occupied by a large candelabrum filled with red votives. Ramón had never seen it burn so brightly; each candle was flickering from the villagers who paid their respects that morning for the president, all except one. The scent of cinnamon and burning wax filled the sanctuary. Only one *jíbara* remained, kneeling at a pew, her hands cradled in her face, her head covered in a black *mantilla* and veil.

Ramón walked to the alcove, dropped a nickel in the metal box secured to the wall and lit the remaining candle. He kneeled, made a sign of the cross, bowed his head with his hands crossed in front of his chin and closed his eyes to pray.

Merciful God, please give President's Roosevelt's family and our country the strength to carry on without him. He was such a noble president, only to die before he saw the end of the war. And please, please, make this war end, which has gone on far too long. Please grant Tío Victor the strength to continue on as he was before he lost his leg. Please send my brothers, Rafael and Isidro, and all the other soldiers home unharmed. Please let the army leave me, and let me do my work here. He paused and took deep breath, letting the air out slowly. *And please, God, let me hear from the college soon, and give me the strength to change Capitán Miraflores's ways, even Mamá's thoughts, to open his heart and mind to accept the love between me and Elsie, for I don't know if I could live without her.*

Ramón worked the rest of the afternoon, but hardly made any sales, for the only talk among the villagers who filtered in and out was of the death of President Roosevelt.

He knew what he had to do. If he didn't hear from the college in one more week, he'd ask Don Pablo to use his phone again to call Michigan. And he'd request a meeting with Elsie's father to ask for her hand in marriage. Despite his mother's warning, he had to try to forge a life with Elsie. He couldn't imagine not doing so.

Still, the irony dawned on him. Only last night, he had come so close to having Elsie for the rest of his life, now that dream might be snatched away. And his nightmare, what of that? He thought things would get easier after that interminable night in jail.

Alone in the store, he asked God, "If you chose to bestow such a gift on me, why are things turning out so hard?"

The only answer was the sound of the wind and the rustling of leaves in the grapefruit tree outside the window.

CHAPTER 30

As it turned out, Ramón didn't have a chance to visit the police chief or to make his anticipated long distance phone call. The day after his proposal to Elsie, Padre Pérez from Yabucoa visited.

Ramón and Chepa were tending to a deep abrasion on the foreleg of their goat, Pepita. Ramón had repaired the spike of barbed wire exposed from her pen, but not before the little goat rubbed against it and slashed her leg. Ramón held his pet steady, petting her forehead to calm her.

"Easy now, Pepita," he soothed while Chepa kneeled to clean the wound and applied a poultice of aloe, covering it with a tight bandage.

Lila, who had come by earlier to help wash the daily laundry in the river, ran into the courtyard and called out, "Mamá, Padre Pérez is here. He wants to talk to you!"

Chepa pushed herself up from the ground and ordered, "Lila, prepare chamomile tea and get the china. Be sure to give the cup without the chip to Padre, and run to the *panadería* to buy almond cookies. Use a nickel from the jar on my dresser, and make sure the baker gives you his six best. Quickly, now!"

Chepa stopped at the small sink on the back porch before she entered her home. She washed her hands, dabbed water on her forehead to clean the beads of perspiration and tucked a few strands of gray hair back into her bun. She smoothed the front of her brown cotton dress.

Ramón washed his hands after his mother, thinking about the day the priest helped release him from jail. Visits from Padre Pérez were rare. What could he want?

After the customary greetings, Ramón, Chepa, and Padre Pérez settled around the kitchen table. Lila had dusted and set out Chepa's delft blue tea cups, normally reserved for Christmas. She added teaspoons of sugar and Pepita's milk to everyone's tea and excused herself to go to the *panadería*.

The priest cleared his throat, his face ashen. "Doña Chepa," he reported, "It is with sadness that I come see you today, to ask you to help Leonardo Trujillo, an earnest boy whose family are important members of my congregation."

At the sound of Leo's name, Ramón gasped. "What happened to Leo?"

A grave look crossed the priest's face.

"I'm afraid his father beat him, severely. Señor Trujillo hired some men to hurt you, Ramón. Leonardo overhead his plans, and somehow his father found out he was going to warn you. Trujillo lost his temper, and beat his son half to death. It's a terrible tragedy, a sin." Padre Pérez paused to shake his head gravely. "The man has sunk to deep despair, has lost his way, and the boy's in bad shape, very bad."

In an instant, all manner of expressions crossed Chepa's face, shock, disbelief, grief.

"¡*Ay, Dios*!" she cried, her hand covering her mouth.

Ramón felt sick, dizzy. He thought of Leo, that sweet boy who would help a beggar without hesitation, getting hurt for *him*. The room was suddenly too small. A thought bombarded his mind: *Why couldn't it have been me?*

"How bad is he?" Ramón heard his voice tremble. "He'll get better, won't he?"

"He's unconscious, badly bruised, probably has some broken

196

ribs, one eye socket is closed. We don't even want to risk taking him all the way to San Juan. He's safe for now, at the home of the neighbor, Señor Herrera, along with his mother and brother. Trujillo's been removed to a sanatorium in San Juan. Señora is doing terribly, can't even manage to take care of herself, let alone those boys. They're arranging to send the older son to a cousin's home in Miami. Leonardo needs the *curandera* with the best skills I know." The kind priest looked at Chepa.

"Of course I'll help him," she said gravely.

Lila entered the kitchen. She looked at everyone's faces and dropped the cookies, wrapped in butcher paper. They fell to the floor with a thud, breaking the ominous silence.

"Oh," Lila exclaimed. She knelt to retrieve the package, unwrapped the paper, and arranged them on the plate.

Ramón looked at the cookies placed in a semi-circle. *Amazingly, they're unbroken, unlike Leo. His whole family's suffering, and it's all because of me.* His stomach heaved into a knot, and the sight of food made the knot twist more.

Lila was the first to speak. "Is everything okay?"

Padre Pérez sighed. Chepa shook her head.

"No," Ramón answered. "Leo needs our help."

The plate of cookies sat untouched.

CHAPTER 31

In the end, Chepa won the argument to accompany Ramón to get Leo. Ramón wanted to go alone, in case one of Señor Trujillo's henchmen made an appearance, but Chepa reasoned: if the boy was in as bad a shape as the priest indicated, she could treat him first at the neighbor's house before Ramón brought him home. It was the first time she had left Maunabo in a decade.

Señora Herrera must have been expecting them, for the front door flew open before they knocked.

"¡*Madre de Dios!* Help us!" Her hands flew to her face. "Ana, they're here!" she called out and motioned for them to come inside.

Ramón stifled a gasp when he saw Ana Trujillo shuffle toward them. He remembered the first time he had seen her with her husband. As a child, he thought Señora Trujillo was a movie star with her hat full of peacock plumes and waves of blond hair. Now he wondered if the merchant had remarried. No, rich older men marry beautiful younger women. But then, Señor Trujillo was no longer rich and this woman, with her stooped shoulders, thinning hair and small mouth twisted, was no longer beautiful.

"Señora, we're here to help—" Chepa began.

"God bless you! I'm sorry. My son, my boy—I can't think. I can't breathe. I'm sorry," Señora Trujillo sobbed.

Chepa stepped forward, and Ana Trujillo clung to her. They stayed like that for minutes, two women locked in each other's arms. Chepa rocked Ana. It wasn't the first time Ramón had seen someone cling to his mother for strength.

Her face swollen and splotchy, Señora Trujillo led them down a narrow hallway to a small bedroom. She stumbled, and Ramón wondered if she had been struck as well, but he saw no bruises. When she opened the door to the room, fresh tears rolled down her cheeks.

Ramón had tried to prepare himself ahead of time, but when he saw Leo lying unconscious and beaten, anger bubbled to the surface. He couldn't draw in enough air and steeled himself not to run to the bathroom and vomit.

The boy's cheeks and eyes were the purple of eggplant, the left eye swollen shut, a deep red welt in the cheekbone, his mouth a misshapen blob. Ramón sat at the edge of the twin bed and gently held Leo's hand. *Dios, why couldn't it have been me that monster went after? I'd go back to that damn jail, give away all that money, to take this all away.*

Chepa wasted no time. She retrieved a tin of unguent from her satchel and applied it to the sores on Leo's cheeks and lips. Still unconscious, the boy shuddered slightly.

"It's a good sign that he feels something when I apply the ointment," Chepa assured.

She pulled back the sheet, gasped, shook her head and crossed herself when she saw the bruises across Leo's naked torso. Ramón had never seen Chepa show her distress while treating a patient. He knew if Leo were conscious, she'd never let the boy see her fear. Quickly, Chepa checked the rest of Leo's body, palpating the bruised areas. Ramón removed his scapular and placed it on Leo's right shoulder, the one with fewer bruises. The boy needed it more than he did.

"The bruises aren't too deep," Chepa explained. "If you're gentle, he can be moved safely. Let's go. God will be on our side. He'll be out for the ride home."

He heard a soft patter of feet behind him and turned. Leo's brother, Héctor. Ramón would recognize him anywhere. He and Leo looked so much alike it made Ramón start; almond shaped eyes the color of chocolate with long delicate lashes and high cheek bones. Leo's brother was remarkable, *the way Leo used to look.*

"You'll save my brother? He . . . he won't . . ." The boy's lips and chin trembled as moisture gathered in the corners of his eyes. He shivered, pressing his elbows into his sides.

Héctor stood a head taller than Leo, and Ramón guessed him to be about thirteen, too young to experience such horror. Ramón took the boy in his arms, and then placed his hands on Héctor's shoulders.

"Héctor, I am so sorry. Your brother means the world to me so we're taking him to my house. My mamá needs to have a steady supply of all her plants and remedies to help Leo. I promise you, as God is my witness, we'll take good care of him. He'll get better, I'll see to it. Please don't be afraid, okay?"

The boy nodded, holding back tears, mouth downturned.

"Can you do something for me, something very grown up?" Ramón asked.

The boy nodded again.

"You need to be the man of the family, to watch over your mamá."

"I will," the boy said in a hoarse whisper.

Ramón embraced Hector again before he cradled Leo in a thick blanket and carried him to the back seat of the Buick. He felt so light, so fragile, that it wasn't even a strain.

Before Chepa climbed in next to Leo, Héctor grasped her elbow and pleaded, "Padre says you're the best *curandera* in the district. I wouldn't let him go with anyone else. Take good care of him."

Héctor let go and ran back to the house.

Ramón drove slowly down the road and thought of Leo's family, the terror they endured, how Héctor had put up a brave front to be the man of the house when he spoke to Chepa. Señora Trujillo had paced the hallway when Chepa tended to Leo. When they loaded Leo in the car, she stood silent on the front porch, hand on her heart.

Ramón turned around briefly, just in time to see Ana Trujillo fall into Héctor's arms.

§§§

Three people gingerly transferred Leo onto a cot in Ramón's bedroom. Chepa supported Leo's head and neck while Francisco and Ramón held his body. It was hard to believe, but the ointment had already seemed to lessen the swelling in the worst of Leo's wounds, the one under his left eye.

Ramón and Chepa took turns applying the unguent every hour. Ramón took a kitchen chair and sat at Leo's bedside, only leaving to use the latrine. He welcomed feeling uncomfortable. When he imagined Trujillo striking and kicking his innocent son, Ramón was overcome with such guilt that the boy endured such pain on his behalf that he bolted to the sink. Ramón heaved, remembering what it was like to be in jail. He would go back without hesitation if it meant none of this would have happened to Leo. He would give all the money back, every cent of his winnings, if it meant saving Leo.

That night, Ramón fell asleep slumped against the mattress, his hand molded over Leo's.

Chepa nudged him awake. "You need to rest. You'll be better

able to care for him if you're not exhausted."

Ramón was reluctant to leave Leo's side, agreeing only if he could push one cot against the other. He wanted to stay awake all night to listen to Leo's quiet breaths, to watch the rise and fall of his chest. God forbid if the boy stopped breathing.

Sometime during the night, exhaustion overtook Ramón, and he slept.

§§§

The next morning, Ramón pushed the cots apart to resume his place on the chair. He ate at Leo's bedside and applied one of Chepa's treatments every hour, alternating between an aloe vera salve, the unguent, or a warm compress laced in oil from her St. John's Wort plant. Ramón insisted he be responsible for nearly all the treatment and learned from Chepa how to perform gentle range-of-motion on Leo's limbs promote circulation and prevent stiffness.

Chepa tended to the store with Esperanza's help, taking breaks often to check on their patient. His mother also taught Ramón how to massage the bruises on Leo's torso and upper thighs: "Use the lightest pressure, like bending a fly's knees. It will increase blood flow, like the trickle of a river, and improve healing."

Ramón gasped when he massaged the bruise on the left side of Leo's chest in the shape of a boot print.

On the second night, he slept again on the cot pressed next to Leo's, although fitfully.

§§§

In the morning, Chepa and Ramón recited the novena to the Immaculate Heart of Mary to pray for Leo's healing. They trickled water into his mouth with the tip of spoon, and placed ice chips on his dry lips. Chepa told Ramón she was reassured that more often during the treatments, Leo would stir and take a breath or a small amount of water, which convinced her that he was coming out of his coma.

That afternoon, Ramón cradled the boy's hand and prayed: "Leo, please wake up. I love you. I don't know what I'll do if you don't wake up soon." He hung his head and began to sob quietly.

"¿Tío?" Leo croaked.

Ramón's head snapped up. Leo's eyes were vacant, lifeless, but they opened a crack while he licked his lips.

Hope had been growing slowly in Ramón, like rain fills a puddle, one drop at a time. But now, relief flooded his heart. He wanted to shout to Chepa, "He's awake!" knowing somehow she would hear him in the store. He even wanted to shout loud enough so he could be heard miles away, but he didn't want to frighten the boy.

"*Gracias a Dios*—you're awake! Don't try to talk. I'll get you water."

As gently as possible, Ramón placed another pillow behind Leo's head. He grabbed the cup of water on the nightstand and held it with a straw to Leo's lips.

"You need to drink. Sip it slowly," Ramón instructed.

Leo did as asked. Ramón thanked God a few drops went down easily.

Frightened, Leo's eyes darted around the room.

"You're in my house. Doña Chepa and I have been taking care of you. Do you remember anything?" Ramón asked gently.

Leo nodded. Tears squeezed out from his eyes. He hitched in air, began to cry harder and winced in pain.

Ramón was glad he had only coffee and no solid food for breakfast, for the way his stomach twisted. He had to stop himself from standing up and pounding the wall in anger for what Trujillo did to his son. But what would that solve? Anger had done unfathomable damage already.

Instead, he remained at Leo's side, rubbed the back of his hand.

"You'll get better. Mamá and I will see to it," Ramón promised, clenching then unclenching his jaw. "I am so sorry, Leo, for what happened to you." A lump shot up in his throat. "I won't let it happen again." He held the straw to Leo's lips once again. "Don't try to talk, just sip."

§§§

The following days, Ramón continued to dedicate himself to Leo. He brought him boiled oats and tea in the morning, spoon-feeding him. By the third day, Leo could chew well enough to eat a soft buttered roll, and for dinner, fried plantains and a few spoonfuls of the mashed chicken and vegetables from Chepa's *asopao*. Ramón continued to apply the unguent, or a compress of aloe or sage, and helped Leo in and out of bed, in and out of the latrine. The first time he helped Leo up, they only walked around the room once, a trip which took minutes, a success nonetheless.

Every afternoon, he read *El Mundo* to Leo. When Leo began

to sit up for longer periods, they played checkers at a table in the courtyard. The first time Leo looked up at the sun, he blinked painfully, after which Ramón gave him his favorite sombrero. Leo spoke very little during that time, mainly just to answer Ramón's questions or to thank him or Chepa.

On the fourth morning of his stay, he looked Ramón directly in the eyes.

"Tío Ramón," Leo's voice choked. "Will God put my father in hell for what he did?" His small face grimaced under the brim of his hat.

Ramón pulled him close. *Dios, the boy is actually worried about his father, after what he did to him.* "Good people sometimes do bad things. Your father will get the help he needs. He'll get better," Ramón assured the boy.

Leo's small body convulsed in Ramón's arms as he sobbed. For the umpteenth time, Ramón wished he could have taken the blows for the boy.

Ramón knew helping Leo through the most painful experience in his life had irrevocably bound them. Their times together playing checkers in the courtyard reminded Ramón of teaching Doctor Roberts the game and it made his heart ache with how much Leo reminded him of himself as a boy, how their relationship was becoming as magical as the one he shared with Doctor Roberts. He still felt sick that he was indirectly responsible, yet Ramón felt the inkling of a sense of peace, a sense of hope. He prayed the feeling would last.

CHAPTER 32

Señora Lepe bound into the kitchen after calling Ramón's name and tramping up the front steps. "It's here, Ramón. It's here!"

She waved a white business sized envelope in the air, shouting, "The letter from the college is here!"

The door banged behind her.

Ramón's breath caught in his throat. The letter. He hadn't thought of anything but Leo all week, had poured all his energy into caring for the boy. He and Leo were sitting and enjoying the quiet and the increase in Leo's appetite, savoring *tortilla española* and coffee laced with Pepita's milk.

"*Dios,*" Señora Lepe murmured and shook her head when she saw Leo.

His bruises had faded some from the unguent, and the scars wouldn't be as severe, thanks to Chepa's aloe vera gel, but his mouth and cheek were still swollen, the stitches still raised below his eye.

Ramón watched Leo's shoulders slump and tried to hide his annoyance. Señora Lepe's mouth still hung open, and Ramón pushed her outside.

"*Dios,*" she repeated. "I heard the boy was bad, but . . . *Dios,*" she said for the third time.

"He's just starting to feel better, but he's still fragile. Shame on you, be more careful what you say. Enough. Give me the letter!" Ramón demanded.

She thrust it in his hand and clapped like a school girl.

"Quick—open it! It's postmarked April 1st. Ay, how long some things take to get here!"

Then it dawned on Ramón. Why such a slim envelope? If it had been what he had spent the prior four months dreaming about, wouldn't it have been thicker? Shouldn't it have forms to sign, maps, booklets, all kinds of things a new student would need?

A sensation thread its way through his body, like fingers that had been submerged in ice, like all the blood draining from his body. Ramón couldn't breathe. He forgot for a millisecond about Señora Lepe. He turned the envelope in his hand.

"Don't stand there like a dead rooster. Open it!" Señora Lepe cried.

Ramón wished he were alone, but he had asked her to deliver the letter personally. His hands trembled as he opened it, and unfolded a single sheet of paper, folded into three equal parts.

We regret to inform you . . .

His eyes saw the words, but he didn't believe them. It got worse, around the middle of the page: *did not meet the minimum English language proficiency requirement . . .*

Weakness surged down his legs. He couldn't translate every word quickly enough but got the gist. The English in his essay wasn't good enough. Ramón dropped the letter to the floor. It fluttered as it fell, seeming to take much longer than it should, taunting him, chastising him.

It was as if he were sliding down the cliff at *Punta Tuna.*

The look on his face registered. Señora Lepe shook her head and said, "They turned you down?"

Ramón couldn't speak. He felt the last of the air drain from his body, and he felt hollow, crushed, a former version of his three-dimensional self, as flat as the paper that mocked him.

"I'm sorry, Ramón." Her eyes fell. After an awkward silence, the postmistress whispered, "Well, there's one good thing, what you're doing for that boy."

Ramón nearly collapsed. He stumbled back into the kitchen.

Señora Lepe followed him and asked, "What do I do with this?"

Ramón turned to see her hand outstretched with the letter of rejection. He shook his head. He went into the bedroom and lay on his side on his cot. He drew his knees to his chest in the fetal position to try and dull the pain.

Leo appeared at his side and said quickly, "Tío, what's wrong? I've never seen you like this, I'm scared. Did I do something wrong? Am I too much trouble? The way that lady looked at me—did she say something bad? She left a piece of paper—do I need to go home? I don't want to go home, please, don't send me there!"

They were the most words Leo had uttered since he woke. Once again, his true nature presented itself. He was the victim, yet still he worried about Ramón more than himself.

Ramón made a choking sound that turned into a word. "No."

After a minute, he sat up. Leo's face was as pale as the moon, which made his fading bruises look even purpler, just as he was starting to look like his old self. Tears welled in his eyes.

Ramón motioned for Leo to sit next to him. He still couldn't believe the news. He wanted to pound the wall in frustration, to stride outside and scream at God for allowing this to happen. Yet it had. And he had himself to blame. He let Antonio write the essay.

Was this his punishment? Perhaps it was, and justly so.

Ramón found his voice. "It had nothing to do with you. Don't ever think you're too much trouble. I love you." *Dios*, thought Ramón, *I have to tell Mamá.*

208

In spite of Ramón's reassurance, Leo's lower lip quivered.

"We won't send you away," Ramón reassured.

§§§

Ramón wanted to wait until Leo was stronger to tell him the news that had spread through the village about the Trujillo family but knew he couldn't wait any longer. Leo would hear soon enough and it should be from him.

"Héctor's in Miami, with your cousin, but don't worry, he's fine," Ramón began. "Your mamá is staying in San Juan with your tía so she can be near your papá. He's sick over what he did, so he's in a special hospital to get well. That means you're staying here. You can go to my grammar school—you'll like it. And you won't go home until you're ready, when your mamá can take care of you. I promise."

"And my pony?" Leo's voice shook.

"He's fine too. I made sure Señor Herrera will take good care of him. We'll bring him here soon, okay?"

Leo couldn't speak. He nodded and leaned into Ramón, hugging him in a wordless embrace. His small body convulsed in agony or relief, Ramón was unsure which. He rubbed Leo's back until he quieted. Now he'd have to tell everyone about the letter. No, maybe not. Señora Lepe would no doubt take care of that. *Dios, all those people in the plaza. I stood there and promised them. And Elsie, who wants to come with me to Michigan; how can I ask for her hand now? And Doctor Roberts, if he knows in heaven. Dios. This is bad as it can get. I'm sure . . . nothing else this bad can happen.*

CHAPTER 33

"There's a reason God kisses some and not others," Chepa said when Ramón spilled his news. "Apply again, or choose another school. This is your destiny." She echoed her words from before.

Señora Lepe did her job as usual, for many people came to the store in the day following the arrival of *the letter* to offer condolences. Ramón dreaded going to work, but he knew people would expect him. He went to face them.

"Ay, Ramón, what does that school know? You'll be a great dentist someday," Guillermo, Ramón's boyhood friend, reassured.

Antonio couldn't look Ramón in the eye yet claimed, "Well, they have all those chaps coming back from the war. They take those guys first, you know. I swear, I did a good job on that essay."

"You swear. I'd like to swear at you," Ramón said.

It was like being struck by a fist. For the millionth time, Ramón regretted letting Antonio write that essay.

He made a mistake, and he would make it right. He had to find a way to fulfill his promise.

The *público* driver whom Ramón spoke to in front of the crowd in the plaza showed up to say, "Well, for all your talk, what are you gonna' do now?"

Ramón swallowed hard and said, "Señor, this is not what I expected, but I'll improve my English. I'll study harder. I'll reapply and make it right."

After the man strode out, Ramón felt like a puppet severed from its strings. He still had to tell Elsie. And her father.

He had only seen her once since Leo had come to recover.

He and Elsie had been alone in the kitchen while Leo slept. When Ramón nuzzled her neck, Elsie closed her eyes.

"Oh, that tickles," she murmured, clearly enjoying the feathery flicker of his tongue on her skin.

"It will be like this when we're married, in Michigan." Ramón moaned and felt a visceral response from his pumping heart all the way to his thighs.

Then Ramón heard Leo's coughs from the bedroom and pulled away. Elsie put her hand on his cheek.

"It's okay," she whispered. "I love that you're so devoted to him. Go."

He remembered what he told her in the heat of the moment: *just the two of us, in Michigan.* Now the words came back to choke him.

§§§

The power to work deserted him. It was five o'clock, only an hour before closing. Ramón wanted to be alone, to think of how to fix things. Esperanza was in the back room altering the bodice of one of the New York dresses for a customer from Patillas. One good thing was that their new merchandise had become so popular that they were busier than ever.

"I'm going home early, Esperanza. Cover for me, okay?" Ramón asked.

"Of course. Go ahead. I hate the way you look so sad. You'll get to that school, Ramón. I know you will."

"Thanks. I think I'll go to the university in Río Piedras tomorrow, get some other college catalogs, check out a book on writing English essays, and apply again," Ramón remarked.

He thought of Elsie; she could come with him. She'd help him find a solution.

"Great idea. I'll work for you tomorrow, too, but I wish there was more I could do," Esperanza said, trying to sound cheerful.

"Thanks. We appreciate you. You've done more than your share already."

Ramón thought of the many times Esperanza worked with Chepa when he went on buying trips to San Juan; she and the children would stay at the León home for dinner after Ramón returned home. She offered support without hesitation. Would Elsie's family do the same? They were a far cry from the humble girl who had immersed herself in his and Chepa's lives.

Ramón trudged home under black clouds as the sky opened wide and sheets of rain sheared upon him like sodden curtains.

He sat at the kitchen table as the cold from his wet shirt seeped into his bones. He was glad he was alone. Leo was playing with Juanito. Ramón loved his nephew all the more for not staring at Leo's wounds and for playing with him so well, even though Leo was a few years younger.

An inch of coffee was left in his cup from the morning, and Ramón gulped it, bitter, cold and thick. He had that sensation again, a tickling across his shoulders, but not like when he bought his ticket, like cockroaches crawling over him. What worse could happen? After a while, he found the energy to stand up and put on a dry shirt.

From his bedroom, Ramón heard a knock at the door. Someone else about the letter? Ramón didn't want to face one more person, but whoever was knocking was persistent. He made his way through the kitchen and opened the door.

Elsie stood on the porch, an agonized expression on her face.

212

Fear surged into his chest at the sight of her. Her heart shaped face was splotchy, her eyes red and puffy from crying, the long lashes clumped into spikes. Her shoulders slumped, as if she carried a great weight.

He pulled her inside and took her in his arms. "What's wrong?"

"Papá says you've been 'carrying on' with Esperanza?"

Ramón's chest constricted. "What?"

"It's not true, is it?" she asked, almost pleaded.

"Of course not—Esperanza's like a sister!"

"Papá was in Yabucoa. The police chief told Papá that you've been seen going to and from her place in the *barrio*. He was there in the plaza the day you talked to everyone, and when he heard Esperanza going on about you, he started to tell people the story Trujillo's been telling everyone all along, that you're cavorting with another girl, one whose husband has only been dead a year."

"But Trujillo's crazy!"

"Yes, but the police chief in Yabucoa isn't and people believe him. For a second, I didn't know what to believe either! And then it all came out. I told them . . . I told my parents I knew you would never do that. I told Papá you wanted to talk to him about us, getting married, going to school—"

"Elsie, no!" Ramón gulped.

She gasped and wrapped her arms around her rib cage. "I've never seen Papá so angry."

Elsie continued her story, her breath coming in spurts: "He got his gun from the locked cabinet, and he told us there were two bullets in the chamber, one for you if he caught you before we left and one for himself if he didn't. It was awful, and he told me . . . he told me that you didn't get into the college."

Fresh tears sprang from her eyes. Ramón wiped a tear from her cheek.

"But I didn't even have a chance to talk to him," Ramón explained, then pressed on, "I wanted to, but I was so overwhelmed about Leo, I wouldn't leave him. I can still talk to him, I can change his mind—I have to try!"

"He's sending me away for a while, to that damn Vieques Island, to his sister, my *jamona* aunt. I haven't seen her since I was six or seven."

It was as if her words were traveling through mud. Ramón could barely hear them over the thudding of blood in his head.

He held her again, felt her tremble. "When? For how long?"

The words he feared most hung in limbo between them.

"Indefinitely, I . . . I can't be with you," Elsie finally said.

Ramón had never been shot, but suddenly, he knew what it would feel like, the split second of waiting before the pain caught up to the bullet and exploded.

"You can't leave me! We can get married and figure out together what to do! I'll apply to the school again!" he insisted.

She shook her head and clutched her chest as if she had cried so hard there were no tears left. "The news about the school made everything worse. I wanted to go to the states. I wanted to learn English, go to college parties, buy the most modern clothes, get new, modern haircuts, meet interesting, smart people. And that won't happen now."

"But it will happen, it will just take a little longer!" Ramón defended.

"Papá will *never* consent. He got called away on an emergency, that's the only reason I'm here. He'd kill you if he found out, and I never want to see that gun again."

Elsie grasped his hand with a strength that surprised Ramón.

"Please don't come for me," she said. "Being with you, the way you told me to follow my dreams, has been a blessing. For that, I'll always be grateful. But I wanted to be a doctor's wife. I wanted to leave here, start a new life."

Ramón's heart shattered.

"I love you more than I've loved anyone! Tell me you don't' love me." He was shocked at the fierceness in his voice, but he couldn't stop. "Look me in the eye and tell me you don't love me!" Ramón reached for her. He wanted to hold her and never let go.

"It's too late. I'm sorry." Elsie pushed his hand away. "I'm sorry, but let me go. I keep seeing that gun, and I can't stay here." She turned and ran down the porch. She didn't look back.

Ramón felt weak, as if he had run a marathon. Trujillo was in the hospital, but his poison was still able to spread with rumors. Ramón recalled the day he went to the *panadería* to get rolls for Leo, the day Leo woke up. Ramón thought he heard a group of women whisper Esperanza's name before he left clutching his bag of rolls, but he was so excited Leo was getting better, and still so worried, that he ran back home without a second thought.

He collapsed into the kitchen chair and looked at the old framed photograph of his parents that hung on the wall. Taken in 1905, they stood in front of the small church in the Maunabo square, dressed for Sunday mass. His mother looked young and beautiful in her cotton flowered dress, his father distinguished in a dark suit and bowtie, both with the promise of the future that stretched out before them.

No one had taken a picture of him and Elsie. A desperation, a loneliness that he'd never known before crashed upon him as he realized there was no record of them ever having been together.

CHAPTER 34

Ramón had to try. He hated the thought of facing Capitán Miraflores when he knew the man had a cabinet full of guns, but he must. After a sleepless night, he trudged to the other end of *La Calles de los Blanchos*.

He walked up the steps to Elsie's house. He climbed only four, but felt like he had climbed a mountain by the time he reached the top. Yet this was Elsie he was here for. He had to fight for her.

He faced the same black knocker. It was in the shape of a ball, but for a second, it morphed into the face of the devil, with pointed nose and two sharp teeth.

Was Ramón seeing things, hallucinations like before the Faudin nearly made him comatose? He had a flash of a memory, when he was six, and Papá took him and Rafael to a movie in the old theater. It was all in English so they couldn't understand anything but when the crabby old man in the movie reached for his familiar old knocker, it transformed into a scary ghost. Then the man was visited by three ghosts on Christmas Eve. Ramón couldn't remember the name of the movie or how it turned out because he had kept his eyes closed after the scariest ghost appeared.

How odd to remember that after a dozen years. He focused on the knocker. That's all it was, a big black ball. Still, the devil image wasn't good. He knocked, waited interminable seconds, then knocked again.

Capitán Miraflores answered. He said nothing but his eyes were black, hard.

Ramón sensed the man's distaste but was not about to turn

back before he said what he had come to say: "I need to talk to you."

"I was wondering if I'd see you, and now, here you are," Capitán said, his voice like ice.

"Can I come in?"

The police chief nodded and stepped back, making just enough room for Ramón to enter. "That's far enough," he said.

The two men stood facing each other in the foyer.

"I love your daughter," Ramón emphasized. "And just as important, I respect her. I want your permission to marry her. I will reapply to college, complete my studies, and I'll be a good provider."

"We're past that. I will not let Elsie be involved with a man who people say is tarnished, who has dishonored a young woman."

"Capitán, there is no truth to that. Esperanza is like a sister to me, like a daughter to my mother. I gave her a job to help her, and she's turned her life around. That's what people are saying, too. Why can't you listen to that?"

"The damage is done."

"But Elsie wants to be with me. She and I can study together, make a future for ourselves."

"Ramón, you were rejected from college. And even if you get in somewhere, and go off to the states, did you *ever* think I would let my only daughter go with you? I'm here to tell you that in this household, a marriage for Elsie will be arranged with proper regard to a man's fortune and position in the community. I am sending her away, and am arranging for her to meet the son of my associate in San Juan, the son of one of the most wealthy, prominent men in the capital who can offer far more than you. I *will* assure her future."

"I was hoping that your love and respect for your daughter,

the fact that she loves me and wants to be a teacher, would be more important to you."

Ramón revealed the truth that was in his heart, but as he said the words, he saw the look of frigid disapproval on the police chief's face, and knew the man would never relent.

Standing in front of an expert archer whose arrow pierced his heart would have been less torture.

"You thought wrong." Capitán's words cut like a knife.

Ramón had to say more. "I think you're making a mistake. What if this divides you and Elsie forever? What if she never forgives you?"

"Stay away from Elsie. If you try to contact her, I will substantiate the rumors people are saying about you and that young woman. Her reputation will be tarnished. And yours."

Esperanza. Ramón would never allow anyone to hurt her.

Before Ramón could respond, the capitán went on: "And there's the matter of the boy who's in your house. It's bad business, everything that happened. That boy comes from a family whose reputation is ruined. For all I know, he has mental problems. I will not let Elsie be exposed to that."

So the police chief got Ramón where he knew it would hurt the most. Leo and Esperanza.

"We're done here," the police chief insisted.

Ramón found the strength to look into the man's eyes and said, "I've only tried to help people, and that's all I've ever done."

Ramón turned and left. The only thing that kept him upright was the fact that he had got in the last word. Still, he forced his legs to get him down the steps without collapsing.

CHAPTER 35

The heart, the strongest muscle in the human body, has four small chambers. Only the size of one's fist, it can still hold a world of grief. Ramón moved through his days like an old man on his last trip to the graveyard.

At work, when the doorbell jingled, Ramón fantasized it was Elsie, running back to him, to tell him she would be with him no matter what. He imagined Señora Lepe strolling in, with a new letter from the college, telling him everything was a terrible mistake.

Neither came.

When he closed his eyes to sleep, he was tormented by the memory of his and Elsie's kiss on the night he proposed, the heady fullness of her lips, the eager way her mouth molded itself to his.

He crossed the plaza, seeing the familiar group of *jíbaros* playing dominoes on tables in the shade of African Palms. So little had changed in the village, yet so much had changed in his life. Ramón could have sworn the same four peasants sat in the exact same positions, never having moved since the day before, never going home to their dirt floor *bohíos* with rusty zinc roofs. He walked by and heard snippets of their conversation, "*some promise, just another one who never . . .*" One of the men looked over and cocked his head toward Ramón, to alert the others. Their voices fell to whispers, and they looked away.

He had to find a way to continue on without Elsie. He still had his family behind him, Chepa, Leo, and Francisco. His brother was so busy at the store, so happy that he hadn't touched alcohol in weeks.

Francisco had told Ramón, "Little brother, you're the smartest guy I know. Send another essay or apply to another school, they'd be crazy not to take you!"

Leo said the same thing. By then, the stitches in his face were removed, the bruises on his body faded except the one on his left cheekbone that had turned into a sunburst pattern in a shade of a soft pink, one that could pass for a birthmark. Leo sat at Ramón's bedside and pleaded with eyes grown big with fear, "Tío Ramón, I'm so sorry about your *novia*, don't be sad. You took such good care of me, I'll never forget it. You'll go to that college and be a dentist to take care of people like you said. You're so good at it!"

Tenderness for the boy surged in Ramón's veins like a drug. Leo was right and Ramón wouldn't disappoint him.

Later that day, Chepa took Ramón to the cemetery to see his father's grave, etched with the words, "*La Familia León Carrasquillo, Ni Tiempo, Ni Distancia Podrán Separarnos.*" (Neither Time Nor Distance Can Separate Us).

It had been a long time since Ramón had visited this place full of tombs, this quiet sanctuary where the ground gave off the scent of grass mixed with peppermint and rosemary. With all that occurred, Ramón had forgotten those words.

Chepa laid a bouquet of fresh plumeria on the ground. She motioned for Ramón to kneel next to her in front of the grave under the shade of a yucca tree. As she often did, she began with a story from her experience as *curandera* to teach a life lesson.

"A year ago, I was called to attend to a boy that had fallen from his donkey and dislocated his shoulder. He was crying, in terrible pain. I told him something before I set it."

Ramón felt more alert, expectant. "What was that?" he asked.

"I told him he had the heart of a lion. I told him to bite down

220

on his father's belt and to breathe out as the pain left his body. It worked, he squeezed his eyes shut and barely cried out when I set his shoulder." She paused to let the weight of her words sink in. "And I saw that strength again, in Leo. And I've seen it in *you*. That boy loves you, watches your every move. Here's your chance to inspire him, to show him how to behave when life gets hard.

"Many are called, but few are chosen. These things that have happened to you, after one glorious event, have been terrible. This is not the end, *m'ijo*, but the beginning. Perhaps it is a test to see if you possess the heart and strength of a lion, your name, the name on that gravestone."

She pointed to *León*.

Ramón knew he would live up to that name.

He remembered the time after his father died. The entire village came to their home for the viewing of the body. His brothers carried Papá's coffin to the cemetery, and Ramón, only ten, struggled after them with a wreath that was almost bigger than he was, pulling every muscle in his shoulders. They walked through Maunabo and black-clad villagers came out of their *bohíos*, cradling prayer beads. The crowd following the coffin swelled. At the bottom of *La Pica*, Capitán Miraflores stood to watch for traffic since it took so long for everyone to cross the road. Ramón's father had no education, had not been a doctor, but had been loved, had earned tremendous respect and reverence. And he did it from nothing.

Ramón had been granted a tremendous gift. He must use it.

"Mamá," he said, his voice rising, "I'm going to go to school in Río Piedras. I'm going to study English harder than ever. I have to make it right with the college . . . I'll apply to Michigan again! Thank you. I needed this day, this memory of Papá." He hugged Chepa.

Ramón helped Chepa off the ground so they could head

home. She wore a little grin on her face, one that conveyed a secret knowledge that implied she knew what the outcome of this visit would be.

As if reading his mind, she declared, "The road to your dreams is not just an uphill one, but filled with peaks and valleys. Anything is possible for the person who believes."

"You're right, Mamá, you always are. I have a promise to keep."

CHAPTER 36

Ramón forged on. It was May 1st, too late to begin the process of applying to a college so faraway in the states, but there was a fine college only hours away in San Juan. He would start there, study English, and reapply to Michigan.

The day after his visit to the graveyard, Ramón drove to the office of Doctor Roberto Santiago, dean of the *Universidad de Puerto Rico* in Río Piedras, planning to coax, cajole, even beg to be admitted for the fall semester.

"The dean's not here. You only missed him by a few days," the secretary explained. "Six months ago, he lost his son in the war. He finished the semester and went to his summer *casita* in Jayuya. I suppose he's there to lose himself in the fields of coffee beans he loves so much. He and his wife went there to recover. *Ay, Dios.*"

She sighed and said, "I'm sorry. Only he can admit you after applications are closed." She shook her head, her dark curls framing her face, her lips tight.

After losing Elsie, and almost Leo, Ramón could barely fathom what the dean was going through. At least Elsie was alive, and the slightest glimmer of hope began to grow in his heart that when she heard how he was forging his future, she might come back to him. But if he couldn't start his education in the fall, his dream was that much farther away.

"Isn't there anything I can do?" Ramón implored.

"At this point, I'm sorry, but I just don't know."

She went back to filing papers into a metal cabinet.

Ramón left the office with a plan: he must see the dean. He

would drive to Jayuya, one of the most remote places on the island, an all-day trip that would take him up and over *Cerro de Punta*, the highest peak on the island.

§§§

Across the street was a small, gray building with a sign with painted black letters: *La Clínica Dental Gratuita* (Free Dental Clinic).

Before he knew where his feet were taking him, Ramón stepped inside. There were a dozen seats in the waiting room and every one was filled, mainly with women and children. A few men stood leaning against what little wall space there was. Ramón guessed by their worn, stained clothes and dusty shoes they were workers from the cane fields outside San Juan. One man had a rawhide rope in place of a belt holding up his baggy pants. They clearly had no where else to go.

The front desk sat empty but within minutes, a man rushed out from the hallway that lead from the back. He looked harried, but his white smock was clean and pressed.

"I'm ready for the next patient," he called out.

A woman stood up and took the hand of her little boy.

Ramón rushed forward to ask, "Excuse me, are you in charge?"

"Yes, I'm the dentist in charge. But if you want to get seen today, it won't happen. Come back tomorrow and make an appointment. My receptionist is sick. It's just me and my dental assistant today. We're already behind."

"It looks like you need more help around here," Ramón blurted.

The man paused, but by the impatient tap of his foot, Ramón

knew to talk fast. "I worked for a dentist in my village, and I learned a lot. I want to become a student here in the fall, and if I can make that happen, I'll work for you. I'll be your assistant. I'm actually pretty good."

"I wish I had half a dozen assistants, and just as many dentists, but I'm already stretched thin, I have no money for more staff."

"I'll do it for free."

The man raised his bushy eyebrows. Even the woman and child turned toward Ramón, looking surprised.

"Great," the dentist answered. "Come back and see me when you're back and we'll train you. We need all the help we can get." He hurried down the hall trailed by his patients.

Before Ramón left, one of the men standing near the exit took off his sweat stained hat and tipped it to him, saying, "You sound like a fine fellow. Thank you, and *buena suerte* (good luck)."

Ramón removed his hat, too. "Thanks. I'll be back."

He drove home feeling better than he had in days. Strange how that *jíbaro* said good luck, as though he knew Ramón needed it.

Ramón thought of the day months before when he was declared 4-F. He thought God's hand may be in that declaration.

Was God's hand in this too, and could that that humble peasant be his messenger? If that were true, this school, this clinic, at least for this time in his life; it was where Ramón needed to be.

CHAPTER 37

The following morning, the sun rose behind him as Ramón drove over two hours westward to Ponce. From there, the road narrowed heading north into the interior of the island. The Buick slowed to near walking pace as it climbed *Cerro de Punta*. Ramón tooted the horn around each switchback, yanking the steering wheel back and forth like he did as a boy when he pretended to drive. The air cooled as the car chugged higher. Other than the groaning of the engine, the only sounds were the wind rustling the trees and the whistles of the *reinita*.

In Jayuya, Ramón went into the small church in the village center, very much like home. The priest was in the nave and knew where the learned man who grew coffee beans lived. Ramón followed the priest outside where the man drew a map in the dirt.

At the dean's *casita* on the outskirts of town, an elderly woman was sweeping a dirt-packed walkway that led up to the front door. The dust swirled above her broom and as she took a step forward, it settled behind her. Ramón wondered why she bothered; as soon as she got to the end of the short path it looked like she'd have to start all over again.

"Señora, is Doctor Santiago home?" he asked.

She stopped and nodded as she ogled Ramón. Perhaps she wasn't used to visitors.

"Rosa, who's that I hear?" the voice called from inside.

Ramón guessed it was Doctor Santiago and stepped to the front door. Ramón had never done anything like this before, but he had no choice, no way to contact the man other than to show up unannounced. This visit *had* to go well. He wished Doctor Roberts could be with him now, and his father. Their memories helped allay his nerves. He even allowed himself to think of Elsie, painful as it was, but he knew she'd be proud of him.

Doctor Santiago appeared at the half-open door. His gray hair covered his head in thin wisps. He wore a dark sweater and trousers. Although Jayuya was located in Cordillera Central mountain range, the highest and coolest part of the island, Ramón guessed the man used to be more robust. Now slight, he needed a sweater to warm his bones. No wonder with what he had been through.

"Can I help you?" the doctor said as he opened the door wide.

Ramón removed his cap. "Doctor Santiago, please forgive my intrusion. I've been to your office and your secretary told me about your son. I'm so sorry for you loss, Doctor."

"Thank you." The man dropped his head briefly. "You certainly came a long way to offer condolences."

"Yes. I was also told you're the only one who can help me, otherwise, I would not disturb you at this time in your life."

The doctor's eyebrows shot up before he asked, "And you came all that way expecting my help with . . . exactly what?"

"I know I missed the deadline to apply but I need to be admitted to the university in the fall," Ramón stated with as much confidence as he dared muster.

"And why exactly did you miss the deadline?"

"Please, can I come in and explain it all to you?"

The dean motioned for Ramón to follow him inside. Like Ramón's home, they walked directly into a small kitchen. Unlike the walkway, the brown tile floor was swept clean. Rosa had done a better job inside.

The dean sat and indicated Ramón take the chair across from

him. He folded his hands on the kitchen table and faced Ramón. With heavy skin under his eyes, the dean looked pensive.

Ramón guessed the man was thinking of his son, who was probably a few years younger than he was now. Ramón's fingers were tingling. His knee bounced under the table. He cleared his throat. "I missed the deadline because I applied to Michigan State College. I didn't get in. I was over confident. I was such a good student in high school that I was sure I would. See, I have my transcripts. I was third in class." Ramón pushed the papers across the table.

The dean looked them over, all three pages that would help shape Ramón's future. Ramón stopped breathing. The only sound was the rustle of paper.

The dean shrugged his shoulders. "I can see you're an excellent student, one who would do well at the university, but classes have already been filled and as you said yourself, you missed the deadline."

"I know, but ever since I was since I was eight, I knew there was only one thing I'd ever want to be—a dentist. I worked with Doctor Roberts in my village for four years, a *humanitario* who I made a promise to, that I would one day continue his work, and one day open the dental clinic that he dreamed of."

"You worked with a dentist when you were *eight*? That's impressive, and I applaud you, but we don't have a dental school."

"I know. My goal is to apply to Michigan again, to their pre-dental program and transfer."

The next part wouldn't be easy, but Ramón decided to tell the truth. He felt a trickle of sweat run down from his armpit. He felt his heart beat faster. In his high school science class, he had learned about the parasympathetic nervous system and how it calmed nerves, slowed the heartbeat. He used that knowledge, willing his heart to slow, his voice to stay even.

"I didn't get in," Ramón admitted, "because the English in the essay wasn't good enough. And I didn't even write it."

"Really?" The dean cocked his head and raised his eyebrows again, sarcasm in his voice.

"Yes, and I'm ashamed. My . . . umm . . . acquaintance went there and assured me he could write a good essay. I wasn't convinced at first, but Antonio is, well, convincing, and I got very sick, with snail fever, too sick to try and write the essay in English even though I studied it in high school. I'll regret that decision for as long as I live."

The dean sighed as if he understood.

Ramón rushed on, "I will do whatever it takes to succeed at your college and in Michigan. I want to learn English so well that I'll write an essay that the school can't refuse. I've already been to that free dental clinic near your office. They need more staff. I'll work there for free when I'm not studying or in classes. I'm determined to do the right thing."

Something sober melted into the dean's eyes. Ramón held his breath, then added quickly, "I will fulfill my promise."

"I appreciate your honesty, and I can tell how much you want this. I've never admitted a student late before, but something tells me I should make an exception for you."

Ramón tried to maintain his composure. He felt his face break out in a smile, and resisted the urge to hug the dean. "Thank you," he said.

The most ironic thing was he wanted share his joy with Elsie, and for a moment, felt a pang so deep he couldn't breathe.

"There's a caveat. Due to the number of boys, or men who are coming home . . ." The dean's voice became quiet, slower, as if were an effort to continue. "Most classes are impacted. My secretary told me that we're anticipating the highest number of students we've ever had, nearly double due to the GI Bill. English classes are popular, and I'm afraid the only class that has room is quite advanced, a literature class focusing on Charles Dickens. I hope you can keep up."

Ramón swallowed the lump in his throat. He didn't know who this fellow Charles Dickens was, but wouldn't be daunted.

"Like I said, I'll do whatever it takes to succeed. Thank you again. You won't regret it," Ramón assured.

"I expect that. By the way, however did you find me way up here?"

"Your secretary told me where you were and then the priest drew me a map."

"Ah, Padre Díaz knows everyone." The dean nodded. "But I've never had anyone come here before. As I said, I applaud you."

"So, what do I do next?"

"I'll send a telegram to my secretary the next time I'm in Ponce for supplies, telling her I've made an exception. Bring her these transcripts and complete an application in registration. They'll enroll you in whatever classes have room. You may not get your first choices."

"I'll take whatever I can get. I appreciate this," Ramón said, excitement in his voice.

Ramón stood to leave. He thought the dean a strict and professional man, one who commanded respect, but as the man shook Ramón's hand good-bye, his face softened. Right before he let go, the dean put his other hand on top of Ramón's. It was such a tender gesture that Ramón thought of his father, who merely pretended to be strict.

Rosa was done sweeping the walkway by the time Ramón left. He told her to have a good day and rather than acknowledge it, she looked him directly in the eye and asked, "Did he tell you how much you look like *him*?"

"Who?"

"His son, Carlos, the one who was killed." She made a sign of the cross. "When you got here, you scared the *diablo* out of me. It's the eyes I think."

Ramón couldn't believe it. He thought this man was like his father, and he looked like the son.

On the drive home, he allowed himself to appreciate this majestic place on top of the world where green gold valleys tumbled in every direction. *Tabonuco* trees towered on either side of the dirt road and red and pink maga flowers carpeted the roadside.

Ramón had read somewhere that in the universe, Yin cannot exist without Yang. Shadow cannot exist without light. Now he realized, perhaps happiness cannot exist without despair. Could this turn of events strengthen him? Didn't he go into jail for a night, and come out stronger?

He saw a swarm of butterflies so vast that they looked like a dancing tapestry of gold in a sky painted a seamless blue. For that moment, Ramón felt closer to God.

CHAPTER 38

The war raged on. Benito Mussolini was executed on April 26, 1945. Four days later, Adolf Hitler poisoned his wife and committed suicide. German forces began to surrender: in Italy on May 1st followed by forces in Berlin, Northwest Germany, Denmark, the Netherlands and Bavaria. On May 8th, Germany surrendered unconditionally.

People worldwide learned of the atrocities committed in concentration camps. After Dachau and Buchenwald were liberated, their horrors were revealed. Prisoners who were spared the ovens emerged like skeletons; photos in newspapers Ramón read showed people leaving the camps with translucent skin on their faces and bones sticking out of their spines like truncated wings. One woman had the most haunting eyes Ramón had ever seen, made larger and even more stunning by her emaciated face.

Chepa, who loved everyone and preached that all God's children were created equal, cried over the brutality in the world. Every morning, she, Ramón, and Lila went to church to say a rosary and light a candle for something so senseless and horrific, to pray for those murdered and the survivors putting their lives back together.

Despite the upheaval in the world, like many people, Ramón carried on with his daily duties. He completed his application, and discovered the dean had kept his word and contacted the school on his behalf.

Ramón would be attending college, a step closer to achieving his dream.

He spent his days working in the store and passing time with Leo like a son. They had moved Leo's pony to a pen in the *barrio*, and

Ramón and Leo savored each evening at dusk when they took turns riding Manchas along the Maunabo shore, his short legs trotting in and out of the lapping waves.

On June 22, Okinawa—the final ground battle of the war—ended in victory for the allies. A month later, Japan rejected the surrender ultimatum. By the samurai, or military code, they were honor bound to fight to the end. The consequences were grave.

On the afternoon of August 6, Ramón was walking on a busy street in Santurce, heading to Gómez and Sons Incorporated on his bi-monthly shopping trip for the store. A merchant ran out into the street, screaming for everyone to stop and listen. A street vendor turned up the volume of his radio. In a somber voice, the commentator announced: *"We repeat for those now tuning in: The Atomic Bomb, the first of its kind and the most destructive weapon on earth, was dropped today by airships of the United States of America on Hiroshima, Japan. We repeat ... at 9:15, the bomb was dropped by the Superfortress Enola Gay. A black cloud of boiling dust and churning debris rose one thousand feet off the ground. Above it, the white smoke climbed like a mushroom to twenty thousand feet. This will surely bring an end to the war."*

It was if someone had dropped a black cloud over Santurce, too. A hush fell over the busy street. Men and women stopped to gaze at one another in shocked disbelief. Some cheered the end of the war. Some cried.

Dios, Ramón thought, *it's over. Gracias a Dios, my brothers are coming home.*

A woman threw her arms to the heavens and thanked God her sons were coming home. She fell to her knees. Ramón ran to her. She reached for him and he helped her up before she stumbled off, mumbling thanks to the almighty savior.

Two men who only moments earlier had stood outside the market and bickered over the price of a bag of rice embraced. People ran out of shops and restaurants to find loved ones or connect with strangers.

The street vendor selling *bacalaitos fritos* shouted, "Free food for all!"

Ramón remembered another time he heard a shocking news report, the night he proposed to Elsie. The wound she left him was still raw. He wanted to take her in his arms, share this startling news with her as they had done before.

And then he felt a rush of guilt. He was thinking of his own heartache at a time when the retaliation from the Japanese might be unthinkable—and even though they were the enemy, Ramón shuddered when he imagined what was happening at the other end of the world in Japan. If that bomb were as destructive as the radio commentator declared, surely people, innocent people, were suffering horrible deaths.

Needing a friend, Ramón went to find Alberto Gómez. He met him on the street in front of his store. The kind merchant was on his way to *Nuestra de Señora Lourdes Chapel*. Ramón accompanied his friend there. A line had already formed at the door. The sanctuary was filled with people praying and lighting candles. After he did the same, Ramón drove home, forgetting the merchandise he had come for.

By the 9th, when the second bomb destroyed Nagasaki, Ramón was thankfully at home. His entire family, brothers, wives, and their children, met at the León home for a vigil. They prayed for the war's end, and they prayed to see Isidro and Rafael again.

CHAPTER 39

The Leóns gathered in the courtyard the night before Ramón's going away party. All stopped their chatter to listen to Chepa as she clapped her hands for attention.

"Change isn't easy. Often, it's wrenching and difficult. But it's change that strengthens us and makes us better." All was quiet except for the huffing of Pepita in the side yard and a cluck from a chicken. "And Ramón, *you*, more than anyone, are due for a change!" A huge smile spread across Chepa's face.

Everyone laughed with her. Chepa's kitchen was too small to hold her growing family, so Ramón, Juan and Francisco had borrowed metal folding chairs and tables from *Casa Alcaldía* and positioned them in the shade of the grapefruit and mango trees in the courtyard. Five round tables were squeezed together to accommodate everyone: Juan and Amanda with their three children, Francisco and Isabel with their three children, José Luis and Marina and their two children, Lila and her husband, Jorge, and of course, Esperanza, her children, and Leo. The children ran about squealing while the women laid out dinner.

They dined on *asopao*, fried cod fritters and pig's feet with chickpeas and rice, the kitchen steamy from the *fogón's* firing all afternoon, the air heady with the scent of grilled meat, garlic, rosemary and onion. Ramón would miss that enticing aroma.

He wasn't traveling over two-thousand miles to Michigan, yet Ramón and Lila were the first in the family to graduate high school and Ramón would be the first to attend college. It was monumental.

The children settled down, and everyone dined and laughed

as *coquís* serenaded the night. One by one, each child drifted off to sleep, most on the grass curled against each other like newborn kittens. Six-year-old Emma Josefa fell asleep in her mother Amanda's arms, Francisco Junior in his Tía Lila's arms and despite trying to stay awake to listen to the adults' chatter, Leo dozed after midnight, his head turned sideways on the table.

When the time came to say good-bye, each brother embraced Ramón before returning to his own home. Francisco held on the longest, again, his apology for everything that had occurred between them.

§§§

The next morning, Chepa stirred Ramón awake. "There's one more person who wants to say good-bye," she said quietly.

Ramón stepped into the kitchen where Isabel sat, a steaming mug of coffee in front of her. Ramón poured himself a cup and joined her at the table.

"Looks like everyone had a good time last night," Ramón commented as he added Pepita's milk to his coffee.

Isabel nodded. "Yeah . . . It was a good party."

They sat in silence for a moment. Ramón inhaled the earthy aroma of Chepa's coffee combined with the rich creaminess of Pepita's milk. He thought of the savory dinner last night; he would miss this aroma, too.

"So, how are—" Ramón began to say.

"Are you ready—" Isabel said at the exact same moment.

They laughed in unison, and it was the first time they had laughed together since that uncomfortable time in the store, when Isabel flirted and Ramón sent her off.

Isabel was the first to speak: "So, you're off today. Good luck. We'll all be praying for you, and something tells me things will work out."

Ramón noticed how different she looked, a softness about the eyes and face that weren't there before. Relaxed and happy.

"You look good," he said.

"Thanks, and I came by to say I'm sorry for the way I acted, umm, you know . . ."

"It's okay, I'm just glad things are good now between you and Francisco."

"You know something, Ramón? They are. The store is good, Francisco is happy and he pays more attention to the kids and me. Things are better than they've been in a long time, so thanks," Isabel repeated, her voice tender, full of understanding.

She pushed a package wrapped in butcher paper in front of him and spoke again before Ramón had a chance to respond: "I made you lunch, I thought it was the least—"

"Thanks!" Ramón interjected and they laughed again.

It was one of his favorites. A *pastele* stuffed with pork.

They finished their coffee and spoke about simple things: the kid's schoolwork, and what Isabel would serve that night for dinner. And it felt good, the ease between them.

§§§

It was the hardest to say good bye to Leo. Lila and Chepa clung to Ramón before he left, but it was Leo who came with him to the plaza to wait for the old school bus, still in operation that Saturday for the workers of the cane fields. Ramón would take four *públicos* to get to Río Piedras. It was the right thing to do, travel modestly, as he did before his life changed forever; he had loaned his car to Francisco, who would take over buying trips for the store in addition to his own.

The rainy season had resumed so Ramón and Leo sat on a bench under an umbrella and chatted about how much Leo was looking forward to resuming grammar school, how good a job he would do taking care of Manchas on his own.

When the rickety jalopy pulled up, Leo held onto Ramón. It was the first time he had cried in months, and when Ramón folded his umbrella and stepped on the bus, Leo ran "home" to Chepa.

It poured so hard that Ramón could barely see out the steamy window with a huge crack in the middle. The old woman seated across from Ramón reminded him of Chepa, and he found himself telling her he was going to college. She was so pleased to meet a smart college boy that she insisted he share her hunk of bread and white cheese. Ramón didn't have the heart to tell her he already had lunch. The driver glared. Obviously he didn't like passengers eating in his bus, but when the old woman grinned with an almost toothless smile, he huffed and kept his eyes on road.

The road flooded and traffic backed up for miles. Ramón thought of the letter he sent to Elsie. He had agonized over it so much he knew it by heart. The day before, he had gone to the post office and asked Señora Lepe to send it.

She had hesitated, then admitted, "I have her address but Capitán Miraflores said not to give it to anyone, especially you."

"Just send it," Ramón said. "Don't tell me the address. I don't want to get you in trouble."

She simply nodded. "All right, Ramón, for you, I will."

Now Ramón closed his eyes and recited it silently in his head:

Dear Elsie:

I leave tomorrow for college, for a semester in Río Piedras. You left me to continue on without you and that's what I'll do, to be the best that I can be. I'll get to dental school in the states, somehow, sometime. What I really want you to know is this. I wouldn't give up the time we had together for anything. You made me a better man. Whatever you do, please, don't give up on being a teacher. You'll be great at it. I know that. You can follow your dreams, too, and I won't stand in your way. Perhaps one day, if God wills it, we can be together.

I will always love you,
Ramón.

§§§

The *público* finally arrived in Río Piedras. Ramón had answered an ad in *El Mundo* and rented a room in a building that had once been a private home, but had been divided in half with a two-room apartment in the back behind a bar facing the street. His bedroom contained a cot under a mosquito net, a dresser with three drawers, a small desk where he placed the framed picture of his parents, and a chair. He shared a bathroom and kitchen with a couple renting the second bedroom. His spartan accommodations seemed fitting considering everything he had been through, and it was crucial he save the money for college. This was his second chance, especially after what Doctor Santiago had done for him.

When he first walked into the room, he shuddered at the thought it was almost as small as his jail cell. But no, this room had been swept clean and gave off only a mild scent of mildew. He missed the heavenly aromas of Chepa's cooking. At least he only had a married couple for housemates, and not a creature or two scurrying across the floor. His new home had two things he considered luxuries: electricity provided by a bare bulb hanging from the ceiling and hot running water in the bathroom and kitchen. He wouldn't have to wait until midday for the sun to heat the large drum of rain water on the roof to take a shower, or to boil water for drinking.

He thought of Elsie's letter again. What was her new house in Vieques like? The thought tugged at his heart like a festering wound, but he believed everything fell into place for this crossroads in his life.

CHAPTER 40

In Río Piedras, Ramón was relieved by his anonymity in the city where no one knew his history. He worked at the dental clinic three nights a week, in addition to carrying a full course load: Algebra II, History of Civilization, and Inorganic Chemistry. Ramón was thrilled the classes had openings, and as Doctor Santiago had informed him, Advanced English Literature.

Algebra II was manageable. Ramón had always enjoyed equations and word problems. In the first day of class, he smiled when he solved one of the problems like an old friend:

> *Two high speed públicos leave two villages that are fifty miles apart. They travel toward each other at rates of 30 mph and 20 mph respectively. A bumblebee flying at the rate of 50 mph starts out just as the faster público departs the village, and flies to the slower público. The bee then turns around and flies back to meet the first público. Then it turns around again, etc., and keeps flying back and forth until the públicos meet. How far does the weary bumblebee fly?* [1]

The History of Ancient Civilizations was fascinating. In the first class, Ramón learned that archeologists in Western Europe were discovering skeletons and artifacts that exposed the mysteries of what ancient men looked like and how they lived and worked.

---

1   50 miles.

Inorganic Chemistry would be a challenge, but he'd had Biology in high school and loved science. It always made sense.

Yet from the day he first walked into Advanced English Literature, Ramón knew it would be his Achilles heel. The students were about his age, but were probably in their third or final year of college. It was clear they already knew one another; when Ramón heard snippets of their conversation, he deduced they had been taking English together since they first came to the university.

The requirement of the class was to speak English as soon as one walked through the door. No Spanish allowed. Ramón was dumbfounded; he had made it all the way to "P" in his dictionary, *puzzle: rompecabezas, acertijo*, but it did nothing to help him engage in conversation. The other students had an easy camaraderie that he envied, and when he posed a question in Spanish to one of them, the instructor, Professor Rolf, glared at him. After that, the other students went back to chattering in English and left Ramón alone.

Ramón sat in front with his dictionary, hoping that placing himself front and center would improve his understanding. He was lost from the moment the professor first opened his mouth to say, "This class will consist of dissecting the work of Charles Dickens."

Ramón began to flip through his dictionary, which was already so worn he'd had to tape the front cover. Dissect, that word sounded familiar like *disecar* but that was odd. *Disecar* was done to a lab animal or frog after it was dead. He recognized the word <u>work</u>, but wasn't this a class to read English books?

The instructor kept right on using words Ramón didn't understand. The man ceased speaking. Ramón looked up from his dictionary.

"That is extremely distracting, Señor . . ." the professor said as he made a dramatic show of grabbing his class roster and running his bony finger down the row of names as if it were a tremendous burden, " Carrasquillo. If you plan to continue using *that book*, please move to the back," the man demanded.

¡Dios! What the heck did he say? The only word Ramón got was <u>back</u>. Everyone looked at him. No one made a sound. Ramón felt heat flood his face. He imagined he turned the color of that silly apple that nurse brought to his grammar school years ago. He was used to being called on for the right answers, for receiving praise from his instructors, not for being ridiculed as the class idiot.

"Well . . ." Professor Rolf added, pointing the same knobby finger to the back of the room. He glared, and his eyes got smaller, blacker, as if he were sending Ramón to the gallows.

Ramón stood and walked to take the seat in the last row. He felt the collective eyes of the class follow him. When he sat, the students were kind enough to turn away. The first day of class, and Professor Rolf already hated him.

The professor droned on. Ramón heard the word <u>essay</u> and of course, knew what that meant, but he was so flustered that nothing else made sense. A man in the class was selected to pass out a book. He smiled when he placed it on Ramón's desk: *Great Expectations*. On the cover was a picture of a pale boy who reminded Ramón of Leo before he got his color back and a pretty girl who held a book open and appeared to be reading to the boy. She didn't have that spectacular copper hair; hers was a shade lighter, but she looked a little like Elsie. Ramón missed her all over again.

The book felt thick and heavy in his hands at 454 pages. Ramón walked away from the class and out into the street, wondering how in the world he would manage with a teacher who looked at him like he was a murderer. The sidewalks were filled by the chatter of students rushing to their classes and the echoes of street vendors haggling their wares. Ramón felt someone tap his shoulder and expected to turn to see the professor telling him not to bother coming back. It wasn't.

"Hi, I'm sorry about what happened. I'm Carlos Busch," the young man stated in Spanish with a slight accent. A couple years younger than Ramón, he thrust out his hand to shake. It was the man who passed out the books, the one with the friendly smile. He had the same name as Doctor Santiago's son, Carlos, whom Ramón resembled, perhaps part of the reason the dean made an exception in Ramón's favor. Carlos was a common Spanish name, but this man didn't look Spanish. He had hair the color of sand and intense blue eyes. He smiled and his dimples became even deeper, making him look younger, angelic even.

"Ramón León Carrasquillo. Nice to meet you," Ramón said as he returned the hand shake.

"Same here. Where are you from?"

"Maunabo."

"Ah, that explains it. Professor Rolf is German, from Berlin. He speaks four languages and considers himself a city slicker, doesn't take too kindly to country folk. Maybe that's why he picked on you. He only came a few years ago, but I hear he can be a real bastard, the toughest teacher in the school."

"Just my luck," moaned Ramón.

"I know what you're going through," Carlos commiserated. "I moved here when I was thirteen, after my dad was transferred. I had a rough time learning Spanish. I was born in Germany but we moved to New York when I was little, so I speak English, and this class won't be hard for me. But I think you'll have a devil of a time passing. Why did you take it? Most of us are third or fourth years."

"I got admitted late," Ramón explained. "I really want to

improve my English, and this was the only class with room left. Damn. Maybe I should switch to a different one." Ramón thought of pleading his case again to the dean.

"Yeah, if only you could. I've never seen classes so full, all those returning soldiers, God love 'em, but this class is going to be a killer."

Ramón felt his shoulders slump.

"You know what? Don't leave the class," Carlos suggested. "I'll help you. Someone helped me when I could hardly get by. I've always been grateful to the guy. Now it's my turn to do the same."

"Thanks, Carlos. By the way, if you're German, how did you get a Spanish name?"

"Oh, my grandmother lived in Barcelona when she was young and she used to take my mother there for vacation. They loved that city. My mother loves all Spanish things, so she named me Carlos."

"I think my grandmother's from Barcelona, but I never knew her. Who knows, maybe we're related!"

Ramón thought of Carlos as a gift, possibly sent by God, or by Ramón's father in heaven, or Doctor Roberts. He also remembered how he told the dean he would do whatever it took to succeed. It was yet another promise. The dean had already done Ramón a huge favor; he wouldn't trouble the man again.

He thought of Carlos's calling the teacher a bastard and remembered the spiteful look in Rolf's eyes. The professor reminded Ramón of the hateful jail guard, Boudreau. The two had similar accents and stocky bodies. They both moved as if they needed no provocation to lash out and strike, would even do so with fierce delight.

Ramón got that inkling again, that tingly spread across the shoulders that something was brewing.

CHAPTER 41

Ramón immersed himself in to a life in which there was no room for distractions. Three days a week he attended all five classes. Tuesday and Thursday mornings were reserved for three hour Chemistry labs. Every afternoon he spent hours studying until his back ached so much from the hard chair in his bedroom that he was forced to get up and move.

After his evening shifts at the clinic, he picked up studying where he left off until the wee hours of the morning. It was part of his plan; he made sure he was so exhausted that sleep came easily in his bedroom behind the bar despite the jukebox's incessant blare of lovers' troubles and the shouts of drunken patrons.

Professor Rolf continued to pick on Ramón. In the fourth class, he announced there would be a *quiz*. A what? Ramón knew it wasn't good news by the groans of his classmates. He paged in his dictionary to cu, only to remember that qu in English and the cu in Spanish were similar sounding but he hadn't got to qu yet. Papers were distributed. Of course, quiz was another word for test. He stared at the question: *Identify the quote and its meaning: "Be grateful, boy, to them which brought you up by hand."*

By hand; Carlos had helped him translate what "by hand" meant: that Pip's aunt, the woman who raised him, beat him. Ramón couldn't imagine that. He knew the answer in Spanish, but it took him so long to translate to English as he frantically turned the pages of his dictionary that Professor Rolf snatched the paper away while he was still writing and growled, "Time's up."

In the following class, Ramón's first take-home essay was

returned with so many glaring red corrections that Ramón was unable to make sense of them. Worse, there was a big "F" emblazoned on top of the paper with the remark: *Halfhearted attempt, poor use of English*. He had never received an F before, and now had two, counting the damn quiz he was sure he'd get an F on.

When Ramón told Carlos, they agreed to begin tutoring sessions. Nearly every night, later after Ramón's work shifts, they met at the library and shared a table in the corner. Every hour or so, in between doing his own schoolwork, Carlos would correct and suggest changes in Ramón's writing or help Ramón with a difficult translation. Carlos would head home at ten or eleven when only the most diligent students remained. By that point, Ramón was so saturated with *Great Expectations* he couldn't read another word. He'd study an English grammar book—he'd never get over the endless amount of contractions—or the two-inch thick English dictionary. He reasoned that looking up the meaning of words exposed him to even more words.

Ramón was the last to leave the library when it closed at midnight. As he walked home, he'd look inside some of the windows that were still lit in the small wooden or cement houses with wrought iron porch railings. Although modest, they all had electricity, which amazed Ramón. He imagined the city dwellers who lived there, what kind of work they did, if they were married or happy. It was a good distraction from thinking about Pip, Miss Havisham, Estella, all from *Great Expectations*, Elsie, and the headaches he suffered.

Once home, he'd work another hour with cotton balls in his ears to drown out the noise from the bar. He used that time to study his other classes, which required less of his concentration. At least he was getting B's in those. He'd fall asleep with his chemistry or history book open on his lap, only to awake several hours later and start all over again. He even studied while he ate, tackling *Great Expectations* while he sipped thick black coffee and ate *pan dulce* from the *panadería* across the street.

§§§

After a month of his grueling schedule, Nitza Ortiz announced her concern when Ramón walked into the kitchen he shared with her and her husband, Chico. He greeted her and began to heat rice and beans on the electric stove; a marvel, no *fogón* to wait for charcoal to heat! As usual, she worked at the table that served as her desk, where she and Chico composed letters to send to their customers' relatives in New York. Illiteracy was rampant amongst the *jíbaros* who worked in the country surrounding San Juan and letter writers with Nitza and Chico's skills were scarce. Ramón suspected many of the relatives on that side of the world couldn't read or write well either. Who wrote for them?

She stopped writing to say, "Ay, Ramón, you look like death! What have you been eating, or more likely, not eating, away from your mamá?"

Ramón shrugged.

"Rice and beans, or fried plantains but sometimes I forget to eat. My school work is endless, and there are always too many patients at the clinic. Last week, I cleaned a lady's teeth and taught her how to take care of her children's teeth—I'd never seen such decay. She must have told everyone what a good job I did. There's a waiting list of people from her *barrio* to see me. As a matter of fact, I need to be at work in an hour."

"Let them wait!" Nitza exclaimed. "You need to eat a good meal. I'm going to make *mofongo* for you! I need to fatten you up."

Like Chepa, Nitza was a marvel in the kitchen. She chatted while she fried chicken and plantains in separate pans on the stove top, then mashed the chicken with onion and garlic in the *pilón* before stuffing it into the plantains.

"It's a tragedy that so many of our people don't know how to write or read. Chico and I are trying to change that. If we teach them something with our writing, even a little, it can empower them, or their children, some who go off to school with the hope they'll get good jobs. We don't make a lot, but we can pay the rent in this place," Nitza said and rolled her eyes.

"And you can cook as well as my mamá and sister," Ramón complimented Nitza as she laid a platter in front of him. The aroma of the meat and garlic made him salivate. He savored every bite.

Nitza shook her head. "You don't get out enough either. Why don't you go out dancing, maybe even find a pretty girl to cook for you? You're nice looking. I see how some of the ladies turn their heads when you cross the street. Ay, if I didn't love Chico so much." Her voice was light, teasing.

Ramón was shocked. The girls in Maunabo were never so bold, but this was the city. He'd never known a modern woman like Nitza, who only a few years older than he, had earned a college degree. This was a rarity among women, especially those from the *barrios*.

"I'm too tired all the time to go out," Ramón said.

In truth, he had noticed when women on the streets or in the shops glanced at him, but when he thought of talking to them, he could only think of Elsie, which opened up a fresh wound to bleed all over again.

§§§

As he walked ten blocks to the clinic, Ramón thought of his housemates. They were trying to change lives, and had the same dreams as Doctor Robert's: to improve people's station in life.

Ramón was beginning to accomplish that. At the clinic, there was only one dentist, one assistant and Ramón. At first, Ramón performed rudimentary tasks, such as cleaning instruments and convincing the patients to make more appointments. Yet in Ramón's first week, the dentist witnessed him teaching a patient how to clean in between his teeth with a toothpick as he explained that a cleaner mouth would help control his diabetes. The *jíbaro* kissed Ramón's hand afterward, and insisted on calling him "Doctor."

"How do you know all that? You certainly made that frightened fellow happy," the dentist had exclaimed. It was Ramón's chance to shine. He told Doctor Cerna about his tutelage under Doctor Roberts and offered to clean his teeth, an offer Doctor Cerna accepted. After that, Doctor Cerna allowed Ramón to clean patients' teeth, and they no longer had to send the *jíbaros* at the end of the waiting line home without treatment.

Ramón's work reinforced that he was in the right place. He had no time for parties or bars, but his patients provided more gratification than any social life would.

If only his damn literature class were going as well as his work. He had earned Ds in two more essays, and Carlos agreed Rolf was unduly harsh.

Ramón knew the professor disliked him yet he didn't know why. The day before, he had tried to talk to Professor Rolf after class, but the man's accent sounded so different from Ramón's teachers in high school that he was incomprehensible, and he refused to switch to Spanish. When Ramón asked for an interpretation of some of the comments on his essay, the professor tapped his watch, and strode out of the room in a huff. Perhaps it was what Carlos alluded to, that Ramón was from a backwards country village. His work at the library improved his vocabulary but not his pronunciation, and that clearly annoyed the professor.

Ramón arrived at work and scrubbed his hands. He knew what he had to do. He would try and reason with Professor Rolf again. He couldn't let this angry man stand in the way of his future.

CHAPTER 42

Ramón sat across from Professor Rolf at his desk, and forcing his hand to stop shaking, he pushed the paper covered in red marks in front of the man.

"I'm sorry. I am trying my best. Why did I get a D?" Ramón asked.

"I'mmmm sorry," the man hummed his *ms* in mimicry. His black eyes sank into his fleshy, pale face. "But your grades reflect your work."

"Re-f-l-eeect?" Ramón stumbled over the combination of f, l, e and c. He wasn't sure what the word meant.

"It's obvious you don't understand much. Write clear sentences with correct use of tense that show you've *absorbed* the theme of the novel," Professor Rolf stated. His face tightened before he added, "That's what's required for an acceptable grade, that's what *some* of your classmates do. But then, a genius such as Charles Dickens didn't write masterpieces for the likes of students at this university!"

Ramón got a fraction of what the man said but couldn't frame a reply.

"Are you deaf?" Professor Rolf demanded.

In his nervousness, Ramón switched into Spanish, then back to English as he stumbled over the difficult combination of e, x and c as he said, "*Con permiso,* I mean exxx . . . cuse me?"

"Never mind," the professor harrumphed. "Your work is substandard. It takes me longer to correct, and frankly, I don't have the time."

The meeting ended. It accomplished one thing. It made Ramón

angry. He had come to this man with sincerity, and the man mocked him. People had always recognized Ramón's industry; his previous instructors, the villagers in the plaza the day of his proclamation, Doctor Cerna, and the patients in the clinic. Why couldn't this man do the same?

Ramón would do whatever it took to get passing grade on his next essay question: *Why does Pip refuse to take any more of Magwitch's money? Was this the correct choice?*

He would prove what he was made of.

§§§

Ramón began with an outline. He discussed the essay question with Carlos, after which he wrote down all the possible answers, in Spanish. He carried a writing tablet with him for the next week. When an idea struck him at odd times, like strolling to work, or in between patients, he wrote it down before he forgot. Then he ranked his ideas from best to worst, and began the laborious task of translating to English. Ramón had been reluctant in seeking Nitza's help as she seemed as busy as he, but one night when Carlos was unavailable, he asked Nitza what she thought of his writing. She was even better than Carlos. She taught him to choose strong verbs in his writing, and that just as in Spanish, English verb tenses are divided into three main groups of time: past, present and future, and to be consistent choosing one tense in a piece of writing.

Ramón spent at least twenty hours on the essay. When he was done, it looked good. Nitza agreed.

"I've never seen anyone work so hard on anything. If he doesn't pass you, I'll kill him myself," she declared.

After class on that Friday in October, Ramón turned in on what he considered his very best work.

He could hardly wait until Monday.

§§§

"Who wrote this for you?" Professor Rolf demanded as he handed the essay back to Ramón without a grade. Only one student remained in the room. When he heard the tone of the professor's voice, he flinched and hurried out.

Ramón clenched the paper, his knuckles turning white. He got the gist of the question. "Me . . . I mean . . . I did," he stuttered.

"I suspect not. It's so much better than your usual work, I think someone wrote it for you."

Ramón couldn't believe his ears.

"No!" Ramón tried to keep the tremor out of his voice. "I wrote it, myself. These are my ideas. I worked very, very hard."

"Well, I may have to bring it . . . something something . . . the review board."

"*Bring* it?" Ramón said and tried to process most of Rolf's words.

"I mean show it, present it to the disciplinary committee, comparing it to your former work. In cases of cheating . . . something something . . . termination."

Ramón remembered the word discipline. He hated the sound of that committee. And the word termination, *terminación* in Spanish, *Dios, I could be kicked out of the class or worse . . . out of school!*

Rolf droned on: "Something something . . . Thursday night at 7 P.M. I'll be there. I make carbon copies of some of my students'

254

work, the best and worst, and I have copies of yours . . . something . . . to defend yourself, you need to be there." He turned and left the room.

Ramón's mind worked at double speed to process Rolf words: an accusation of cheating. The blood pounded so hard in his temples, Ramón could barely hear the clicking of the man's polished heels on the linoleum floor as he strode out. Ramón understood why men commit crimes, why he tried to strangle Señor Trujillo that day. He wanted to hurt this man. After all that work, Ramón was so proud, and Nitza too. Damn. He wouldn't give up. He would do whatever it took for the committee to believe him. He needed some way to prove the material was his.

§§§

"Ramón, how about I put some powder under those eyes? You look terrible!" Nitza suggested.

Ramón had slept only in snippets since the horrible accusation. Carlos had confirmed what the outcome of the meeting would be if Ramón were found guilty of cheating; he would have to leave the university.

"Powder that ladies use? Thanks, but no thanks. And thanks again for coming with me, both of you," Ramón said as he turned to Nitza first, then Carlos. They had both insisted they come to the meeting and were having coffee in the kitchen before they walked to the admissions office for the 7 P.M. meeting. Doctor Cerna had given Ramón the night off, stating if the clinic weren't so busy, he'd have been there as well.

The three of them, Ramón, Nitza and Carlos, had formulated a plan. Ramón had, thank *Dios,* kept his outline, writing tablet and notes that he wrote for the essay. He would show them to the committee, and Nitza and Carlos would back him up. Simple. Still, they walked to the meeting in silence.

§§§

Three men, the disciplinary committee, sat in black chairs behind a long table in front of the classroom. They faced a sea of empty desks, all save one, occupied by Professor Rolf. One of the committee members was Doctor Santiago. Ramón's heart danced in his chest, but then sank. He thought the dean would believe him, but then Ramón remembered: the man knew about the essay for MSC that Antonio wrote.

Doctor Santiago looked at Ramón and his friends and said in a firm voice, "Have a seat, all of you. Professor Rolf will speak first."

Thankfully, the meeting would be conducted in Spanish; Professor Rolf's rules didn't apply here. Brief introductions were made. Ramón was so nervous he forgot the names of the other two committee members.

Ramón, Nitza and Carlos took their seats behind Rolf. Ramón looked at the back of his head, imaging how it would feel to strike it.

Professor Rolf stood and showed the committee Ramón's first essay. It was a carbon copy showing all the blatant corrections. Ramón couldn't believe Rolf copied it.

The professor talked while the three men looked at it in turn. "As you can see, the work is poor, with little to no comprehension of the proper use of gerunds, past and present tense, and with multiple spelling errors and shocking grammatical errors. The papers submitted after were just as bad."

Damn, his Spanish is really good, fumed Ramón.

Ramón knew the second and third essays were better, that Rolf was lying, but in a fit of anger and embarrassment, Ramón had thrown out his papers emblazoned with Ds. *Damn that man*, he seethed again.

"Then," Professor Rolf continued, "I received this. It's far too improved to explain other than this man, Ramón León Carrasquillo, in desperation, had someone write it for him. And I caught him."

The accuser turned and pointed his bony finger at Ramón. He looked gleeful.

The three committee members each read the newest essay. Minutes passed. Ramón heard Nitza breathe quicker. He wondered if everyone could hear his own heart pound. Drops of sweat trickled down his arm and popped out on his brow. He wiped his forehead with a clean handkerchief.

"Well, it's markedly better, a very good effort. How can you explain it, Señor Carrasquillo?" asked the examiner sitting in the center.

Ramón stood and swallowed the taste of his fear. He stepped in front of the committee, his entire body trembling. He focused on quieting it, took a deep breath and began with the speech he had rehearsed.

"I worked harder on this essay than I ever have on anything. I was determined to improve. Here's the outline I made, the notes I wrote to organize my thoughts, even a writing tablet I carried so I could record my ideas at any time when they came to me."

Ramón handed all his work to the committee, who passed the material between them.

Ramón continued: "These are my friends, Carlos Busch, who's in the class with me, and Nitza Ortiz. In no way did they write that essay for me, but they helped me edit. They've helped me from the

257

beginning. Carlos meets me almost every night at the library. I do all the work of translating *Great Expectations*, and he helps when I have questions. And my English has improved. I also brought my dictionary—I take it everywhere I go and study it whenever I can."

He handed the group his book. By then, the cover had fallen off and the pages had rolled up to the letter F.

Nitza, God bless her, jumped up. Her short, black curls bounced around her head in all directions. "It's true," she agreed. "I graduated from this university, and I write letters for people in the *barrios* to send to their relatives in the states. I've seen Ramón's English improve tremendously since he came. I'm very proud of him. He wrote that essay himself, without a doubt!"

With the look on her face, Ramón was happy she was on his side.

"I agree," Carlos said and stood. "Ramón stays at the library studying long after I go home. I've never seen anyone work so hard."

Ramón noticed a subtle shift in the postures of the three committee members. They seemed to sit more upright, intent on his friends' words, contemplating his innocence. The intuition gave him the confidence to confront Rolf, who had remained standing.

Ramón faced his professor, who stood inches taller, yet Ramón lengthened every vertebra until he was nearly eye-to-eye.

In his best English, he asked, "Why are you so hard on me? Isn't it your job to teach, to inspire, not to try and ruin a student's life?"

Ramón saw a flash in the man's eyes, one of surprise.

Rolf seemed to grow smaller. "I still think your friends or someone had more of a hand than you state," he declared, his voice weaker and less certain now.

Ramón couldn't believe it. He had intimidated the man.

"We need several minutes to take this under advisement," Doctor Santiago announced. "Please wait in the hall. I'll come for you when we've decided."

Ramón looked at Rolf as they waited in the hallway. The man looked away. Ramón paced. So did Rolf. Nitza gave Ramón's hand a squeeze. It had gone better than expected, yet the verdict wasn't out yet, the one that could change his future. He thought of the *jíbaro* who kissed his hand, and that calmed him. In fifteen interminable minutes, Doctor Santiago called them back in.

"We've reached a unanimous decision," Doctor Santiago informed. "We vote in favor of Ramón Leon Carrasquillo." He looked at Ramón. "It's obvious how hard you've worked. You can stay, but we expect you to continue to produce work of similar quality. Good luck."

"Thank you!" Ramón exclaimed.

He couldn't say more as he feared he would break down in front of the committee. The man from a backwards country village had defeated the city slicker who spoke four languages. Ramón was elated but for a moment, he wished Elsie were there; how proud she'd be.

Nitza kissed Ramón on each cheek. Carlos embraced him and slapped his back two times. Rolf was the first to leave.

After three beers back in the bar, Ramón experienced his best night's sleep since he arrived in Río Piedras.

CHAPTER 43

A new day dawned. A future full of promise. In the class following Ramón's victory, Professor Rolf handed back the essay with a small B in the top margin. Ramón didn't care that the man failed to include any comments. It was as if the B were embossed in gold.

Rolf neither said a word nor made eye contact when he placed the essay on Ramón's desk. Again, Ramón thought of Marco and Boudreau, and remembered how hard the heinous guard had kicked him in ribs. All three men disliked Ramón for no good reason. They had tried to beat him down, but he had gotten up.

That day in class, Rolf posed the question: "Who said, 'If you can't get to be uncommon through going straight, you'll never get to do it through going crooked?'"

The professor paced. No one's hand went up. The students glanced at one another. Carlos shrugged. A man in the front row looked at the ceiling. Rolf harrumphed, "Well, the answer won't come out of the sky."

Ramón raised his hand, the only student who did. All eyes turned to him. Clearly as possible, he explained, "Joe said that, when Pip told him he lied about Miss Havisham's house. It was in chapter nine. When Joe said that, it showed he was smart." Ramón paused to formulate how to express his conclusion. "Even though he was poor, and common."

Ramón sat up straighter and smiled.

"Fine. Now, moving on . . ." Rolf resumed his pacing.

Ramón left class feeling lighter with an energy that carried him through the rest of the day.

§§§

Before Ramón went to work that night, the bartender pounded on the door of his apartment and shouted, "Carrasquillo—get your ass to the bar. You got a phone call. Hurry up, I'm not running a damn switchboard!"

For a moment, Ramón panicked. Had something happened to Chepa? He ran to the phone.

"Tío, I need your help. Something bad happened to my papá. They can't find him." Leo's small, tremulous voice crackled across the phone line.

"What do you mean they can't find him? Who can't find him? And why isn't he in the hospital?"

"They sent him home, since he was doing better, but he ran off last night, and no one can find him. Capitán is looking—"

Ramón's thoughts spun. Wasn't Leo safe at home, with Chepa?

"Where are you calling from, Leo?" he asked quickly.

"Don Pablo's house." Leo's voice quivered.

Good. A safe place, thought Ramón.

"Leo, you and Doña Chepa can stay there or go to Francisco's house, or Lila and Jorge's, okay? I'm gonna' come help, as soon as I can."

"Okay," Leo managed to say.

Lila came on the line and said, "Leo insisted on calling you himself. Hold on a second."

Ramón heard her shift the mouthpiece away from her chin, then heard her muffled voice in the background saying, "It's gonna be okay, Leo, let me talk to Tío Ramón now. Señora Cadiz will fix you a drink in the kitchen, okay?"

She came back on the line. "It's not good, Ramón. Miraflores came here. Trujillo got sent home from the hospital. We heard he was better, but he got bad again real fast. He ran out of the house, and he was looking for you. Stories are flying around; he wants his money, he wants his son back, but the weather is horrible and no one can find him. The Yabucoa police asked for Capitán's help. They're looking everywhere, but they can't find him!"

Ramón glanced out the window. The rain was hitting the thick glass pane like bullets.

"I'll be there. I'll come help find him. I'm the one he's after," Ramón insisted, his voice rising.

The bartender flashed an irritated look.

"Are you crazy? How are you going to get here in this weather?" Lila said on the phone line, her voice rising, too.

"I'll find him. I don't want him hurting Leo again. I'll find a way to get there."

Not giving Lila a chance to protest, Ramón hung up, then said to the bartender, "I need a ride to Yabucoa, or Maunabo."

Ramón strode toward the bartender's brother in his customary spot at the other end of the bar, where he was a fixture every night, nursing beers or rum. "You have a car—I need to borrow it!" he practically shouted.

The man turned his bloodshot eyes to Ramón. "Yeah, *compadre*, but look out the window, the road's gonna . . ." The man licked his lips, swallowed another slug of beer before he continued. "The road's gonna' be a river soon," he said, his words slurred.

The bartender interrupted, "You can use his car, but it will cost you, in this weather."

"I'll pay whatever you want," Ramón finished.

He looked outside at the teeming downpour. What a night for a search party.

CHAPTER 44

It took over three hours to get to Maunabo in the Ford truck. The engine coughed black smoke out the tail pipe the entire drive there, but one thing was good; the larger tires raised the truck a little higher, allowing it to roll through the mud. Ramón had agreed to pay ten dollars, an exorbitant amount. He talked the bartender into accepting an I.O.U. The man was reluctant, but since Ramón had paid twelve dollars rent up front for three months, the man agreed. If he had known about Ramón's money, he surely would have asked for more, and Ramón would have paid.

He debated where to stop first, in Yabucoa at Trujillo's house, but no, surely the search party had been there. Straight home to Chepa's? Or Don Pablo's where everyone might still be gathered, waiting for news? Then he had a flash. Something told Ramón there was no time for that.

Ramón hunched forward and gripped the steering wheel, forcing his eyes to try and make out the road; as soon as the windshield wipers sloshed the rain away, it pounded the window again. He drove straight past Yabucoa, up and over *La Pica*—thank Dios it hadn't flooded—and toward the sugar cane fields on the outskirts of Maunabo. He pictured the miles of cane fields in his mind; a place someone could get lost, maybe someone who wasn't in his right mind. His vision told him with a force similar to when he bought his ticket. Trujillo was there.

§§§

The headlights of the Ford shone like beacons in the rainy, black night surrounding the cane fields. They lit up a black De Soto, angled and stuck in deep mud at the side of the road with the driver's door flung open. Ramón was right. Trujillo had ended up here, but there was no sign of him. Still, he couldn't have gotten far.

Ramón slowed the truck to a snail's pace as it rocked through the muddy road alongside dripping sugarcane stalks taller than its roof. The entire time, he kept his eyes peeled for the merchant. Then he saw a body lying by the side of the road. Ramón stopped, rushed out of the truck and sprinted to the man.

The headlights illuminated Trujillo's face; he looked unconscious, but then opened his eyes that looked black against the ghostly pallor of his skin. His clothes and face were soaked to the bone and saturated with mud.

"What were you thinking? You could die out here!" Ramón shouted.

"You." Trujillo coughed weakly. "Looking for you."

"I have to get you out of here," Ramón insisted, raising his voice against the rain that fell in sheets and the thumping of the truck's windshield wipers.

"Not you, never," Trujillo whimpered, shuddering with the effort.

"Keep quiet. I'm taking you home. I won't let you die." Ramón's voice was hard.

Trujillo didn't have the strength to protest as Ramón lifted the man from under his shoulders and almost dragged him through the mud to the truck. Trujillo's legs began to give way, but Ramón found the strength to help him into the back seat. By then Ramón was soaked. His shirt was plastered to his back, and his old Converse sneakers were so full with water they sloshed like puddles. An old work shirt lay on the back seat. Ramón wrapped it around Trujillo's chest before he gunned the engine and drove as fast as the road would allow.

§§§

Chepa hovered in the door when Ramón pulled up, clutching her rosary beads. Despite everything Trujillo had done, Ramón knew she prayed for him.

Ramón flung Trujillo's arm over his own shoulders to help the man into the house. The merchant continued to cough and stumble.

"You found him, I knew you would," Chepa declared. "Let's get him to the bedroom, quickly!"

"Get me out of here," Trujillo gasped.

"Stop protesting—save your energy," Chepa scolded.

"Where's Leo?" Ramón demanded.

"At Lila and Jorge's, thank *Dios*," Chepa said.

Ramón struggled with Trujillo, who was so weak Ramón supported all his weight and dragged him one step at a time, the merchant's feet unsteady like a toddler just learning to walk. Ramón was glad Leo didn't have to see his father like this.

Chepa hurried ahead, pulled off the mosquito net and the sheet down on the bed, the same one in which Leo had recuperated. Despite her age, she moved fast.

"By the sound of that wet cough, he may have pneumonia. Let's get him dry," she demanded.

Ramón helped Trujillo to a chair. He collapsed into it. His

head fell forward and his chin snapped into his breastbone. Then silence. The merchant sat utterly still.

Ramón panicked. Was Trujillo dead? Then he started coughing again, but weaker.

"Let's get the clothes off, *now*." Chepa produced dry towels, a long-sleeved night shirt and thick blanket. She and Ramón began to undress the merchant.

"No," he sputtered and clutched Ramón's forearm.

"Stop it. Let us help you," Ramón demanded and pried himself loose.

He and Chepa worked fast. Chepa, as usual, showed no emotion when working but Ramón had to stifle a gasp when he watched the man's chest and bony ribs heave as he tried to breathe, producing a wet, wheezy sound.

They dried him, put the shirt on that fell below his hips and helped him walk three steps to the bed. Trujillo allowed Chepa to place his head carefully on two pillows. She tucked the blanket around him.

"Clean yourself up, Ramón, I can't have two of you sick," she insisted. "He needs to be in a hospital, but it won't happen on a night like this. I'll be right back, with the pleurisy root I prepared. I can get him through tonight."

Chepa hurried out. Ramón turned his back and took off his wet clothes, plastered with mud that had rubbed off Trujillo. He laid them in a corner, toweled off and took dry clothes out of the dresser. The merchant stopped coughing but Ramón heard his labored breathing, reminding him of the day he almost strangled the man to death. Ramón shuddered, although not from the cold in his bones. He pulled on his pants, his back turned to the merchant. As he buttoned his shirt, he heard Trujillo speak. Ramón turned.

"Why are you helping me?" The merchant's voice was hoarse.

"Because harboring anger is poisonous."

Trujillo let out another spasm of coughs.

When the man stopped coughing, Ramón said, "I have this ability. Sometimes it's stronger than others, but I can sense things, see things. I saw that number that day, and it was your number. Strangely, it bound us together. And tonight, I had that sensation again and it brought me to you."

The oil lamp on the bed table cast a dim yellow light, making Trujillo's pale face look even gaunter, and his temples more hollow. His eye sockets were deeper than Ramón remembered. The man was wasting away.

"Thank you," Trujillo said, his voice thickened.

"Like my mother said, save your strength. We'll get you through the night. I'll take you to the Yabucoa clinic tomorrow, or the hospital in San Juan."

"Yes," he rasped. Then his face contorted in pain, as if an arrow pierced his head.

"What is it? What can I get you?" Ramón asked urgently.

"Nothing. You've done so much," he said, his voice weaker now.

Right before Trujillo turned his head away, Ramón locked eyes with the man, and saw a look beyond rage, one of powerlessness, even shame.

§§§

After consuming Chepa's pleurisy root tea, Trujillo slept. Chepa and Ramón alternately applied tinctures of pleurisy root and echinacea to his chest. Twice during the night, Ramón turned him on his side while Chepa cupped her palms and held her fingers together to perform a percussion treatment on the backs of his ribs. Ramón was amazed; despite her arthritis, Chepa's blows were firm but gentle, her hands moving in an unbroken rhythm. Their patient remained asleep, his breathing more regular.

"At first light, take him to Yabucoa. They'll stabilize him before they transport him back to the hospital. You're exhausted, Ramón, but I know that look, too tired to fall asleep. I'm making valerian tea. We'll both get a few hours rest before you have to leave. I'll pray for a safe journey."

"Me too, Mamá," Ramón said.

CHAPTER 45

The next day dawned brilliant. The storm had blown away the clouds, leaving the scent of damp earth and a sky of endless blue.

Trujillo's condition did not mirror the weather. He looked like death was only hours away, feverish and clammy, his eyes glossed over with a film of blue. He was barely awake, unable to sit up or speak.

"He's worse off than I thought," Chepa cautioned. "He needs an ambulance. We're leaving it in the hands of the doctors and nurses, and God."

She rushed to Don Pablo's. First she called the hospital in San Juan, and then called Francisco to help.

Ramón and Chepa tried to save the man, but what if he died? Ramón hated that Leo may lose his father, despite what the man did, that his death would be senseless. The night before, Ramón had missed work, had fled San Juan without even contacting Doctor Cerna, who trusted and respected him. Ramón imagined the patients who desperately lined up in the clinic. Without Ramón's extra help, many of them would go without treatment. What must the dentist be thinking?

And today Ramón would miss his classes. Would Professor Rolf somehow take it out on him? Then Ramón chastised himself for thinking of something that seemed trivial when a man hovered near death, a death Ramón felt indirectly responsible for.

He felt an even deeper heartache, for when he stepped outside to wait for the ambulance, the visibility was so clear that he could see Vieques Island, only thirteen kilometers away, knowing Elsie was there. How he wanted to hold her at this moment, to hear her say everything would somehow turn out all right.

Chepa had given Trujillo more pleurisy root and valerian leaves seeped as tea to help him sleep. The whole time she treated him, he seemed oblivious to her presence.

It would take an hour for help to arrive, an interminable time to wait.

§§§

The ambulance raced into town with the red light on its roof blaring its arrival. Two medics in crisp white uniforms sprinted inside, and inserted a hose into Trujillo's nostrils connected to an oxygen tank before they transferred him onto a stretcher. Such a vehicle, pure white with a large red cross painted on each of the tall side doors, had never been seen in Maunabo. By the time they carried the merchant outside with Ramón and Francisco's help, a small crowd had gathered to ogle. They spoke to one another in hurried, hushed tones as the medics loaded Trujillo in the rear of the ambulance.

Don Pablo rushed over to Ramón with Señora Lepe close on his heels.

"I phoned Capitán Miraflores to call the search off," the don said. "You've done a remarkable thing, Ramón, to bring him here."

"Yeah," Francisco interrupted, "my brother saved that bastard's life."

"Mamá was the one who did the hard work," Ramón said.

Francisco quickly added, "If he was left out there last night, he never would have made it, not that he'll ever admit it."

"Hush!" Chepa scolded. "That man is only steps away from

death's door—do not speak of him that way!"

"What happened, how did you find him, Ramón?" Señora Lepe pleaded to hear the story, her eyes as big as mango pits.

"I got lucky. I guessed where his car would get stuck. I'm exhausted, I don't want to talk about it any more," Ramón said, then felt a pang of guilt for the sharpness in his voice. He turned toward the crowd and said, "Please, all of you, pray for the man."

The look on his face silenced them as the ambulance sped away.

CHAPTER 46

Ramón dreaded going back to Advanced English Literature class. In his course syllabus, Rolf wrote that attendance was of utmost importance and students must inform him when they would be absent. Ramón imagined Rolf's eyes boring into him as he tried to explain why he missed class. Would the explanation that he had a family emergency suffice? Leo was family, after all, and that was why Ramón fled to find Trujillo as he did.

At least Ramón had comfort in the knowledge that Leo was safe and healthy. Before he drove back to Río Piedras in the truck, Ramón had stopped at Lila and Jorge's. He told Leo the bare minimum: his father had been found, and he was back in the hospital in San Juan, where the doctors there would do all they could to make him well. The small boy nodded, and Ramón could see the tumult of emotions cross his face. Leo was worried about his father, but feared him as well, then appeared relieved as he said, "I hope he gets well fast, so he can be the papá he used to be. He was trying his best." Once again, Ramón was astonished at both Leo's bravery and empathy.

§§§

Ramón shuffled into class. Right away he noticed the energy in the class was different. Professor Rolf was absent from his vigil in the front of the room and the class buzzed with conversation and whispers, in Spanish!

Carlos ran over and sputtered, "Can you believe what happened?"

"What's going on?" Ramón asked.

"Rolf's gone. He's a Nazi, can you imagine? He won't be teaching anymore," Carlos blurted. "And he's under investigation. The story flying around is he lied about his brother. He told the school the guy was a poor refugee, who he was trying to get out of Germany, to come here. But guess what?"

"Nothing you tell me about that man would surprise me," Ramón said as his heart beat faster. Whatever else Carlos had to say wouldn't be good.

"The brother was no refugee—he was a guard at a concentration camp, and people are saying that Rolf did a lot of Nazi propaganda writing before he came here, maybe even wrote plans for starting those horrible camps. Can you believe it?"

"Yes." Ramón felt sick. He remembered the photos of the concentration camp victims. To imagine Rolf and his brother had a hand in that.

"The disciplinary committee checked his background after our meeting! When Rolf turned in some report about you, they suspected him of something after they read it. It must have been pretty bad. Everyone's talking about it. Can you believe it?" Carlos repeated.

Ramón guessed Carlos was thrilled that he, too, had a hand in catching the duplicitous Rolf.

Carlos quickly added, "My parents are sick about this. I told them what happened and they want to meet you, the guy who stood up to Rolf. Who'd have thought this is the way things would turn out?"

For a moment, Ramón was too stunned to speak, even forgot Carlos was standing next to him as he processed the news. He hated his literature class, even hated Rolf, and wished that he and he and the man had never met. Then it dawned on him. God had put him in Rolf's path for a reason: to be a conduit to the discovery of the man's horrific past, perhaps even to keep him from trying to ruin another student.

"Well, can you believe it?" Carlos continued to probe.

"Actually, I can. And you know something? I'm glad I got into this class, and that things worked out the way they did."

"No kidding, really?"

"Yes, really," Ramón confirmed. "Everything about Rolf accusing me was awful, but my English got a whole lot better. And I think there's a reason why I met the man, so, indirectly, I could help expose who he really was."

Ramón paused. He could tell by the contemplative look on Carlos's face and the way he nodded his head slightly that he was taking in the information as well.

"Carlos, thanks for everything," Ramón emphasized. "I don't know if I could have done that essay and faced Rolf without you. You helped expose him, too by helping me. And you know what? I think there's another important reason why we met, but I just haven't figured it out yet."

CHAPTER 47

Ramón wanted to hug the Western Union delivery man who showed up at his apartment door, but by the time he read and processed the news, the man was gone.

Days after the exposure of Professor Rolf, Ramón received a telegram:

RAFAEL HOME LAST NIGHT. ISIDRO IN PONCE NOV 9. MAMA PLANNING CELEBRATION. COME HOME SOON AS POSSIBLE. SAFE TRAVEL.

LILA

Rafael was home, and Isidro would be home in two days! The news was a blessing on the heels of all that had happened. His brothers had done it, made it through the war. They were among the lucky who survived. Ramón could hardly wait to embrace them, their bodies still whole. He prayed their souls were unscathed as well.

§§§

Without delay, Ramón arranged to be gone, this time for several days. Advanced Literature was on hold until a replacement could be found, and Ramón's other professors were supportive in light of the reason for his impending absence; they were used to students and staff missing classes to welcome their loved ones home.

Doctor Cerna accepted Ramón's request for a few nights off with the same civility and calmness that had allowed him to withstand the never ending demands of his clinic for years.

"We'll miss you, but you must be home at this time!" Doctor Cerna said, the joy genuine on his face. "Your family is blessed to be together again."

There was one more commitment Ramón needed to fulfill before he left, to see about Trujillo.

§§§

The nurse at the front desk sat like a sentry with her tall starched cap atop her shoulder-length black hair.

"I'm here to see Señor Trujillo," Ramón said, keeping his voice even with the emotions bombarding his brain.

How would Trujillo look? What would Ramón say to him after all they'd been through? What would the merchant say?

Her eyes scanned the list of names on the open ledger before her. After a minute, she shook her head to say, "He's in the consumption ward. No visitors."

Consumption. Tuberculosis. That wasn't good at all. Worse than Chepa's thoughts the man may have pneumonia. A chill ran down Ramón's spine.

"Can you find out how he is?" Ramón asked.

"Are you family?" Her tone was crisp.

"Ahh, no . . ." How could Ramón ever begin to explain who he was, the relationship between him and Trujillo?

"I can try and find the doctor. Who should I say is asking?" she said.

"A friend of the family. I'm from the village next to his. I know his son very well."

She cast him a suspicious glance.

Ramón thought she would tell him to leave. "Please, señora. My mother is the *curandera* who treated him before he came in here," he said, his tone urgent.

"Fine. Wait here," she quipped, then strode behind a locked door.

Ramón paced the small waiting room, which smelled of polish and disinfectant. At least the place was clean. The clock on the wall ticked. Five minutes passed, yet it seemed like fifty before she returned and resumed her position behind the desk.

"He's in quarantine in a ward for patients who have nervous disorders of the mind as well. He'll be here for at least a month or two. The doctor said his chances are fifty-fifty." She might as well be reciting the weather report.

"Thank you for telling me," Ramón said, his voice tight with the ache at the back of his throat.

The man had done some horrible things, yet the thought of his death from consumption and a mental disorder still made Ramón feel as if all the air were punched out of his stomach. If Ramón hadn't won that day, hadn't bought that ticket, would the merchant be lying in that bed right now? And Leo never would have been harmed.

Please God, he prayed silently. *Show mercy and give this man another chance. You gave me a miracle, bestowed Your love upon me. If You can do the same for him, from now on, I promise: for every person I come into contact with, I will give them all the love, kindness and compassion I can muster, without any thought of a reward. Please.*

§§§

As he took the half day's journey home on the *públicos*, the events of the past days filled Ramón's mind. He was thrilled to soon reunite with Isidro and Rafael, yet his excitement was marred by Rolf's exposure and Trujillo's prognosis. It troubled Ramón and made him sad at the same time. He was another one of Rolf's victims yet the others, those at the concentration camps, had been much worse off. And what would Ramón tell Leo of his father? What if Trujillo died? Ramón had to believe it wasn't completely over between him and the merchant; they still may come to some resolution, to allow his prayer to come to fruition. He thought again of Yin and Yang, the opposing forces of life, how joy and sorrow exist side-by-side.

When Ramón finally stepped off the last *público* in the Maunabo plaza, Leo threw himself into his arms to tell Ramón, "Tío, you're home! You'd be so proud of me. I'm doing great in school."

Leo pushed his shoulders back and jutted out his chin, the scar on his left cheekbone even more faded and boasted, "I raised my hand and answered a question in class. It was really hard, too, about the Magna Carta."

"Good for you, Leo." Ramón's mood couldn't help but be buoyed by Leo's exuberance.

"And guess what else? The teacher says I remind him of you! He says I improved so much that I can be whatever I want. I want to be a doctor, and do all that schooling, just like you," Leo said with new confidence.

Ramón was overcome with emotion. "You'll be a great doctor," he said with conviction. After all the boy had been through, Leo was back to his old self, if not better, with an uncanny knack for saying

279

the right thing at the right time.

Ramón experienced a flash of a vision: Leo in the future as a tall, handsome young man with angular features. Wearing a white lab coat, this older version of Leo counseled an elderly woman, telling her how the surgery he was about to perform would cure her.

Ramón knew that Leo would achieve everything he wanted, and warmth radiated through Ramón's entire body with the thought that his and the boy's lives were so intertwined.

Then he remembered his silent prayer for Trujillo. Would the man live to witness his son's endeavors? Ramón shivered. He dared not allow his mind to see into the merchant's future.

CHAPTER 48

On November 9, 1945, Ramón and Lila began their two hour trip to Ponce, to meet the surviving soldiers of Puerto Rico's famous 65th infantry, Isidro amongst them. Their tour of duty began in 1942, and took them to Panama, North Africa, Casablanca, Germany, Italy and the Maritime Alps. On October 27, they sailed from France for the last leg of their trip. Their men were coming home.

Chepa, Esperanza, and the rest of the family stayed home to prepare for the celebration. Doña Chepa said a prayer of thanks for sending both her sons home as she sprinkled *adobo* seasonings— oregano, peppercorns, garlic and salt—over a pig to prepare it for the barbeque. The kitchen chairs were pushed aside to accommodate the crowd, and the chickens and goats were herded from their courtyard into a neighbor's to make room for dancing.

As Ramón drove his Buick within several miles of the city center, the normally lightly traveled road became clogged with traffic. The entire island had men considered heroes to welcome home.

"This is so exciting, Ramón," Lila exclaimed and clapped. "First Rafie, now Isidro. I can't wait to see him, it's been three long years—what a happy day!"

"We're truly blessed, having our brothers back," Ramón agreed, then with thickness in his voice he could barely contain, he added, "Safe and home."

After slowly rolling along with the multitude of cars, they finally neared the center of Ponce and the *Plaza de Las Delicias*. Ramón found a parking spot several blocks away. He and Lila

281

continued toward the plaza on foot in the middle of a throng of well-wishers. Mambo blared from roadside bars. Patrons spilled out into the streets happy, drunk, cavorting and swirling their hips to the sounds of drumbeats. Bartenders shouted, "Free Drinks for all. This is a day to celebrate!"

Ramón and Lila arrived at the plaza and waited with the boisterous crowd near the Cathedral of *Our Lady of Guadalupe*. Four buses rumbled into view. A hush came over the crowd. Lila grabbed Ramón's hand and squeezed it as they stood on tip toes to look over people's heads and the waving of Puerto Rican flags.

The buses rolled to a stop, the crowd cheered, and the first soldiers stepped out. Flowers and confetti flew into the air. Women held bouquets of plumeria that filled the plaza with the sweet scent of orange blossoms, mixing with the diesel fumes of the buses.

After five minutes, Lila pointed and pulled Ramón to the front of the crowd. "There he is! I see him!" she shouted.

Isidro's face brightened when he spotted his siblings. He dropped his duffle bag and ran forward to embrace them. The three hugged for minutes amidst the rest of the families shouting and crying. Joyous pandemonium reigned.

Isidro kissed Lila two times on each cheek and turned to Ramón. He placed his hands on Ramón's shoulders and held his little brother at arms' length.

Ramón returned his gaze in awe. Somehow he thought seeing Rafie first and breaking down would have prepared him for seeing Isidro, but it didn't. Ramón was near to tears all over again.

Isidro was twenty-six, only six years older than Ramón, but his eyes were more soulful than before; Ramón imagined he had witnessed things no young man should see. Yet Ramón had never seen his brother look as handsome as his did on that day, straight shouldered in his crisply pressed uniform with its glittering brass buttons.

"Is Rafie home?" Isidro's eyebrows drew together, his shoulders stiffened.

"For a week now, home safe from Panama, waiting for you. He's as good as expected," Ramón assured.

Isidro let out a big breath and his shoulders visibly relaxed. "And you, little brother, you look different. Winning that lottery, it made you grow up. You can't imagine how I felt when your news reached me. Even the censors must have liked it, because they didn't use their razor blades on a single word of your letter!"

Isidro's comment, *it made you grow up*, if only he knew . . . For a moment, Ramón couldn't speak.

"It's amazing, isn't it?" Ramón managed to say, his voice tight.

Isidro nodded. "It kept us going, the guys and me. When times were dark, we talked about you, the richest kid in Maunabo."

The richest kid in Maunabo. Ramón felt rich beyond money at that moment. Moisture gathered in his eyes, and held his breath to keep from crying. Conversations and people's squeals of joy filtered in around him.

"Let's go, I have something to show you," Ramón shouted above the noise of the crowd.

Isidro retrieved his duffle bag and the three made their way out of the plaza. Isidro whistled when he saw Ramón's Buick and claimed, "Hey little brother, that's a beauty."

Ramón laughed. "Yeah, it's the biggest thing I bought, foolhardy on my part, but it's come in handy. I gave two hundred dollars to everyone in our family, except Mamá, who refused. She insisted I save it for college. I put yours and Rafael's into bank accounts, waiting for you to come home."

Ramón had so much more to tell his big brother, but that could wait. This was a time for joy.

"No kidding. *¡Dios mío!* Thanks, little brother, I knew you were born under a lucky star. How about I drive this baby home?"

"Well . . . sure, but when did you learn to drive?"

"Oh, I had lots of practice driving jeeps in the army. You'll see, I'm a good driver."

"I haven't felt this good since the day I won the jackpot. I love you, my brother," Ramón declared, his eyes dry but voice still quivery. "It's your lucky day, too. Welcome home . . . at last."

Ramón grabbed Isidro's duffle bag, threw it in the trunk and tossed the keys to his brother.

The three passengers traveled east on the seaside road to Maunabo. Ramón and Isidro rolled down the windows and placed their elbows on the door frame. Ramón admired Isidro's driving skills and relaxed.

Isidro pointed out the window at a large Puerto Rican hibiscus tree and said, "Look, the Roses of Althea. I smelled them once in a dream, so real I thought I was home. Then I woke to that damn smell of the foxhole—dirt and men who couldn't bathe for days or weeks. But it was more than that, it was smell of fear . . . I've been waiting for this for a long time. It's good to be home."

The sun began to set over the Caribbean. Ramón admired the pink and red hues spreading over the sea, reminding him of the sangria that had flowed in the bars in Ponce.

Lila smiled and exclaimed, "Look, Isidro, I bet you haven't seen a sunset like that since you left. God ordered it—just for your homecoming!"

When they arrived home, Chepa ran from the house as fast

as her arthritic knees would carry her to throw her arms around Isidro. Her tears had barely dried since seeing Rafael. After Isidro was surrounded by the rest of his family, the first partiers began to trickle in. Villagers came in and out all night to embrace Rafael and Isidro, and to praise the saints for sending the two León men home alive, and to share Chepa's culinary delights.

After the last guests left and the platters were cleared, Ramón and Isidro retired to the small bedroom they shared as children. Leo was fast asleep on his cot, his breath coming and going in slow, even waves. They had told him his father was getting better in the hospital and Leo seemed at peace. And the boy had a gift; he could sleep through anything, including their parties.

Isidro closed the door firmly, sat on the edge of his cot and whispered, "Ramón, I have something to show you, but please, don't tell a soul, especially Mamá. She would never approve, and I don't want her to become upset, especially today, of all days."

Ramón, lying on his cot, propped himself up on his elbow to ask, "What is it? You're making me nervous."

Isidro reached under his mattress. He removed a German handgun, a Luger.

Ramón gasped. "*Dios*, it's not loaded, is it?" He kept his voice low, just in case it would wake Leo.

"Of course not. You know how strongly Mamá feels about guns and violence."

"Where did you get it? Did you get if off a German? Did you kill him?"

Isidro didn't answer. Emotions flitted across his face, and he made a sign of the cross.

"What are you going to do with it?" Ramón asked.

"I don't know. Maybe I never should have brought it home."

"Put it back under the mattress, it makes me nervous," Ramón pleaded. "Isidro, I have a confession to make."

"What can you say that's as bad as what I went through?"

Ramón began his story. "I got drafted last year. When I went to the physical at Fort Buchanan, they found snail fever. Who knows how long I had it? The doctor said people can take a while to show symptoms, but if it goes untreated, the bug can get into your brain and cause all kinds of problems, even death."

"What happened?" Isidro looked shocked.

"They declared me 4F. I got the medicine, Fuadin, from Señor García, the pharmacist who tried to save Papá. It made me sick as hell, but after I felt better, I went to a lab in San Juan and they said I was cured. Part of me wanted to report the cure to the army, somehow reverse the 4F, but I didn't."

Ramón paused, lowered his eyes before he continued, "I've had to live with myself for that, but somehow I knew that if I went to war, I wouldn't come back. I think it was like my other premonition, about the number, and you know what happened after that one. But, *Dios*, after I won that lottery, things happened that you could hardly imagine."

All of the events of the prior months spilled out. Ramón glanced over to check that Leo still slumbered, and left nothing out, the attack on Trujillo, the night in jail, how Leo came to the house, and what happened with Rolf. Even though it pained him, he divulged how things ended with Elsie.

Isidro remained mostly quiet during the story save a few quiet gasps, and then whispered, "You went through a kind of war yourself, didn't you?" He shook his head as he clucked his tongue, like Chepa often did. "But think about it—in spite of everything, you were lucky, *two times,* when you won and then got the 4F. I think God was showing us you're meant for something else. Plus, I wouldn't have wanted you to be in that hell. I'll never forget the noise, the scream of the shells overhead, the planes' engines that almost made you deaf, the awful pop-pop of machine guns, the wounded and dying men, *Dios*, the moans." Isidro stopped speaking for a moment.

"And some of the guys treated us like shit for speaking Spanish. They said we weren't real Americans, called us 'American Joes' and gave us the crappiest jobs, like burying bodies. I heard something even worse. On San Jose Island, our guys were part of these experiments, sprayed with mustard gas to see if they reacted differently than the other soldiers."

"*Dios mío*, I can't believe it. How can the country we're fighting for do that to us? We're just as American as they are," Ramón insisted.

"I suppose the US Army thinks we're not as smart as other guys. But you can prove them wrong, Ramón. You can go to college and show them what a Puerto Rican's made of when you become a dentist, like you always talked about. You're smarter than anyone I know. I remember how you used to read all those books as a kid when the rest of us were out catching lizards to see who could dangle the little bastards the longest off our earlobes." Isidro grinned.

Ramón was lost for a moment in a memory. As a child, he would stay after class in the one-room schoolhouse to read what few books were salvaged from *Huracán San Felipe* and beg the teacher to tell him stories about pioneers like Doctor Bailey Ashford, the first doctor to treat parasites and anemia in Puerto Rico, saving thousands from death. Ramón never tired of hearing the tales of such revolutionary healers.

Isidro became pensive. "It's God's plan for you, to be healer like Mamá, just like He had a plan for me. He made sure I got home."

He rested his hand on Ramón's shoulder.

Too overwhelmed to reply, Ramón simply nodded.

CHAPTER 49

After Isidro's proclamation, Ramón returned to Río Piedras with renewed purpose. The first place he went was the hospital. The same nurse nodded at him in recognition after he inquired about Trujillo. She reported back in the same monotone voice but with news that lifted Ramón's spirit: "He's improved. The doctor reports his chances of survival are sixty or seventy percent. He may return home by the new year."

Ramón had the nerve to ask if he could visit, and the nurse's response was more sober; all visitors had to wear masks and the rules were family only, and that only included Señora Trujillo.

Still, it was an improvement.

Ramón ran to the bar. The bartender glared but agreed to one call for twenty cents, so Ramón called Don Pablo who ran to get Leo.

When Leo picked up the phone, Ramón reported, "I've been to the hospital. Your father's much better; he may even be home after the New Year. Your mamá visits every day."

Leo accepted the news with his customary quiet resignation. "That's good. Thanks for telling me, Tío."

§§§

In his literature class, it was as if a switch went off in his brain. All the work Ramón did on his essay propelled him to a higher level of English. Without the brooding, overbearing presence of Professor Rolf, Ramón began to relax, and surprisingly, began to enjoy *Great Expectations*. He felt sorry for Pip, who seemed unemotional when describing his work, whereas work was the reason Ramón got up every morning.

He couldn't help compare the snobbish Estella to Elsie, especially on that last awful day he and Elsie were together. Yet Estella changed, and she and Pip rekindled; might the same happen for him and Elsie? Ramón remembered the good times they shared and still missed her with a hurt so profound he could barely breathe, especially when he saw a couple together on the street, or when he observed the tender moments between Nitza and Chico as they sat together at the kitchen table, heads bent close, writing a letter or laughing.

Part of him was happy, yet he still carried around the weight of his sadness from missing Elsie, and it was his work that buffered his heartache. Ramón remembered his prayer, his promise to God that day in the hospital; he treated each patient, no matter how dirty, no matter how poor, as if he or she were royalty.

When Ramón finished reading the novel, he actually missed Pip. Like Ramón, Dickens's hero was a poor boy who made it big. But sadly, Pip had been ashamed of his past. In the end, Pip realized that the friends who helped him and loved him were golden and that fortune does not equate to happiness. It was a brilliant story, and Ramón couldn't help but see the parallels with his own life.

The new literature professor had retired but returned to work due to the lack of teachers during the war. Professor Guadalupe loved spare, tight prose and in particular, Ernest Hemingway. He let the students choose which novel they'd like to analyze. The choices were: *The Sun Also Rises* or *A Farewell to Arms*.

He was tired of war, as was the rest of the world, and still harbored guilt over not serving, so he didn't choose *A Farewell to*

Arms. The logical choice was *The Sun Also Rises.* He had to admit, it was appealing as it was the shorter of the two and part of it took place in Spain in the bull fighting ring.

He expected to enjoy it but when he read about Lady Brett Ashley he found his thoughts drifting to Elsie. Even though he was shocked by Brett's behavior, might Elsie show even a fraction of Brett's bravado and run off with him? Would he ever read something and not think of her? The best character of the story was Jake Barnes, a working man who seemed to be searching for integrity in a morally crazy world.

Ramón also had to admit: reading this novel, as painful as the memories that it dredged up were, had only improved his English more for the one essay his future depended on, the essay for MSC.

Ramón continued to study and work at the free clinic. He went to the hospital every Monday afternoon at three o'clock to inquire about Trujillo. Bit by bit, the merchant improved. Surely Ramón's prayer, his promise, had helped. He sent a letter to Leo, telling him his father was even better, to share with Chepa.

Ramón kept as frantic a schedule, but by the first of December, was thrilled that his English had improved to the point where he received "B's" and even one "A-" on his essays. Hemingway was a far cry easier to read than Dickens, whose prose went on so long Ramón often wondered if he'd ever stop.

And then an amazing thing happened: Ramón had his first dream in English. Of course, it starred Elsie who remained by his side, helping him run his own dental office. Was it even more of a sign that he and Elsie might have a chance together, even after all these months?

One thing he did know. His dream told him he was ready to tackle the MSC essay. The college required applicants to answer one of two questions. Ramón had tucked them away in his desk drawer months earlier:

1. Describe an experience, passion, or characteristic that illustrates what you would contribute to the MSC community and how this will add to the overall richness of campus life.

2. Describe a significant experience from the past two years which required you to interact with others outside of your own social or cultural group and how you resolved it.

The obvious choice was the second question. A significant experience—how about a life-altering experience? He'd have to describe the last year in five-hundred words or less. Two pages to change his life, his destiny.

CHAPTER 50

Ramón studied for finals each available minute and carried his writing tablet everywhere. Anytime a thought struck him about his college essay, he jotted it down and began his first drafts. Doctor Cerna gave him a week off to write and study. It paid off when he received his final grades:

Algebra II: B

History of Civilization: B

Inorganic Chemistry: A-

Advanced English Literature: C

A "C!" It wasn't close to the grades he was accustomed to, but Ramón would take it. The time for a celebration was long overdue. Carlos and he blended in with the rest of the students at one of the popular college bars where the drinks flowed freely. After three beers and only one small pork empanada, Ramón felt a lightness he hadn't experienced in months. He danced with a young coed with red ruby lips and brunette hair clipped short into a page boy, which she insisted was all the rage.

As they swayed and gyrated to the live band and the sounds of percussion and mambo, all his problems seemed to float away; the essay, Señor Trujillo's downfall, even Elsie. Why hadn't he allowed himself to have a little fun before now? He had been out with Carlos once months before, but all night, worried he should have used the time to study. Yet what a night this was!

After the woman pecked his cheek good-bye to run off and powder her nose, Carlos and Ramón stumbled to the bar in front of his apartment for more beers.

"It's about time you came out for a little fun, *compadre*. I've never seen you with such a big grin on your face. You usually look like you swallowed a lizard!" Carlos said and laughed as they sat at the bar for their fourth, or was it their fifth beer? A couple hours earlier, they had stopped counting.

"You're right, why haven't I done this before? What was it you said I swallowed?" Ramón laughed and threw his arm around Carlos' shoulder.

"A *largatito!*" Carlos chortled.

"No kidding! My cousin Albertito used to hang those off his ears! Hey, speaking of Albertito, that kid had the thickest hair I've ever seen. Mine's gotten so thin, maybe if we shave it off, it'll grow back twice as thick. Cheers to Albertito and his hair!" Ramón realized he was shouting and some of the older *jíbaros* glared at him and Carlos.

The two boisterous college boys left the bar and practically fell through the door of Ramón's apartment. Nitza must have heard them because she came out of her bedroom in housecoat and slippers.

"It looks like you two have been out cavorting after finals. I'm glad you boys made it back safely, but keep your voices down. You'll wake Chico," she scolded.

"Pardon us, fine lady," Carlos nearly shouted. "Ramón wants to shave his head. He wants his hair to grow out thicker. Ha!" He grabbed his side, bending over to stifle his chortle.

"Shhh," she chastised. "Are you *loco*, Ramón?"

"Oh no. My cousin had a thick head of hair. I don't know what happened to me." Ramón shrugged and laughed.

"Hey, I bet there's a pair of scissors in the kitchen. I'll give it a try." Carlos giggled.

"*Dios*, in the state you're both in, I don't want either of you handling anything sharp. I'll do it for you, Ramón. At least I won't cut off anything other than your hair!" Nitza shook her head, crowned with a set of pink rollers, and went to get her clippers.

§§§

Ramón woke the following morning shocked to see his nearly bald head in the mirror. He grinned as he ran his hand over his newly shaved scalp. The tiny bristles scratched it pleasantly. He couldn't stop a huge smile from breaking across his face. He didn't look half bad, with none of the lumps he saw on some men who shaved their heads.

That night at the clinic was his last. The patients, Doctor Cerna, and the other assistant all teased Ramón for his "new look." In spite of their good natured ribbing, Ramón was touched at how the patients bid him farewell. They gathered together in the reception room and chipped in five or ten cents each for his college fees to become a dentist. Some of them gave speeches, telling how Ramón helped them and in many cases, tears were shed. One of the patients—the *jíbaro* who'd held Ramón's hand and insisted on calling him doctor—tried to speak and froze. Unable to go on, he shouted, "Three cheers for Ramón!" after which everyone laughed and joined in.

Later that evening, Ramón was so inspired by his patients, all poor people who obviously didn't know his past and had sacrificed for him, that he wrote the final draft of his essay. They had all toasted him, "A new look for a new life."

He prayed it would be a new life in Michigan.

CHAPTER 51

My name is Ramón León Carrasquillo. I am a 20 year old Puerto Rican American. The past year has been the best and worst of my life.

On November 17, 1944, I had a vision that changed my future. I saw a number in the sky. It burned so bright I knew it was something remarkable so for the first time in my life, I bought a full sheet of tickets in the Puerto Rican lottery with all my savings.

I won. It was a miracle, a sign from God, the chance to keep a promise I made years before to a man who was like a father to me, the man my village called "humanitario."

Doctor Roberts was the dentist who saved me when I was eight from the worst infection in my life. After that, I worked with him as a dental assistant for four years in his shack in the jungle. We treated villagers for nothing but a chicken or a coconut, improving their looks and lives. Everyone loved him and so did I. He had a dream of opening a clinic to help even more people, but he got sick and his son took him back to New York. I promised him on his deathbed that when I grew up, I would carry his vision, our vision, through.

My childhood passed happy and I watched my family shape their futures, wondering when my opportunity would come. I studied hard in high school, and graduated third in my class, but what's a poor village boy to do? My brothers are honest, hardworking merchants, but none ever finished high school. I bided my time, helping my mother in her textile store, until I saw the number.

My number was the same a rich merchant had played for years until that day. He was bent on revenge. He stalked me and my girlfriend and attacked my mother. He tried to ruin my family's business. In a fit of anger, I attacked him back and spent a night in jail. Once released, I renewed my honor and that of my family. The man became so despondent he beat his son badly and my mother and I nursed him back to health. I gained a wonderful friend in that boy, but I lost my girlfriend and true love.

I've done things I'm not proud of, but I've made it right. I learned English and improved so much I had to defend myself against a false accusation of cheating. I won that too. I did it not only for me, but for my village, to fulfill the promise I made to them, my mother, the memory of my father, and to my mentor.

If you admit me to your college, I promise to you and God, it won't be in vain. This is my life's purpose. This is my dream, to become a dentist for my people. I'll do whatever it takes to see it through. Thank you.

Four-hundred-and-ninety-eight words. Ramón wrote, corrected, rewrote and counted the words a hundred times to make sure he didn't go over the limit. Nothing was left to chance.

On the night before leaving Río Piedras to go home, Ramón gathered with Nitza and Carlos around their kitchen table to have them approve the final copy. He believed it adequate, but would rewrite it another hundred times as needed.

"I have to get in," he told his friends, "because if I don't, all this work will be worth nothing."

He held his breath as Nitza read. Her eyes filled with moisture as she chimed, "I helped you with part of this but I had no idea, it's wonderful. I feel honored to know you, to help you. I can't see why that school wouldn't want you after reading this. And I'm going to miss you!"

Carlos read it and had a similar reaction: "She's right, but Ramón, I never knew all this about you—why didn't you tell me?"

Ramón shrugged and answered, "I came here because no one knew what happened to me. I wanted people to like me, for me! You and Nitza are great friends, I feel blessed. My mother says that it's important to not to talk about yourself but to share in other's glory and if you do something nice, you don't have to tell anyone, just revel in the joy of giving. I guess that's why I didn't tell you all that stuff."

"You're quite a guy, Ramón. I'll miss you, too," Carlos said.

Ramón felt a bubble burst inside his chest, and then a waterfall—the essay was okay, even better than okay. He looked around the table. His friends wore looks of pure joy on their faces, and it was for him. He hadn't become close to many people since he moved to the city aside from his patients and their families, and other than Doctor Cerna, Carlos and Nitza were his only friends, but they were golden.

Then an idea struck him. Ramón saw the grin on Carlos's face, the unmitigated happiness, and he thought of Esperanza. They were two of the same. He had a vision of them sharing their lives, forging their futures.

"Hey Carlos, I knew there was another reason why we met. As soon as you can, come to Maunabo," Ramón insisted. "There's someone you have to meet."

Ramón hadn't felt this happy since long before Elsie left, since Rafie and Isidro came home.

CHAPTER 52

"It's time for Leo to go home. Señor Trujillo is back," Chepa remarked.

As usual, Chepa spoke in a tone that left little room for argument, but Ramón detected a hint of sadness in the slower way she moved about her kitchen, her domain. She made a pot of chamomile tea and sat at the kitchen table with Ramón and Lila and her shoulders fell.

The only sound was the cooling and popping of the charcoal of the *fogón*. Leo was asleep in the room he shared with Ramón.

Ramón heard the words he feared but one day knew would come. He prayed for Trujillo to recover, and Leo returning to his family was the consequence. Still, the news sent a dull and heavy ache to his heart.

Ramón recalled the last time he went to the hospital.

The same nurse had been there, and said, "I know you're not family, but you've been coming here for what, a month or more? I suppose I could bend the rules. We've done all we can for him here, and he's not contagious any more. Do you want to see him before he goes home in a few days?"

Her face had softened, showing a glimmer of compassion.

Ramón shook his head. On some level, he knew it wasn't time. If the man was finally getting better, finally feeling some peace, Ramón dared not risk upsetting that peace.

"No, señora," Ramón told her, "But thank you, just hearing he's better is enough for me right now."

§§§

Ramón felt an enormous lift after finishing his essay, after sealing the envelope and blessing it three times before sending it off to Michigan, and after his final night at the clinic. Now, he felt a great weariness. Yet now, he didn't have his work as an escape.

"I missed all of you in the last few months, especially during that awful mess with my professor," he told Chepa. "I couldn't wait to come home, to spend more time with Leo, but I have to admit, it's time to let him go."

Chepa nodded. "Padre Pérez came to see me again. He assured me Trujillo has paid for what he did. That man is sick over what he's done; he begged for forgiveness, and is asking for Leo and his brother, who is coming home from Miami. The man's crippled by rheumatism, and he needs to be comfortable—he doesn't have much time left." She made a sign of the cross. "Trujillo needs to be with his sons and so does la señora."

"I don't want him to go, either. I'm used to having him around," Lila added. "He reminds me of so much of you, Ramón, but it's time."

Lila stood and refilled their cups.

"Okay," Ramon said. "I'll drive him home tomorrow."

§§§

Leo and Ramón cleaned Manchas's stall, carpeting the floor with fresh hay and grooming him until his coat shone. The pony shivered in happiness and stuck his nose in Leo's pocket, seeming to know he would get a treat after the bi-weekly cleaning and rubdown.

"It's great to have you home, Tío," Leo exclaimed. "Manchas thinks so, too!"

"Speaking of going home, it's time for you to go to your other home, to your parents," Ramón said gently.

Leo stopped brushing Manchas's left hindquarter. He stood ramrod straight and said, "But this is my home. I love it here."

"And we love having you here, but the time is right. Your father and your mamá miss you. Your father is *so* sorry. He loves you and your brother. Héctor's coming back, too."

Leo's lip quivered. His dark brown eyes had different depths. Sometimes they were flat, but now Ramón could see deeply into them; he knew how hard Leo was wrestling with his emotions so he assured, "You're a special person, Leo. You really helped me when I had almost given up. After I found out I didn't get into college, you were the one who talked me into trying again."

"I did? Really?" Leo's voice raised in doubt.

"Yes, you sure did. Where would I be without you? You have a gift, a way of making people feel better. You know exactly what to say at exactly the right time, even if you don't realize it." Ramón fought hard to betray his own emotions. Part of him didn't want Leo to leave, but he had to convince the boy. "We'll always be your family, but now I think it's time for you to help your first family. They need you."

Absently, Leo moved some hay around with his toe. "I'll go back."

Ramón kept his voice even. After all, he was the one who was supposed to be brave. "I want you to do something for me, okay?" he asked.

Leo nodded.

"Forgive your father," Ramón told him, and then let the weight of his words sink in. "And keep taking such good care of Manchas. When you go back to your old school, I want you to keep studying, keep doing so well in school. I'm really proud of you."

Leo raised the hand that had been holding the brush and wiped a tear.

"You won't forget me? You'll come visit?" Leo pleaded, with his eyes looking directly into Ramón's.

"I could never forget you, and of course I'll visit." Ramón took Leo in his arms. "If I ever have a son, I hope he's half as brave as you."

CHAPTER 53

The light of the full moon danced off the canyons surrounding *La Pica* as Leo and Ramón rode in the Buick to Yabucoa to bring Leo home. They wanted to get an earlier start, but Ramón's entire family, his brothers, wives and children had all come by to bid good-bye to Leo. It had taken all day and now only the stars and the moon kept them company.

Unlike the one-story houses that abutted one another in Río Piedras and the small wood houses in Maunabo, the Trujillo home was two-storied and set back from the street by a long driveway lined with towering palms. Ramón drove to the end, which swept around in a curve and ended in a parking spot for visitors adjacent to the two-car garage, the only one in town. He parked the Buick.

They sat for a minute while the engine pinged and cooled. Ramón looked at the house. Two sconces burned brightly to illuminate the front door. Trujillo's home was one of the few with electricity and the largest in Yabucoa with a sprawling verandah in front, over which there were double leaded windows with red shutters. It reminded Ramón of a villa from a fairytale owned by a king in Spain. He imagined the white stucco must have been brilliant years ago in the tropical sun, but now at night, it had decayed to the color of Chepa's old aluminum pot.

Ramón and Leo walked up the front steps of the verandah. Ramón's hand strained to hold onto the handle of a metal bucket filled with water with a ladle hanging off its rim, the healing water from *El Chorrito*. In his other hand he held a small package wrapped in butcher paper. When he sensed Leo hesitate beside him, Ramón looked at the young boy, smiled and nodded as if to say, "It will be all right."

Leo returned a shy smile. Ramón knew he got the message.

The ornate wood door was flanked by two black urns filled with dead flowers, hanging their weary heads two feet over the edge. At one point they must have been stunning. Ramón placed the bucket and package down and knocked. He hoped Leo couldn't hear his heart pounding when the large black doorknob turned.

Ana Trujillo opened the door. Her hands flew to her face, and her eyes went wide as she cried, *"¡M'ijito!"* She stepped onto the porch, embraced Leo fiercely and began to cry, mumbling and repeating how much she loved him, missed him, how this would make his father so happy.

"Me too, Mamá," Leo whispered.

When Ana pulled away, Ramón looked at her face and saw where Leo got his expressive eyes. He remembered how she looked that day months earlier when he picked up Leo after the beating. Now Leo's mother looked so happy that Ramón witnessed a flash of who she used to be.

She turned and embraced Ramón as well. *"Gracias a usted* (Thanks to you)," she whispered and motioned for them to come in.

Ramón felt his hands turn clammy, his heart palpitate at the prospect of seeing Trujillo again. The last time he and the merchant had been together, the night Ramón found him in the cane fields, the man has shown some gratitude, some desire to heal the wrongs between them. Now it was their chance to finish what they started.

Ramón reached down and lifted the bucket to explain, "This is water from *El Chorrito*, the spring at the top of *La Pica*. It's so fresh that people go up there for buckets of it." Ramón showed her the package. "And this is a poultice for el señor's rheumatism, sent by my mother."

"*Gracias a Dios* for you and Doña Chepa," she murmured.

"They say this water can heal," Ramón said. "Can I bring it to him?"

"Yes, but . . ." Ana flashed Ramón a warning with her eyes and then glanced at Leo, as if she wanted to say something but couldn't in the presence of her son. "Padre Pérez came by, said to let him rest. I pulled back the mosquito net, to give him fresh air, like Padre said to do," she defended.

Ana turned to Leo, who clutched a paper bag with some clothes and two books he had borrowed from Don Pablo. Ramón watched Ana searching for words. "Put your things in your room, *m'ijo*. You can see Papá soon. He's been waiting."

Leo nodded and walked inside. He crossed the vestibule, turned and disappeared down a long hallway.

"Come with me," Ana told Ramón.

Ramón followed her down the same hallway. At the end stood a grandfather clock with a plume of peacock feathers fanned out on the wall above it and a mahogany table with a phonograph surrounded by piles of records on the floor. Ramón had never seen so many, a library for records. He read the title of one on top: *Le Nozze di Figaro*.

They turned into what Ramón deduced was the master bedroom. Ana Trujillo stopped and stood silent at the door, then walked away as Ramón entered the room and pulled up a seat at her husband's bedside. Could this be the same man Ramón remembered? Trujillo had shrunken, even from the night of the rescue. The room smelled of illness, unwashed flesh and mildew. Ramón imagined it must have once held the scent of fresh flowers, the smell of life and wealth. Now it smelled of death and decay.

Ramón placed the package on the nightstand and the bucket on the floor, where it landed with a bang, sloshing water on the floor and waking Señor Trujillo.

"Who's there?" the merchant whispered, his voice labored. "Turn the lamp up, my eyes can't . . ."

"Señor, it's Ramón."

Ramón reached to the nightstand and twisted the knob of the oil lamp. It cast a luminous yellow glow, making the merchant's face appear even more sallow.

"Who are you?" Trujillo rasped. "I'm nearly blind."

Dios, can't he remember me? Ramón wondered.

"It's Ramón León, from Maunabo. I've brought your son—I've brought you some medicine."

Trujillo stared at Ramón vacantly. His eyes had a bluish cast to them, looking waxy and unreal. Then the pupils became sharper and Ramón saw a flicker of recognition cross the merchant's face as he uttered, "It's you. With my son?"

"Yes." Ramón took his handkerchief out of his pocket and knelt to wipe the floor. "I'm sorry for your pain and everything we've been through." He sat again.

"What we've been through, I've never in my life . . ."

Señor Trujillo began to hack. Ramón handed him a clean handkerchief from the nightstand. The merchant coughed into it.

"Do you know the legend of *El Chorrito*?" Ramón asked.

Señor Trujillo shook his head weakly.

Ramón said, "They say once you go there and taste the water from the spring, that you'll always come back. It's so clear that people come from all over to drink it, for better health. My mother infused it with lemons. I'll get you some."

Ramón took an empty glass from the nightstand and used the ladle to fill the glass with water, careful this time not to spill. He reached behind the frail man's head to support him and held the glass to his lips.

"It's delicious." Señor Trujillo licked his dry lips. A frown crossed his face. "Why are you being so kind to me, after everything I've done?"

"I must do what my conscience tells me. It's what my mother taught me. I also have a poultice of St. John's Wort and juniper leaves for your legs."

Ramón unwrapped the package. He removed the leaves and strips of gauze. He pulled back the sheet and held back his gasp at the skin-covered skeleton covered with bruises. He thought of the pictures of the gaunt people from the concentration camps and his stomach clenched. With a steady hand, he placed the poultices on the man's knees and pulled the sheet back up.

"Young man, do you know the story of Wolfgang Amadeus Mozart?" Trujillo asked.

It was Ramón's turn to shake his head.

"Mozart's rival, Antonio Salieri, went mad with jealousy over the brilliance of young Mozart, who became one of the best composers of all time." Señor Trujillo's voice became hoarse from exertion. "Mozart's music moves me like no other."

Trujillo continued the story, and his voice grew stronger: "It's a tragic tale of betrayal. Salieri wrote a silly little march to welcome the young Mozart to Vienna. Mozart memorized it and transformed it into genius, *El Nozze di Figaro*, his most glorious opera. Salieri tricked Mozart into writing a requiem for mass which Salieri claimed as his own—how devious!"

He stopped to cough. He called to his wife, "Mami, come!

Tell Juana to play the *Duettino, Che soave zeffiretto*, from *Nozze di Figaro!*"

Ana Trujillo appeared at the door to call out, "You old fool, we got rid of her weeks ago!"

She left with a wave of her hand, but in moments, two voices like songbirds filtered into the room.

"Ahh, that's right, the maid is gone, but Mami plays it for me on my phonograph. Listen, this aria is exquisite!" Señor Trujillo claimed, his eyes misting. "You come here to help me. You helped my son, whom I betrayed as Mozart was betrayed. Will he ever forgive me?" The man shuddered. "That boy, he's always been different than his brother, so sensitive. Perhaps that's why I took my anger out on him, but I love him so . . . I don't know if I can forgive myself."

Ramón placed his hand on the man's shoulder. In a few minutes, the merchant's shivering stopped.

"Leo is a very special boy. He'll forgive you, señor," Ramón assured.

Trujillo's expression changed. The waxy appearance of his eyes evaporated like a drop of water on a hot stone left in the tropical sun, leaving the whites of his eyes brighter, more lucid. "It was you who came all those times in the hospital, wasn't it?"

Ramón nodded. "I just had to know that you were okay."

Minutes passed to the strains of music. "This is beautiful. I've never heard anything like it," Ramón said, in awe.

"Yes, the voices of these sopranos have souls," Trujillo whispered.

Ramón listened to the two singers and experienced a tingling to all his extremities. He felt more alive, euphoric, in their presence.

"It took me almost dying to see the light." Señor Trujillo turned to look directly at Ramón. "God sent you here to restore my faith. I feel as if I'm in the presence of an angel."

Ramón felt heat flush his face. It was the second time someone called him an angel. The first was when he brought food to Esperanza, and her daughter called him an angel.

Señor's eyes opened wider as he said, "I became so distraught after you won and I didn't. Ay, such divine unfairness! My heart filled with hatred for you. For the first time in my life, I knew violent thoughts, and God forbid, I harmed you and my son. Unforgiveable! I have begged God for mercy, to enter me so I know He still loves me. And when I heard the overture to *Nozze di Figaro* in my head, it struck me: I was like Salieri, who went mad, claimed he had killed Mozart, tried to commit suicide. I ran out that awful night in a rage, and who of all people found me? *You.* Why did you do it? You helped me when you had nothing to lose, everything to gain from seeing me gone. Did God send you to teach me a lesson in humility?"

Ramón felt a sudden release of all the tension he had been holding through his body. Had this been one of the reasons why he won and Trujillo didn't? Was the man always due for a fall, and was Ramón the one meant to catch him? And what of Ramón himself? Didn't the very act of struggling against the merchant result in Ramón's finding great inner strength? He felt warmth fill his chest, a lightness.

Ramón said, "All men are equal in the eyes of God, señor. I did what He would have asked of me. You and your son will find each other again."

"When I die, and I think that time is not so far away, I want people to speak my name with honor for what I've done, not shame."

"Don't talk like that! The water from *El Chorrito*, it will help you—"

"Young man," the merchant interrupted, "Your money comes

with a burden. Mozart went mad, as did his rival, and died a pauper, buried in a mass grave. Don't squander your money as I have and as he did."

"I won't! I'll use the money to become a dentist. I'll come back and help people. No matter what it takes."

"I know you will. You're destined for it. You have grit, honesty and unlike me, integrity."

Ramón placed his hand on top of Trujillo's. The skin was as translucent as onion paper, the bones as fragile as a pile of twigs. Señor Trujillo closed his eyes and smiled like a child at his birthday party. For a moment, he looked at peace. Completely.

The two men listened to the masterpiece of Mozart. Ramón knew that Señor Trujillo agreed with him: God celebrated His glory in the voices of those two sopranos. Ramón saw the love of a father for a son, the regret of what Trujillo did that he could never take away.

It took Ramón's breath away.

Ramón had no idea what the two ladies were singing in Italian, but at that moment, their voices soared to the heavens, and he knew that both he and Trujillo would be free.

CHAPTER 54

It was the first Christmas and New Years in years that Isidro and Rafael were home for, the entire family together. All except Leo. For him, there was no papaya candy wrapped in a silk square under the bed on *El Día de los Reyes Magos*, so the León family recited a special prayer for him.

On the day Ramón brought Leo back to Yabucoa, the boy was very brave when he said good-bye. He embraced Ramón fiercely, yet shed no tears. Ramón arranged for a goat herder to deliver Leo's beloved pony, Manchas, in the back of his old truck and he pictured the pony and the boy happy together, riding along the shore.

Since then, Ramón allowed the Trujillos their privacy, their time to become a family again. He prayed many times for their healing. He knew children had an amazing capacity for recuperation, and at times, wondered if Leo, back in his familiar surroundings, might even begin to think of his recovery at the León household as a dream. Yet he had seen Leo's uncanny knack for helping those in need, had witnessed the boy's selfless nature, and knew Leo would probably never forget. Leo, like Chepa, would become a great healer. Ramón must make sure he would do the same.

§§§

One morning two months later as the light of the new day began to make the eastern horizon pale with its first light, Ramón tended to Chepa's herb garden. Falling back into his old routine was comforting, and he loved this time of day before the rest of the village woke, when the only sounds were the chirps of the *coquís* and the high pitched tweets of a *reinata* high in the treetops. He worked for an hour in silence. As he picked a batch of *culantro*, something made him look up.

Don Pablo hurried around the corner. The look on his face reminded Ramón of the way Alberto Gómez looked the day Ramón won the lottery. Ramón wondered what made his friend and neighbor so giddy.

"Ramón, thank your lucky stars, thank God, thank your mother, and praise the skies!" Red-faced, Don Pablo placed his hands on his knees and bent over, gasping to catch his breath from running.

Ramón stood. His knees wobbled. He felt that tingle across his shoulders and up and down his spine, that same gooseflesh the day he bought the ticket, and then on the day he won.

"Thank God for what!?" Ramón exclaimed.

"YOU GOT IN!" Don Pablo stood and began to clap. "The school just called. Praise God," he shouted again and threw his hands up to the sky.

Ramón embraced his friend and picked him up to twirl him around, then collapsed with the effort; Don Pablo outweighed him by forty pounds.

They both landed in the dirt and began to laugh . . . and laugh and then laugh some more. Ramón laughed so hard, the muscles in his stomach ached as if he'd done a hundred sit-ups. He laughed so hard he began to cry. And so did Don Pablo.

Ramón didn't know what to say. He thought this day would come, prayed this day would come. And now here it was. He got to a kneeling position, pushed himself back up to standing and then helped the don up before he gave the man an enormous *abrazo* and exclaimed, "Thank God my friend, thank God indeed."

Don Pablo reached into his back pocket to grab his handkerchief and wipe the tears off his face as he explained, "A man from admissions called. He said he read your essay last night and that he hardly slept until he showed it to the president this morning. They want to put it in the school's newspaper. They want you to call the president of the college!"

The news sank in as Ramón remembered the application asked for a phone number. As Ramón still didn't own a phone, he wrote Don Pablo's. Ramón believed that if he were ever in the presence of an angel, she would be delicate with beautiful features. This day, some angel, or God himself, delivered a message in the form of his rotund, jolly neighbor. Ecstatic, he hugged Don Pablo again and kissed his cheek before he raced inside to tell Chepa.

§§§

The news traveled as fast as a mangy cat being chased by a hungry dog. Ramón was accepted at Michigan State College for the fall semester, 1946. Chepa had clapped her hands when Ramón told her, looking as giddy as a school girl. People came to the store all morning to congratulate him.

The two people he wanted to share the news most were Leo and Elsie. He believed it was time to visit Leo, but what of Elsie? In spite of their last time together, Ramón harbored the hope she would change her mind, her father's mind, and come with him to Michigan, to fulfill the dream she had shared with him of becoming a schoolteacher. Surely that hadn't changed. He remembered the good times they had, that first date at *Casa Alcaldía*, how she cried when he told her about the draft, her birthday dinner and his proposal. She had to remember those times, too, didn't she?

He had to see her. For one last try.

§§§

That afternoon Ramón called the college in Michigan. In Río Piedras, he had a few months to learn what college was like, and one thing he knew for sure; asking a student to publish his personal essay in the school newspaper was no every day occurrence. He used Don Pablo's phone. Ramón stood alone in the kitchen, listening to the muted voices of Chepa, Don Pablo, and his wife, Rosario, in the adjacent dining room. Sunlight arrowed into the kitchen through the large plate glass window.

With trembling fingers, Ramón dialed the operator and asked her to place a call to Michigan. After endless clicks and whirls that finally connected Ramón to another world—something he still found unbelievable—a woman answered the phone.

"Good afternoon. President Hannah's office."

"Ahh, hello, may I speak to the president?"

Ramón could hardly believe it. He might as well be calling President Truman!

"What's this regarding?" she said in a clipped tone.

"Ah, my name is Ramón León Carrasquillo. The president wants to talk to me about my . . . ah . . . essay."

There was a delay as the words traveled through thousands of miles of phone wires. Ramón felt sweat trickle down his arms. Had she hung up?

And then finally, "Oh, yes! You're the fellow whose essay he showed me. It was absolutely charming."

315

Her tone changed from a bull dog to a songbird. "He'll talk to you. Hold on please."

She was gone. Instrumental music played. Ramón shifted weight from one foot to another. If the phone cord were longer, he would have paced. The phone clicked. The music ended.

"Mr. León? President Hannah here."

Ramón swallowed hard. "Hello, señor, I mean, sir. Yes, I'm Ramón León Carrasquillo." Then a quick thought followed: what a dumb thing to say! Didn't they already know that?

Another delay. More sweat.

"I know who you are, Mr. León. I generally don't get involved in the application process, but Mr. Smith in admissions read your essay last night and was so moved that he called me first thing this morning. I was impressed, too. Your application is complete so we'd be pleased to accept you. Your official letter will go out in a day or two."

The president paused, then said in a lighter tone, "I hope you'll be joining us in the fall, because if your personal essay is an example of what you sent to other schools, you'll have your choice of where to attend. I can only hope it's with us."

Ramón translated all the words as quickly as he could. Ironic how all that suffering in Advanced Literature paid off. The president was much easier to understand than Professor Rolf, even thousands of miles away. Ramón wished his father were here. He wished Doctor Roberts were here, and maybe, somehow, they were. He swallowed again, this time a lump in his throat as large as a *coquí*.

"Thank you, sir. I only applied there. I would be honored to attend."

"Excellent!" Ramón could almost hear the smile in the president's voice as he continued on. "With your permission, we'd

316

like to reprint your essay in *The State News*, our school newspaper. I must say, I wish more of our applicants could have penned such a heartfelt personal statement. Our students deserve to read it. Congratulations."

Ramón was at a loss for words. He thought again of how persistence and honesty pays off. He had poured all his emotions into that essay.

"Mr. León, you're still on the line?" the president asked.

"Ahh, yes, sir. I'd be honored to have you print my story," Ramón answered with adrenaline coursing through his veins.

"Very well. It will run in the first issue in the fall. If there's anything I can do for you, don't hesitate to contact me again. Welcome to MSC."

Ramón hung up. He felt like he did when he won the lottery, when he stepped off the bus for his coming home celebration. If he had a hat on, he would have tossed it in the air, just like he did that day. Only this time, it wouldn't tumble back down. With the exhilaration he was feeling at the moment, he would have tossed it so high, it would have reached the angels or God Himself.

CHAPTER 55

Ramón paid a fisherman a dollar to take him to Esperanza, the small fishing village on the southern side of Vieques. He had begged Señora Lepe to give him Elsie's address, and she relented, scribbling it on a square piece of paper, which he folded in half to place safely in his pocket.

The fisherman aimed his sailboat toward the dock at Esperanza. The man had the biggest arms Ramón had ever seen, almost as thick as the posts of the dock he headed to, no doubt from a lifetime of hauling and lifting baskets of lobster and fish. Ramón viewed the coastline as they approached: the crumbling remains of the *Puerto Ferro* lighthouse and the old *Playa Grande Sugar Centrale*. Smoke no longer billowed from the twin stacks of the sugar mill after it closed when the Navy took over the island years earlier. The beaches were pristine and uninhabited except for two wild ponies and a few seagulls cawing and hovering on air currents before diving into the sea for fish. It was sad to imagine visions of days gone by when the island was more prosperous, yet breathtaking.

The floor of the sailboat gave off the pungent smell of fish. Ramón hoped the scent didn't stick to his clothes for his first meeting with Elsie in seven months. She'd be surprised, shocked even, to see him, but he had no way of contacting her and didn't want to wait until he sent a letter. He hoped she'd be happy to see him and to hear his news. Ironic, she now lived in Esperanza, *hope* in English, the sentiment he felt for their future, and the name of his friend, Chepa's apprentice who had shown such gratitude to their family.

The sailor tied the bow of the boat to the dock where it bobbed gently. He stood solidly on the floor of his boat and offered his hand to help his passenger up. Ramón shook his head and proceeded to the end of the dock where he found his land legs again. He checked the paper in his pocket.

A few establishments remained in Esperanza, a bar, cantina and a store selling groceries and newspapers. Ramón tried to imagine what it was like a few years earlier, when ten thousand people had moved there to build navy bases. Now most of them were gone.

He asked directions from an old man sitting in front of the sundries store, whittling a figure from an oblong piece of wood. Ramón then walked into a neighborhood of modest homes where a group of four boys played baseball with the branch of a mango tree used as a bat.

Ramón arrived at the address Señora Lepe wrote. He took one last deep breath, noting the faint scent of pomade and Lux soap from the shower he took before he left home.

The home of Elsie's aunt was a modest peach colored bungalow fronted by a garden with bushes weighed down with pigeon peas and morivivi plants, their pink blossoms and green leaves open to the sun. A brilliant green hummingbird fluttered around a magenta hibiscus. The air was filled with the scent of lemon and grapefruit.

He walked up the short paved path lined with rosemary and climbed up two steps to the porch. He stood at the screen door. Someone must have heard him approach. Ramón sensed movement and saw a silhouette of a woman. Elsie.

The door opened. Her eyes flew open wide in recognition and she said, "Ramón! What are you doing out here?"

She stepped out onto the porch. Her face looked more beautiful even though she wore no lipstick or blush. Her hair was pulled back in a tight ponytail, and cascaded down her back, longer than he remembered. It made her cheekbones appear even more sculpted, her neck and shoulders even more graceful. She was slimmer, and it made her look taller, even in flat sandals.

"I came to see you. I have news. How are you?" Ramón blurted, the thoughts jumbling in his head so fast that he said everything in one breath.

"My life is different here, it was hard at first, but I love my tía and I help her quite a lot around here," Elsie said and waved her hand to sweep the view of the garden.

"It's beautiful," Ramón said.

A moment of awkward silence passed.

"I got into MSC," he announced. "I finished a semester at Río Piedras, I did pretty well, so I reapplied. They took me and they're even going to put my essay in the school's paper!"

Ramón heard the excitement build in his voice.

"Oh, that's great," Elsie replied in a tone that was neither friendly nor unfriendly. She bit her lower lip with a sharp intake of breath.

Ramón recognized that familiar expression. He knew she was thinking of what to say next. His heart sprinted. He waited a second, and plunged on with his heart spilling from his lips: "So I'm going to Michigan in the fall. And I'd hoped, I thought, well, with everything that happened, there was still a chance for us, for you to come with me, become a school teacher. I still love you. We could try and change your father's mind."

"I guess you haven't heard," Elsie said as her face paled.

"Heard what?"

Ramón's knees felt wobbly again, like getting off the boat.

"I'm engaged. To a lieutenant, from the navy. We met a few months after I got here. Everyone's gone now, and he had to go back to San Juan, too. We'll be married in less than a year. I'm . . . I'm sorry."

Of course Ramón hadn't heard. Neither Capitán Miraflores nor his wife came by to congratulate Ramón. Now he knew why.

"What about becoming a teacher?" Ramón said quickly.

"I'm moving to San Juan to live with my other tía and I can go to college, too. Hernán doesn't mind. In fact, he likes the idea. His mother is a professional woman. She owns one of the finest boutiques in Condado."

Ramón couldn't breathe. So she was marrying someone else. Someone named Hernán. For a moment, Ramón imagined striking the man, then regretted it. Hernán, whoever he was, had done him no harm. Ramón wanted to ask about the man, but he couldn't find the words. He felt ill.

"Are you okay? Do you need some water?" Elsie asked, her voice now showing concern.

"No. I don't need anything. I . . . I think I need to go."

"Please don't be mad, not after all we went through. You know, I hurt, too, after Papá separated us. I wanted a certain life with you, and it didn't look like it would turn out that way—"

"Well, it looks like you got what you wanted. Good luck."

Ramón was surprised at the sharpness in his voice.

"I'm glad you got into college in the states. You deserve it." Elsie's eyes fell, her cheeks flushed. "You need to know something, Ramón. That time we had together, watching all you went through, it changed me. I wanted to do something special with my life, too."

Elsie paused to sigh and release a deep breath. "Remember I told you my father chose a man for me, the son of an *associate* of his? Well, I met the man in San Juan, and he was awful. He was so old, thirty at least, and he reminded me of a bull dog who barely spoke,

321

mainly grunted. And around that time I heard what happened to you in school with that professor saying things about you and how you won over him."

"You heard all that?"

Elsie continued before Ramón had a chance to say more. "Yes, and it made me speak up for myself, too. I told Papá 'no'. I couldn't believe it but Papá relented. And then I met Hernán. He's so nice, so considerate to me. He's letting me go to college, and I know I can do it, partly because of you, and because of that letter you sent. I kept it, you know."

"Why didn't you try to call me, tell me all this before?" Ramón pleaded.

"I'm sorry," she repeated in a gentle voice. "It was too late. That last day, the things I said—I didn't want to stand in your way. I wish things had turned out different."

Ramón heard the sadness in her voice. For a moment, with the rose colored bloom across her cheeks, Elsie looked like the same girl at his coming home party.

"Me, too," Ramón said, regretting the tone he used earlier. "Elsie, I have to go . . . " He turned and left before she saw the look he knew was on his face.

When he passed the garden on the way out, the morivivi leaves had closed, even in broad daylight. He had never seen that, but someone had told him once, perhaps it was Chepa, that they close when threatened from predators.

Ramón had arranged for a return trip with the brawny sailor, mentioning to him that he might have another passenger accompanying him, a young lady. Now he'd have to tell the man that he'd be going home alone.

CHAPTER 56

Ramón was going through it all over again: heartache, a hurt so profound he could barely breathe. He could pick a winning lottery number, but he didn't know much of the nature of women.

He slept more than usual for the first few days after he arrived home from Vieques, waking up after a restless sleep at eight or nine in the morning, long after the rest of his family had begun their days.

And then something happened. He looked in the chipped oval mirror one morning and studied the face that stared back. The skin on his cheeks was still as smooth as the gleam on a fine piece of furniture; his dark hair grown back after he shaved it all off, although not as thick as he'd hoped. Yet his eyes looked older than he remembered, with faint lines at the corners. Wisdom lines. He'd earned every one. He had defeated the awful jail keepers, and the conniving Rolf. He had saved Leo and his father, particularly Leo, whom he should be celebrating his college acceptance with.

The entire village was counting on him. Michigan was waiting for him and when he got there, the other students would read his essay. If Elsie didn't want to be a part of that, so be it.

He had to move on.

First he went to Don Pablo's to phone Nitza with the news of his acceptance. Ramón pictured her at the kitchen table, a pot of steaming coffee in front of her as she and Chico began their morning of writing letters. The same cantankerous bartender answered the phone and grumbled about the trouble but agreed to summon Nitza. Her reaction was just as Ramón expected. Her enthusiasm and pride for him was palpable through the phone line.

"I'm so thrilled for you, Ramón. After hearing this, I'm barely going to be able to concentrate to finish my work today! Wait until I tell Carlos and Chico. We'll have a beer tonight and toast you!"

"And speaking of Carlos," Ramón said, "Remind him that he needs to come to Maunabo as soon as he can. There's someone he needs to meet, *rápido!*"

Ramón remembered his vision of Carlos and Esperanza together. If he couldn't find love, at least he could assure that one of his best friends did.

§§§

Later that day, Ramón drove to Yabucoa to share his news of Michigan with Leo, the one who really counted in his life. He ended at the Trujillo house. It looked better. Someone had replaced the dead flowers in the large black urns with fresh ones. Yet something felt wrong. He sensed it. Ramón experienced a moment's panic. He parked and rushed up to the front door.

Héctor answered it to say, "Papá died three days ago."

Ramón stepped inside and put his hand on the boy's shoulder. "I'm so sorry." What else could he say? What would Chepa say? "Is there anything I can do for you, for your family?" It sounded cliché, but Ramón meant it. He had changed tremendously in the past year. Perhaps his strength could help this family. Perhaps it already had.

Héctor shrugged.

"How's Leo?" Ramón asked.

Again, no response from Héctor.

Señora Herrera rushed forward, wearing a black dress, her hair pulled back severely in a bun tied with a black ribbon. "Ay, you heard. Señor is gone." She clasped her cross necklace and kissed it.

Ramón asked about Leo again, and about Ana.

Señora Herrera replied, "Señora Ana is in bed. She was doing better, but today is a bad day. This family needed help and I'm it. That smaller boy, he hasn't said much, has hardly said anything since he came home." She paused and lowered her voice. "After the trouble."

"I need to see him," Ramón demanded, then added, "please."

She nodded. He followed her down that same long hallway to Leo's room. Someone had polished the floor. He remembered how it was dull and scratched at his last visit. The same grandfather clock was there, but someone had removed the stacks of records. He guessed Señora Herrera had done so. As if reading his mind, she announced, "Ay, the state this place was in when I got here."

Ramón entered Leo's bedroom.

Leo sat at the head of the queen sized bed, which nearly swallowed his small body. His eyes grew twice as large when he saw Ramón and cried, "Tío Ramón!"

Leo jumped off the bed, and they embraced.

"I'm so sorry about your father, Leo," Ramón said as he hugged the boy harder. They sat side-by-side on the edge of the bed.

"Thanks." Leo looked up at Ramón and tried to smile, but it was like someone trying to hide his grief, his pain. "He was so nice to me after I got back. It was like we were a family again. We all thought he was getting better. But . . ."

Ramón heard the quiver in Leo's voice.

"I know what you're going through," Ramón began. "I lost my papá when I was about your age, too. I can still see him in my mind, dream about him coming into my room when I was sick and trying to make me feel better."

"Really?" Leo's eyes widened again. "I always wondered what happened to your papá."

"I've never told anyone this story, but when he got really sick, I snuck out of bed one night and hid near the door to my parent's room. The pharmacist was there, and he put a jar with a candle in it on Papá's chest. Mamá moved it around to different spots, to try to draw the toxins out of his chest."

Ramón continued his story, forcing his voice to remain strong for Leo's sake.

"The next day I went into the kitchen and Lila and I got in a fight. She wacked my feet with the broom, screaming at me to get out of the way. I screamed back. Papá yelled at us to be quiet. I ran to his room and he was sitting up in bed, coughing so hard . . . he fell back and he died, only a few hours later. I ran so fast and so far I thought my chest would give out like Papá's. I climbed a ceiba tree way out in the cane fields. No one could find me for a while. I always felt like it was my fault."

Ramón remembered Chepa later that day. Her sister, his Tía Aída, came and tried to comfort her. Aída lay in the bed next to Chepa, holding her, stroking her long white hair. It was the first time Ramón saw Chepa's hair loose, not in its tidy bun at the nape of her neck; it looked like a silken blanket that covered her, but made her look smaller. It was the only time he had seen his mother fallen.

Leo shook his head. "It wasn't your fault, Tío. It was his time to go to God."

And there it was again; Leo comforting Ramón, when he was the one who should be doing the saving. It was so alarmingly adult of him, at his tender age, that Ramón was silenced for a moment.

"Yes, Leo, like with your papá, too. You brought him a lot of happiness, and pride. In spite of everything that happened, you know how much he loved you, right?"

"Yeah, I know," Leo agreed.

"And unlike me, you didn't run, right?"

Leo shook his head.

"You were here, for your mother, for your brother, right?" Ramón said.

Leo confirmed, "Yeah, I was. I'm the one who sits with Mamá, holds her hand. She isn't doing too well, and Héctor has never been good around her when she's having one of her spells. But how did you know?"

"I know. It's in your nature to be that way, and I just know." Ramón paused. "Hey, I got some great news. It's why I came to see you today."

Leo sat up straighter. "What?"

"I got in to Michigan. They want me, and they liked my essay so much that they're going to put it in the school newspaper!"

"That's great news!" His voice was happy, but then fell. "But, it means you're leaving."

Ramón nodded. "I'll be gone for years. When you're a kid that seems like forever. But trust me, it goes fast, and the way you study so hard at school, you'll be too busy to think of me."

"I'll never be too busy to miss you," Leo defended. "Tío, you deserve it, more than anyone I know. I need to give something back to you. I kept it just in case, well, you know, after everything that happened . . ."

Leo reached under his short-sleeve button down shirt and retrieved the scapular.

"Are you sure? I gave it to you," Ramón reminded him.

"Yeah." Leo handed it to Ramón. "I think you need it more than me now."

Ramón pressed it back into its familiar place. It felt as if he had never taken it off.

"Thanks. I'll write to you. I'll tell you all about life in the states," Ramón said.

"Promise?" Leo looked like his old self again, the kid he was before and then weeks after his father's attack. The small semi-circle scar on his left cheek was almost invisible.

"Promise," Ramón affirmed. He embraced Leo again, and this time, he didn't want to let go.

CHAPTER 57

What Ramón told Leo was right. When you study hard, time passes quicker than you can imagine. Ramón spent the first half of 1946 continuing to memorize his dictionary, reading as far as the Ts: tireless, adjective: *incansable, infatigable.*

He started reading *The Grapes of Wrath,* just for the fun of it, and to learn more words and grammar. When he got to the states, he'd try to see the movie, although people always told him books were better.

He worked at the store, played basketball with Leo every Sunday, and enjoyed Chepa and Lila's cooking. He still thought of Elsie. Although it pained him immensely, he hoped she'd find happiness. The profound hurt that tightened his chest lessened a little with each passing month. Plus, knowing Carlos and Esperanza found happiness was a buffer.

Carlos had come for a visit in the spring. Ramón would always remember the first time he and Esperanza met.

They had all joined at Chepa's house for dinner. Over *polvo de amor* for dessert, Carlos's and Esperanza's eyes locked across the table. Esperanza quickly looked down. Ramón guessed it was because of her acting so boldly with the first man since her husband, but before her eyes fell, he saw an expression never seen before, the flash of a smile that lit up her entire face.

The next day, Carlos called on Esperanza with a bouquet of pink maga flowers, and drove her and the children to the beach for the day with the lunch Chepa had packed. They had such a good time they went again the following day. Before he left to return to

Río Piedras, Carlos asked Chepa and Ramón for permission to court Esperanza.

"I've never felt this way about a gal before. I'd like to come to Maunabo on the weekends to see her, if that would be okay with the two of you," Carlos said.

"Of course you can, that would be better than okay. That would be great!" Ramón replied. He had never seen his fun loving friend so smitten.

Chepa gave her consent, embraced Carlos and told him, "Ay, young love is a beautiful thing. I never get tired of watching it grow."

Chepa's words went straight to Ramón's heart, for the joy his friends deserved.

§§§

In August, Ramón took his last buying trip to San Juan. Alberto Gómez sold three fine suits to him for the discount price of $15.00 each, his going away present. He had tailored each, explaining to Ramón he left a little extra room in the waistline, hoping the food on the mainland would treat him well.

Alberto embraced Ramón farewell and kissed each cheek. He wished him good luck and told Ramón he was the most admirable young man he had ever done business with. He also added this: "Once your luck gets a little momentum, there's no telling where it will take you, ay, my friend?"

For a moment, Ramón was so moved he was unable to answer.

§§§

The night of Ramón's going away celebration arrived. August

24, 1946. Chepa prepared one of the finest meals outside of Christmas day: a roast pig donated by Don Pablo, chopped peppers, *arroz con pollo*, stuffed plantains, empanadas, crescents of mango and papaya laid out on platters, and rum. Ramón's mother had a heavy heart, but her pride overshadowed it. She invited the entire village. With Don Pablo's phone, Ramón had called Nitza again, and she, Chico and Carlos came from Río Piedras to celebrate.

"I wouldn't dream of missing it," Nitza had exclaimed from the phone in the bar.

In the courtyard of the León home, Juan offered a toast: "Here's to my little brother. God has certainly granted him luck to get to this point, and may it continue in Michigan."

Juan lifted his glass of rum and swirled the amber liquid.

Everyone looked at Ramón as they held up their glasses. "To Ramón!" they shouted.

Don Pablo Cadiz ambled to the center of the group.

"I have something for the guest of honor." The courtyard became quiet. "The whole village is proud of you, Ramón," Don Pablo announced. "On behalf of all of us, I have a gift, something I know you'll need."

The don motioned to Francisco who walked forward carrying a new russet colored valise. The crowd clapped as Ramón's brother handed him the gift of fine workmanship. The smell of the new leather was one of the richest scents Ramón had ever experienced. Friends and family rushed forward to kiss him. For moments, he was unable to speak, relieved for the distraction of people milling around him, admiring his gift.

"Don Pablo," Ramón began, his voice breaking before he cleared it, "*Muchas gracias.* I . . . I'm honored to receive something so beautiful. I would also be honored if you would carve the pig for us tonight. Please, you must be the first to try my mother's exceptional cooking."

The guests crowded around Don Pablo as he expertly carved the pig on a platter surrounded by pineapple. He took the first bite, licked his lips and the tips of his fingers, grinned widely, and shouted, "Superb!"

Everyone clapped again and lined up at the tables full of food. The rum began to flow. Juan played his *pandereta* and José Luis played his trumpet, accompanied by drums, *güiros*, and maracas. The children ran about, squealing and dancing with each other and the adults. Ramón had driven to Yabucoa earlier that day to pick up Leo and Héctor and they joined the raucous. The courtyard swelled with more visitors, who began to spill out into the street and shake their bodies to the tunes of the Caribbean Kids.

After most of the guests had eaten at least two plates of food each, Ramón slipped away to his bedroom for a private moment. He walked back to the courtyard and stood unnoticed at the door. Many people were still dancing, and some gathered to converse in small groups. Francisco was standing and talking to Juan and Amanda with Isabel at his side; he stood close to his wife, with his hand nestled against the small of her back, and Ramón couldn't help but notice how much easier they seemed with each other. Francisco looked better than he had in as long as Ramón could remember, his eyes clear, the puffiness gone. He hadn't touched liquor in many months. The two brothers had embraced that night without a word. When they pulled apart, Ramón looked at his brother's face and saw love and admiration.

Ramón watched as Lila stood in another group with Jorge. She looked stunning in her rose colored dress fashioned by Chepa for this party, a dress that covered the bump that was just showing in her belly. She and Jorge were thrilled, expecting their first child. Someone had pinned a white orchid to her collar. Lila and Jorge chatted with Don Pablo, his wife, and Ramón's trusted friends from Río Piedras, Nitza and Chico. Carlos was off dancing with Esperanza, newlyweds who married only weeks before when a beaming Ramón walked Esperanza down the aisle. The young couple settled in Río Piedras, and Esperanza planned to work a few hours at home, tailoring for a fine clothing store. Twice a week, she and the children would come to Maunabo and help Chepa.

Ramón's heart ached at the thought of leaving them all. He remembered the celebration the day after the lottery. This was so similar, yet so very different.

He listened to snippets of conversations, realizing how his family and friends would move on without him, sharing news of their lives, their work, and having parties when there was cause for rejoicing, such as engagements, weddings and births; Lila's baby and the babies Esperanza would surely add to her now complete family. He would miss it all for years to come. Yet now was the time to start his new life, to celebrate change. He squared his shoulders and strode into the courtyard to rejoin the party.

§§§

"Come, my son, walk with me on the beach. It will be years before you return," Chepa requested on the night before Ramón's flight to the mainland.

Ramón drove his mother down the steep dirt road she could no longer navigate on foot and parked his Buick. He held her hand, as fragile as the gauze she used in wrapping her poultices, and guided her through a grove of African palms to the Maunabo Beach.

Ramón paused to remove his sandals, to appreciate the fine, warm sand beneath his feet, a sensation he would miss.

They strolled along the shoreline, arms intertwined.

"You're ready to leave, Ramón, now more than ever," Chepa said. "The store is better than ever, thanks to you, and the world is working toward peace. It's a time for change, for growth."

"I'm excited, scared, and nervous, all at the same time," Ramón admitted.

They stopped walking. Chepa turned toward her youngest son and reached up to place her palm on the side of his face.

"That's no surprise. The men in our family are quite emotional, especially Papá, may God rest his soul. Take care of yourself, get enough rest, exercise, and eat well. You're a sensitive man, more than most, but you'll be fine. I'll pray for you. We all will."

"I can't fail, Mamá, not after the promise I made to everyone. I have to come back a success. And speaking of Papá, I know he would want more for me in life, so doing this, becoming a dentist, is like a gift to him, to his memory."

"Your hard work will pay off. It already has. Be an honorable man, as you have with everything you've faced. Be true to yourself, and you'll get your reward. You were a gift to me in my later years, after losing so many."

Chepa took her hand from Ramón's face and withdrew something from her dress pocket, a St. Christopher medal on the end of a gold chain. As it lay nestled in the palm of her hand, she explained, "This belonged to your father. I knew there'd come a time when I'd give it to one my children, the one who would leave me. Somehow, I always knew it would be you. God willing, this will see you safely on your journey. Our family's hopes and dreams will travel with you."

Ramón's voice quivered. "Thank you."

"Your compassion is a gift, Ramón. Carry it with you always and forever," Chepa added as Ramón leaned down and she placed the medal over his head.

The two joined hands again and resumed walking, forearms wound like the roots of a tree, comfortable in the silence save the songs of the *coquís* and the gentle wash of waves. His mother had given Ramón other gifts along with his father's medal: emotional strength, support and love, and the ultimate gift, that of letting go.

CHAPTER 58

Ramón rose early the morning of his flight. He donned his chalk stripe suit for his long trip, the favorite of the three he purchased from Alberto. He smiled when he buttoned the pants, for they fit perfectly. Alberto claimed he left some extra room in the waist, but Chepa and Lila had spoiled him with his favorite foods in the months before his departure, and now the pants felt just right.

Francisco and Ramón drove to the airport, after Ramón decided that the Buick would be shared amongst his brothers.

The two began their trip, appreciating the quiet company of one another. It was Francisco who broke the silence to say, "You're going to make it, Ramón. I've always known it. Ever since you were a kid, all those books you used to stick your nose in, how well you did in school. It's not just that you were smart, you had something else too, determination. For years, I was jealous. Now, I'm just proud."

"Thanks," Ramón answered. "I needed that, because right now, I'm terrified."

Ramón drove and stole a look at his brother. Francisco looked forward with his arm propped against the window, his face reflecting a contentment not there before. Even the lines around his eyes seemed softer.

"Francisco," Ramón began, "It's your family, your friends, and our belief in one another that count most in the end, isn't it?"

Francisco nodded. "That's the truth if I've ever heard it, *hermano*."

Ramón wished they could drive forever but they arrived at the airport. Once out of the car they embraced.

336

"*Buena suerte, mi hermano. Vaya con Dios,*" (Good luck, my brother, go with God) Francisco uttered before he jumped in the car and drove away.

Ramón stood on the sidewalk and watched the taillights of the Buick fade until the car was out of sight. He turned and entered the airport.

After receiving his boarding pass, Ramón walked across the airfield to the four-engine propeller Pan Am plane. The air felt dense with the humidity of summer in the Caribbean. He glanced at a group of iguanas languishing in the sun on a grassy area next to the take-off strip. He knew everything would feel and look different when the plane landed in New York, and it already made him homesick. He also had another feeling. For the first time since winning the jackpot, he felt completely confident that his future would unfold in the way he wanted it to. In many ways, his life was just beginning.

Ramón climbed the steep steps of the mobile staircase and despite his 5'7" frame, had to duck to enter the airplane. He walked down the narrow aisle and turned at the seventh row, taking the window seat. He hoped the metal box that called itself a plane would get him to the continent in one piece, but his fear only lasted for a moment, for just then, a rectangle of sunlight from the port-hole sized window illuminated the air in front of him with a bittersweet dusky light, filling him with joy.

The stewardess smiled. She chimed on as she welcomed Ramón and the other passengers but Ramón barely heard her.

Instead, he heard Doctor Robert's words: "Make the world a better place."

And Chepa's words: "There's a reason God kisses some and not others."

And Leo's words: "You deserve it more than anyone I know."

And Trujillo's words: "You have grit, honesty, and integrity."

Ramón had all those people and their memories behind him, the village counting on him. He knew what they already did. He'd make it, and like the cannons at El Morro Fort, this plane would catapult him from one life to another.

As sharp as that morning's daybreak and as clear as the water from *El Chorrito*, Ramón knew he would succeed.

Doña Chepa.

Ramón age 3, Lila age 7, circa 1928.

Ramón at Michigan State College, 1946.

Ramón in dental school, circa 1953.

GLOSSARY

Abuelo, abuela: grandfather, grandmother

Abrazo: hug, embrace

Arroz con pollo: a classic Spanish dish of rice and chicken

Asopao: a kind of gumbo made with vegetables, chicken, or seafood

Bocadillo: a sandwich made with bread cut lengthwise

Bacalaitos fritos: seasoned cod fritters

Barril de bomba: traditional drum made of wood from rum storage bottle with goat skin, used in bomba music

Barrio: a neighborhood, particularly in the outer rim of villages or cities

Bohío: a simple zinc-roofed dwelling of the barrio

Carnicero: butcher

Casita: little house

Ceiba tree: the commonwealth tree of Puerto Rico which can grow over 100 feet and many consider a symbol of strength

Chancletas: inexpensive slip-on sandals

Compadre: good friend, comrade

Coquí: tiny tree frog native to Puerto Rico known for its distinctive song

Cuidado, m'ijo: be careful, my son

Culantro: a biennial herb know for its medicinal qualities, not to be confused with cilantro

Curandera: a woman healer

Doñ, Doña: a title of esteem for a person of social or official distinction, such as a community leader of long standing

El día de los Reyes Magos: Three Kings Day, celebrated on January 6

El Mundo: The World, a Puerto Rican newspaper founded in 1919.

Empanadilla: empanada, a pastry stuffed with meat

Frigoles Negros: a nutritious dish made of black beans

Fogón: a cooking fire, a charcoal stove

Farmacia: pharmacy

Guaracha: a genre of Cuban popular music, of rapid tempo and lyrics

Guarapo: sugarcane juice

Guïro: musical instrument made from a dried gourd, played by rubbing metal tines to produce a scratchy sound

Hermano: brother

Huracán: hurricane; In Puerto Rico, named for the saint on whose day it occurs

Jamona: a woman who has never married

Jíbaro, jíbara: A mountain or country dwelling peasant, a rural Puerto Rican with the traditional values of hard work and simple living

La Calle de Los Blancos: The street of the Whites

La Monjas Hippodrome: a horse racing track built in Ponce in 1927

Lo siento, m'ijo: I'm sorry, my son.

Macheteros: workers of the cane fields

Maga flower: The commonwealth flower of Puerto Rico with large red flowers and five bell shaped leaves, the Puerto Rican hibiscus

Mambo: a dance of Latin American origin and the music accompanying the dance, similar to the rumba

Manchas: patches

Mantilla: a lace veil or shawl worn over the head and shoulders, often over a high comb called a peineta

M'ija, m'ijo, m'ijito: daughter, son, little son

Mofongo: fried plantains stuffed with vegetable and meat or fish

Novia: sweetheart, fiancée

Novio: fiancé, bridegroom

Paella: a traditional Spanish dish consisting of rice, saffron and seafood or meat

Panadería: bakery

Panderata: tambourine

Pan dulce: sweet bread

Pastele: a meat and spice-filled pastry with a masa of plantain

Pendejo: fuckin' idiot!

Pesos: Puerto Ricans refer to US dollars as "pesos."

Pilón: a wooden mortar and pestle

Plena: folkloric music, dances or chants native to Puerto Rico

Polvo de amor: a popular desert of sweet coconut crisp

Público: a public van or bus

Queso blanco: white cheese

Reinita: little queen, Puerto Rico's national songbird

Sinvergüenza: without shame

Son: a style of music originating in Cuba that combines Spanish Guitar, percussion and African Rhythms, a precursor to salsa

Tienda de ropa: clothing store

Tabounuco: the large green, leafy trees of tropical rain forests, often reaching up to 100 feet

Tortilla Española: Spanish omelet

Trepado: climbing

Vellonera: jukebox

ACKNOWLEDGEMENTS

This story would have not come to fruition without the help of many people. Thank you to my wonderful critique group, Writers Unanimous, for your encouragement, untiring comments and for listening to the many versions of my manuscript over the seven years we were together. For Karin DeRocco, Mary Lee Fulkerson, Vonda Novelly, Joyce Phillips, Carol Purroy, and Helen Stevens, my life is better with all of you in it.

And thank you to David Sundstrand, for being a champion of my work and encouraging me throughout the years. To Alex Espinoza and my fellow workshop attendees at the Squaw Valley Community of Writers, thank you for your honesty and thoughtful critiques. We really are a community.

To editors Lorin Oberweger (thanks for pushing me!), Leyla Namazie, and Roberto Cabello-Argandoña, thank you for your time and expertise. To readers Carol Evans and Joanna McMullen, thank you for your knowledge and kind words.

To my parents, Ramón and Evelyn León, many thanks for passing on to me the tenacity to tell this story and to see my dream of publication through.

To Brad and Elena, thank you for giving me the freedom to accomplish this mission, and never complaining, yet always supporting me. I know you've witnessed my acting a bit loca at times, and I realize how lucky I am.

And to my father, my sincerest thanks for your patience, time and willingness to share the intimate details of your life with me so honestly. I am blessed.

Reading Group Guide

I have been a tried and true member of a book club since 2003 and love book clubs! I am available to travel to your meetings in Reno, NV, the Tahoe Basin, and some communities as far as the Bay Area. For almost anywhere else, I'm available through SKYPE. Please feel free to contact me at my email or websites, cjl@usamedia. tv, www.celesteleon.com, www.celestejleon.blogspot.com, or on www.facebook.com/AuthorCelesteLeon to arrange a meeting. Thank you for your interest!

For discussion:

1. What are Ramón's expectations after winning the lottery? How do they change?

2. Ramón's mission in life is to keep a promise to his humanitario. What are his other goals?

3. Ramón forges several relationships in the novel. Which are the most meaningful and how do they change?

4. How do the characters feel about World War II? How do Ramón and other Puerto Ricans feel?

5. Is Elsie a "good girlfriend?" How does she change? How do others view her?

6. What are the themes of Luck is Just the Beginning and what scenes illustrate those themes best?

7. Who is the strongest character in the story? Who is your favorite character or who are your favorite characters and why?

CPSIA information can be obtained
at www.ICGtesting.com
Printed in the USA
FSOW01n2104140217
30848FS